The Ides of March Conspiracy

CLYDE MATTHEWS
The Ides

*The Year the IRS
Got What It
Deserves*

# of March
Conspiracy

ARBOR HOUSE

New York

ACKNOWLEDGMENTS

I am indebted to two brilliant computer scientists, Charles Lecht and Ralph Stout, president and vice-president, respectively, of Advanced Computer Techniques Corporation, New York, N.Y., for providing the expertise on computer technology. I am likewise grateful to highly accomplished attorneys John H. F. Shattuck of the American Civil Liberties Union, Washington, D.C., Andrew T. McEvoy and Lawrence M. Monat, New York, N.Y., for advice on legal aspects of this novel.

Special appreciation is due my editor, Jeanne Bernkopf, for her well-known skills and insightful guidance in bringing it all together.

TO FLORENCE, my resident critic and indispensable friend

Foreword

When the computer was first developed in the nineteen-forties even its designers could not envision its awesome potential. It has since become a highly sophisticated, increasingly virtuoso mechanism which has penetrated almost every facet of our lives, reaching out to the farthest planets and operating everything from global communications, complex industrial processes and mammoth government programs to supermarket checkout counters. Our society itself is dependent upon the computer's incredible capabilities.

This space-age genius which can perform unimaginable feats, such as placing men on the moon, can also be an evil genius. Like nuclear energy and the automobile, the computer and its data banks have a dark side. They can invade our privacy, compromise our civil liberties and commit major crimes-for-profit. They have in fact been doing these very things, largely in secret, for some time and on a shocking scale.

The Ides of March Conspiracy is based upon these actual violations of our rights by government and industry, as well as the very real potential of computer-assisted terrorism and the subversion of democracy itself. Fiction begins as the story proceeds from its realistic base.

The proliferation of computers and data banks—and their inadequate control—comprises one of the greatest threats to the Bill of Rights and to our individual liberties. This novel projects what might well occur if effective safeguards are not instituted and enforced before it becomes too late.

—Clyde Matthews

East Hampton, N.Y.
July 1978

The Ides of March Conspiracy

Chapter One

Taking long strides across the wooded campus, Kermit Nordstrom was oblivious to the soft winter sunshine filtering through broken pewter clouds and to the crisp air mentholating his nostrils. Pressure was escalating in his head at the realization of the intimidation he had just been through. He was furious with himself for having taken it in such a civilized manner.

He bounded up the broad masonry steps to the low, modern Light Engineering building and rushed down the empty corridor, his leather-heeled boots clicking out his frustration like a sullen-faced male flamenco dancer. His office door was locked. He fumbled clumsily with his keys until he found the right one, flung the door open, and banged it behind him, its glass panel shivering in its frame.

He sat on the edge of his desk, picked up the phone and dialed the Computer Center. Dana wasn't there. He dialed her apartment and let it ring six times. Where the devil was she? He hung up and dialed again. Ten rings. No answer. He slammed the phone down, filled his pipe, lit it with fast, hungry puffs, looked at the fat manila folders piled on his desk which required his attention, said "fuck it" with some satisfaction, got up and walked out of the quiet, smoke-filled room and out of the building into his chocolate-brown Alfa Romeo in the tree-lined faculty parking lot.

As he threaded through the winding roads of the rolling university campus, he berated himself for not squarely facing up to Gideon Chappell.

Forty-five minutes earlier, Kermit had been sitting in the light-oak paneled reception room of Dr. Gideon Chappell, the president of South Hanover Institute of Technology, trying to relax his longish body in the sleek chrome and leather Eames chair. He had flipped the pages of *Scientific American* as he speculated about why Chappell wanted to see him. The only time he ran into Chappell was at faculty dinners and receptions for visiting VIPs. He had been in the president's office just twice in the five years he had been on the teaching staff: once when he was hired as an instructor and the second time when Chappell informed him of his promotion as associate professor of Computer Science soon after the publication of his book, *Computers and Society.*

Kermit had tried reviewing all the possibilities which could account for this unusual summons. He couldn't think of anything which made sense. There was his testimony before that congressional committee when he had tried to get those characters to see the dangers of the invasion of data banks and all those other computerized surveillance shenanigans by the government. But that was months ago during the last session of Congress. It had to be something else.

It was Monday, January 14, 198–. Not only a new year, but into a new decade. He was still writing last year's date on his checks and letters sometimes; somehow he hadn't yet accepted the two new digits. His head was still back in the seventies—a time of so much frustration around the country.

Kermit remembered the cliff-hanging series of student deferments which had kept him on the Northwestern University campus as a math major during the Vietnam War and afterward, when he got his master's degree and finally his doctorate in computer science at M.I.T. Now, in his mid-thirties, he was working with a new generation of kids who were frighteningly bright and yet apparently unconcerned about the accelerating social and political problems. They were a generation that absorbed computer printouts through their bloodstream, their minds programmed with unparalleled knowledge, their psyches inured to violence and immoralities and dehumanization. And now a new decade. What kind of people were they becoming?

He looked at his watch; it was 3:15.

4

"Do you think it will be much longer, Mrs. Bausman?" he finally asked Chappell's secretary, trying to smile pleasantly and recrossing his long legs. It was about as far as one could safely go with her. Her manner was studiedly gracious, as long as you obeyed the rules. Just don't push her or cause her boss any problems.

"I shouldn't think so." She smiled beneficently, looking up from her paperwork. "Dr. Chappell has, of course, been quite busy today."

No doubt, he thought, going back to his magazine. A minute later, a buzzer sounded on her desk. She picked up the intercom phone, listened for a moment, then announced, "You may go in now, Dr. Nordstrom."

Chappell met him at the door, a not quite tall man in his late forties, narrow-shouldered, with clear blue eyes set in a rather large, light-pinkish face with trim silver-black hair over a high forehead. He had a scholarly but eager look which reminded Kermit of a motivational research executive from Madison Avenue. Perhaps that was why he had been such a successful fundraiser for the university.

Chappell gripped Kermit's forearm with his left hand as he grasped and shook his visitor's hand with the other, leading him into the spacious room dominated by the long, pickled-pine table with an inlaid green leather top that served as the executive desk. It was centered on one wall in front of French doors.

"It's good to see you, Kermit," Chappell said in his rich, well-groomed voice. "We don't get to see each other nearly enough. My fault of course. I don't know where all my time goes. Sit down, sit down."

Kermit murmured his agreement as he sat down facing Chappell across the desk, the bright block of sunlight coming through the French doors making a smoky void of the president's face and turning his hair to matted straw.

"Well, then, Kermit . . . how goes things in your department?"

Do you really want to know? Kermit thought. "No special problems. I think we're making progress. We got some new and more sophisticated equipment this year, as you know, and we've just about finished debugging it. And, of course, the incoming kids get smarter each year—it's frightening. But we somehow manage to keep a step ahead."

"You do better than that, I happen to know. I also understand you're writing another book."

Kermit was surprised. He smiled self-consciously. "Well, I'm researching one that I hope to write. But I'm quite a ways off from the writing yet."

"That's fine." He paused and looked across the room reflectively. "I don't believe in the 'publish or perish' garbage as university policy. But I do feel that those who have something really authentic and original to contribute should."

He smiled benevolently at Kermit, his cerulean blue eyes steady and guileless. "What's the subject going to be this time?"

So that was it? Chappell was worried about what he was writing. He felt a sense of relief to know it was as simple as that. But he was also surprised that Chappell should be so clumsy in trying to find out.

"I don't actually know at this point. The book could go in any one of several directions in computer technology. I just haven't yet decided what the thrust will be."

"I see," Chappell said slowly, shaking his head up and down solemnly as though perceiving an esoteric truth. "It will be on some new technology then." He was still fishing.

"Not necessarily," Kermit said crisply, anxious to pinch off any further definition. "But some technology will inevitably be involved simply because of the nature of the field." He hoped that his non-answer would end it.

"I understand," Chappell said in his most open-minded manner, understanding only that he was getting nowhere on this tack. "You know, Kermit," his voice softer and more confidential, "one of my main concerns as the head man of this institution is to see that the quality of our performance keeps rising and that what we do here is relevant to the needs of those who come here to learn, as well as to the needs of society itself."

What the hell?

"It's not an easy thing to do, as you well know. We've got to keep looking at our physical plant, the courses we offer on both the undergraduate and graduate levels, our admissions policies, our teaching standards, our faculty and, of course, the way we administer the whole kit and kaboodle. And while we're looking at it, others are looking over our shoulder. You know, the proverbial fishbowl. So what does that bring us up to? Well, one of the key elements that makes any college or university what it is, is of course the quality of its teaching personnel. And that brings us up to Kermit Nordstrom." He smiled mysteriously at Kermit.

The bastard is playing with me, Kermit thought.

At that moment—as though stage-managed by Chappell—the door opened and Mrs. Bausman walked in with a silver serving tray holding two small cups of fine English china and a sterling coffee service. She smiled solicitously at both men, primly set the tray down on the desk between them and carefully filled the cups, her round, matronly breasts overhanging the desktop. She straightened up, a smile on her middle-aged Shirley Temple face, and marched out straight-backed.

"Thank you, Nancy," Chappell called after her, seemingly as an afterthought, as she went through the door.

They sipped their coffee in formal silence. After a minute, still holding his half-full cup, Chappell looked up. "Well . . . to get back to you, Kermit. I've been watching your work and of course I've been aware for a long time what your associates and your students think of you. I'm convinced that you are an important asset to the university, not only because of the excellence of your teaching, but also because of the originality of your thinking. You are favorably known in educational and industry circles around the country. And that is good for South Hanover. Top-notch instructors help attract top-notch students and that's what we're always looking for. Now the point of this little chat, Kermit, is that we'd like to consider you for an appointment to a full professorship with expanded authority in your department and, of course, the rather substantial salary increase that goes with it."

Kermit's eyes widened, but he noted the word *consider*.

Sensing an interruption, Chappell raised his hand quickly. "That's only part of it. . . . We're also expecting a sizable grant from the federal government—something in the mid-six figures, I would think—for a comprehensive computer study involving a major government agency. The funding would come directly from that agency. We would naturally want to recommend the professor who is best equipped to take on the assignment and I happen to think that person is you. You have the creativity and the expertise which this project needs. I can't tell you more about it now because it's very confidential at this point. Besides, I frankly don't understand it all. Of course, it would bring great prestige to the university and to the man who heads the project." Chappell paused, his face brightening. "Well, Kermit, what do you think?"

"Well, I'm very flattered of course, and I appreciate your confidence in me. But I'm also a little confused." He knew he should phrase this discreetly. "Is there any connection . . . between the professorship and the government grant?" It sounded blunter than he intended.

Chappell didn't seem to notice. "Not necessarily, but hopefully." He smiled a bit self-consciously, and Kermit liked him for the first time.

"I know that sounds cryptic, but I'll decode it for you." He smiled again and took a deep breath. "You *are* being seriously considered for the professorship. Now the person who will head the study project must be a full professor according to the terms of the grant. As I said, I would like to recommend you for that. So while the two are not tied together, I am hoping they will both be you. Does that answer your question?"

Kermit nodded, though it didn't entirely.

"I am sure you realize," the president continued, "that these things will take a little time to come through. The professorship appointment will have to be passed upon by the committee during the upcoming semester and the federal grant should become available toward the end of the year. I don't foresee too much problem on the professorship. As far as the grant is concerned, I think that the powers-that-be in Washington will simply want to be sure that whoever gets it at South Hanover is clean and trouble-free and not involved in any activities which might embarrass a government agency. For the rest, I'm certain they'll be guided by our recommendation. I'm sure you understand."

"I'm not sure I do. What do you mean by 'activities which might embarrass a government agency'?"

"I don't think there's any mystery about it. Just as we are concerned about anything our personnel may do which would in any way reflect adversely on the university, I believe the federal government would be concerned about whom it made grants to, especially one as significant as this. They wouldn't want, for example, to have anyone running an important and highly visible project for them if that individual was involved in something which might be questionable."

Kermit sat silent, a sick feeling rising in his stomach.

"I don't think there's anything to worry about, do you?" Chappell's manner was offhand but crisp.

"I don't know. I would hate to think that a person's rights as a citizen would be a factor in whether or not he received a grant for a government study rather than his qualifications." He knew it sounded pompous, but Chappell brought out the worst in him.

Chappell smiled. "I don't disagree with you, Kermit. In fact, I couldn't agree more. But politics and even industry are rough on scholars and idealists. What seems right and proper in academe is often considered naïve to those who run our country and industry. As long as we stay in our ivory towers, we can keep our ideals. But once we try to play in a bigger ballpark, then we've got to be prepared for some disillusionment."

"I don't think we're talking about the same thing, Gideon." It was the first time Kermit had called him by his first name. He felt the anger rising, tried to contain it. "I'm prepared to be disillusioned. I have been many times, that's not any problem. But I'm not prepared to give up any legitimate activities—even in theory—if that's the price of receiving the grant. Frankly, Gideon, I still can't understand why you're bringing this up. Do you feel I'm involved in anything questionable?"

"Do *you* feel you are?"

"No!"

"Then there is nothing to be concerned about, is there?"

"I'm not sure. I'm not the one to make these decisions. Do *you* see anything in my background or in my present activities which could possibly hinder my candidacy for a professorship?"

Chappell spoke slowly. "No . . . neither in your background nor *present* activities, as far as I know them. And your record as a scholar and a teacher is, of course, exemplary. But I must make two points to answer your question accurately. The first is that your *future* activities —between now and the time of those decisions—would naturally come under scrutiny and be considered. And, secondly, my own opinion is just one of many in authorizing a professorship."

"Fair enough. But that raises another question—maybe more than one. I can't project what my future activities will be, except that they will be legitimate and legal. But it would be helpful if I knew how you felt about what I've already been involved in—off campus, I mean—up to now. It hasn't exactly been a secret."

"I can't give you a simple answer to that. To be perfectly honest, I haven't always been happy with some of your activities in Washington because there are always political overtones. And motives, however worthy, are often misunderstood. If you were, let's say, to continue or to accelerate those activities—although you'd be entirely within your rights to do so—then the increased publicity might very well tip the balance and make it difficult for me to support you in any meaningful way. I'd still be in your corner, of course. But it could be tough. I'm sure you understand that."

"I see. . . ."

"I suggest you give it some serious thought. I am sure you know how anxious I am to have you get that professorship, and how pleased I would be to recommend you to head that project. You have to decide how important they are to you. Whatever you decide, I'll be on your side." Chappell's smile was brief.

As they rose, the president put his hand on Kermit's shoulder and walked him to the door. Kermit resented the patronizing gesture and, anxious to get away, did not notice Chappell's proffered hand as he walked unseeingly through the reception room and past Mrs. Bausman's organized jungle of intertwined potted plants.

Chapter Two

Dana had heard Kermit's footsteps approaching on the hard vinyl floor of the hallway after the elevator door opened and closed, and she had the door of her apartment open before he could ring. She looked at the expression on his long face with its full, high forehead, long-lashed blue eyes and strong jawline. She reached out for his arm and pulled him in.

"You look as though you need more than a drink," she said.

"I need to talk."

She walked into his arms and put her head on his shoulder and pressed her body to his. "Talk later. Unwind first. I'll fix a drink."

Dana stepped back and spun around with her back to him, showing a neatly carved profile with a short, fine nose, a high, delicately curved cheek and a firmly angled chin, tendrils of burnished red-brown hair wisping at the base of her slender neck.

Kermit watched her walk to the kitchen, so slenderly graceful and feminine. He wondered how far in his life he might go with this lovely, independent young woman. Would it ever be more than an affair? She was so super-alive—even in odd moments of repose she sometimes seemed about to take wing—it sometimes frightened him.

He remembered the first time he had lunched with her six months earlier, soon after she joined the upstate New York institution's Computer Center staff as program analyst and director. Her wide-set, gray-green eyes had challenged him almost arrogantly from three tables away. Without thinking, he'd just gotten up, food tray in hand, and walked to her table. "May I sit down?" he had said. "Why not, it's S.H.I.T. property," she had answered looking at him levelly, referring to a traditional campus joke on South Hanover's initials. For two months they had met for lunch whenever their schedules permitted, usually two or three times a week, seen each other occasionally in the adjacent Computer Center building and then had begun having dinner off campus a few times a week. After their second dinner date they had made love for the first time. She had come to him so freely, so openly, with such sensual exhilaration, it made him feel there was a whole generation gap between them rather than just eight years. She turned lack of inhibition into an art form. Their relationship had become a steady one and they usually met in her apartment because it provided more privacy. Faculty friends and an occasional student would sometimes ring his doorbell unannounced.

Philosophically and psychically they were on the same wave length although they had arrived from different directions. Their serious talks about social matters made their lovemaking more intense, as though they were nailing down their convictions through the confirmation of the flesh. They enjoyed laughing together—at themselves, at each other, at the world beyond the campus.

Dana returned with two highball glasses tinkling with ice cubes. She smiled empathetically as she handed him one and sat down close to him on the sofa, placing her head on his shoulder. They sipped their drinks for a minute in silence.

Kermit was staring blindly at a woven Indian wallhanging across the room. Finally, he said, "I almost let myself be had today. You won't believe what a Machiavelli our good doctor turned out to be. I used to think of him as a Madison Avenue smoothie—but, believe me, we underrated him. And I'm afraid he took me by surprise although I still can't figure out why. It *was* our Washington lobbying he wanted to see me about. I've been kicking myself for letting him get me in a corner the way he did. Oh, I twitched a little but I sure avoided a showdown."

Dana touched his hand. "Before you kick yourself anymore, tell me what happened—from the top."

When Kermit finally had disgorged himself of the distasteful episode, they sat huddled together quietly for a full minute before Dana spoke.

"This must be an awfully big thing for him to put such obvious pressure on you. It's hard to believe that it's only the image of the university or that some of the trustees don't like what you're doing—what *we're* doing. Who the hell could be against preventing theft or sabotage or invasion of privacy by computer? It's like motherhood and the Bill of Rights."

"Not exactly. We've been through this before, Dana. The ones against it aren't the crooks, it's the agencies and institutions—federal, state, municipal—that have been getting away with it. The law-and-order boys who think it's their duty to break the law to control lawlessness. It's been many years since Watergate but still we haven't learned. Police departments around the country, the FBI, the CIA, secret government military apparatuses, all find computer invasions of confidential files on people and organizations very useful. And because the government does it, it's still largely covered up."

He would never forget what they did to Dr. Gar Lassiter, his professor and mentor at M.I.T. It was a recurring nightmare. After being appointed Science Advisor to the President in 1972, Lassiter was forced to resign by the White House chief of staff when the FBI belatedly turned up an army dossier on him indicating a homosexual incident with another soldier during the Korean War when he was twenty-two years old. While Lassiter told the press he resigned for reasons of health, a White House aide leaked the contents of the dossier. The humiliation he suffered among his family, friends and colleagues, and the public disgrace of being dismissed from a high post under such demeaning circumstances was more pressure than this brilliant, sensitive man could handle. A month later he cracked up and was committed to a psychiatric hospital where he had been ever since. Kermit later learned from Lassiter's wife that the report was untrue and was based solely on a charge of his superior officer, a sergeant who was offended when the young private he fancied rejected his advances. A dossier with unsubstantiated information had destroyed the fine man he felt so close to, and he never quite got over it.

Dana nodded, then brightened. "Do you think Chappell is fronting for someone higher up? Some big wheel in Washington is turning the screw to get us to stop? Using educational funds from HEW or from a foundation as leverage . . . or maybe even the promise of a juicy appointment? After all, that's the game he's playing with you."

"We just may have stepped hard on someone's toes, who knows?

Remember the last time round we made some pretty big waves? My testimony urging stronger controls on the government's computer operations before that congressional committee got a lot of press coverage. A couple of wire service stories made the first page of the *Times* and a lot of other papers around the country. Even *Newswatch* ran a piece on us, remember? Nothing happened, of course, even though a couple of senators called for a congressional investigation of my charges." Kermit's thick eyebrows climbed. "But why *now?* What suddenly popped up to get Chappell to try to blackmail me into keeping quiet? If he were doing this on his own, he would have tried stopping us months ago when we were getting all that publicity. So there has to be some pretty important reason why he's so anxious to stop us at this particular time. . . . Whatever the reason, we have to *do* something. To do nothing would be a decision in itself, and a bad one."

Dana's hand was on Kermit's thigh. "I agree and I've made a decision. I've decided that we've done enough talking for a while." She got up and raised both arms to undo a hook at the back of her dress. "Help me with this," she ordered.

He undid the hook and unzipped the lavender dress. He watched her as she stepped out of her dress, her back still to him, pale yellow panties fitting snugly on her slender, curving hips, no bra. She pivoted around, facing him with her arms flowing at her sides, her head cocked sideways and her deep-set eyes, dark green in this light, smiling pointedly. Her small firm breasts were delicately molded into her square-shouldered, light-boned torso. Each time he saw her like this was almost like the first time. He marveled at the exquisite modeling of her petite yet long-limbed body.

She took his hand and led him into the bedroom.

An hour later, lying there in the early darkness of a winter late afternoon, their moist bodies just touching at the shoulders, Dana raised herself on one arm, her shadowed face looking down on him.

"You're looking much better, friend," she said lightly. "How do you feel?"

"Like I look—much better."

"Would you care for any more therapy?"

He smiled at her. "Not right now, thanks."

"I should think not. You were pretty violent there for a while."

14

"I guess I was." He smiled self-consciously. "I had to get it out of my system."

"Uh huh," she said, rising from the bed. "And now, if you'll excuse me . . ."

A few minutes later Dana emerged from the shower with a large towel around her middle and with a small towel wrapped in a turban around her head. Sequins of water glistened on her face in the light of the shiny yellow ceramic table lamp on the night table. Tufts of wet dark reddish hair stuck out beneath the turban and a marvelous scent came from her warm, moist skin.

She sat down on the edge of the bed, leaned over and kissed him. The scent of her was overpowering.

"Well, what will it be, lover—talk or an encore?"

He thought for a moment. "We better make it talk."

He patted the spot beside him. "Lie down."

Dana threw off the bath towel, settled her still-turbaned head on the pillow and lit a cigarette, blowing the first puff at the soft-edged geometric shadows on the ceiling. "Okay, let's add up the options," she said. "If we were to stop lobbying in Washington, that would make Chappell and a lot of other people happy, and the old boy would probably come through with the professorship. About that pie-in-the-sky grant—who knows? Maybe. But if we keep needling Congress and the press to start an investigation or to pass some meaningful legislation, then we'll probably be out on our academic asses. You're up for tenure in June so you're vulnerable as hell. I'd have to be marked for slaughter too. So what do we do, look for new spots somewhere else? We might be lucky but it would be tough. We might try for private industry, but no thank you. So what's *left?* We could go underground."

"Underground? Are you serious?"

"I wasn't, but encourage me."

"It's your idea. You write the scenario."

"Well, first we publish a newspaper anonymously. We present computer-based crimes against individuals, companies and the government too, all documented, along with proposals for corrective action. We circulate it among senators, congressmen, committees, the press and—"

"Forget it, Dana. It would never work. We're too well identified with the whole business. They'd spot us in a minute."

"Okay. What if we were to organize a citizen's group—keeping ourselves strictly out of it—to draw up petitions with thousands of signatures in major cities around the country. . . ." Her voice trailed off as she anticipated his reaction with a negative shake of her head on the warm pillow.

"Same thing."

"I have no pride of authorship," she said. "Suppose you try your hand at it."

Kermit ran his hand over the smoothness of her hip. She took his hand off her hip, raised it in the air and dropped it at his side. "Keep your mind on business, smartass."

"I was just trying my hand at it." He turned serious. "We need to dream up some dramatic action that would galvanize public opinion, that would be the direct opposite of what we've been doing . . . something so different no one would ever connect us with it."

"That's a tall order. A dramatic action . . . that would shake up the country . . . and go in an opposite direction. What kind of action?"

"I don't know. . . . Something that would have broad impact and in some way be a threat to the entrenched system. Like an act against a major bureaucracy. A government agency or a private institution. A government agency would probably be better. It would have to be a real blockbuster. Something to foul it up good, maybe even shut it down entirely."

"A computer crisis?"

"Of course . . . but what kind?"

"Oh . . . a little steel wool in their equipment . . . maybe erasing their key tapes . . . breaking their entry code and modifying their programs through a remote terminal or accessing their data banks—"

"Dana, you're talking about invasion—"

"It's exactly what we've been warning against, so we have a perfect cover."

His voice became quiet. "This is pretty extreme stuff, you know—"

"You're the one who drew the picture, Kerm, I'm just filling in the blank spaces."

He kicked off the thin sheet covering the lower part of his body, suddenly felt hot. "If we knock out a government data operation, what effect would it have? It would have to raise hell with that particular agency and possibly with interconnecting ones. The amount of hell

16

would depend on how vital the agency was and how sensitive the data was—"

"It should be the most vital and sensitive we can find. The point of the whole thing is to dramatize how serious the problem is and the fact that no data processing operation is invulnerable. It wouldn't be worth the risk otherwise."

"The question is can we control the thing so that no one gets really hurt? . . . so that it just becomes a huge headache and a temporary panic. We've *got* to be able to turn it off again. After all, we're out to prove a point, to make the country aware of how vulnerable it is and that the government has been playing Russian roulette with our privacy and violating our civil rights a dozen different ways that nobody still would believe, even with all the little previous attempts at exposure—including our own."

"Let's say we do it. What happens then?" she asked, suddenly uncertain.

"They'll probably catch us, if that's what you mean. Whatever outfit we hit will be crawling with the FBI within hours. Probably CIA too. They'll suspect everyone—from old-line urban terrorists to Soviet agents. I'd hope to turn off the action and restore the operation before they found us. Then we could call a press conference and tell all. It would be one hell of a forum, wouldn't it? But we'd still be guilty of a crime and there's no telling what they'd do to us. It's a big risk."

Dana moved closer to him, and Kermit held her tightly without realizing it. He was thinking of the endless months they'd spent writing articles and delivering speeches before professional groups, meeting with senators in their offices and with newsmen in Washington bars and at the National Press Club to urge overdue action against uncontrolled computerism. And the tiresome flights to and from the capital, their hope draining away over the months as nothing was done. Finally he said, "It could mean imprisonment and the end of our careers. It could be very, very rough . . . but what an opportunity to tell our story while the country was still shocked enough to listen. There would be worldwide press coverage . . . probably a trial in federal court . . . investigations by congressional committees. . . . It would grab attention like nothing else. It would be a hornet's nest, but that's what we would want. Some kind of solution would *have* to come out of it. And if we really believe in this thing, it may be the only way—"

17

"Then let's get with it."

"Hold it, Dana . . . a hot-eyed revolutionary I'm not. I'm a scientist and if we're to succeed in this thing we've got to keep everything tentative, fluid until we evaluate all our options, press each button until we get to the final one. In fact, I think we should try to design a fail-safe plan so that if anything goes wrong, at least we won't be ruined—"

"I don't disagree with you, but let's be as *definitely* tentative as possible."

He ignored her dig. "The first step is to select the target—based on how vital the data is . . . how sensitive . . . how valuable to the government . . . how well protected they think it is. What effect breaching it would have on government operations . . . on the economy . . . maybe on relations with other governments. Certainly on people, the individual . . ."

"Also, how vulnerable the system is. We have to be able to gain access."

"That shouldn't be a factor except in a negative sense. Every data system can be breached if the right technology is brought to bear and if the invaders are expert and persevering enough. That's one of the things we want to prove. So we should look for an operation that's considered virtually impregnable. That's what I meant by how well protected *they* think it is."

"Can I start a list?"

"Why not."

"Should we include private financial institutions?"

"Like what?"

"Oh . . . the New York Stock Exchange. Think of what would happen if we were to trigger their computers to exaggerate the sales of stocks of well-known companies. There would be mayhem on Wall Street and panic in the economy. Sound good?"

"An interesting start. Let's list anything that sounds possible. We can evaluate later."

Dana sat up quickly, reached over to the night table beside her, pulled open the top drawer and took out a pad and pencil.

Kermit turned his head on the pillow and looked admiringly at her slender nude figure, legs pulled up, ivory skin tones amber in the glow of the table lamp.

She scribbled as she spoke. "How about the Chicago Commodity

18

Exchange? We could create artificial shortages in wheat, soybeans, maybe even pork bellies. How could we ever survive without being sure of our pork bellies?" She giggled. Kermit, his arms folded back behind his head, smiled, but he was beginning to wonder how much of this was an intellectual exercise in frustration, and how much they really meant it.

"Put it down," he said, "and keep going."

"I may be running dry—at least on private companies. Hey, how about the insurance industry? They've got a lock on half the country's money anyway. They're totally dependent on data and statistical information to process policies, pay claims and dividends, make investments . . ."

"Why don't we swing into the government sector? I really think that's the way we should go. After all, our real bogeyman isn't industry or the public. It's the damn federal bureaucracy and the leadership—executive, legislative and administrative. We've got to make *them* look bad and shock the public into learning how dangerous the situation is so they'll demand action." He paused. "I'll start with the FBI."

"Okay, I'm starting a separate list for government agencies. The FBI," she repeated slowly as she wrote it down. "Boy, that would be a sock in the head. I can see those reels of magnetic tape jumping their sprockets and the G-men in their crew cuts and blue serge suits running through the aisles of their computer center with their guns drawn looking for the subversives to shoot at, and ending up pumping the 360s and 370s full of holes. What a scene! Okay, your turn." Her pencil was poised and she looked at him expectantly, his head still propped on his folded arms.

"Well, there's the FCC . . . HEW . . . Department of Agriculture . . . Commerce . . . SEC . . . the Treasury . . . Defense . . . CIA, the General Accounting Office. They're all as vulnerable as hell, once you gain access. The CIA, I understand—and this is hard to believe but I'm told it's really true—has a mediocre protective system against data invasion. But I still don't see them as a good candidate for what we have in mind. The GAO, on the other hand, would be beautiful. They're the central point for accounting for all federal agencies and departments. If we hit them, the government wouldn't be able to pay its bills. The shock waves would temporarily screw up the economy. As for the . . . hey—what about Social Security? Put that down. The only trouble is, it would hurt the wrong people. The elderly who need it most." He paused. "You know,

Dana, a *lot* of people could be hurt if we go ahead with this thing, and that's the last thing we want to happen. We've got to keep in mind that the purpose of the exercise is to *protect* the interests of people. We don't want anyone to suffer, even temporarily, from what we do. That would defeat the whole . . . well, ethical reason for doing this—"

"But if we louse up the programs or files of any major industry or government agency, don't a lot of people have to get hurt, even for a limited time?"

"That's what worries me. That's why we can't just pick a target. We've really got to be sure it's do-able without hurting innocent people."

"Even temporarily?"

"Even temporarily. Besides, we need public opinion on our side. If a lot of people get hurt, they won't care *why* we did it. Assuming we can find—"

"I've got it! Eureka and all that, but no kidding . . . I think I've got it," and she bounced against the headboard, making the entire bed jump. She spoke, slowly, in a theatrical monotone, pausing dramatically between phrases. "I've found a way . . . to sabotage . . . the computer operations of a vital and sensitive government agency . . . which will rock the establishment and the economy . . . *without* hurting the general public or jeopardizing their interests. In fact people may even love us for it. And it covers all our criteria."

Silence. She was looking at the dark mirror on the opposite wall.

"Well?" he said, mystified and slightly irritated at her silence. *"Well?"*

"I thought you'd never ask." She turned to him and burst out laughing, her lovely face glowing with excitement, her voice still teasing. "The target is . . ."

"Yes? . . ." He was impatient and annoyed.

"Beg me."

"The hell with you."

"The IRS!" she announced triumphantly.

"The Internal Revenue Service? Well . . . *that* would certainly stop the clock. The country's cash register . . . we knock it out and no money can go in or out. We make their computers go berserk and they've got to shut down operations. Everyone hates the tax collector anyway. *Taxes take a holiday.* People will love it, I bet we could win any popularity contest in the country. It's the perfect target, Dana . . . I congratulate you . . . I adore you. You're, as they say, fucking fantastic—"

"That's true. I am," she said, and jumped out of bed, running quickly across the room, kicking off the clinging sheet as she ran.

Kermit went after her. As he cornered her between wall and a chest of drawers, her slender back to him and long hair in disarray across her shoulders, she wheeled around suddenly, her eyes intense and smiling.

He pressed his body against hers, flattening her against the wall.

"What, sir, are you *doing?*"

"Trying to gain access."

"Get your remote terminal out of there. You don't have the entry code and that's sabotage." Her breath was on his neck.

"Negative. That's rape."

She threw her arms about him and pressed her hips forward. "That's what you think."

They stumbled their way over to the bed, knocking over some bottles of toilet water on the dressing table. And they made love, charged up with the excitement of their conspiracy, of attacking the target object together.

Afterward, lying there side by side, perspired and sticky, Kermit said quietly, "You were very exciting . . . more than I can remember. . . ."

"There's an old Phoenician saying: *Today I made a war—tonight I'm worth the taking.*"

"Where did you dig that up?"

"From an archaeologist friend of mine."

"Was he a Phoenician expert?"

"No, just an expert phony."

"Just like you. You made it up, but I'm not complaining. And now if you'll excuse me, I think *I'll* take a shower."

When Kermit emerged from the bathroom fifteen minutes later in a white terrycloth robe, Dana was still nude on the bed. "I've been think-ing," she said, "you're such a slow showerer I had plenty of time. You know, there are so many ramifications to this IRS thing, I don't know how we're going to chase them all down. We can't just go in blindly and hope everything will come out all right—"

Kermit sank into a small upholstered chair, extending his long legs and crossing them at the ankles. "What's bothering you?"

"Wouldn't it prevent government employees from getting paid? And what effect would it have on federally funded social services? We've got to make sure it's not a Pandora's box."

"Who's getting cold feet now?"

"Not really, but it would be stupid to tackle this thing without knowing where the booby traps are. We're not a couple of wide-eyed kids hot for adventure—"

"You're right, but you're forgetting something: payments to public employees and other commitments come out of general funds already appropriated. No one will lose any money if taxes stop coming in for a month or so. Remember, we're not fouling the system permanently. But we do have to face up to the fact we're talking about a dangerous project and there's no way of really knowing how it will come out." He paused. He knew now that it was no longer a game plan they were playing at to exorcise their frustration. It had grown deadly serious. "Do we quit or go on?"

"Are you kidding? Professor, I wouldn't miss this for the world."

Chapter Three

After a long night of troubled dreams, Kermit went through the next day by rote. He conducted his two intermediate classes and one advanced class in computer science feeling like an instructional cassette playing itself back. He heard himself say all the right things and answer questions by reflex . . . except once when he was challenged by an aggressively bright student with his own counter-theory.

Sitting in his office between classes he found himself doodling abstracts on his calendar pad with a sharp black pencil. The lines were straight and assertive and sharply angled to each other in an overlapping network of grids. He saw all kinds of ominous possibilities in them, but none he could quite define.

He knew what was bothering him, of course, but that didn't help. It annoyed him that as a mathematician, a scientist, he was reacting so emotionally. Instead of putting it aside until he could sit down and analyze it properly, he was letting the IRS project bounce around in his head, creating disjointed images of the myriad things that could go wrong. Was this his way of getting psyched up for what was ahead or was *he* getting cold feet? Where was the alleged Romanian gypsy blood that presumably flowed through him from his mother's side a few generations back?

He picked up the phone and dialed Dana in the Computer Center. She wasn't in and he had an itchy ten minutes shuffling the papers on his desk until she called him back.

"Hi. What's up?"

"How do you feel?"

"Fine. Why?"

"That makes one of us. I've had a lousy day. I can't get this"—he was about to say IRS but stopped short, remembering it was an open phone line—"thing off my mind. How about an early meet this afternoon, about four o'clock. We can linger over a drink, then have dinner."

"I'm not cooking tonight, friend."

"No, I thought we'd go to Constantine's and spend a few hours there. Can you be ready at a quarter to? I'll pick you up."

"Make it a quarter after."

Constantine's was located in a side street in downtown South Hanover on the edge of the old shopping district of late nineteenth-century store fronts, their detailed wooden façades abraded and discouraged by neglect as rows of new glass and chromium stores had appeared along North Main Street and a couple of large shopping malls blossomed on paved-over apple orchards to the west. The restaurant itself had been renovated some years before with gray and pink imitation stone front and one discreetly small, heavily curtained window.

There were only a few people at the bar and George, one of the owners, shrugged with surprise when Kermit said they wanted to sit in the empty dining room. They normally sat at a table in the bar when they arrived this early. They took a booth and ordered drinks.

Dana seemed so alive and free that Kermit wondered again whether she was really aware what they were letting themselves in for. "We've got some serious talking to do," he said.

"Don't be so grim about it. We've got some serious drinking to do first." She raised her glass, and her eyes, amber green in this light, looked steadily at him over the rim of the glass as she sipped.

"First we've got to set a couple of ground rules." He kept his voice low. "Rule number one: we never mention the target by name. Next, we never discuss this with anyone else. Anyone. Even obliquely. We don't talk about this on the phone or in a place where we might be overheard or where there is any possibility of being bugged. And nothing should be put in writing. If we have to make any notes, they should be burned immediately afterward. Can you think of anything else?"

"How will I know if I'm bugged?"

"I'll check both our apartments, especially the phones. I don't think there's much likelihood of that now, but we may as well get used to maintaining security."

Her eyes suddenly lit up. "I think I've got a code name for you-know-what . . . *Azimuth.*"

"Azimuth?"

"Yes, Azimuth. A-z-i-m-u-t-h." She spelled it slowly. "The azimuth circle is one of the great circles in the galaxies and it intersects with other celestial circles along its perimeter. Actually at its zenith and nadir. I see it as a huge target interconnecting with other targets."

"I *know* what it is, teach . . . well, why not? It's irrelevant and hard enough to say. Okay, Azimuth it is. Now to the real business of this meeting. How do we check out the possible side effects of Azimuth to screen out negatives?"

"I can handle that. You know I once worked on a research project for . . ." She looked at him. "You mean I can't mention it even now?"

Kermit shook his head.

". . . for Azimuth while I was a research assistant at SRI, and I know—"

Kermit looked at her sharply. "Are you playing games, Dana?"

She threw her head back and her full-throated laugh echoed around the empty dining room. "SRI, professor, is Stanford Research Institute. You know I worked there, dummy." She reached out over the red tablecloth and grasped his hand. "You think too hard."

He nodded. "Yup, and we've got a lot of hard thinking to do. Maybe you don't know what you've let yourself in for. So how do you propose to check on possible side effects?"

"I'm not sure yet, I want to think about it some more." She tossed her head back, resettling the full, soft strands of hair on her shoulders. "But I can't think on an empty stomach. Let's order."

"It's only five-thirty."

"I had no lunch. If you want me to think, you've got to feed me. I've got to store up some BTUs."

They ordered from the outrageously bastardized Greek menu, with dishes like moussaka and souvlaki side by side with veal parmigiana and corned beef and cabbage. The brothers Constantine stayed in business by accommodating a broad range of tastes from the campus community to local businessmen to mechanics. Kermit ordered a second round of drinks while they were waiting.

"Well, now that you're about to be fed, let's think about how we invent our way into Azimuth. What access technology can we use?"

"As a starter, there's ARPANET, which now has about one hundred terminals from Maine to Hawaii interconnecting with seventy-five or more Host computer systems in universities, think tanks, research centers and some of the government agencies like DOD and FEA. Maybe we can tap into it from our ARPANET terminal here at the Computer Center."

"I don't think ARPANET can lead us there. Besides, it's too visible a network. Let's think in terms of getting the entry code and then working backward as to how we'll tap in."

"I may be able to get it from someone I know who works for Azimuth in Martinsburg, West Virginia, where the master files are kept. Maybe I can con him into helping us without his knowing it."

"Too dangerous. We should stay away from anyone connected with the target. We'll have to do it another way. We might try electronic eavesdropping. We could rent a tractor-trailer equipped with special magnification microphones, antennas and oscilloscopes and make an acoustical intercept of entry codes, programs or whatever else we're interested in. It's expensive as hell, but it's one way of doing it. Or we could wiretap a telecommunications setup from computer to computer. But we'd have to figure out how to bypass the cryptography trap."

Dana's eyes widened. "That's an exciting idea. But we don't have the know-how for it—or is there something in your past you haven't told me about?"

"No, that's exactly the problem. The best ways of doing all this are probably beyond our capabilities. Why do you think I'm having bad dreams?" He smiled ruefully.

"But there are quite a few outside contractors, consultants and think tanks doing work for government agencies, and some of them must interconnect with IRS—" She clapped her hand to her mouth and looked around with an embarrassed smile—the room was still empty. "It slipped. I'm sorry. Well, anyway, that's one possibility. And then there

26

are all those federal and state agencies which have computer contact with Azimuth. Maybe we should work that side of the street because there we know what we're doing."

Kermit sat there, looking glum. The waitress, a smileless flat girl in a black dress with a white sash, arrived with a basket of bread and the salad. After she left he said, "It's more and more obvious to me that we can't do this by ourselves. And yet I don't want to involve anyone else. If we get others into it—assuming that they feel the same way we do about it—we increase the chance of detection before the target is hit. I'm not too concerned about afterward. My only concern is failure."

She put down the breadstick she was nibbling on and leaned forward. "I don't think we have much choice. If we're going to do this thing, the extra risk has to be taken."

His nod confirmed it. "So now all we've got to do is find ourselves a uniquely qualified person who is willing to join us. Someone who's very very sharp on systems architecture and computer penetration technology. Someone who is ideally situated in a sophisticated facility, with access to major government computer operations or to institutional data centers that interconnect with agencies. And someone who happens to think as we do that our individual privacy is threatened and that the country is in real danger of computerized totalitarianism. That's not all . . . this person must also have the guts to put his career and his entire future on the line by becoming a criminal. And he—or she—must have cool nerves, a closed mouth and no personal entanglements that could jeopardize the project. Simple, huh?"

Their project was the kind of fantasy he'd often dreamed about and thought he would never actually do: he was too damned analytical, cerebral, to expose himself to mischance or high risk. . . . Well, he could, of course, play it safe and keep a low profile at least until his tenure was secure and the professorship and grant came through. But if he did, he knew he just couldn't live with himself. His friend's tragedy had taken care of that. Chappell's crude attempt at coercion just made this next step almost inevitable.

Kermit sipped his second scotch sour. "I may have a candidate. . . . I got a letter a couple of weeks ago I haven't answered yet, from a former student of mine—a brilliant kid I was very close to. He's not a kid anymore. He got his bachelor's and master's here and then went on to M.I.T. for his doctorate. He's working at the Parkinson Institute now.

He probably has the best computer mind, and instinct, I've ever come across. He's capable of developing the most abstract theory and then devising intricate engineering solutions to make his theory feasible. I got him a teaching fellowship for his master's. He was sort of my protégé. Anyway, he sent me a reprint of a paper he delivered before the IEEE Computer Society International Conference recently. He keeps in touch with me at least a couple of times a year. His name is Yukio Ishizaka. He's a second generation Nisei. His grandfather bombed Pearl Harbor. He's also Jewish. He converted about two years ago when he married a girl from an orthodox Jewish family. I guess Yuki is a year or two older than you, Dana."

"He sounds fascinating. But how does he measure up to your impossible list of specifications?"

"I'm not sure. I haven't seen Yuki in the last two years and he may have changed. But I have no doubts about his expertise. He did his doctoral thesis on *Computer Penetration Technology and Protective Counter Mechanisms.* Perfect? It was one of the most sophisticated pieces of work on the subject then, and he's gone way beyond it since. He really knows his stuff on a very practical level. Besides, at Parkinson he's in a beautiful spot since they're one of the top systems consulting outfits and they have access to plenty of sensitive government data operations. His job is protecting the integrity of client computer systems and data banks. . . . His doctoral thesis—I have a copy in my office—makes it clear how strongly he felt about privacy, mass surveillance and data theft of all sorts and the shocking inadequacy of protective measures. But what I don't know is whether he's willing to risk his career and maybe his marriage on this deal. And *that's* one hell of a big question."

"How do we find out?"

The skinny waitress in her straight black dress served their entrée. Dana had broiled trout and Kermit the moussaka. A bottle of cooled Portuguese green wine was opened and placed before them. They began eating, welcoming the silence.

By the time they were having their coffee it was after six-thirty and a few of the other booths were taken but none so near them that they couldn't talk.

Dana lit a cigarette and looked at Kermit. "Let me tell you what I dreamed up. I'm almost positive I can get an accurate analysis of possible side effects of our project. Do you remember the comprehensive Hillden-brand Foundation study that Professor Chakraverty did last year for the Council on Social Priorities? It was to determine the effect of government fiscal policies on social programs between 1962 and 1977, beginning with the 'Great Society' years. He computerized a simulated socio-econometric model that interfaced the effect of the major government departments and agencies. I'm quite sure that . . . Azimuth had to be one of the agencies included. And if I'm right about that, I should be able to run a query program focused on that segment. It should give us a good printout of what we want to know."

"And how do you plan to access the program without authorization? And if you get around that one, how can you do it without identifying yourself? And if you get over those two, how do you prevent *your* job from being recorded on the log?"

She smiled mysteriously. "You underestimate me, professor. I don't know if I should tell you this." She cocked her head teasingly. "Access is no problem even with a classified program. I use the entry code of an authorized person. It gets me in and it doesn't identify me. As for logging, there are a couple of ways of keeping the job invisible. One is by erasure—you know about that—and the other is by fooling the housekeeping devils. Now please don't ask me any more questions. The less you know the better."

"All right. I take your word for it. How soon do you think you can do it?"

"Will tomorrow be soon enough? . . . Now tell me more about Yuki. What's he like?" She put her elbow on the table and cradled her chin in her hand.

"You'll like him. He's kind of intense and . . . I guess sexy—in a Japanese sort of way, of course." He said it with a straight face. "He has straight black hair and he smiles a lot when he isn't scowling—a big toothy smile. The girls used to think he was cute."

"He's probably cuter now. There's something about married men. Especially Jewish married men."

Kermit shrugged at that, paid the check and they left. They walked around the block once to stretch their legs and feel the cool, dry air on their faces before getting into his vintage Alfa Romeo.

He drove slowly through the dimly lit streets of the business district where most of the shops were closed, then past the prim old residential area of South Hanover with the large Victorian houses and modest clapboards giving way to ranch homes and modern Colonials as they passed from town to surrounding suburb to dark open country. But Yuki's shyly smiling face kept coming between Kermit's inner vision and the dark winding landscape before him.

Finally he broke the silence. "There's something I better tell you about my relationship with Yuki. He started out as an admiring student—we really got along fine—but after I got him the teaching fellowship at South Hanover, he seemed to be competing with me. All the more so once he got his doctoral degree. I don't fault Yuki on this," he said, glancing at Dana's dark profile as they entered a broad highway. "After all, in a way it's flattering, and Yuki is too decent to be arrogant about it. Still, it's there. I'm telling you all this because it creates a problem. . . . I couldn't get close enough to him now to be sure about his motivation for joining up. And yet, in another sense, I'm still too close to him to want to influence his decision if I could. You just don't put that kind of heat on a protégé, even a former one."

"So you want me to turn the heat on."

He ignored her tone. "It would mean your going up to Boston to sound him out. I hate to ask you to do it—"

"Ask, ask. I'd love to."

On the rest of the drive back, they discussed the best way of determining Yuki's convictions and his interest in joining them without giving away the actual project. . . . There would be plenty of time to tell him the truth later.

It was only a little after eight-thirty when Kermit arrived at the big white frame house on the edge of the campus after dropping off Dana at her apartment house. His second-floor apartment was dark but lights shone in the downstairs apartment where his landlord lived. He went upstairs through the separate side entrance. There were only three rooms: bedroom, living room with kitchenette on one wall, study, and bathroom, but the rooms were sizable and the ceilings were old-fashioned high. It was a 1920s house and it had a nice feeling of solidarity and warmth.

He went into his study. The semitechnical article he was writing for *Datamation* lay on his desk with a partly typed page still in the typewriter. He read what was on the page, decided it sounded pretty good. It would be easy enough to finish at this point, just a couple of pages of

30

summation. He sat down at the typewriter to knock it off, but he found himself blocked, staring at the paper in the machine. The only thing going through his mind was the talk of the evening. He saw Dana's face across the red tablecloth, so touchingly beautiful, apparently free of any sense of apprehension, never mind guilt, about what they were planning to do. He couldn't help wondering if this child of privilege and gentility was equal to the commitment she made so easily, even gaily? Was this too much a game for her, a way to certify her liberation by rebelling against her affluent, old-American background? And was *he* being fair to her in letting her share the dangers of this act and its unpredictable aftermath?

Kermit got up from behind the typewriter, turned off the desk light and walked into the living room. He picked up a pipe, stuffed it from the ceramic tobacco humidor on the oval mahogany coffee table and dropped down on the green Lawson sofa, stretching out his legs on the worn oriental rug.

Lighting the pipe in a slow clockwise circle until the flame of the burned-down match caught his finger was a hypnotizing ritual which focused his thoughts. A ridiculous idea crept up on him and got larger and larger until he couldn't ignore it. The deadline for filing tax returns with the IRS was April 15. So what would happen if the data operation was shut down exactly one month before, when the flood of tax filings was beginning to peak? March 15 . . . the Ides of March. What a dramatic time to strike when the agency was most vulnerable. As soon as the news got out, millions of taxpayers would stop filing tax returns while they waited to see what was happening. No amount of exhortation from the government would persuade the majority of them to send their forms and checks to an agency so resented and now in disarray. What a blockbuster the timing would be. Then, after a week or two, the operation would be turned back on again and the mission would have been accomplished. What could be more perfect!

He was itching to discuss the idea with Dana but the phone was no way to do it. He would have to wait until tomorrow.

Kermit felt suddenly buoyant and energetic. He had to do something. Then he thought of the magazine article unfinished on his desk. He bounded over to the refrigerator, threw together a corned beef and Swiss cheese sandwich, poured a glass of tomato juice, took them into the study and placed them within reach of the typewriter. A half hour later he had added the final two pages to the manuscript and done a little superficial editing.

When he went to bed, his mind was alert and he felt an exhilaration coursing through his veins. It took him a long, long time to fall asleep.

Chapter Four

April was bending over the Xerox machine, her back to the door, when Kermit walked in at ten o'clock the next morning. As he entered his office, her voice came after him. "Oh, I almost forgot. Miss Haverhill called just before and said she couldn't make it for lunch but she would call you later."

The morning went quickly and routinely. He reread the article he had written for *Datamation* and gave it to April to type and send out. He had a student conference on a program change and gave a class in the arena-type lecture hall from eleven to noon. Just before the lecture, Dana called and told him cryptically that she didn't have time for lunch because she had a more interesting appointment elsewhere. They arranged to meet at three-thirty.

Kermit was waiting in the crowded parking lot next to the Computer Center building when Dana arrived wearing a soft blue wool pantsuit with large white cartwheel buttons on the jacket which was open and flowing as she strode, showing a heavy-knit gray turtleneck sweater circling high under her chin. She had the casual elegance of a slender high-fashion model on campus location for a magazine layout.

Kermit felt a rush of admiration, and just a touch of unease, every time he saw her like this: so cool, sleek and sure of herself, and devastatingly lovely. She was effortlessly superior to the girls he had grown up with in his middle-class suburb of Chicago.

She smiled at him with her wide-set eyes, her lips remaining unparted. It was a look of controlled excitement. "Hi. Waiting long? Take me for a quick hamburger."

He opened the car door for her with an elaborate flourish.

As they roared away out of the parking lot down a curving road past clusters of modern concrete university buildings. Kermit said, "Did you get it?"

"Yup!" she shot back gaily.

"I did too."

She turned her head quickly, her long russet hair swirling over her mouth and cheek. "What did *you* get?"

"Tell you later." He was enjoying her puzzlement.

They drove to a roadside hamburger joint about five minutes from the edge of the campus. A lot of students frequented this place so he pulled over to an empty corner of the parking area, got out and brought back hamburgers, French fries and coffee so they could eat and talk in privacy.

"Well, I did it," she said. "I accessed the Hilldenbrand program and asked it a lot of questions and I got a printout. I did it during lunchtime when the place was practically deserted. I got some great answers. Basically what I asked was what the short-term effects would be in three different categories—financial, operational and social—of a two week scramble of Azimuth's data center. I won't go into all the details but the net of it was that there would be no discernible effect on the economy and no financial penalties to government employees or the public. Also there would be no cutbacks in federal spending for social programs, defense or anything else. There would probably be some devaluation of the U.S. dollar abroad and increased buying of gold, but the effect would reverse itself when the operation went back to normal. The printout also said to expect confusion in the stock market and in business circles and also concern among U.S. allies. Then I threw in the question of what the reaction would be in the Administration. The printout said: *Reaction is logical. Not programmed to give details.* She chuckled. "I guess I was getting too nosy. But we can take a stab at it—panic . . . charges that the government is being subverted by American Maoists or Soviet agents, titters from communist and Third World countries— but what counts is that we got a clean bill of health as far as any damage to the country or the people is concerned. Isn't that marvelous?"

Kermit put his arm around her shoulder, pulled her toward him and kissed her. "That it is. I think, as they say, we're in business. Only one thing, though . . . how sure can we be that there's no record of your waltz with the program today? Because if there is any mark at all it means that we've got an electronic stool pigeon to contend with or else a coconspirator."

She looked at him intently for a moment, reviewing what she'd done. "I don't think there's anything to worry about. I took all the precautionary measures so there would be no record of the job. I used the entry code of one of the people who worked on the Hilldenbrand program so there's no possible way of tying me to the entry. I instructed the job to erase itself on completion and I checked it afterward, and it did. And I used a preset modifying technique to insure that the log would ignore the job. There's no way I know of in which the entry and the job itself could be anything but invisible. Satisfied?"

He wasn't. "Isn't it possible that Hilldenbrand's program may contain a hidden instruction providing that a record be made of any job performed on it regardless of instructions to the contrary. Maybe done by a dual taping system so that only one could be erased?"

"It's conceivable. But that wouldn't make any sense in this kind of program because the government doesn't consider it sensitive and most of the information was digested and released some time ago. Chakraverty just wanted to make sure that no one modifies his program. Whatever protections are in there are just to insure its integrity."

"Okay, I'm convinced, I guess. And, lady, you've done a sensational job. I'm mighty impressed . . . and proud of you—"

"Oh, don't sound so damn paternal." But her pleasure showed in her eyes. "If you're impressed, it simply means that you underestimated me again. Hey, didn't you have something great to tell me?"

"I was just waiting for—"

"Wait another second. There's one more thing I forgot to tell you. This is absolutely fascinating. I threw in another question. I asked what was the best date to shut down Azimuth's data operation to have the maximum impact. Guess what the printout was."

"March fifteenth."

Dana looked cheated.

"How did you figure *that* out?"

"With my head. It's the critical point to stop the flow before the filing deadline. I keep telling you that the human brain is the best computer. We've gotten so dependent on the monster to solve our problems that we've almost abdicated our right to think. After all, thinking is the hardest and loneliest work in the world, so now that we have this brute with a brain, why think at all? Just program it and forget it. Which plays right into the hands of the bureaucrats, private and government. Computerize everyone, manipulate what they can and can't do and reduce their need to think. It's all worked out for them."

Dana's sigh was theatrical. "That sermon sounds familiar, professor, but this is me, your friendly coconspirator—remember?" She reached for his hand, squeezing it. "I adore you anyway. Are you listening?" She cocked her head to one side and leaned toward him. "I've got something else to tell you—no, I'm not pregnant . . . I'm meeting Yuki Ishizaka tomorrow in Boston. I phoned him this morning—from a pay booth— and asked him if I could see him tomorrow for an hour or two on a research project I was doing for my doctorate. And he said okay."

"Just like that."

"Yes, just like that. I did mention that I knew you slightly. . . . Okay, I told him that we worked closely together and that you thought he was the greatest, and recommended him as the supreme authority for my research."

"What did he say to that?"

"He said it sounds like the same old S.H.I.T."

Kermit's sudden laugher resounded in the cubicle of the car. "Did Yuki really say that?"

"I love to hear you laugh like that. You don't let go often enough. No, of course he didn't say that. But he sounds delightful."

She had to make a nine o'clock flight that evening out of the Albany airport, an hour's drive away. They drove back to her apartment so she could pack an overnight bag, they made love, they stopped at his office to pick up his copy of Yuki's doctoral thesis for her to read on the plane, and on to the airport.

Dana woke up the next morning to realize it was Saturday and the large room she was in was at the gracious old Ritz in Boston. She looked at her watch: eight-thirty. She was meeting Yuki in two hours. Plenty of time to shower, dress, and have breakfast, then finish reading his three-

36

hundred-page thesis which she had been reading on the plane and before she went to bed. It was an impressive piece of work. Kermit had not exaggerated his expertise and technical brilliance.

When the phone rang at ten-fifteen, she was ready. Yuki was downstairs and willing to wait if it was too early. She told him to come right up. She was sure they could talk better in private. She felt him hesitate a moment before he agreed.

She straightened the blanket and pillow on the bed and threw on the bedspread. Then she spotted the bright green cover of Yuki's thesis, tossed it into her overnight bag and paused in front of a mirror to adjust her hair. She wondered whether his hesitancy to come up was Japanese delicacy, plain shyness, fear of compromising himself, or something else.

She opened the door to the knock; he was medium height, wiry slim, black straight hair, strong face with a broad, self-conscious smile. He was dressed in a blue denim jacket and pants with a maroon turtleneck pullover and he carried a trenchcoat over his arm.

"Hi. I'm Ishizaka."

"I'm glad you could make it. Come in."

As his eyes went around the room, Dana realized that the room hardly had the impersonal ambience in which a stranger could feel comfortable. The two upholstered chairs and coffee table didn't counterbalance the bed and mirrored dresser with the hairspray can.

"I'm sorry, Yukio—"

"Call me Yuki."

". . . If you'd rather go downstairs to the coffee shop or—"

"No, this is fine. We can talk here. It's perfectly comfortable, Miss Haverhill."

"Dana."

He sat down in one of the club chairs facing away from the window and folded his arms over his midsection. "How is Professor Nordstrom? I haven't seen him in quite a while."

She noted the defensively folded arms and his selection of a chair away from the light. "Oh, he's fine. He asked me to send you his best regards. I'm in charge of operations at the Computer Center so we work together quite a bit. Kermit says you have the best systems mind he's ever known. And of course he's very proud of how far you've gone so quickly."

There was the suggestion of a smile on his shadowed face. "He is an excellent teacher."

"I read your doctoral thesis and I was very impressed, though I admit a lot of it was over my head. I was especially impressed with your obvious concern about the effect of computer abuses on people. Kermit says your thesis was, quote, 'an important contribution to the art of penetration prevention.' Unquote."

Yuki was smiling broadly—and somewhat uncomfortably. "That's almost more flattery than I can stand for one morning. It's good for my ego but I'm not sure it's so hot for my character."

"I didn't mean to embarrass you. It's just that because of your expertise in computer security, Kermit thought you would be the ideal person to help me with my project. It would mean a great deal to me, obviously, if you could. But please . . . I don't want you to feel obligated. If you don't have the time or the interest, please say so. I'll absolutely understand—"

"Tell me about the project."

"Well, it's research for my doctoral thesis. It starts out with the premise that since data communication via satellite has grown so explosively in recent years—I think it's up to five billion dollars a year now, isn't it?—and multipoint data transmissions are hitting to different places around the globe simultaneously, *and* compact terminals are becoming available—we have a serious potential problem of data invasion or tampering on a global scale via satellites."

Yuki nodded his head slightly.

"Of course, I've got to develop this premise with facts and statistics and with as many examples as possible of ripoffs and sabotage and other serious abuses of COMSAT's or INTELSAT's data transmission facilities. And then I hope to be able to devise some countermeasures, or at least some approaches, to make it more difficult to gain access to satellite communications. You can see why I need a lot of help from the right authority. What I would love to have from you would be some guidance about resources to use for my research and for the technical expertise to assemble those countermeasures. That is, if you think my premise is valid."

Yuki rested a hand over his mouth, his thumb alongside his long, flat nose, and stared at her. It seemed like minutes before he spoke and she began to feel that maybe he wasn't going to say anything at all.

"I wonder if you know what you're getting into, Dana."

"Not entirely. That's one of the reasons I came to see you."

"I don't want to discourage you or question your qualifications, but I think you should know that you'd be stepping into a rattlesnake's nest. Let me explain." He stood up, dug his hands deep in his pants pockets and began pacing back and forth, looking at the floor. "This is one of the most . . . sophisticated areas of computer technology and it involves the space sciences as well. There are a lot of people engaged in satellite data transmission but they each know only a small part of the operation. Only a comparative handful really understand all the technologies involved, and it's very difficult to get them to talk. With good reason. We're now getting into our fifth generation of equipment, all-digital systems for data and voice, with transmission speeds of up to eighty-thousand bits of information per second. And the new compact terminal, DICOM, makes it easy to send or receive data signals from practically anywhere. So you see, satellite data *is* becoming more vulnerable and this is causing worry. There have already been a number of unauthorized entries, but the facts have been suppressed." He stopped pacing and looked at her.

"Then my premise *is* valid."

"That's the problem. It's critically valid. They're classifying a lot of the new material, so they're not about to open up to someone doing research for a doctoral thesis, especially on this jackpot theme. In fact, if you were to tell them what you had in mind, I'm quite sure that the FBI and the CIA would do a thorough job of investigating you."

"Even if I made it clear that the whole purpose of my thesis was to develop techniques for *preventing* invasion?"

"Especially. If you *were* able to develop it, it would mean you would also have the penetration capabilities. They couldn't risk that."

"But it seems to me the far greater risk is in *not* having better methods of protection. In your case, for example, when you devised new ways for preventing invasion of computers and their data banks as you described in your thesis, did anyone try to stop you? And weren't some of your techniques later adopted by computer manufacturers?"

"Yes, but I was dealing with the broad field of computer operations and a lot of the information was pretty much generally known. And I was a research assistant on a federal project and my doctoral research was supported under a grant from the National Science Foundation, so I had official authorization. With COMSAT or INTELSAT, we're dealing with what's in effect a closed corporation."

"I see." She sounded deflated. She turned toward the thinly curtained window. In arguing for her thesis she had almost convinced herself that she was actually planning to carry it out. Now that that ploy hadn't worked, she needed another approach. Fast. "I've got to break through this problem in some way and I have no idea how. So much depends on it. . . ." She heard herself speaking her thoughts aloud, recognizing the double entendre, and a spontaneous notion formed as she spoke.

Yuki sat down on the chair and leaned forward. "Are you that committed to this subject for your doctoral?" His voice was sympathetic.

She realized at once she'd struck the right note. "Oh, it's not my thesis I'm thinking about. It's something more important than that. . . ."

He took the bait. "Which is?"

"I kind of thought you'd know."

He shook his head.

"It's what we've both been talking about . . . but from different directions. The problem of satellite vulnerability. I'm very concerned about it. I think that invasion of satellite data transmissions is one of the great dangers facing this country, and many other countries too. Think what would happen if national computer utilities linked together among nations by data transmission satellites were successfully accessed by . . . well, unauthorized elements." She heard her voice rising. "We could have electronic terrorism with economic and political blackmail and chaos on an international scale. Those extremist groups that take government embassies hostage or kidnap prime ministers or hijack airplanes to extort money for their causes might learn to invade satellite transmission, and then they could blackmail several governments into meeting their demands. A hostile group could actually overthrow governments. The warnings of your own thesis would be a child's nightmare in comparison."

"You put that very well . . . I don't know how to say this, Dana, and I'm afraid I may put it badly." He paused. "You are obviously a very bright person and I'm certain that you are an extremely competent systems analyst. But what you are trying to do in this research project of yours is . . . well, probably beyond your competence. I mean, it straddles two different disciplines: computer technology and a difficult area of space science. There are not too many people qualified to handle both. And, without access to the right resources, it would be impossible."

"I understand that . . . can you help?"

"Dana, I'm going to tell you something that I never intended to tell

40

anyone." He paused for a moment and clasped his long, bony fingers together on his lap. "When I was hired here at Parkinson over two years ago, it was as Data Security and Privacy Manager. My job was to protect our own data and systems and those programs we conduct for our clients —mostly government agencies and corporations and some private foundations. Sort of a private eye on computers. Well, in the process I got to see some things which were . . . serious. I've been working with COMSAT on certain developmental projects, many of them in the laboratory stage, and for the last year I've been urging my firm to present a comprehensive proposal of mine to build a wall of protective mechanisms—hard- and software—around COMSAT's and INTELSAT's data transmission operations for exactly the reasons you guessed at. Because the tremendous growth of data communications via satellite— with the multiaccess systems and the new miniterminals—makes the global system penetrable by a highly knowledgeable and determined terrorist, subversive agent, thief, whatever. But the top guys at Parkinson haven't been able to sell the program to COMSAT management, or so they say. I have to assume that they tried because I've been bothering the hell out of them.

"It's not just the U.S. that's involved. About ninety countries around the world, with earth stations for transmitting and receiving data are part of INTELSAT—alphabetically, from Argentina to Zaire—and many of those countries have become dependent upon satellite transmission not only for telephone, telegraphy, radio, television and weather signals but also for all kinds of data that affects their economies and their political stability. The point is that this global superstructure, created in the nineteen sixties, is in great jeopardy now in the eighties. But the powers that be refuse to do anything about it. Believe me, Dana, I'm not a visionary or a kook. I don't see bad guys behind every tree. I'm a practical scientist—and I *know*. I've tried to get the message across, but the Parkinson brass says, 'If the client doesn't think it's that important and says stay with the programs we've contracted for, then that's what we've got to do.' You don't know how that made me feel."

He turned away and she saw only the back of his head with its long, shiny black hair hanging straight down, and the edge of his cheekbone touched with light. She wanted to reach out and touch his hand, but she was afraid to.

Yuki turned back and surprised her with a self-conscious laugh. "I've just decided that the only way I can get out my ideas on protecting the satellite data system is by cooperating with you. Do you mind?"

"*Mind?* I think it's great."

"It means I will be violating my security clearance because I'll be giving you classified information on satellite technology. Some of it will deal with potential access techniques and some of it will describe protection mechanisms. But it's only a technical violation, and I'm sick of all these damn restrictive technicalities. All I'm out to do is to help prevent invasion by forcing them to *do* something about it. If we hothouse this thing together, I think you should be able to get your thesis finished and published within a year. I'm counting on you to keep this absolutely confidential—you can't even tell Kermit. Just tell him I'm sort of guiding you in your research—or I'll be dishonored and have to commit hara-kiri." He smiled weakly. "Okay?"

"I'm speechless." She really was. She didn't know what to tell him. She hadn't expected him to, in effect, proposition *her.* But what she still had to find out was whether Yuki, through Parkinson, had any channel or chain of interconnects for reaching into Azimuth—through a satellite or otherwise. And so far she hadn't even been able to approach the subject. She'd been sidetracked by her own ploy. "I need a little time to absorb it all," she said. She looked at her wristwatch. "Look, Yuki, it's getting on to lunchtime. Why don't we go downstairs, have a slow drink and then some lunch."

He sprang up from his chair, smiling easily. "I've got a better idea. Why don't we have a fast drink and a slow lunch. I'm suddenly very hungry."

Seated opposite him at a corner table in the dark-paneled, red-carpeted hotel dining room sipping a cocktail, Dana contemplated the striking personality change in Yuki. He spoke easily about his early interest in math and space science and how he had devoured the details of all the exciting preparations for NASA's first moon launch when he was barely a teenager. Remembering what Kermit had told her about him, Dana steered him into talk about his family. His father had been born in Japan and had emigrated to the United States as a young man several years after World War II. His mother was a native Californian of mixed American and Japanese parentage and she became a high school teacher. Yuki was born in the fifties when the impact of being a Japanese on the West Coast was still a difficult experience. He mentioned that his grand-

42

father had been a wing commander in the air attack on Pearl Harbor. While he spoke calmly, it was clear that Yuki still had ancestral feelings of guilt about that. Although he thought of himself as an American—*not* as a hyphenated Japanese-American—during his growing-up years in California Yuki had been constantly reminded of his ancestry by his friends and schoolmates on the one hand and by the basic ethnicity of his family on the other. That was one of the reasons he came east as soon as he finished high school at sixteen as a top honors graduate. The schizophrenia of feeling entirely American, and yet realizing that he was just one generation removed from growing up in Osaka, had lessened over the years, but the image of Pearl Harbor in ruins remained as an occasional, recurring twinge.

"Tell me about your wife, Yuki. What's she like?"

"Harriet? I met her at a party the day after I landed my job here in Boston. On our first date I told her I never went out with a Jewish chick before. She said, 'That's okay, I never went out with a Jap before. My parents would die if they knew.' Then she said something about our having a lot in common—that she was a JAP too. I asked her to explain and she did: 'Jewish American Princess.' It was only partly true. Her parents had given her everything she ever wanted, but basically she wasn't really spoiled. I liked her immediately. We did have trouble with her parents but we gradually wore them down. They just couldn't deny their little girl anything. I even converted to Judaism, to satisfy them . . . and I found it very interesting. . . ."

Dana decided that it was time to get down to business—to find out about his firm's computer relationships. She started by casually asking him who some of Parkinson's clients were, aside from COMSAT. Yuki immediately looked uncomfortable.

"I'd rather not talk about it here." He looked at his watch. "It's getting late and I told Harriet I'd be home before this."

Dana had a queasy feeling in her stomach. She had squandered the time thinking that she would have the opportunity to find out what she needed to know over lunch. She saw her mission disappearing down the drain.

He read the disappointment on her face. "Tell you what. If you can be ready in a flash, I'll drive you to the airport. It's practically on my way. We can talk in the car. I'll call Harriet and let her know."

"Perfect . . . be down in a minute." She got up from the table and hurried to the elevator.

Dana was not going to waste the thirty precious minutes they would have together on the way to the airport. As soon as Yuki's blue Chrysler Imperial pulled into traffic—it was a gift from Harriet's parents, he said apologetically—she reopened the subject of Parkinson's other clients.

"Do your computers interconnect with the government agencies you do work for?" She kept her tone as bland as possible.

He stared ahead, switching lanes in the downtown traffic, the turn signal ticking metallically in the quiet, plush interior of the car. "Yes, they have to. Our computers talk to theirs all the time."

"I suppose you do work for several government agencies?"

"Like which?" He turned his head to her momentarily.

She tried to sound random. "Oh, like HEW, Agriculture, Commerce, IRS, Interior and so on."

"No, none of those. But the agencies we're programming for do interconnect with them and *our* terminals interconnect, of course, with theirs."

"Then you could have access to any of those government agencies through your terminals here?" The jackpot question, finally. She hoped it didn't show.

"It's technically possible . . . but we'd have to get clearance for it, and that's unlikely unless it was under an authorized contract. Why?"

She settled back in the deep leather seat and stretched out her legs, crossing them at the ankles. "I'm curious to know if government agencies are as vulnerable to penetration as COMSAT or INTELSAT."

"Much more. No comparison. That's why I have a job." He turned to look at her again. "I hope I didn't give you the wrong impression. Satellite data transmission is extremely difficult to breach, but it's getting easier as time goes on and that is why I'm so concerned. Security must keep three to five years ahead because systems architecture is involved, and it takes time to design protective hardware and techniques."

He accelerated suddenly and the heavy car shot ahead as they entered an open stretch of highway. Dana rolled down her window and felt the cool air of the winter afternoon wash over her quiet exhilaration. *She had her answer:* it was technically possible! That's all she needed to know for now. She took a few deep breaths, turned and looked at him as he peered

44

intently through the windshield. He seemed so young—a long-haired boy still on campus nurturing visions of a better world. She felt a real rapport with him. But she still owed him an answer to his earlier question. "You've been very helpful and I'm grateful for your confidence and your offer." Her voice was low and intimate. "I would love to accept, of course, but you've given me a lot to think about. Would you be annoyed if I postponed my answer just a bit?" She just couldn't lie to him anymore, and this way she didn't have to.

"No, of course not. I realize that what I am asking you to do is, in a way, unethical—to use classified information for your research. I have my own reasons for doing this, but you have to consider your own situation. When you didn't answer me before, I thought that the answer was no. I'm glad that the possibility is still alive."

They were now at the airline terminal building in Logan International Airport and Yuki stopped the long car in front of the main entrance.

"Don't bother to get out," Dana said quickly. Her gray-green eyes held him and her voice became intimately warm. "I want to thank you so very much for everything, Yuki. I hope we're going to get to know each other much better. I'll be in touch." She leaned over and kissed him softly on his cool cheek.

Dana jumped out of the car, her small overnight case swinging in her hand. She walked a dozen steps, turned around and saw him standing at the curb. She waved with her free hand, and he nodded in acknowledgment.

Something, she decided, had happened.

Chapter Five

It was just before dusk when Kermit met Dana at the Albany airport. As she emerged wearily from the terminal building, he pulled her toward him and kissed her, immediately sensing that she had been through an ordeal. As they drove away, the sky was already darkening, a violet-leaden tinge foretelling snow. Dana sat without saying a word, her eyes straight ahead. He had never seen her like this.

"Was it that bad" he said finally.

She made a little grimace that he didn't see. "Oh, I feel ugly. I tricked him into telling me something he shouldn't have and I feel awful about it. I broke him down with a lie, and it happened to be the perfect lie, so he turned himself inside out for me, and I know it hurt." Her voice was suddenly low, intense. "Kermit . . . Yuki is such a sensitive, vulnerable person and I feel rotten about conning him with my phony story of needing his help for my doctoral thesis." Her words hung there . . . a rebuke.

"Maybe I should have been along, after all. I'm sorry you had to go through all that. Well, then you don't think he's our man?"

"That's the trouble. I'm sure he *is*. And I hate the idea of involving him."

As they drove under the rapidly darkening sky, Dana recounted in detail her long conversation with Yuki. "It was," she said, "like mugging a guy and then having him invite you home for dinner." She saved for the last the astonishing revelation that Yuki had actually offered to provide her with classified information on penetration and prevention techniques on COMSAT's and INTELSAT's data transmission operations.

"I'll be damned," he said. "While we were cooking our conspiracy, Yuki had his own simmering on a back burner waiting for the right moment. And you showed up at the perfect time with the right entry code." He shook his head. "It's one helluva coincidence, but really not such a surprise. His thesis showed how strongly he felt about computer surveillance and electronic totalitarianism. But we still don't know if he will work with us. We know we need him and that he has the technology and motivation. But would he be willing to come in with us—is he willing to commit a major crime, even if it is reversible and for a good cause? Would it be fair to ask him to? I'm not so sure. . . ."

It was dark when they arrived at her apartment house; the lighted windows looked like a distorted checkerboard in the building's half-dark façade. Upstairs, she resisted his embrace, too wrapped up in what to do about Yuki.

Stretched out in easy chairs facing each other halfway across the large multipurpose room, they discussed every aspect of Yuki's possible involvement. And although they talked about alternate possibilities—other people, other approaches for activating the Azimuth scramble—it was, ultimately, just an exercise. They already knew, each one privately, it had to be Yuki.

Finally she said, "Okay. We'll put it to him and let him decide. If he doesn't want to, that's his protection. He'll stay out of it. If he isn't sure, we won't persuade him. If he wants to . . . but we won't push him into this—he's got to sell himself. Is it a deal?"

"Deal." Kermit got up from his chair and walked toward her playfully. He reached down, and pulled her flying into his arms. At almost the same moment he sensed her nipples harden against his chest and she felt a bulge pressing against her.

"What do you think you're doing?" she said as he unzipped the back of her blouse. "That's not the deal I had in mind." She stepped out of her skirt as he continued undressing her. "You're an old lech, you know that?"—as he crouched on his knees pulling off her body stocking that he hated. "What's taking you so long?"

Their lovemaking went on longer than usual. It was a way to release, explode the pressure. They made love violently, casually, teasingly, inventively, and in between they sat on the rumpled bed watching the television news and talking back to the screen, stopping to eat a warmed-over Quiche Lorraine with Rhine wine when they got hungry, then probing the filaments of love once more and finally falling asleep, limbs in disarray, like kids under a Christmas tree.

On Monday between classes Kermit phoned Duane Crozier, a political reporter for the Washington bureau of *Newswatch*, a weekly national newsmagazine. Crozier, a thirtyish, pudgy, very bright tongue-in-cheek cynic, had been the only newsman they'd met who seemed to empathize with their lobbying for legislation to crack down on computer-based crime and invasion of privacy. He had given them one of the most favorable write-ups they'd received, and a rapport had built up between them. Crozier was the best pipeline Kermit had to what he was burning to know.

Kermit didn't immediately recognize the flat voice at the other end. "Duane?"

"Who else? How are you Kermit?"

"Good, and you? Yes, Dana's fine too. . . . Look, Duane, I wonder if I could get your advice on something. It may be nothing at all but I'd appreciate if you could check it out." He took a quick breath. "I think I'm being, well . . . blackmailed . . . by, if you can believe it, the president of South Hanover—yes, Chappell . . . Gideon Chappell. That's right, blackmailed, I don't really know any other good word for it. What? . . . It's okay, I'm using a pay phone. I have a feeling that there may be a connection in Washington. I think they're trying to stop us, you know what from. I know it sounds weird, and it could be all in my head, but let me tell you about it. . . ."

Kermit sketched the highlights of his strange meeting in Chappell's office and he found his anger reigniting as he spoke.

Duane was fascinated, his newsman's instincts piqued. "And you want me to dig out the connection, if there is one. I'd be surprised if there isn't. But let me tell you something, Kermit. Even if I find something that smells, these things are almost impossible to prove. The members of the club know how to protect themselves and each other. Yes, I have a few obvious places to start and I'd like to help you hang the bastard. I mean *your* bastard. I don't know who mine is yet, but I'm going to love finding

48

him. Okay, I'll look into the angle of the phony grant too but I wish I had more to go on. Don't worry, nothing will hit the ink if I stumble onto something. What kind of a bum do you think I am?''

They left very early on Saturday morning to catch the first Allegheny Airlines flight from Albany to Boston. Dana had set up the meeting with Yuki without mentioning that Kermit was coming.

As they drove to the Albany airport, Kermit told Dana of the hand-delivered invitation he had received to play tennis with Chappell on a private indoor court near the campus the following Tuesday. No question that this was a command performance. Well, he did owe the president an answer to his camouflaged ultimatum. But at least this time he knew what the rules of the game were. He winced at his unspoken pun, then decided he was entitled to it. Unlike some other things, it didn't, after all, hurt anybody.

It was a chilly ride in a taxi with a broken window from Boston's Logan International Airport to Chelsea and Yuki's house, a long, contemporary, hip-roofed ranch filling a well-landscaped property and framed by older traditional homes. Yuki answered the ring promptly, clearly though politely uncomfortable at the sight of Kermit.

"Kermit . . . what a surprise. Come in, both of you." The floor felt unsteady beneath his feet as he turned from Kermit, managing to dispose of the coats in the entrance closet. Stiff-kneed, he led them into the large, whitewalled living room heavy with handsomely framed modern paintings and graphics, obviously expensive contemporary furniture, several pieces of abstract wood and soldered metal sculpture perched on marble cubes. White, deep-piled carpeting flowed throughout the visible areas and track lighting ran the length of the ceiling focused on the paintings, the graphics, and the sculpture. A small chandelier of hand-blown tubes of rippled Venetian glass suspended over a corner table shimmered in the sunlight from the adjacent picture window. Lots of taste and money.

"Harriet was an art major and she enjoys this sort of thing," Yuki said self-consciously as he noticed them studying the room.

Kermit settled into one of two chromium and tan leather Barcelona chairs sitting side by side like headless horsemen astride their steeds, the huge matching hassocks. "It's very comfortable and attractive," he said.

Yuki gave him a quick, cautious smile.

Determined to dissolve the awkwardness as quickly as possible, Dana plunged in. "Yuki, I know you were expecting me alone, but there's a very good reason why I asked Kermit to come with me. I know you'll understand why he *had* to be here with me, and that I really didn't betray your confidence. Let me tell you before I bust. . . . When I first came to you and asked for your help with my thesis on preventing satellite data invasion, I was lying about the thesis. I've got to tell you that right off. I'm not working on my doctorate—at least not yet. But I . . . I mean we" —she nodded in Kermit's direction—"do need your help on something that I think you'll agree at this point is far more critical. The trouble is it requires an illegal act on all our parts and we didn't want to burden you with this . . . guilty knowledge, I think they call it, because we didn't know how you'd feel about it. We didn't want to involve you unless you wanted to be, and the only way I could find out was to lie to you about the thesis. I'm very sorry about that, but it was the best way I knew. But everything else was true. I still feel exactly the way I told you about satellite penetration and so does Kermit."

Kermit raised his shoulders to loosen up the back of his neck. He felt very uncomfortable as a silent spectator in his own defense, in front of his former protégé.

"It's all part of the same thing, really," she was saying, her face striving for conviction, "whether it's satellite data transmission or computer data banks." She paused momentarily, monitoring Yuki's eyes for a sign. "I know you told me a lot of things you undoubtedly never would have if I hadn't deceived you, and I hope very much you won't regret it. But believe me, our purpose from the first was the same as yours— to prevent the violation of computer systems, yours by satellites, ours by land-based computers."

"You told him everything we talked about?" Yuki said in a flat voice.

"Well, yes . . . but you've got to understand, Yuki, that . . ."

Kermit could wait no longer. "If you don't mind, Dana, I feel *I* owe the explanation to Yuki. . . . Yuki, there's something I want you to know because it's important . . . at least to me. Dana didn't tell me anything about you I wasn't aware of. We did work together rather closely for a couple of years, remember, and I knew how strongly you felt about our responsibilities as computer scientists and how concerned you were about the threats to our civil liberties from misuse of computer technology. Besides, it's all spelled out in your doctoral thesis for anyone to read.

In fact, it's required reading in my Comp Sci 2 class." He looked for a sign of response, saw none. "So what does that leave? . . . the fact that you're willing to reveal some secrets of satellite transmission penetration in order to force those jerks to let you build higher walls to protect them better? That doesn't surprise or shock me. Quite the contrary. If you're worried about betraying a trust, then you should forget the whole thing. But I'm sure you meant what you said to Dana, and we both admire your guts for proposing it and being willing to go through with it, to go out on a limb like that." He paused, hoping he wasn't overdoing it.

"I think it's obvious we all have the same motives and goals. What we came here today to find out, Yuki, is whether the three of us can and should work together on one project to achieve that goal. We think it's an absolute natural. And to be perfectly frank, we feel that you're indispensable to what we have in mind. The question is, can *we* serve *your* purpose? We think it's all the same package. But you'll have to decide that for yourself."

Yuki looked uncomfortable. "I don't know how to answer that. I would have to know a lot more about what you propose."

"Of course," Kermit said quickly.

For the next half hour Kermit leaned forward on the tan leather chair, hands occasionally cutting the air in short, crisp motions. When he had finished outlining the plan to penetrate the IRS, and the three of them had discussed how the satellite's computer vulnerability could be made an integral part of the project, Kermit finally leaned back and studied the intense young man seated across from him; his eyes were a damn sight more responsive now. "You'll be running the same risk we will. We could all end up in jail, who knows for how long. I think you should consider that carefully before you decide."

"I've already done that, while we were talking."

"How do you think Harriet would take it?" Dana said, getting to her feet.

"I want to keep her out of this. This is nothing for her to have to worry about."

"You're *sure* then? . . . You'll do it?" Kermit said, anxious to make the commitment clear-cut.

"I'll do it," Yuki said quietly.

Kermit stood up, took a few steps and clasped Yuki's hand. Dana hugged him as he stood there rather stiffly, smiling self-consciously. "Welcome to Azimuth," she said, releasing him.

"To what?"

Finger over lips, she said, "I'll tell you later. For now, do you happen to have a chilled bottle of champagne in this joint?"

Chapter Six

The tennis match with Chappell was at the old brick factory converted to a luxurious tennis club. It started out as between gentlemen, Chappell gracious in his white shorts, insisting that doubtful calls on line balls be resolved to Kermit's advantage. But by the time the score in games was four to two in Chappell's favor, it suddenly became a high-noon duel.

The transition started when Gideon, standing at the net toweling his pink sweaty face and neck between games, said casually, "By the way, Kermit, since I haven't heard from you following our chat at my office, I assume that you've decided to discontinue your lobbying activities. Am I correct?"

"You are correct," Kermit said with matching insouciance, walking away from the net bouncing a ball he had just retrieved.

"Just a moment," Chappell's voice took on an imperious note.

Kermit turned and stood there flatfooted in his tennis shoes, racquet in hand facing his opponent. He tightened his grip.

"I'm afraid I need more assurance than that. I must be certain you've put the subject out of your mind completely. To be frank, Kermit, more than a professorship and that government grant are at stake. It could affect your tenure at the university and conceivably even your career." No one was in earshot.

"That sounds like a threat," Kermit said, smiling.

"To the contrary. It's a prediction. I would hate to see it happen, but as I explained last time, I would have no control. I would much prefer to have you stay on and get your promotion and the grant—"

"I'm sure . . . I really don't like to be threatened, and I already told you I've stopped all my lobbying activities. But my word should be good enough." He hoped he'd struck just the right blend of indignation and surrender.

"Excellent. . . ." Chappell's voice was oiled with victory. "Then you've nothing to worry about . . . we understand each other."

That did it. Chappell was clearly the more expert player, and Kermit remembered the collection of gold-plated tennis trophies in the wall niche in the president's office, but he was determined to wipe that goddamn smile off the suave face on the other side of the court.

Kermit's two first serves went in clean and strong, but Chappell put them away easily beyond the reach of his backhand. Down love-thirty on his service, Kermit began hitting the corners just inside the baseline on his returns, softened his serves and angled them carefully, forcing Gideon to rush in to reach them and to overhit them beyond the baseline. In a seesaw battle of ad-ins and ad-outs, Kermit finally took the game.

On Gideon's serve Kermit developed a strategy of undercutting the ball so it stopped nearly dead before Gideon could rush in from the baseline. To do that Kermit lay back as the serves boomed in and started his swing further back. It worked just well enough for him to take that game too, evening the score to four-four. Once Gideon solved the underspin return, Kermit varied the pattern, keeping his opponent off-balance with occasional slices, top spins, alternating hard and soft service and placing his returns, sometimes shallow and sometimes deep, actually catching Gideon flatfooted a couple of times. It was the only tactic he could use to prevent Gideon from bringing his superior game to bear, and it took tremendous concentration.

By the time they were six-six in games, Gideon's smile had withered. He managed to take the next game from Kermit after going to deuce three times. In the next game he double-faulted twice in a row, and when Kermit took the next two points—one on a well-placed passing shot and the other with a teasingly effective offensive lob after Gideon had rushed the net—Gideon threw his racquet to the ground in disgust. Embarrassed, he said, "I've never done that before. Sorry." He retrieved the racquet and walked slowly back to position to receive service, his face a pink mask.

After that he bore down hard but was clearly unnerved by his loss of composure. His best shots went off, and Kermit's accuracy increased as Gideon's game stayed erratic—though he held steady for short periods, burning brilliant, unreturnable shots at Kermit. They were playing silently now, tensely, Kermit with craft and sweat, Gideon with stony desperation—each conscious of the high psychological stakes. Gideon had the game point advantage several times in each of the remaining games but in duels involving flashy returns on both sides Kermit either lured him into error or Gideon netted the ball himself on critical points. The set and match ended nine-seven, Kermit's favor. He had beaten the champion of South Hanover.

On the way to the locker room he hoped it was an omen of a far more important victory.

A few days later in his study, while Kermit was editing the first typewritten draft of his article for *Datamation,* the phone rang once and stopped. He went to his desk, picked up a pencil and waited. A minute later it rang again. He picked up immediately. The voice on the other end asked, "Is this two-five-four-nine?" Kermit replied, "No, I'm sorry, you have the wrong number." It was Duane Crozier using the prearranged signal to be called back from a public telephone at the Washington number just given where he waited in a phone booth.

Kermit put on his leather jacket, went out to his car and drove five minutes through the quiet, dark residential streets to the gas station just off state highway 23. He entered the phone booth and punched out the number, his left hand cupping coins. He knew the area code and three digit prefix that Duane purposefully omitted.

"I've been digging in some fancy cesspools," Duane began, "and I've come up with a few items."

Duane's findings centered on Senator Gunther Morstan, a hard-line, hawkish Democrat from South Carolina, the powerful longtime chairman of the Senate Committee on Military Affairs. Until 1976 when it was partially revamped as the result of a series of sensational revelations, Morstan had been a member of the congressional watchdog committee which was charged with overseeing the CIA but which instead gave it virtual carte blanche.

"So you think Morstan is the one pulling the strings on Chappell to shut me down?" Kermit finally said.

"No proof, but it's a good bet. They're both Dartmouth alumni just one class apart, they were fraternity brothers and still are—Sigma Alpha Epsilon."

"That's interesting but hardly conclusive."

"It gets more interesting. This wasn't easy to come by, friend, so please don't ask me how I got it, but listen to this: two members of the senator's staff are quietly writing proposed legislation to authorize linking the time-sharing computer systems of over twenty federal departments with state and municipal agencies so they can automatically plug into each other."

There was a momentary silence from Kermit. "Are you *sure* of that?"

"I'm sure."

"God. Do you know what that means? Hundreds of these systems will be interchanging data of all kinds on people and organizations that are absolutely none of their damn business. Those data banks are full of personal information that's inaccurate, irrelevant and never belonged there in the first place. A lot of it was gotten illegally anyway by the FBI and other government intelligence units. It means wholesale slaughter of privacy."

"Don't get excited. The best is yet to come. Wait till you hear about 'the police state provision.' That's my phrase, not theirs." He paused. "They're writing a provision which will *mandate* setting up a massive multiaccess computer system inside the FBI which would let them monitor the computers of every city and state police department in the country—there are about 4,000, I understand. The FBI has been trying to get this kind of authority for years. Their National Crime Information Center has been a valuable tool for law enforcement, but they got the taste and now they want the whole thing. That's the trouble with computers. They've got such a gluttonous appetite they'll eat anything people give them. . . . Tell me, Kermit, how's it technically possible for them to do this? There are all different kinds of systems—so many unrelated pieces of equipment, it seems to me. . . ."

"Because about five years ago—in the late seventies—the Department of Defense developed a technology that made it possible for incompatible time-sharing systems to communicate with each other despite the different systems and types of equipment they used. It was a big breakthrough and opened up a lot of doors for the industry. Still, I don't see

56

how they'd be able to get away with this. It's so obviously illegal—"

"I'll tell you how. I was able to get a pretty good rundown on how the legislation will be written and presented. The bill will be presented as a crime-fighting resource to enable the FBI to help local law enforcement agencies reduce the level of crime across the board. The pitch would be that more comprehensive computerized data would give the FBI and the local police more advance information on criminal activities so they could react faster—"

"And violate the rights of those they only suspect," Kermit finished.

"And they also have another angle. It would give greater protection to our national security through better surveillance of potential terrorists, subversives and so forth. And they've got a really good argument for that other provision—the linkage of federal, state and city multiaccess systems. They'll say it will speed the flow of important statistical information among the various agencies for more effective planning of the nation's economy."

"They've got it all blocked out. Do you think Congress will buy it?"

"I think it will have tremendous appeal to a lot of people, especially when they get through packaging and promoting it. You've got to remember the mood of the country and of Congress. The swing is still toward conservatism, or away from liberalism. Even the liberals aren't very liberal anymore. Everyone's fed up with crime, racial problems, inflation, First Amendment cases that turn out to be partly hustle. Invasion of privacy is so pervasive, it's hardly noticed. I don't know if anyone gets excited about it anymore."

"I'm afraid you're right . . . but it seems to me that such legislation could be stopped on constitutional grounds—"

"I don't think that would be a factor in Congress. Then it would be up to the Supreme Court. And remember who we've got sitting up there. They reflect the mood of the country too. But the bottom line, Kermit, is that I'm sure that Morstan is your man. His tie-in with Chappell, and this legislative abortion being prepared, *and* Chappell trying to muzzle you. I just don't believe in that much coincidence. . . ."

Driving slowly back to his place, Kermit felt a strange kind of relief. Any reservations he had had about the advisability of Azimuth were now dissipated. A few of them, at least, weren't going to stand around and watch invasion of privacy and political manipulation of U.S. citizens become a daily commonplace, while thousands of civil service clerks sat at terminal consoles and mindlessly punched holes in the First Amendment to the Constitution.

Chapter Seven

The three were sitting in Kermit's large living room with a round oak dining table on one end and a compact kitchenette wall of white appliances and cabinets just behind. It was late Saturday morning, February 2—a week since their last meeting. Yuki had just arrived from Boston.

Glancing around the room, Yuki said, "It hasn't changed much since I was here last, except maybe for a few extra cigarette burns. . . . I've worked up a specific proposal for the Azimuth job," he began matter of factly. This was a looser Yuki than either of them had seen. "It did take a while to figure it out. It involves a certain amount of fairly exotic satellite technology, so feel free to stop me if you have any questions. Nothing's fixed. It's just a sort of blueprint for discussion and change. Okay?"

Leaning forward from his seat on the sofa, he went on, "We start with the fact that IRS is heavily computerized and has a very sophisticated query processing system for information storage and retrieval on some ninety million private individuals and fifteen million businesses. We also know that the central computer system is in Martinsburg, West Virginia, and that there are ten computer Service Centers serving seven regional offices. The Service Centers receive the tax filings and data on taxpayers in their areas and use a Honeywell 4020 to directly transcribe the data to microfilm tape, and then the individual returns are processed and the data verified on a Honeywell 2058. Then they send the data to the central system in Martinsburg, which analyzes and programs the accounting, billing, issuing of refunds, delinquencies and so forth. The incoming data from the Service Centers and the programs created in Martinsburg, as well as the data on individual taxpayers, are stored in the master data bank in Martinsburg. Okay?" He looked at one and then the other. "Programmed instructions are then sent back to the Service Centers to be acted on. In other words, Martinsburg is the brain center that receives the data, makes the decisions and tells the Service Centers exactly what to do. They carry out the instructions on a Control Data 3500, a real-time system which Martinsburg loads. The Service Center computers then print the notices of whatever type—bills, audits, delinquents, refunds, etcetera—and sends them out to area taxpayers. Martinsburg, of course, has a collection of IBM 360s and 370s all tailored to the agency's specifications, about ten in all, and they're experimenting with a more advanced model now . . . a real monster."

Dana broke in as Yuki paused. "Don't forget that the real brain of their computer system is the National Office of Computer Facilities in the IRS headquarters building in Washington. They develop all the software and programming, they select and test all computers before they go on line and they oversee quality control for the system generally. I had a lot of contact with them when I was doing my research project for the agency."

Yuki nodded and resumed his explanation. "The fascinating thing to me about this whole setup is the newness of their telecommunications network. Until the last year or so they had no means of instantaneous communications between their Service Centers and the master computer. They actually shipped their tapes by truck, rail and, if they were in a great big hurry, by air freight. Can you believe that? A huge, vitally important government computer system from Maine to Hawaii with computers that couldn't talk to each other? It's incredible . . . a sophisticated system using a horse and buggy delivery mode. Well, anyway, that means it would have been almost impossible to break into Martinsburg using a terminal a year or two ago. We would have had to have someone right inside the walls. But now with telecommunications they've become more vulnerable but you can be sure that their security on the new network is very tight. There's more system integrity built into the hardware and an extremely rigid protocol would have to be followed to bypass the cryptography trap and access the central computer from a remote terminal. So we take an entirely different route. Invade them by a route they have no defense against . . . because they don't know it exists. . . . The beautiful thing about it is that it integrates terrestrial computers with satellite computers so we invade *two* systems with *one* terminal. Nice?

"What I've worked out is based on one of the weaknesses of COMSAT security that I uncovered a while back and couldn't persuade them to plug up. This is the thing you and I discussed, Dana, and it's what decided me to go into this thing with you. A couple of years ago I acted as a consultant for COMSAT Labs in Clarksburg, Maryland, on a very sophisticated Advanced Message Switching Program—AMSP—they were developing for their own domestic satellites as well as for INTEL-SAT's. As you know, when a computer sends a message to a distant computer via satellite, the message goes through telephone circuits to the nearest earth station, which beams it via the satellite to the earth station nearest to the destination where it is relayed to the intended computer. My job was to help insure the security of the new AMSP. After the program was completed, approved and inserted into the satellites, I kept experimenting with ways of breaking it down from Parkinson's computers. That kind of testing is also part of my job. In the process of testing, I discovered a penetration bug I considered serious. I finally worked out a method of eliminating it which I demonstrated to the Parkinson brass and then to the COMSAT officials. But they turned it down. They said the degree of access was so marginal it wasn't worth the cost of modifying the program. I thought it was very bad judgment on their part because it could turn into a security nightmare." His eyes were intense.

"Anyway, what I discovered during my testing of the new program up there in orbit was that during abnormal peaks, when the computer's circuits exceeded certain electronic load levels, messages from the satellite could be rerouted to addresses *other* than those ordered. In other words, if someone wanted to send data through a satellite from an unauthorized source to a computer system which was not accessible to that source, he conceivably could do it *if* he had a means of rigging the message-switching program in the computer or if he already had a private arrangement with the computer system to handle it that way. That's a lot of ifs, but it is possible for a number of people who, like myself, do have the technology and enough motivation." He looked from one to the other for questions.

61

"I'm with you so far . . . I think," Kermit said. "Go on."

"Okay. What I plan is to rig the program by inserting a new bug of my own. I've already worked it out. It's a carefully coded alteration to look like a correction and what it will do is route messages transmitted via satellite within IRS's computer network to me, on command. When I say to *me,* I mean to Parkinson's computer, where it will be transferred automatically into my file. That won't be noticed because it's the normal way I work in testing systems for penetration."

He drew a deep breath. "Now for the rest of the scenario. Once I've piggybacked my bug into the existing program in the satellite's computer, I give the command via a terminal—I'll either use one at Parkinson or a remote terminal I have at home—to go ahead and monitor all IRS traffic from their central computers to their regional network and back again. The monitoring can go on twenty-four hours a day if necessary, not just during those peak hours . . . because once I've inserted my correction, it's like a wedge. I can keep the door open as long as I want, and all that data speeding back and forth within the network will also enter our computer memory subsystem which controls access to my files."

He paused momentarily. "I'm writing a program to analyze and then summarize the data we've retrieved and also to instruct the computer to load the discs onto magnetic tape and store them in my files. Of course, I've got to break their code so I can identify their incoming data and that won't be easy. But we've got a library full of all kinds of exotic decoding programs and I'll just experiment till I find one. . . .

"All right, here's the rest of it. I want to command the satellite as soon as possible to tap Martinsburg's computers and monitor its two-way traffic through its network because we don't know what we'll find and we don't have a lot of time. Once we see what we have, we can decide what to do with it. What kind of foul-ups we perpetrate on whatever data we've selected. I should be able to figure out by studying the incoming data how to activate instructions to replicate the role of IRS Central and have the satellite send *our* messages directly to the Service Centers looking exactly as though they had come from Big Daddy."

Kermit nodded. "That's where the code comes in again, doesn't it?— to identify the programs and give us the command instructions and addresses of the Service Centers."

"Exactly. Then I intend to insert a real-time clock in this operation so that I can set the trigger for a certain hour on Saturday, March fifteenth—which, folks, is exactly six weeks from now. IRS's computers work round the clock seven days a week this time of the year and their automated equipment—printing, typewriting, stuffing, stamping—can process whatever it is we decide to have them do even on the weekend. And there will be no reason for anyone to suspect what's happening because the instructions coming in to the regional Service Centers will be arriving in the normal way, ostensibly from Martinsburg, and it will take a long time to discover otherwise. By then the fireworks have started . . . and all hell breaks loose, we hope."

Kermit and Dana sat there, fascinated. "That's brilliant, Yuki!" Kermit told him, and meant it. "I don't know anyone else who could have figured out how to do it."

Yuki's face creased into a self-conscious grin. "Thank you," he said quietly. "Now all I've got to do is make it work."

Dana's forehead wrinkled beneath the center part of her hair, which separated to either side. "Is that the whole thing? Your plan is marvelous, but in a way it seems almost too simple, or neat. . . ."

"It isn't really. Maybe I was too smartass glib. It's really pretty complex, and it'll take some doing to bring it all together. For example, devising the bug to get the message-switching program to misbehave was tricky. And breaking IRS's code is not going to be easy. And, of course, I don't know just how the monitoring program will work out. What shows up will depend on the kind of traffic going back and forth this time of the year, though I'd think it would be a rather fertile time. . . . Those are just some of the complexities."

But what happens if you can't break the code?" Dana asked.

"We're out of business."

Kermit tapped his pipe into the metal ashtray. "I'm curious how you were able to create a bug to alter the message switching program. That was really the starting point."

"The program is in the memory of the satellite's computer, okay? A copy is also on a disc at Parkinson and that's the one I experimented with so I know it works. Without getting too technical, it meant my working out a set of instructions which cause monitored messages to be rerouted to me while the original messages still arrive at their assigned destinations. In other words, it sends the same message to my computer as it does to the place where it's supposed to go."

63

"Okay, that's all clear," Kermit said, "but won't the presence of your bug show up in some way? Won't they detect that something abnormal's happening?"

"Nope. It will be invisible. Only what comes out of the pipeline at the end of a whole series of actions—the act of disruption itself—will be visible. And then, like I said, it will be too late."

"And Central will know nothing because it will receive nothing," Kermit tagged on. "That's beautiful."

"One last question," Dana said. "It seems to me that you'll have to put in an awful lot of time in Parkinson's computer center managing all these operations, maybe some of it after hours. How do you expect this not to be noticed?"

"Remember, I'm the top cop there. What I'll be doing is the same as my normal activities. It's my job to be suspicious and to pry and to probe. Besides, I can do a lot of the heavy work away from the office."

A look of quiet satisfaction flitted across Yuki's face. "So we've established our pathway. What do we do when we get there? Most of the input for that has to come from you two."

Kermit took a last puff from his pipe. "Ah, yes . . . that's a problem with all kinds of possibilities. All right, let's kick it around—" He stopped suddenly. "Oh, I almost forgot. I thought it would be helpful to have a list of criteria to measure our ideas against." He leaned over to the desk near his chair as he spoke and picked up a few sheets of white paper. "And to make it easier, I did a little homework." He handed each of them a typewritten sheet and kept one for himself. "See if you agree with this or want to add anything."

The three of them read their copies:

AZIMUTH CRITERIA
1. Must be quick acting.
2. Must be quick surfacing (visibility).
3. Must cause serious problems—throw scare into Administration.
4. Must arouse (preferably shock) public opinion.
5. Must be identifiable as external sabotage rather than internal technical breakdown.
6. Must not injure general public.
7. Must not damage the structure of government (temporary disruption only—readily restorable).
8. Preferably cause taxpayers to withhold filing annual returns.

Dana looked up from the paper first. "It looks good to me. The only thing missing is that it should lead to a presidential pardon for the perpetrators."

Neither man reacted to the tongue-in-cheek comment. They didn't even want to think about it.

"All right," Kermit said. "Who wants to start?"

Dana shrugged and made a self-effacing little expression she sometimes affected. "I guess I'm a professional volunteer. What about scrambling some of the key programs to make them unusable?" She shrugged again to identify it as a throwaway.

Kermit shook his head. "I don't know. It would paralyze those programs, it's true, but it wouldn't surface. They'd keep the lid on. But if we could figure out a way to break it open, then people would certainly stop filing tax returns. Let's hold it over." He looked at Yuki.

"A few days ago," Yuki said, "I learned that IRS has no lists in its files as such—which isn't exactly good news. All ninety million individual taxpayers are listed *only* by their Social Security numbers; companies are listed by their employers' numbers. The only pattern that I can see is that individual taxpayers are apt to cluster in ages through the sequence of Social Security numbers indicating when they came into the job market. Otherwise, they haven't anything else in common—income, vocation, geography, alphabetical sequence of names . . . anything. How do you grab onto that?"

"That *is* a problem." Dana's eyes seemed to deepen. "That's an area I never got into when I did my thing for IRS. Without lists of different categories of taxpayers, there just aren't any targets. That leaves us with practically nothing to work with."

The air in the room went suddenly dead as the impact of the apparent impasse hit them. The three of them sat there, three points of an unhappy triangle, trying to get their thinking back into gear. Finally Kermit said, "It's not as bad as it sounds . . . the answers are there, I'm sure of it, we've just got to work a little harder and dig them out. Okay . . . let's start. . . ." His eyes brightened as he thought he saw a small cut through the jungle. "For one thing, who says we must have special lists handed to us on a platter? Why can't we bypass the taxpayers' list entirely? Dana already suggested one way—scramble the programs and make them unusable. There have got to be others." It was the way he often challenged his students in the lecture hall.

Yuki reacted. "How about scrambling the data on communications so that it would go out as analogue gibberish to taxpayers? The printing of notices is activated by the CDC 3500 so they'll go out automatically."

"It *might* get by the office staff, I'm not sure. It would raise hell if it did." Kermit was subtly steering the meeting back on the track. "Okay . . . there's another idea that doesn't depend on lists. Let's have some more."

"Who says there *aren't* lists?" Dana suddenly demanded. "Martinsburg must be creating new lists every week as part of the programs they send out to the Service Centers. Lists of people who owe money . . . lists of people to get refunds . . . lists of those to be audited . . . lists of delinquents to be dunned and god knows what other categories. We don't have a list shortage—we have a bonanza!"

She's right," Yuki mumbled as though convincing himself. "Those are functional categories, and we missed them before. Actually there's no reason why we can't mess around with those. With a terminal to play with, we should be able to invent some very interesting games. . . ."

". . . called 'Screwing the Inscrutable,' maybe?" Kermit added.

"Is that an Oriental slur, sir?" Yuki said straight-faced.

"No, it's strictly occidental—"

"Cut the crap, kids, and let's get down to business," Dana said pleasantly.

"Okay, there is another possibility," Kermit said, referring back to Yuki's last serious statement. "We can create our own list-building programs. We can use the terminal to instruct an existing program—say, one which picks accounts to be audited—and tell it to pick out of the general file accounts with certain data characteristics. For example, federal employees making over $50,000 a year or corporate executives earning over $100,000 a year. That's one way of defeating the anonymity built into the system. Then we instruct the program to add these accounts to those scheduled to receive audit notices or any other kind of notice. We can do this with as many different categories of people as we want to target. The possibilities are unlimited."

"An easier way to do it," Yuki said, "would be to encode a macroexpansion within an existing program that would do the same thing, and the alteration would be virtually invisible. Otherwise, we'd be creating a program that wasn't in the data bank before and then we'd have to bury it."

They became silent and thoughtful. Finally Dana looked up. "Why don't we send out wrong notices, like penalties or fictitious bills, randomly or to selected individuals. That should stir up a ruckus . . . or better yet, why don't we just send audit notices to every one of the ninety million taxpayers in the country. Can you *picture* that? . . . millions of furious taxpayers, the country would be in an uproar, local IRS offices would have to close down . . . what do you think?"

Kermit looked up. "Ninety million notices printed and mailed? That would cost a fortune in paper, processing and postage. The taxpayers might hold it against us for wasting their money and for causing them all that trouble. It would give us ninety million enemies. It's a blockbuster, all right, but I'm afraid it would defeat our purpose, Dana. Now, on the other hand, if we could send out *refund* checks to everyone, it would make us a whole lot of friends, *but* it would break the Federal Reserve and then we'd all be in trouble. And that suggests another nasty idea . . . what if we sent dunning notices to the heads of all federal agencies—executive, regulatory, administrative—and to federal judges . . . or audit notices to members of Congress of the minority party. Half those guys must be cheating anyway. It would seem like a White House plot to embarrass the opposition, especially since this is an election year. . . ."

Dana smiled. "I like it."

"So do I," Yuki said.

Kermit's face went sober. "Except it won't get people to stop filing their tax returns. . . ."

"No, but it would give millions of just plain citizens a lot of pleasure to see those VIPs squirm," Dana replied. "However, if you're hungry for another idea, here's one: who are the most vocal and affluent people outside of government? Doctors, lawyers, union leaders, top management executives, right? And they're not above ripping off the public with big bills, secret slush funds, excess profits, unconscionable salaries and fringe benefits. How about selecting those with incomes of, say, $100,000 and over and sending *them* audit notices, making sure to include heads of oil companies, multinational companies and large defense contractors. Those fat cats would squeal like stuck pigs, you should forgive the horrible mixed metaphor."

Kermit nodded. "That one certainly goes into the hopper."

Yuki was poised with his contribution. "We could alter the code so that everyone who's entitled to a refund check would get a bill for the identical amount instead. They'd realize it was a mistake and their angry letters and phone calls would give the IRS's offices around the country one awful headache. It would be simple to do—we'd alter a small code reversing refunds into bills. Can you imagine the effect?"

"I think it's a definite possibility," Kermit told him, and Dana agreed.

"Talking about making headlines," Kermit picked up again, "what about sending dunning notices for the delinquent taxes *actuo'ly owed* by prominent public figures—senators, judges, governors, cabii.et officers— to newspaper, radio and TV news editors, as though by error?" Kermit looked expectantly at the others.

"You're a regular devil, professor," Dana said.

"But in a good cause . . . anyway, we have enough to go on—at least until we can get a dump of the current traffic between Martinsburg and the Service Centers and see what the inventory looks like. Maybe the smart thing to do would be to program two or more separate but simultaneous explosions . . . like one to scramble a program and find a way to make the news public so that tax filings will stop dead . . . and another to get a lot of influential people or just plain citizens so mad at the agency that they'll shout their heads off."

"Like a *Chinese* menu," Yuki said pleasantly. "One from column A and one from column B."

Dana rose suddenly, smiling sweetly. She glanced at her wristwatch. "Which reminds me, gentlemen, I'm starved. And oh, yes—let's not forget to burn the criteria sheets."

Chapter Eight

Lyle Gabriel looked irritable as he stood in front of the Shoreham Americana Hotel in uptown Washington, a cigarette burning unheeded in his hand, his sad gray eyes searching up and down the avenue busy with morning traffic. A minute later, a shiny car pulled up at the curb and he walked quickly toward it.

As Gabriel opened the door and slid inside next to the driver, Duane Crozier said, smiling grimly, "Don't say it, Lyle. I'm sorry I'm late. I got stuck behind a guy with all kinds of problems at the car rental office. My, you look slick today . . . going to the races?" He put the car in gear and took off turning left into the stream of northbound traffic.

Lyle always reminded Duane of an undernourished sea gull—gaunt, long-legged, a thin, sharp nose, and gray all over from his colorless once-sandy hair to his large, deep-set Lincolnesque eyes, which saw too much and rememberd what was best forgotten. Each time Duane saw him, he was surprised by Lyle's fashionable attire, which was at such variance with his no-nonsense newspaperman's personality. He had first known him several years back when Lyle was still a fellow member of the White House press corps and reported for a chain of South Carolina dailies—before he became a speechwriter for Senator Gunther Morstan. Although their political philosophies and their personal backgrounds were very different and Lyle was at least a dozen years older, they shared a passion for good writing, fine restaurants, good government and forthrightness—the latter two, they agreed, validating their cynicism.

Since Gabriel married his second wife—a beauty contest winner from Charleston—two years back, they no longer played cards or tennis nearly as often as they used to but they still kept in close touch by phone or an occasional lunch or drink.

"You chronically late characters always have a great cover story," Lyle said in his softly accented Southern voice, "but I assure you it's not part of your charm."

"Okay, dad, what's up?" Duane ignored the reprimand. "Why did I have to rent a car and pick you up in this end of town? Couldn't we talk at a bar or on a park bench?"

Lyle stared ahead, frowning. "We could but I preferred that we not be seen together."

"Is Marilyn that jealous?" Duane couldn't resist.

"Come on, Duane. I didn't come for the ride . . . the other day I let you coax some very confidential information out of me with the understanding that it was off the record. I thought you might care for some more . . . on the same basis."

Duane smiled gently in apology and nodded.

"Okay then, let's set up a couple of ground rules. What I'm about to tell you is top secret and counter to my responsibilities. You know my motivation in this. I'm disgusted as hell with what the senator is doing and I'm worried right down to my socks with what could happen to this sweet ole country of ours." He took a deep breath. "So-o . . . I'll use the Deep Throat technique. I won't volunteer anything. You make an assumption and I'll confirm or deny it. Make the right assumption and you'll get answers. Otherwise, nothing." He stared ahead.

"All right, I'll play," Duane said. "If it worked for Bob Woodward, why not for me? First try . . . is it related to what you told me about the bill your boss is drafting?"

"That's not an assumption, that's a question—but *yes* . . . I'll give you that one."

"It has to do with the purpose of the bill."

"Yes."

"All right, then . . . this purpose goes beyond the free access to all levels of government agency data banks by certain federal agencies."

"Yes."

"Great, where do I go from here?"

70

"Your prot¹em."

"You're making it tough . . . there's some other individual, or organization, coming into the picture."

"Correct, and I'll make it easy. It's an organization of sorts."

"The organization is a right-wing political group."

"Negative."

"It's a right-wing businessmen's organization."

"Negative."

"Okay, it's a government department or agency—"

"That's close enough."

"Yeah, but there are too many to pick from. I'll assume it's one of these . . . DOD, Justice, Treasury, FBI, CIA, FCC, GAO, IRS . . . let's see . . . Agriculture, Labor, Interior, Commerce, HEW, Nuclear Regulatory . . ."

"No cigar."

"Oh boy," Duane said in disgust. "You sure make a guy work for a living." He thought for a moment, and the only sound was of the car's tires gripping the highway. "I assume that it's not a secret agency tucked away underground somewhere."

"No, your assumption is not correct."

Duane was nonplused for a moment, then: "You mean it *is* a secret agency."

"It is a secret operation." Lyle's voice remained bland.

Duane swerved the car to the right, pulled over on the shoulder of the road on a windswept rise on the Capital Beltway and stopped the car. He turned off the engine. "You let me go through the alphabet of government agencies when the operation is a secret one and I couldn't possibly know it?"

"That's not a statement, that's a question."

"Okay, wise guy—game called on account of dirty play. What's the agency?"

Lyle's dour expression tightened. "I shouldn't be telling you this because . . . oh, screw it, I *want* you to know." He paused, then: "It's the National Personnel Advisory Council."

"The National Personnel Advisory Council? I never heard of it."

"I know. Almost nobody has. It's an obscure bureau that was set up quietly after the Korean War as a sort of executive talent agency to find and screen qualified appointees to high-level federal posts. It was organized by a hotshot management consultant—Conger Mayberry, I think it was—and he apparently installed one of the best computer systems in the country with the dossiers of tens of thousands of top people from business, the professions, the sciences, universities, politics, of course—from everywhere that mattered. It was so damn good that somewhere down the line—I don't know exactly when—it was expanded and secretly funded by a handful of federal agencies to do some of their dirty work. So now, NPAC hires free-lance spooks and private eyes to dig up incriminating information, some of it pretty sordid stuff, on anyone those agencies want to discredit or intimidate for political reasons. If they can't find anything damaging, they're not above manufacturing it, from what I hear. But if you dig enough you can generally find something in a guy's past that he wouldn't want known. Then they plant this stuff in their data bank and it becomes forever gospel. When an inquiry is made by a federal agency or someone high in the Administration, the computer spits it out. There it is in black and white. The individual doesn't know what's in his dossier because he doesn't even know that it exists. So the guy never gets the chance to prove that he doesn't go in for sodomy with borzois, or that his Cuban mistress doesn't smuggle the Congressional Record to the Algerians in exchange for hashish. All he knows is that his tries for public positions are stymied, federal grants for scientific research or whatever are denied . . . and he never gets too far up in the hierarchy of big industry or the academic world or government.

"NPAC used their original charter—finding and screening appointees for top federal jobs—as a cover for the rest of the operation. This means that its data bank is filled with enough legitimate stuff to make the whole thing look like motherhood. Its front office is in a sedate little brownstone in the Embassy Row area, But the real work comes out of a high-powered computer center located in a small industrial plant operating under a phony name. I don't know what it is, but the plant is somewhere outside of Harrisburg, Pennsylvania."

Duane sat there, arms resting on the wheel. "So we can assume that Morstan intends to use his bill to legitimatize the National Personnel Advisory Council by wrapping it in the American flag. Make their dirty work kosher so that he can get them large open funding to help certain federal agencies and the White House spy on more citizens and thereby save the country for one hundred percent Americans, by his definition, of course . . . turn the place into an electronic police state—"

72

"You got it. And there's one other point . . . NPAC would remain an independent, freewheeling operation responsible only to the President—not subject to congressional oversight."

"Do you have anything on the kind of data they've accumulated in their bank?"

"You-all name it, they-all have it. Every citizen who calls attention to himself in ways critical of the current Administration or of the military or police establishments may have a dossier drawn up on him and entombed in their data bank. That could include members of consumer and political activist groups, people who write dissenting letters to high public officials, leaders of people's lobbies, and even rival politicians . . . not to mention selected newsmen too critical of Administration policies or of the big man himself. It's been going on quietly under a few Presidents. They must have several million people locked away in that data mausoleum by now. I'd be surprised if you weren't among them."

Duane looked at him. "What do they do with all that stuff?"

"There are all kinds of ways those files could be used to intimidate or punish individuals if the data in them is at all incriminating. I know for a fact that some of this stuff has been used to inspire punitive IRS investigations and gratuitous probes by regulatory agencies such as FCC into the licenses of radio and television station owners who were considered particularly hostile to someone high up. Those files were also used to force some pretty good citizens who were involved in some hanky-panky at one time to become informers for the FBI; others were black-mailed into becoming agents for the CIA overseas . . . and lord knows what else."

Duane felt closer to his friend amidst this wintry landscape than he had for some time. "You know something Lyle," he said kindly, "you're starting to sound like a, watch out, liberal . . . maybe even a civil libertarian—"

"Not quite. I'm for the rights the Constitution guarantees. To hell with labels."

"Okay . . . and you're worried that Morstan wants to turn this whole underground spying operation into a legitimate government operation?"

Lyle was looking out the car window to the declining hills and shallow valley below powdered with a hint of snow. "More than that," he said glumly without turning his head. "I'm afraid that he intends to use those files to stifle enough of the opposition within the party—particularly the northeast wing—to insure his candidacy for the presidency." He suddenly faced Duane. "I know it sounds crazy but it just might work. Some of those dossiers on party leaders around the country are dynamite. And then if he ever makes it into the White House, think of what he could do with that data bank out of Harrisburg. It wouldn't be an imperial presidency—it would be an imperial dictatorship." His thin creased face seemed drained by the thought.

"But if you feel this way about him, why are you staying on as his speechwriter . . . and helping him? You've turned out some great stuff for him lately. How can you go on working for him?—"

"Two reasons. One, I want to see him stopped, and I figure the only way I can do it is from the inside. If I left and turned against him, I wouldn't have much credibility. And two, I'd have big trouble finding a decent job. No one likes a backstabber. Who'd trust me? I can't take that chance now, I've got a wife to think of. I can't go back to a newspaperman's salary. Marilyn is an expensive woman, and I just can't risk losing her."

Duane had never seen his friend so vulnerable, so openly frank. "Then why tell me—especially since you won't let me use any of it for publication? How will that help stop the bastard?"

"I'm not exactly sure yet. But when you came to me last week looking for some dirt on Morstan, and I told you about the bill the boys are drawing up, I figured that maybe in some way you could be the pipeline for pulling him down—if I gave you the right stuff. I haven't worked it all out in my mind yet, but I know you're one helluva reporter, and you'll do the digging I can't. And when the time comes, I'll tell you . . . okay, let it roll . . . use it all . . . blast him for all you're worth. Jesus, this country just can't *afford* a man like that . . . certainly not as President."

Dana was just finishing dinner with Kermit in his apartment when the call came in from Duane. She drove him to a phone booth in a nearby supermarket parking lot and waited in the Alfa Romeo as Duane told Kermit about his meeting with Gabriel.

As he listened, Kermit was once again reassured that even his wildest fears weren't neurotic in the least. His worst suspicions were confirmed. Yes, Virginia, there is a devil—and he lives in a big beige box with rotating red discs for windows. And they can be activated in secret by amoral adults playing wicked unseen games. . . .

As Kermit fed coins into the box, Duane emphasized that Morstan being Chappell's connection was no longer theoretical and that Kermit's earlier warnings to Congress were more real than Duane had realized. Then he came to the point. "What do you plan to do about it?"

"What do *I* plan to do about it?" Kermit was startled by the question. "What do you think I *should* do about it?"

"Well, it seems to me you have two possible courses. You can restart your lobbying now because it is about to become a legislative issue. There'll be people in both Houses very interested in hearing your expert testimony. "Of course, you'd go down the drain at S.H.I.T.—I'm sure Chappell wasn't bluffing—and you might have trouble getting a good spot at a top university. The senator does have powerful friends in many places." He paused, hoping for a reaction, then continued. "Or . . . you can simply do nothing"—his tone put down the thought—"and hope that the press and some of the organizations like the ACLU, People First, the Council on Social Priorities, Common Cause will stir up enough public opinion to stop the legislation . . . if there's time enough to do it."

"When do you think the bill will come up for debate?"

"I'd say in about two months. It will probably be a couple of weeks before it's introduced, then it will have to go through committee."

Kermit felt reassured. There was a little over a month to go before March 15. Time to spare. But he couldn't tell his friend about The Project. "Okay, Duane, you've spelled out my options. I'm going to take the second one . . . do nothing, let the concerned power blocs and activists do the job. I wasn't very effective before and I'm afraid my credibility is pretty thin. Cried wolf too often, I guess. Now that it's the real thing—well, you know how the story goes. Besides, this may be a lost cause and it would be stupid to sacrifice job and career and come out on the short end all around. The cost-ratio relative to risk is too far out of balance." The words tasted bitter.

"Cost-ratio! You're beginning to sound like a middle-level Washington bureaucrat. What ever happened to the idea of civil liberty?" He waited for his friend's certain rebuttal and after moments of painful silence, realized with shock it wasn't coming. "That professorship and grant must be awfully important to you."

Kermit felt as though he'd been hit, and couldn't fight back. "I'm sorry you feel that way." He hung up quickly.

That night, Kermit's dreams churned with involuted political horrors . . . He had accepted the directorship of the National Data Treasury of the Computrol Party, which ran the country by printout edicts based on input from thousands of terminals around the country, all shaped like juke boxes and playing the Marseillaise backwards. Whenever the input from local terminals varied more than one-tenth of one percent from the "norm," edicts were telecommunicated to those locations for immediate corrective action, upon pain of crucifixion on a TV antenna. Kermit was in the process of secretly spiking the system when he woke up covered with sweat. Something was insistently pounding his thigh. He heard a familiar voice next to him say, "Darling, I wish you'd stop that moaning. Can't you just go back to snoring?"

"Chappell must have kicked the shit out of him—I don't know how else to put it," Duane said heatedly into the phone.

"What are you talking about, anyway?" Dana replied, still surprised by Duane's call to her apartment at eight o'clock in the morning. She was in her pajamas, not entirely awake, and not at first aware that Kermit had left.

"I can't believe that Kermit suddenly folded that way under pressure. It's just not like him. Unless there's something he's not telling me. If there is . . . and I hope to Hannah there is . . . then he owes me an explanation. I'm on your side, you know."

She wavered. He could be an important mouthpiece for them when the time came. She wished that she had a cup of coffee inside her to clear her head. "How far would *you* go if your career was threatened?" It was more than a debater's question. In that instant she decided to test him, knowing there was a risk.

"I hope I'd do what I believed in."

"Suppose it meant committing a criminal act."

"Short of murder or mayhem, or hurting a lot of good people—I'd at least consider it . . . provided it was really important. . . . Now I have a question. Is Kermit keeping something from me? All I was asking him to do was to come to Washington and speak his mind."

"You'll have to ask him that yourself."

"Well, you can tell him something for me. Tell him I'll help if there's anything he has in mind. Will you do that for me?"

"You've got a big mouth, Dana," Kermit exploded when she related her phone conversation with Duane as they drove to a restaurant that evening. He lowered his voice. "What the devil possessed you to tell him I was considering a criminal act?"

"I never did!" she flared. "I simply asked him if *he* would commit a criminal act if his career was threatened."

"You must be kidding! Do you think he's stupid? How are we going to maintain secrecy on this thing if you—"

"I *told* you—I was half asleep. You know how I am at eight o'clock in the morning! Besides, you said we ought to think about bringing him into the operation. I wanted to find out if it was safe to approach him in case we decided to. We've a better idea now."

"Not much. Not until he knows what's really involved. And why in God's name didn't you call him back from a phone booth? He would have understood."

"*Because* . . . it was eight o'clock in the morning," she said irritably, emphasizing each word. "Not everyone thinks that clearly early in the morning." She stared at him resentfully.

Kermit kept his eyes on the road. "Look, kiddo—this is not a dilettante exercise. We can't afford to make mistakes."

"If I'm such an impediment to the *goddamn* project," she said heatedly, "why don't I just drop out? You and Yuki can go it alone. I set him up for you—now I'm unimportant. Don't worry, you can count on my silence, even though I am a dilettante broad."

Kermit looked at her in a moment of fascinated disbelief, then burst out laughing.

"What brought *that* on?"

His eyes returned to the dark road washed down the center by the headlights, the faded white line defining the curve. He reached over and put his hand on her knee. "Because, idiot, I love you."

She smiled. "What a sexist answer. However, you may say it again." He did.

Over a cocktail at a highway restaurant, they talked over the merits and risks of letting Duane into the act, and between the shrimp cocktail and the veal paprikash they decided to invite him in if Yuki agreed.

During her lunch break the next day, Dana phoned Yuki's direct dial number at his office and gave him the last four digits of the public telephone booth just outside the ladies' room of the Student Center. He returned her call five minutes later from a nearby Boston restaurant.

"I'm glad you called, Dana," Yuki said immediately. "I was going to call you this afternoon. I've got bad news. I haven't been able to break the Azimuth code. I've been working on it all week. I must have run sixty decoding programs and none of them fit. I know I can lick it eventually but it'll take more time than I have. And I need the time to insert my wedge in the satellite and keep it open so that I can collect all the communications traffic between Central and their regional centers. Then I've got to write programs to select out and boil down the stuff and to analyze it. That's weeks of work. Without the header codes to identify the programs and to give us the address and command instructions, we're out of business. We must have those codes, Dana. You said you had entrée at Azimuth headquarters."

"I know a couple of people there, yes. But I don't know if I can work it." The thought of even trying awed her. "How soon do you need it?"

"Today—now. That's the problem." There was a pause on the wire. "A few days at the latest."

"And if I can't get it?"

"We're in trouble. I know it's a big risk to try to . . . uh, get the codes but what choice do we have? I was sure I could come up with the answer but . . . hey, why did *you* call *me?*"

It took a moment for her to remember. "I was going to tell you about a possible new partner, a journalist. But let's find out first if we still have anything for him to join."

Immediately after she finished her work in the Computer Center she sought out Kermit in his office in the Light Engineering building. They discussed Yuki's news on the drive home.

"If Yuki says he needs the time, he needs it," Kermit said. "But I don't like the idea of your stealing the codes. If you were to get caught it would blow the whole thing—"

"Not to mention blowing me with it, brother. It's not my favorite notion. Why don't we let Yuki keep trying to decode it and whenever he does, we'll take it from there?"

"It could be too late. We've got to hit Azimuth on March fifteenth—March thirtieth at the latest."

"Maybe we can find a way of tampering with IRS's programs without the codes."

"Possibly. But we wouldn't be able to do the kind of things we talked about. Yuki wouldn't be able to identify the stuff coming in or have the necessary instructions. We might be able to cause some trouble at Martinsburg . . . destroy master programs and records or make some of their systems malfunction . . . but it would be like using a sledge hammer instead of a surgeon's scalpel. We would only be defeating our purpose."

Chapter Nine

As she left the plane at National Airport in Arlington on Monday, Dana was still thinking on how she was going to do it. Or, actually, if she *could* do it. She regretted being so damn glib in giving Kermit and Yuki the impression she could pull this off.

It had been two years since she was last in Washington. As the taxi crossed the Fourteenth Street Bridge entering the District of Columbia, the old excitement came back to her. The sweeping views down the Potomac, the majestic Jefferson Memorial astride the Tidal Basin, the curving parklands into the city, the clusters of dignified public buildings and the inspiring shaft of the Washington Monument overawing the long, sloping greensward around it.

Dana got out of the taxi on Constitution Avenue directly across from the IRS Building and stood there, facing it. It looked different, somehow, from the way she remembered it when it was a workaday place for her —challenging and a bit fearsome now. She felt like an invader checking the facade of a fortress: the long, gray limestone Greek revival structure six stories high, its three tall arched entrances set back from the seventy-five-foot-wide deep stone steps. Across the entrance just above the austere Doric columns was an inscription chiseled in stone: TAXES ARE WHAT WE PAY FOR CIVILIZED SOCIETY—Oliver Wendell Holmes. And then some, thought Dana.

Her eyes moved to its neighbors—the Department of Justice cheek by jowl on the right and just beyond the National Archives; to the left the immense Interstate Commerce Commission structure. She couldn't see it but she knew that the FBI's ugly, contemporary J. Edgar Hoover building was diagonally in back of the IRS Building just across Pennsylvania Avenue.

Mounting the broad, flat steps she noted that signs on the right and left entrance doors directed: USE CENTER DOOR ONLY. She didn't recall that. She was being funneled into the narrow neck of the structure, presumably for security reasons. At the top step she checked her watch. It was 1:25. As she walked through the door, the roar of a jet taking off from National Airport followed her in.

Although she'd been through this lobby a hundred times, it all seemed new to her: the vast marble floor inset with tan and dull-pink circles and squares; the ornate, two-story-high ceiling intricately sculpted with small bronze rosettes framed in squares with a Greek key border.

At the security desk a uniformed guard was examining the contents of an attaché case of a man ahead of her. A young woman in uniform asked Dana her name, whom she wanted to see and her identification. Her driver's license sufficed. While the female guard telephoned upstairs, the other guard went quickly through her handbag and returned it. "You may go up—room 6333, sixth floor."

A typist behind a desk greeted her when she entered the room. The young woman picked up the phone, spoke quietly into it, then rose quickly and led the visitor to a door marked N.O.C.F., the National Office of Computer Facilities. As she walked through the doorway of the modestly furnished office a rather large man in his late thirties sprang up, beaming. His blond hair was thinning and his light features were vague but pleasant.

"Dana!" Charles Braithwaite bellowed. "It's been a *doag's* age. Let me look atcha . . . gorgeous as ever, kiddo." He leaned over and kissed her enthusiastically on the cheek, held out a side chair for her next to his desk stacked neatly with papers.

She sat facing him and smiled. "I see you've moved up, Chuck."

"Yup. Deputy Assistant N.O.C.F., Master File Programming Division for Martinsburg."

"Terrific!" And it was . . . a stroke of luck to start.

He grinned. "Thank you. Yes, it was a nice break. There's been a lot of changes around here." He leaned forward. "Well, Dana . . . you said

81

on the phone that you're doing something on your doctoral—was that it?—and you needed some help from me. What's it all about?"

She shrugged. "Nothing too earthshaking, but I know you can be a big help." She favored him with an intimate smile. "I'm considering doing my doctoral thesis on evaluating the premise that computer-controlled robotic watchers can guarantee security on federal agency and military computer installations. I'm contacting Social Security and DOD on this as well."

"Nothing earthshaking, she says." He shook his head. "That's heavy heavy heavy."

"There's nothing definite about it. It's just one of the possibilities I'm considering." Her eyes held his. "After all, Chuck, I want to move up in the world too. I don't want to spend my life on a campus. I thought you might like to help me." She wasn't being too subtle, but with Chuck, she remembered, she didn't have to be.

"You know I want to help, Dana"—he smiled, showing his large, uneven teeth—"but you know, kiddo, on this I gotta get an okay from upstairs."

I've laid it on too thick, she thought. "You're jumping the gun, Chuck. I'm just looking into feasibilities right now. Like I said, I'll decide later which way I'll go. All I want to do now is update myself, get an idea of what's changed in the last two years. In this business that's a long time. . . . So if you think you can arrange it . . . well, I'd really appreciate it. . . ."

"Well . . . say, let's get some lunch," and he got up abruptly. "I've been waiting for you and I'm starving."

Dana got up too. "Oh, I'm sorry, Chuck. I had lunch on the plane. Besides, I don't have lunch with married men." She smiled when she said it. "But how about dinner? I only have this afternoon and I want to get started looking around."

"Do you mean that? . . . Okay, it's a deal . . . I mean a date—"

"You've got it, either way. Now . . . let's get started, okay?"

They walked down the long corridor with its succession of doors until they came to one marked 6200 and entered a stark reception area with two security officers standing behind a gray metal desk who greeted Braithwaite and put a security log book in front of Dana. She signed her name, listed South Hano er Institute of Technology as her address and, glancing at her watch, wrote in the time, 1:40 P.M. One of the security officers handed her a plastic identification card on a beaded chain to place around her neck. Braithwaite signed in too.

He took her through a door to a large computer room where long rows of horizontal disc drives, vertical tape drives and a large IBM 360 computer lined the walls and bisected the area. Some of the reels in the tape drives were spinning. Several terminals with console readouts were being operated in various parts of the room. The air was cool and dry: the required computer room temperature of 70 degrees and 50% humidity.

"This is Herb Ferrar," Braithwaite said as an amiable-looking, sharp-featured man approached. "He's the panjandrum of our computer center. Knows everything. Herb, this is Dana Haverhill of South Hanover Institute of Technology. She runs their computing center. But let me warn you about her, Herb. She's not just an academic, she's a computer-nik like us. She used to work here a couple of years back on a six-month tour for SRI. She's priming herself for a doctoral thesis. Show her around and tell her whatever she wants to know. Now I've got to get the hell out of here before I starve. I'll pick you up later, Dana. Take good care of her, Herb."

Ferrar took his superior's words literally and gave her even more answers than she wanted. Most of the equipment he showed her was familiar, including the Remote Job Entry terminal which connected with both Martinsburg and the Old Post Office Building around the corner where most of IRS's programmers worked. Somehow she had to manipulate him in the direction of the command codes used between Martinsburg and the Service Centers around the country. Instead he bombarded her with statistics on the National Computer Center in Martinsburg—that it had 75,000 square feet of space, over 21,600 feet of which was utilized by the computer room, that the individual master file held over 700 reels; she learned the exact processing time for the various transactions, and even that the parking lot held 204 cars, for god's sake. She was getting no closer to the target.

Finally, though, she got him to take her into the adjacent tape library, a compact room that held several thousand metal canisters of reels filed upright on wall-to-wall steel shelving. He told her, "The tapes identifying the codes on master programs are here. Our programmers keep updating them as programs are modified and new legislative changes come along."

"Does one reel contain all the codes?"

83

"No, there are quite a few." He picked out a canister sitting on its end in a shelf. "Here's one," he said casually, and squeezed it back in.

She still wasn't getting anywhere. Even if he pointed them all out, there was no way of getting the reels out of the building. She'd try another tack. She knew that over five hundred programmers worked in the Old Post Office Building which she had no access to now. The programmers had to come here to test out their programs on the terminals. "Are any of the programmers testing their programs now?"

"Oh, sure, they're always testing, correcting, modifying. Would you like to have a look?" He led her to an area where two young men were sitting at terminals and a young woman was working on printouts at a desk.

Ferrar introduced her briefly with a wave of his hand.

"I don't want to interrupt you," Dana said. "I'll just kibitz, if it's all right."

She watched first one, then another at work. She asked a question or two, then moved on. They were correcting routine programs of no interest to her. Still going nowhere.

She turned to Ferrar. "Is there a programmer who happens to be working on, let's see . . . command codes? That's an area I'd like to know more about. . . ."

"Right now, you mean? I don't know. Let's see what Angela's working on. She often updates the codes." In a far corner was a desk piled with several orderly stacks of printouts. But no one was there. Ferrar asked a girl passing by, "Do you know where Angela is?" "On a coffee break, I think," she answered without stopping.

Dana said quickly, "Why don't I just wait for her here? I'm sort of bushed, and I don't want to take any more of your time—you've been very nice but you must be busy. . . . I'll find you when I get through talking to . . . Angela, was it?"

He hesitated. "Mr. Braithwaite wanted me to—"

"That's okay, Mr. Ferrar," she cut in. "Really. I'm grateful for all the help you've already given me. We can chat again when I get through here."

"Well, I guess . . . okay, but if you need me, just whistle." And he finally left.

She thought he damn near winked. Well, be grateful for God-given advantages, she told herself, and turned her attention to the printouts.

There were five stacks of them. People were walking back and forth and Angela might show up any minute. She reflexively looked at her watch —2:37. She looked around, picked up the first batch and began flipping through. Nothing. The next stack was a cumulative reference register program. She riffled through it hurriedly, looking up nervously every few seconds. The third stack was a program for transaction processing, including sorting, merging and Social Security number and ZIP code validation. Dana was itchy with tension. Angela might be back at any moment.

Eyes flicking upward every few seconds, she nervously thumbed through the remaining two stacks. Still nothing. Obviously, Angela was not working on the codes today. That was too much to expect. She realized she might have to come back a couple of more times to run into the right program printouts. Which was clearly impractical. She thought about gathering all the printouts processed during the day, after they were carted away but before they reached the shredder, for analysis later, and quickly realized she'd need a truck and security was too tight anyway.

Well, it had been a longshot to begin with. Unless Yuki could break the codes quickly, they'd have to scuttle the whole project. She felt lousy about it, but there was nothing she could do. She leaned back in the chair to let out the tension. It didn't matter if Angela came back now or not. She even considered going to bed with Braithwaite, doubted she could hack that, and even if she could, how would she ever get him to give her a copy of the command codes? . . .

Frustration made her desperate . . . what the hell! She looked about carefully. Two people were bending over machines at the other end of the room. She eased open a long, shallow drawer of the gray metal desk. Paper clips, note paper, a stapler, odds and ends. She quietly slipped the drawer back in, her eyes monitoring the room. Slowly, she drew open the top left drawer. There was an official-looking hardcover directory and a quantity of blank file cards. The next drawer was a deep one that pulled out with some difficulty. It contained green folders, the top edges labeled by subject—

"Are you looking for something?" A young woman was standing beside her. It was the same woman whose work she had observed earlier.

Oh, my god, I've really blown the whole thing now, Dana thought, sliding the drawer closed. "I was looking for a Kleenex," she murmured, not knowing where the silly idea came from. "Mr. Ferrar asked me to wait for Angela. . . . I'm sorry, I shouldn't have gone rummaging through somebody's desk like that, but this damn cold . . ." She smiled weakly —felt weaker.

The woman looked at her for a moment, then said casually, "Here, have one of mine." She reached into a skirt pocket and took out a small packet of tissues, then walked off after Dana had accepted one from her. Did she suspect something? . . . Would she report her? She thought of Kermit and Yuki depending on her. She'd *have* to chance it. She had to have a look at those file folders. Slowly she pulled open the heavy drawer. Half lifting out the first folder, then the second, then the third, she hurriedly scanned them. Printouts, but nothing of consequence. She flipped through three more. The next after those was labeled "Miscellaneous Completed." Halfway through her eye caught something . . . she lifted the batch of printouts from the folder and held them on her lap, below the level of the desk top. Her heart was thumping. It was the Executive of the system—a program describing the contents of all the master programs used by Martinsburg, listing and interpreting the command code for each. From the description on the header, she could tell that Angela had been cleaning up any inaccuracies in the program and testing it for integrity. And on the fourteenth page she found it—the coded headers that identified and would activate the relevant programs. It was in her hand. But how could she get it away? She looked at her watch again. 2:49. How could she get that single page to a copying machine without being seen? Impossible—security clearance would be required. Take the page and hope it wasn't missed for a while? Too risky, they'd trace it to her and it could blow their whole project.

She cursed herself for not having a minicamera in her purse. She might have been able to sneak a quick shot—*if* she could have hidden it from security. Writing it all down was out of the question—there were an even dozen header codes plus descriptive titles, and she couldn't take pencil and paper and write them down without being seen. What to *do?* Angela would be back any minute and that would be that. She looked around desperately, then picked the single page from the stack and studied the code list. Nothing else for it, she would have to memorize them. Each consisted of four characters: two alphabetic letters, one punctuation mark and one number—but in varying sequences—plus the title of each master program. The first one was F5,V; the descriptive title was too long but the key word was Billing. She added the initial B to the code, repeated the code several times to herself like an alphanumeric catechism until she felt she had it. Then she went on to the next, adding the key word initial. But she stopped every ten seconds to look down the aisle from which the programmer would be approaching. It was totally nerve-wracking, particularly since she had no idea what Angela even looked like.

It took her four minutes to fix the codes in her mind—at least she hoped she'd gotten them . . . she had to get the page back in the stack—

"Miss Haverhill, I'm sorry to tell you that—"

Her heart pounded in her chest; she thought she'd have a stroke. She looked up, her face drained. "Oh, Mr. Ferrar, you scared me . . . my mind was somewhere else." She still held the incriminating sheet in her hand.

He smiled apologetically. "What I started to tell you was that Miss Inamorata had to go back to her office across the street in the Old Post Office Building and she may not be back for a while."

"Miss *who?*"

"Angela Inamorata, the programmer. Some name, huh? She takes a lot of flak about it around here, but she's a good kid and one of our best people."

"Oh," Dana said, mightily relieved. She forced herself to look at the paper in her hand. "I hope you don't mind my looking at one of the printouts on the desk. I got tired of waiting and—"

"It's all right, Mr. Braithwaite said to show you anything. You can look but you can't take." He smiled as though he had made a joke.

Dana felt sick. She casually put the paper down on the desk and got up, not knowing what else to do. She had to get out of there quickly and write down the codes while she still retained them.

"You asked before about how our 360 integrates with the new support equipment. If you'll just follow me. . . ." He was off and running, talking enthusiastically as he went, and she had little choice. She felt like a zombie trying to keep those code characters from jumping around in her head while she blocked out as best she could the sounds of other data assailing her.

Suddenly she said, "I'll be back in a moment, Mr. Ferrar. I left my compact on the desk." She turned and walked quickly away before he could answer. When she got back to the desk she confirmed that it was out of sight of where Ferrar was standing. She sat down quickly, replaced the page she had separated out, slipping it back into the proper folder, and quietly slid the drawer closed. She got up and walked back to the microfilm conversion printer, where Ferrar was waiting. He began speaking animatedly, his hands moving for emphasis. Some of the words even filtered through ". . . with high-speed magnetic tape-to-microfilm plus one seven-track half-inch tape unit which . . ." She tried to run the code characters through her mind but he was going on and on, his face a moving sequence of blurred mimes. He was taking her by the arm now . . . "and I'd like to show you—"

She pulled her arm away, too abruptly, she feared. "Mister Ferrar," she said, "I'm sorry, you'll have to forgive me, but I simply must go. . . ." Reading his puzzled face, she tried to compensate. "I'm afraid I'm just not feeling very well. Can you point me to the ladies' room?" She smiled wanly.

"Of course, I'm sorry. It's outside and down the corridor. You'll have to sign out first." He was very solicitous, as though he was in some way at fault. "Do you want someone to go with you?"

She shook her head. The last thing she wanted. In the reception room she quickly signed out in the security log, handed the plastic card to the guard.

Ferrar was at her side, apologetically. "It was just that Mr. Braithwaite wanted me to—"

"I understand," she interrupted, and hurried out of the room and down the long corridor. It *was* a genuine emergency. As she rushed down the hallway, she intoned to herself, "F5 comma VB . . . J3 slash WR . . . M9 semicolon YA . . ."

In the ladies' room she entered a cubicle and bolted the door behind her. She opened her purse and took out a pen and a matchbook. Carefully, she transferred the sequence of characters from her brain to the inside of the matchbook, pausing frequently and mumbling some of them sotto voce when she wasn't certain. Finally she felt she had them all down, spelling out key words like Billing and Refunds and Audits to make sure she wouldn't forget them. She hoped to god it was all accurate. Fortunately she had the visual faculty to hold on to it for this long, but soon it would have disintegrated. She heard someone come in, quickly flushed the toilet. A large dark-haired young woman was wiping her hands on a towel. As Dana walked by her, she glimpsed an ID badge pinned to her blouse. It read: ANGELA. She didn't make out the last name, or try to. Jesus.

On the elevator down, she remembered her promised dinner date with Chuck. She'd call him from the airport and tell him she was sick, bad cold, felt like flu . . . the lady with the tissues and Ferrar would corroborate that.

The security guard in the lobby stopped her and asked for her pocketbook. He opened it and took out her compact, looked inside and snapped it shut. Then he picked up the matchbook.

Oh, my god, she thought, I should have stuck it in my bra—she felt like throwing up. . . .

The guard dropped the matchbook back in, closed the pocketbook and returned it to her. She walked blindly through the lobby and into the bright light and the sounds of midafternoon traffic on Constitution Avenue.

"C for Charlie . . . five . . . colon, L for Lewis . . . Delinquent Account," Yuki repeated carefully into the instrument. "Correct? That's the last one then. Excellent. Terrific. That should do it."

Dana stood shivering in a drafty, unlit phone booth in the supermarket parking lot near her apartment. Kermit was waiting in the car. "Let's hope it does," she said. "I wouldn't want to go through that again. I couldn't. When will you know whether these codes work?"

"Well, the wedge is in and the stuff is piling into the memory subsystem at the office and dumping into my files. I'll test it out in the next couple of days. Meanwhile I'm working up those programs to boil down and analyze the stuff so we can figure out what to do with it. Now that I've got the master codes I should be able to identify the programs and figure out the destination addresses and command instructions. If the codes work, we're in business."

"Do you think they will?

"We'll soon know," he said. "At least you bought me that extra time."

She hung up the phone and stood there for a minute, thinking, boy, is this an oddball conspiracy. Here we are, about to rip off the government, talking with the detachment of a classroom exercise. We should feel passion, exhilaration . . .

The whole thing was getting mixed up in her head as she walked over to the brown sports car where Kermit was waiting.

Chapter Ten

On Lincoln's birthday Senator Morstan held a secret meeting in his apartment in The Westchester on the northwest edge of the District. It was a holiday the southern senator most particularly did not observe. Present were three senators who had been strong supporters of his political views over the years; two representatives who favored the bill about to be introduced; Russell Waggoner, the Democratic Chairman of the Senate Subcommittee on Government Operations, which would report on the bill; and Gideon Chappell.

With his seven guests seated in a living room filled with antique oriental furniture interspersed with African drums, spears and fearsome tribal masks, Morstan conducted the informal meeting with the skill he had acquired in six years as a congressman and sixteen as a senator. He began by setting a strongly positive tone, polished sales manager style, reporting that the Committee to Strengthen America formed the year before by one hundred conservative businessmen of both political persuasions, and Americans United, a grassroots conservative citizens' organization founded July 4, 1976, were joining in a twenty million dollar advertising campaign and public relations media blitz. They would also wage a lobbying campaign directed at Congress and the Administration to sell the importance of the Morstan Bill and to show that the majority of the American public favored it. The campaign would be timed to impact before and during the debate in Congress.

90

Waving a glass of bourbon and water, a thin forelock of silver-blond hair dipping over an eyebrow, Morstan was all assurance. "Gentlemen, the majority of Americans sincerely feel as we do—they aren't stupid, they have been misled—and they are out there . . . waiting for a recognizable signal. We won't keep them waiting much longer. We've heard talk the country is going more conservative for years. Well, it was and is the truth. . . . The trouble has been that people haven't had any real organization or leaders to identify with . . . the Republican Party has been a joke, and I must admit my own party hasn't been much better. They may have meant well, but they just weren't up to setting this country back where it belongs—at the top, number one . . . not coequal with but superior to any other power . . . and, damn it, cleaned up here at home so decent people can live free of fear from the self-indulgent animals that have taken over our cities. As you know, I'm neither a racist nor a saber rattler. I am, though, a man who cares about his country—it's my supreme love, after all—and I know I share that with all of you here."

Russell Waggoner applauded, smiling and nodding his pink bald head vigorously; the others joined in politely. Senator Waggoner then assured the group that his Senate subcommittee would give the bill priority consideration and schedule hearings as promptly as feasible. He was confident he could produce the votes to clear it through. "But," he said, squinting myopically at the lounging figure sprawled on a red brocade Chinese loveseat across the room, "I'd feel a whole lot better about it if I knew that Charlie Windmiller over there would get a joint bill going in the House so that we could make it up more or less together and get it on both floors at the same time. That would give us a hell of a lot more momentum and save a bundle of time."

Gunther Morstan looked at Windmiller, waiting for a reply.

Windmiller, a small compact Hoosier with thatched colorless hair and bright knowing eyes, stared back at Morstan with a detached air. He was Chairman of the House Subcommittee on Government Operations *and* a Republican, and thus not one of the senator's boys, and he wanted to signal that. Unhurriedly, he replied in a flat, midwestern voice, "I'm not as certain as Russ here seems to be that my committee would go along on this. I've got some difficult people on my committee as you all know. They don't think the way we do on a lot of things. I don't expect we'd have the votes. If Gunther has something up his sleeve, well then, I'd like to know about it. And by the way, Gunther, take it easy on us old Republicans, if you don't mind. . . ."

Morstan smiled. "Oh, sorry about that, Charlie, and I confess I do have something up my sleeve, which I intend to pass along. You'll know how to make good use of it, Charlie, I have no doubt of that. How many votes would you have to swing back . . . three . . . four?"

Windmiller nodded. "About that."

"Well, if that's all your problem is, you've *got* them. I'm not presuming to tell you how to run your show—it's been too many years since I sat in the House and frankly I didn't do too well there, but I have some ammunition guaranteed to change those three or four minds and I'm sure you'll know how to use it. I've admired your talents for many years, Charlie. I think it would spare everyone a little embarrassment if you and I were to take this up later. I'm sure none of you would mind." He looked around at the faces. "Good! Cloakroom protocol."

"If you can guarantee that, senator, then I would be pleased to sponsor your bill in the House," Windmiller said grandly.

"It's settled then," Morstan said, toasting the agreement with a raise of his empty bourbon glass. "To the Morstan-Windmiller bill. This is a great day for America. The first of many, I'm sure."

Someone said, "Hear, hear," and the meeting dissolved into a generalized discussion of various ideas for maneuvering the bill into more rapid transit through the maze of congressional procedures.

Gideon Chappell, who had sat there saying very little, was fascinated, a little shocked at times. Those were not unreasonable men—not at all the monsters that men of Kermit's ilk no doubt considered them to be. They were men of strong beliefs that others could disagree with . . . still, he did feel a bit uneasy, hearing them talk about trading off and collecting favors due from industrialists, lobbyists, and other members of Congress as though they were baseball trading cards—"He owes me for the CAB and FAA approval I got him for that new branch route for that pennywhistle airline of his. . . ." "This will pay off for that no-bid highway contract I wangled from Transportation for his brother-in-law. . . ." "All I have to do is remind them of that price-rigging case I quashed for them with Justice. . . ." Even his own tactics during years of career climbing and campus administration did not prepare him for this. Well, he reminded himself . . . in need of a new shot of rationalization . . . there are different kinds of realities; he would simply have to adjust his thinking. The important thing was Morstan's convictions—which he shared—and Morstan's obvious confidence in him . . . he'd been made privy to a powerful inner council. It was a good portent.

Just before the meeting ended Morstan announced to his colleagues that Gideon Chappell—whom he had introduced originally as "the nation's most progressive educational administrator, a very good friend, and a member of our team"—had a special assignment to persuade university presidents and trustees around the country to support the bill.

He ended the discussion by rising to his full five feet eleven and declaiming, "Gentlemen . . . we all know what we have to do. We cannot let our country go down the wrong road any longer. And if I can presume upon your friendship and your indulgence, I'd like to say that with a Waggoner to carry the goods and a Windmiller to blow down the opposition, we should have no trouble at all." They indulged him with a burst of polished congressional laughter, and he knew it.

As they departed, they all shook Chappell's hand vigorously, saying "it was an honor, sir" and "welcome aboard."

What Chappell didn't know was that when Charlie Windmiller remained on with Morstan after everyone else had left, the ammunition which he received from Morstan was a Xerox copy of a printout of the dossiers of a half-dozen members of the House Subcommittee on Government Operations—damaging information of a personal nature, illegally retrieved from the NPAC data bank.

It was Saturday, February 16. One day short of a month to Azimuth. While they were still nervously awaiting word from Yuki, the other pieces had to be put together quickly. At Kermit's suggestion Dana arranged to meet Duane Crozier on middle ground. It took as long for Duane to fly from Washington to Albany as it took her to drive from South Hanover to the Albany airport. She was waiting for him in the main sitting area of the terminal, reading the Albany *Times-Union,* when she heard a voice behind her. "Hi, beautiful, buy you a cuppa coffee?"

She looked up and smiled, dropping the paper on the chair beside her and rising. "Hello, Duane. You can buy me a whole breakfast. I haven't had a thing this morning."

The airport coffee shop had few people in it at this hour. They took a table in a distant corner where they could have privacy.

"This is all pretty dramatic, you know," Duane said as they sat down.

His thick, dark hair was disheveled and he was looking pudgy in his winter uniform of gray corduroy jacket and bottle green turtleneck shirt. "A midnight telephone call . . . an early morning dash to the airport . . . breakfast in a crummy coffee shop with a red-haired beauty who is being *very* mysterious. Where will it all end?" He gave her a friendly leer.

She smiled back at him with mock sweetness. "Didn't your managing editor ever tell you there'd be days like this?" Her expression turned serious. "Duane . . . I have something important to ask you. Last week you told me you'd consider committing a serious illegal act if it was for something you really believed in—something important to the country, I think you said. Do you still feel that way?"

"Yes, I do. It would have to be damned important, though."

"Do you think that alerting the country to wholesale violations of First Amendment rights is important enough?"

"Of course, but—"

"What if I told you that your arrest would be guaranteed, along with others? No way of escaping the consequences."

"Depends on the rest of it."

She looked at him intently, took a deep breath, and against the background of planes taking off and landing in the distance and the arrival of orange juice, eggs, toast and coffee in the foreground, narrated their plan to invade IRS's master computer system in Martinsburg. She told him that there was a third person participating in the project but she thought it best not to identify him at this moment.

As she spoke, Duane never took his eyes off her face, alternately hypnotized by the intensity of the expression in her deep-set eyes and the sensuality of her mouth. Her manner, though, was businesslike and conversational, counterpoint to the extraordinary story she was telling.

When she finished, he sat there looking at her across the table, his half-finished cup of coffee cold. Finally, he said with a long sigh, "Well, sweetie . . . I guess you rang the bell. Let me tell you something about myself. You're looking at the original liberal manqué—also spelled *schmuck.*" Dana's lips parted as though to smile, and then stopped. "You've no doubt noticed that I talk up a great liberal storm. I even vote for the most liberal candidates on the slate who usually turn out to be indistinguishable from the rest of the crowd once they get to the state capital or to Washington. I've always wanted—or said I wanted—to get out there and *do* something to change things around, instead of hiding behind a typewriter. I also seemed to be out of synch—either in terms of time or place. I was ten when the March on Selma took place. I even missed out on the campus protests against the Kent State killings and never made it to the demonstrations against the Pentagon during the Vietnam War. The truth, at least part of it, is that I was also just too damned lazy. So-o . . . I never did get to picket or pass out leaflets or shout slogans or bean a National Guardsman, or get my own head broken or, far better still, march peaceably with Martin Luther King. And I guess I'm still frustrated as hell about it."

"Well, Duane, I don't want to sound pompous or anything . . . I've hardly been your dedicated on-the-barricades type myself most of my life, but I guess I do have to remind you that this shouldn't be, you know, just an outlet for you or any of us. It's awfully serious, with awfully serious consequences—"

"You're right, and here I go doing it again . . . copping out with easy self-putdowns. But if you can stand it, I happen to be more serious than that. I do happen to believe in old-fashioned stuff like an open society and that there's nothing much more sacred to us than our privacy, our right to be left alone . . . and that's from a snooping newspaperman, who knows something about the subject, since I've had to violate it more than once for a story. It's still in my guts, though, and I believe it. End of speech. I'd like to sign up. I think what you and Kermit have hatched here is tremendous. Just as important, I think there's a chance it might even work."

Dana looked at him seriously. You're *sure* you don't want to think it over first? You're not committed just because you know about it. You can stay on the outside and advise us—"

"*No.* You're not talking me out of this. I've found a way in. Besides, this guarantees me an inside track on the hottest political story since Watergate. I might even make the Pulitzer on this one." He grinned.

"You'll probably make jail with the rest of us."

Morstan's bill went to the Senate subcommittee on February 18, earlier than anticipated. He and his supporters in the Senate were obviously trying to rush it through to cut the opposition's chances to marshal support against it.

The initial press and broadcast reaction to the bill was swift and mixed. It was opposed not only by many liberal but by some conservative newspapers and television and radio commentators for reasons which came out sounding similar. The liberals were alarmed at what they saw as a political surveillance and information control system which would systematically deprive people of civil liberties and lead to a totalitarian form of government. The conservative media tended to emphasize its overkill aspects, warning that the bill's excesses violated various sections of the Constitution. But a substantial number saw merit in the bill's provisions, pointing out that the many crises facing the nation around the world and at home justified strong measures to insure the nation's security. Many of them editorialized that the linkage of public computer systems by federal agencies was necessary for efficiency in government operations, planning and decision-making.

The mood of the country-at-large was one of apathy, or ambivalence and an almost metaphysical malaise resulting from the succession of shocks it had absorbed in the nineteen-sixties and seventies—the assassinations, the My Lai massacre and the general trauma of the Vietnam disaster, Watergate, double-digit inflation, Depression-size unemployment, the economic blackmail of the U.S and the western world by a handful of primitive Arab countries, the U.S. loss of leadership around the world. . . .

It was an ideal—or critical, depending on one's point of view—condition for a takeover, and for its instrument—the computer—which had been operating below the surface for some time.

Chapter Eleven

A motel just outside of Boston was the most practical choice for their meeting—Yuki didn't have the flexibility the others did because Harriet was being kept in the dark. It was now Sunday evening, February 24, almost two weeks since Dana had given Yuki the codes. All that the others had learned from him was that things were "proceeding."

Yuki arrived first at 7 P.M., registered as Yukio Hirohito. Joke. The motel buildings were of a brick and white trim Colonial-style spread out over half a dozen attractively landscaped acres. Yuki had just finished inspecting the two large rooms furnished neatly with light-wood functional pieces and burnt orange broadloom when the others arrived; they had met at Logan International Airport.

Yuki and Duane shook hands with stiff cordiality, each sensing that he was suddenly vulnerable to a strange new face. They eyed each other speculatively as they all seated themselves around the room. Duane was surprised that the new man was Japanese and so young, and Yuki was intrigued that the fourth member was a journalist whose name he had seen on well-written national affairs pieces in *Newswatch*. But the vibrations between them were good.

Yuki eased into things. "I told the registration clerk we would be using the suite just for one night, for a business meeting, and he replied with an 'oh certainly, sir.' "

Dana laughed. "That explains why when we stopped in the office to ask your room number he said under his breath, *'Ménage à quatre.'* Nasty kid."

Yuki looked at his watch. "I told Harriet I'd be back by midnight. She thinks I'm attending a fraternity board meeting. Let's get started."

Kermit nodded. "We're waiting on you. Did the codes work? Are we in business?"

"Well, I've had some luck this past ten days, and I must say I've enjoyed it. I opened up the whole network—Martinsburg to the Service Centers and back—from New York to Hawaii. My wedge in the satellite kept it open for over a week and it spilled its guts into our memory subsystem and right into my files. But none of this would have meant anything if Dana hadn't given me the keys." He bowed his head in her direction.

"You mean they worked? Hallelujah! I wasn't sure I could trust my memory. I was damned sure, though, I couldn't have gone through that again."

Yuki smiled. "I might still be fiddling with decoding programs otherwise. As it was I was able to use those codes from the Executive to identify what was coming in so that I could sort it into categories. I ran my own program to do that, of course, and then another to summarize the stuff to manageable proportions. Even in summary, the printouts were stacked this high"—he held out his hand parallel to the floor—"and with those codes I can now send instructions to various Service Centers which will look identical with those coming out of Martinsburg. . . .

"Most of the data was routine—the kind of traffic you'd expect this time of year: inquiries, verifications, processed individual and corporate tax information, instructions on tax bills, refunds, audit instructions and so forth. Then I ran the whole summarized stack through an elimination program, dropping out the obviously routine transactions. And when I boiled it down to a stack this high"—he held his fingers six inches apart —"I began to see things that looked interesting. Except that I couldn't tell what they meant, they were just random clues. So I wrote a program that refined the analysis of just the particular printouts I'd pinpointed, including the kinds of data and what they were being used for. Some of the results were fuzzy because some of the data was related to things not in the dump. *But,* I did get some answers that were a big surprise—a good one for our purposes but otherwise very scary. . . . Azimuth has been systematically draining the dossiers of data banks of many of the major federal agencies as well as the Associated Credit Bureaus of America, the national banking system, the large corporations, the insurance industry and the major credit card companies. Probably other systems too. And what they find useful is incorporated into their own data bank, adding up new dossiers and fattening up the ninety million existing ones with all kinds of information—a lot of it irrelevant and all of it illegal."

"We knew that other federal agencies were tapping into each other," Dana said, "but we didn't know that Azimuth was doing it too. Why would the private organizations sit still for it? I mean, it doesn't make sense—"

"It doesn't surprise me," Kermit said. "Private institutions are intimidated by the power of the federal government. They assume that if a federal agency asks for something they're better off obliging them. There's always the threat of antitrust action and other federal violations. . . . The other agencies and departments that Azimuth gets the data from do much the same thing . . . especially the FBI, CIA, Immigration, Pentagon, Justice, Treasury . . . and the whole thing is such standard procedure that the question of legality is academic. In any case, as we all know, the law in this whole area is inadequate and largely ignored."

"You ain't heard nothin' yet," Yuki said. "Remember how a few weeks back we were worrying how we were going to get data to use if taxpayers were listed only by their Social Security numbers? Well, it turns out a person's Social Security number is the master key that unlocks his individual dossier in all data banks. If you think about the kinds of information that exist on each one of us in perhaps a hundred or more data banks electronically tracking every intimate detail of our lives—our physical description, family, personal relationships, income, bank accounts, education, IQ, employment record, financial dealings, what we own, what we're worth . . . our political affiliations and attitudes, our psychoprofile, medical history, sex habits, drinking habits, our driving record, the commercial airline flights we've taken and with whom—and things like past unpaid bills even if they were computer errors . . . old lawsuits against us that may have had no merit, whether we flunked out of college, got a dishonorable army discharge or demonstrated for pension reform in front of the Washington Monument . . . well, this kind of data and a lot that's even more damaging is sitting in Martinsburg, West Virginia, in our individual Azimuth dossiers.

"And along the way I stumbled across a program called Project Pygmalion, which is a greatly expanded and updated version of Project Leprechaun, which operated in the Miami area a half dozen years ago. After it was exposed as an illegal operation and the Azimuth brass seemed embarrassed by it, it was *supposed* to be aborted. At that time, if you'll recall, Azimuth used female undercover agents, call girls and police informers to dig out all the sordid stuff they could find on business and professional men and criminal figures to pressure them into paying taxes allegedly due. They dug up things like deviant sex practices, extramarital affairs, drinking and drug habits, involvement with questionable persons and activities. . . . Anyway, the thing of it is that they don't have to use sexy ladies and professional snitches anymore. It's more efficient and milliseconds faster to use all those well-documented data banks to do their snooping. Whatever they may lose in accuracy they overcompensate for in volume. Project Pygmalion is nationwide—all fifty states apparently—and it covers the average citizen now as well as the big shots. It's no longer a local, specialized operation. At least that's more democratic, I guess."

"Yes, democratic like Big Brother," Kermit said, standing up suddenly. He shook his head.

"There's even more," Yuki said. "You know the way I was able to open the door to the COMSAT computer was to hit it during the peak load period when it was vulnerable. Well, apparently it wasn't an entirely original discovery. Someone else was there before me. I have tapes and printouts that show that the White House, Treasury and the National Security Administration have evidently been doing the same thing: accessing Azimuth's master data bank on a selective, short-term basis and withdrawing God knows what."

"And that doesn't surprise me a bit," Duane said. "I guess they preferred not to go through the front door and ask for certain dossiers directly. They've gotten more cautious since Watergate. Hold on to those tapes and printouts, Yuki. They're going to help prove that what we're doing is not much different."

"That's right," Kermit agreed. "It's a bombshell—having the goods on the White House."

"It's fabulous," Dana said.

Yuki looked pleased. "Now to get down to the nitty-gritty. I've also identified a number of special dossier categories that I think are very interesting." He took a small green notebook from his jacket pocket and

100

squinted at an open page. "I'll pick out some at random to give you an idea. Okay, there's the Political Activists Dossier. I suspect that's been culled and updated from the dossiers computerized by the Army's Counter-Intelligance Analysis Division—the infamous Compendium of individuals and organizations involved in protest and other civil rights activities in the late nineteen-sixties and early seventies. Let's see . . . there's the Dissident Clergy Dossiers on clergymen who presumably dissented against the Vietnam War or supported the use of the pill or abortion. I should be kidding, but I'm not. Here's one for you," Yuki said, nodding to Dana and Kermit, "the Campus Radicals Dossiers. There's also the Union Officials Dossiers . . . Mafia Dossiers—well, I'm for that—Journalists and Media Management Dossiers—"

"I'd hate to think I didn't make that one," Duane said.

"A Lottery Winners list . . . a Yacht Purchasers list . . . let's see what else . . . oh yes, they even have dossiers on the Fortune 500 list of America's largest corporations and their top management executives. At least it's across the board." He slapped the notebook down on the coffee table. "There are quite a few others and you may want to look at them. But as you can see, Azimuth is evenhanded and very thorough. They invade the privacy of good guys and bad guys alike."

Dana reached over and picked up the small green notebook, holding it out in front of her. "*This* is really something . . . I mean, we picked Azimuth because we thought it was a provocative target to prove our point—a prototype—but it turns out to be the bull's-eye, the hot center. Maybe they won't think we're such wild-eyed types when we tell them our story."

Kermit moved forward in his chair. "So the big question now is what programs do we go after and exactly what do we do with them."

The next three hours were addressed to that as they tried to narrow the field of opportunities to a manageable few. It was 10:45 P.M. when they arrived at a consensus. As they sat around the room sipping coffee from paper cups and munching on sticky danish pastries from the motel coffee shop, Dana, who had taken notes, prepared to read the decisions they'd made. The room seemed to vibrate. Her voice was low as she read without comment or shading, like a court stenographer's reprise: "Audit all incomes of $100,000 and over for 198– . . . mail list of past due taxes actually owed by federal officials, including senators, congressmen, agency heads and judges to news wire services, major daily newspapers and radio and TV network news departments . . . audit notices to alleged Mafia and union leaders . . . audit notices to all members of Congress who are not on delinquent tax list . . . mail printout of individual dossier to each taxpayer in Project Pygmalion files—"

"Actually," Kermit said, "I don't think we need to hit all five targets to get our story across. But we're only doing this once. This is one time I'm in favor of overkill. Yuki, can you program every one of the five targets we selected? I'm thinking particularly of the program to get printouts of the dossiers from Project Pygmalion. That one seems to me to be something of a longshot. We've dumped this entire responsibility on you and if you feel—"

"I can do it. It's the most complicated to retrieve, but I'm almost sure I can do it. I've got a lot of homework to do on all of them, and I hope to do my final fiddling with the terminal by March seventh or eighth at latest. If I run into a snafu on any of these I'll know this week."

"We've got to decide what happens *after,*" Duane said. He looked around as though expecting an argument from somewhere. "Even if everything goes off perfectly in Martinsburg we can louse up if we don't make the public understand what we did and *why* we felt it was necessary. It's not just the act that will prove the point but the public's perception of it. There will be plenty of people who will be outraged by this apparent sabotage of a government agency—and I don't mean just Morstan and his crowd. In fact, what we do could backfire, prove his point . . . help get his bill approved . . . *unless* we make the people understand quickly what it's all about. Which means that the press conference has to be orchestrated just right and we've got to develop a strategy for a continuing PR program after that. It's one thing to tell people how their rights are being violated and another to make them believe it. The key is credibility."

Yuki looked at him. "But don't you think that the value of what we're doing will be self-evident? Like when the news media print the names of government officials who aren't paying their taxes?"

"Yuki," Duane told him, "public opinion is a volatile thing. It's not always the good guys who win it but the guy the public *perceives* as the hero. Politicians especially learned this a long time ago. That's why they're always so concerned with image—not just what they do, but how what they do *looks.* That's why five billion dollars a year goes for public relations—"

Suddenly Dana sprang up and walked tightlipped across the room, looking down at the floor molding. "There's a bug in the room," she advised.

Yuki jumped up for a look.

"It's a praying mantis, I think," she said, her back still turned.

Kermit shook his head in irritation. "You're a real character, Dana." And then he relented. "Oh, well, maybe that's a good omen. Maybe it's praying for us."

Chapter Twelve

Kermit felt oddly disoriented as he went through his classes, gave exams, met with students having problems with their projects and chatted with the department chairman and other faculty members. He had entered into another state of reality and his academic chores no longer seemed real at all. He knew that soon the bright-eyed young people, his small paper-cluttered office, the chatter of the terminal consoles and the quietly spinning tapes in the Computer Center, the sprawling campus sculpted with strikingly organic masonry structures, the lunches in the faculty cafeteria . . . they would all be gone. Dana would still be with him but she would be different and so would he. *Everything* would be different for him. . . .

Yes, he felt detached from what he was doing but he also felt himself gathering and holding impressions . . . the feel of brass-ball doorknobs filling his palm, the fanlike shape of the beige and brown lecture hall with its sharply angled seats and panoramic multimedia screen, the reflection pool in front of the Light Engineering building leeching the violet grayness of the sky, the contrasting deep and thin voices fracturing down the broad corridors . . . subconsciously storing up these impressions because he was starting to miss the place already. Like knowing he was going to be drafted and getting suddenly sentimental about the old homestead. But not quite. The road to the future was threatening and uncertain. He might never come back to this place, or any place in his profession.

He knew that for Dana it was somewhat different. She was terribly impatient about the intervening weeks before the Day. While sometimes it frightened her, she found the idea exciting and the element of risk made it even more so.

When Kermit arrived at his office on Tuesday morning, March 4, he found a letter from the editor of *Datamation* saying how much he liked his article and saying that it was scheduled for July publication. He tried to visualize where he would be in July and what he would be doing. He didn't like the pictures he was drawing and he gave it up.

When he returned to his desk later in the day between classes, April told him that Mrs. Bausman had phoned and that Dr. Chappell would like to see him for a short time the next morning at 9:45.

That evening Dana cooked dinner in her apartment and they talked about Kermit's morning appointment with Chappell. They agreed that whatever the president had in mind didn't really matter. Time was on their side now. They spent the rest of the evening across the walnut dinette table talking about Kermit's statement for the press conference.

"Enough for one night," Dana commanded sweetly as she rose from the chair, stretched slowly, luxuriously, arms a provocative triangle above her head, and trailed a yawn down the short hall as she walked to the bedroom.

Their lovemaking was gentle, tender as they slipped past their frustrations into fantasies and fears about the future. . . . He wondered whether it was possible to carry the sensitivity of their relationship into marriage without its deteriorating. Dana never raised the subject, but he realized he had been thinking about it lately. It occurred to him that with the uncertainties of the future, it might be overly tempting to seek an anchor to the wind, which was a bad way to go into a marriage. Face it, he told himself, at heart he was practical and conventional.

Next morning as Kermit walked past Mrs. Bausman's terraria and shelf-to-floor terraced jungle, then through the president's office door, it suddenly hit him that something might have leaked, that Chappell might be on to them. . . .

Chappell came around from behind the big neat desk and grabbed Kermit's hand in a hearty clasp. "I'm delighted to see you again, Kermit. How have you been? Sit down, sit down. I appreciate your coming on such short notice." As Kermit sank into a barrel-backed chair, Chappell sat down sidesaddle on the edge of the desk, one leg dangling.

"Tell you what I wanted to see you about"—Chappell clapped his palms together with a round thwack and kept them interlocked in front of him, looking very serious—"I've confirmed something about you . . . yes, and Miss Haverhill too . . . that doesn't surprise me at all."

Kermit thought, What do I do now . . . lie my way through it? I've no other choice.

"I knew when you gave me your word that you had given up lobbying that I could count on you. And that Miss Haverhill would comply as well, although her name never came up. I know you've had every provocation and, yes, opportunity too, to press your position in Washington with the new bill that's been proposed. I'm aware that both of you are opposed to it, and I respect your opinion. Personally, I take no position on this at all—I've got my hands full just running the university. That's my only concern . . . I'm sure you understand that. . . . You've kept your part of the bargain, Kermit, and I will keep mine. I'm delighted to tell you that I am recommending to the board of directors that you be named to a professorship as of the fall semester. I'm sure the board will accept my recommendation."

Kermit started to respond when Chappell said, "No, wait, there's more. As I told you at our last meeting in this room, once you have your professorship I will also recommend that you receive that grant we discussed for a major computer study for a federal agency. I still can't give you any further details on that, but you'll get them as soon as I'm free to give them to you. I should think the grant would be coming through the early part of next year. I would say you can count on that. Yes, definitely." His smile was beneficent, a church father spreading largesse to a prodigal returned.

Kermit went along, hugely relieved. "I want to thank you very much, Gideon. I really am most grateful." His tone was proper, but restrained. He looked at his watch. "I've got a class in ten minutes. If I hurry, I can just miss it," he said, enjoying the old joke, pushing himself quickly from the chair.

Chappell got up from the desk. "Yes, of course." He was taken aback by the sudden exit. He hadn't quite finished the ceremony.

"And I want to thank you again for all your kindness," Kermit said, heading for the door, avoiding the inevitable firm handshake.

"Not at all, Kermit. Let's get together for tennis soon. You owe me a rematch." His voice trailed after Kermit, who was already past Baus-man's jungle and reaching for the outer door. *Rude bastard,* Chappell said to himself at Kermit's broad-shouldered, disappearing figure.

Moving rapidly down the broad walkways, vaguely aware of the weak, still-wintry sun and groups of students entering buildings, Kermit felt light, with a special elation. He knew he had won this encounter just as he had lost the first one. Chappell knew nothing. He was still trying to buy his silence until the bill was voted in Congress.

On Thursday of that week Yuki phoned Kermit and told him that he had worked out the various problems involved in devising and inserting via satellite the five different programs they had decided to impose on IRS's network. Two days later, just one week before "Azimuth Day," he would sit down at the Olivetti remote terminal he kept in his basement study—which he used regularly for his work at Parkinson—and tap out the fateful messages. There was pride and excitement in his normally low-key voice as he talked to Kermit from an outdoor public phone booth in downtown Boston. Did he and Dana want to come and share the big moment?

"Do you need us?"

"No, I can manage it myself. I have all the programs worked out. It's a beautiful operation, if I say so myself. Takes under five minutes to activate. I just thought you might just like to watch it go down."

"You know I would. So would Dana. The problem is I don't think we can. We're supposed to meet with Duane over the weekend to work up our statement for the press conference." He sensed a letdown on the other end. "It would be a helluva thing to watch you manipulate that huge computer system in Martinsburg from that little console in your basement, but I'm afraid we need the time here."

"Look, we each have our own work to do," Yuki reassured him. "And at least now I won't have to worry about getting Harriet out of the house."

Kermit was relieved by Yuki's reaction; it eased the sense of guilt he felt for using his young, vulnerable ex-protégé as a triggerman. He also would have to stop thinking that way.

At 7:30, after dinner, while Harriet was loading the dishwasher, Yuki walked down the shag-upholstered steps to his cedar-paneled study in

107

the basement, just as he so often did. This time it would be different.

A white formica countertop stretched the length of a short wall and in its center was a gray Olivetti computer terminal. It looked like an electric office typewriter with a wide roll of printout paper along the back edge. The only apparent difference was that the keyboard was larger and contained a number of special instruction buttons and symbols in addition to the alphabetic and numeric keys. A telephone coupler was recessed into one side.

Yuki switched on a fluorescent light over the terminal, pulled up a chrome and white leatherette stool and sat down. His black hair had a lustrous blue sheen under the fluorescent tube. He opened a drawer and took out a stack of long printouts and studied them for several minutes. He could hear Harriet's footsteps overhead. He looked at his digital calendar watch: it was Saturday, March 8, 7:35 P.M. Seven days to zero. He turned on the terminal, picked up the black phone instrument sitting alongside it and dialed the telephone number of the satellite network. There were two rings followed by a high-pitched whine; he was connected. He snapped the phone instrument into the acoustic coupler in the left side of the terminal, took a deep breath, then rapidly pecked at the keyboard. The letters *HHHH* appeared in the long horizontal window over the roll of paper: the line was ready to use.

A moment later, the machine chattered briefly, printing: $U\# =$. The Parkinson computer was asking for his User Number. He typed the answer: *RQW 48496*.

PASSWORD = was the computer's next request. His fingers responded quickly: *MKA 752 FMC 30281 00.9*. But the line did not appear on the paper although it did get through to the computer. It was a security measure to eliminate a printed record of the password. *ALT PASSWORD =* the machine typed back. He punched out the alternate password and again the keys moved but did not print on the paper.

ID = appeared next in the window in an instantaneous staccato. This was an identification query for record-keeping and billing purposes. *YIMISEXP*, his fingers replied. It was his own code acrostic for Miscellaneous Experimental account with his initials in front. This was an amorphous, catch-all category that was SOP and would never be questioned.

READY, the computer announced in the little window. Yuki paused,

108

looking down at the printouts on the counter. The room was silent except for the hushed whirring of the waiting terminal before him.

This was a decisive moment, just before the point of no return.

He typed out the first message: *RUN AZIMUTH 1.* The machine burred it out like a muted machine-gun burst, then blandly responded, *READY.* He punched out the instructions on the other programs which were stored in Parkinson's files: *RUN AZIMUTH 2 RUN AZIMUTH 3 RUN AZIMUTH 4 RUN AZIMUTH 5.* The acknowledgment was immediate: *READY.* He wanted to be certain. *CONFIRM RUN AZIMUTH 1 2 3 4 5,* he typed. *READY,* the computer repeated, indicating completion of the instruction.

Yuki looked at his notes on the top sheet of the printout on the countertop next to the terminal. He turned to the keyboard. *ACTIVATE SWITCHERS BW 0000.46. KCU 0000.93 MDM 0000.14 LR 0000.37 TCH 0000.03.* These were the relay switchers in the satellite's computer which enabled him to exploit the loophole he had discovered on COM-SAT's new Advanced Message Switching Program.

If he had designed everything correctly, the programs he had just activated would arrive at the Service Centers looking as though they had originated in Martinsburg. The terminal chattered momentarily and the printout read: *SWITCHERS ACTIVATED.* He studied his notes and carefully compared them with the printout of the switcher characters and digits on the paper roll. They checked. One last instruction. He worked the keys again: *EXECUTE ALL PROGRAMS PER REAL TIME. AZIMUTH 1 2 3 4 5.* His previously inserted programs contained Real Time clock instructions geared to activate on March 15 at 10 A.M. There was a slight pause and the terminal came alive for an instant. *READY,* it read.

Yuki smiled grimly. He one-fingered his standard signoff: *BYE.* The computer answered with a two-line flow of characters and digits indicating resources used in the files and memory bank, ending with *OFF AT 03/08/8– 19:47 EDT*—the date and time.

Just a few minutes and it was done.

He uncoupled the telephone handset and returned it to its cradle, then ripped off the printout of the job from the roll. He sat there, arms hanging heavily at his sides, staring absently at the silent terminal. He saw the satellite rotating with the earth at 22,300 miles in the arctic blueness of space. He had just used its brain to transmit a series of messages for later execution. He had done this sort of thing thousands of times but now it was different. He felt himself trembling with a combination of elation, guilt and uncertainty. What if he had made the smallest invisible error and it caused serious damage and even panic?

Was this his own assault on Pearl Harbor? He stopped himself from thinking about it. His throat felt dry. He thought of the God of Moses, his adopted religion. It was desperately important that this project succeed. He would go to the synagogue and pray. The next moment he rejected the idea; he wasn't a religious man. But if there were a God of the Computer, deus ex machina,—which he often thought there should be—he would program a prayer to him.

He rose slowly, picked up the job printout, placed it in a large ceramic tray and put a match to it. It flamed like a temple offering. The glow danced over his high cheekbones. His face was an opaque mask as he mounted the stairs. When he reached the top, he heard Harriet yell to him from another part of the house, "Yuki, don't forget to put out the garbage."

Chapter Thirteen

The Senate Subcommittee on Congressional Operations had begun their hearings on Monday, March 10, and by the end of Wednesday nine witnesses had been called, questioned and, in some cases, badgered by the chairman and various of the seventeen members present.

The proceedings made the first page of most papers around the country and the highlights were digested on radio and television news around the clock. The early witnesses were heads or high officials of government agencies. The subcommittee chairman, Senator Russell Waggoner, handled them with the courtly deference accorded heads of state by a protocol officer. Seated in the center of the elevated, bow-shaped dais of the formal hearing room in the Dirksen Office Building, he shielded these dignitaries with high cutting voice and an angry wave of his bald head from the sharpest questions of the more critical committee members.

The next morning the Washington *Post* headlines read:

FBI, CIA, ARMY OFFICIALS
SUPPORT MORSTAN DATA BILL

Cite National Security, Crime
Control as Key Factors

On succeeding days the director of the Civil Service Commission and officials of the American Association of Industrial Management and of the Committee on Scientific and Technical Information of the Federal

Council of Science and Technology all emphasized in different terms a common point of view: the need for central, unlimited access to all governmental computer data banks—as well as to many in the private sector—to better analyze, plan and manage the country's resources and technology for greater economic growth and development. The executive director of the Industrial Management organization said that the concept of individual liberties must change in the postindustrial society, declaring, "Many of our civil libertarian values have become obsolete, even dangerous."

When witnesses who could be expected to oppose the bill came to testify, Chairman Waggoner did not make it easy for them. He asked that they give their written statements to the clerk to be printed in the Congressional Record instead of permitting them to read them as the earlier witnesses had. He blamed the pressure of time and overruled objections. This meant that the full text of their statements did not get through to the radio and television audience, although a few papers like the *New York Times* subsequently printed key portions.

Norton Lastvogel, popular author-sociologist, branded the bill "an irreversible first step toward an authoritarian bureaucracy, leading quickly to a faceless society where the individual would become a digit in a dossier." He also said that aside from the loss of privacy, which was already a fait accompli, "the punishment-and-reward aspect of living naked and frequently maligned in hundreds of government and industrial data banks erodes our individuality, sense of selfhood, makes us increasingly dependent on a system that controls our personal data and manipulates our lives accordingly."

The next witness to testify was the chairman of the American Bar Association's Committee on Science and Law. He warned that the proposed legislation was, in his opinion, unconstitutional, violating liberties guaranteed in the Bill of Rights, and that it was a perversion of democracy to place overwhelming power over the individual in the hands of government.

The last witness heard to this point, the director of the National Institute of Science and Humanities' Project on Computer Banks, referred to a little-known quotation from *The Year 2000*, written in 1967 by Herman Kahn and Anthony Wiener, futurologists of the Hudson Institute, which predicted that, "Access to and control of the national computer networks would become the focus of politics, conspiracy and

112

ultra-elite groups." One of the members of the subcommittee responded sardonically, "I find it curious and disconcerting that this prediction by two outstanding authorities of what could be expected in the year 2000 is now upon us almost twenty years early."

It was, of course, more curious than he knew.

Chapter Fourteen

Yuki felt more tired than usual when he swung his car into the driveway. He had left the office an hour early. Tension had drained his energy this past week as the Day drew near, but he had tried to keep everything looking as normal as possible. It was difficult chatting with his colleagues in the office and facing his superiors every day knowing that, in fact, he had betrayed the classified information it was his responsibility to defend. In a way it made him feel like the Japanese ambassador smiling and bowing to Cordell Hull at the U.S. State Department while hundreds of Zeros were making ready to blitz Pearl Harbor. It was a pretty stupid analogy, he knew, but it dredged up the old senseless guilt. He *was* an American, he *thought* like an American, he *felt* American. And then he would look in the mirror.

Harriet was surprised to see him. The only time he had come home early before was months ago when he was feverish with a virus. He put off her questions saying he was feeling fine but just tired and things were slow at the office anyway.

"No come-home kiss?" she said petulantly, standing there darkly petite.

He leaned over and kissed her quickly. "I'm sorry," he said, walking over to a chair in the living room. "I had something else on my mind."

"Obviously. You've had something else on your mind for some time." Her tone was matter of fact.

114

He looked up at her, so well groomed and neat, face undisturbed by emotion. He knew her pride was hurting.

"I'm just tired, Harriet. Really."

She walked over to the off-white velvet sofa and installed herself in the middle, arms winged on the top edge, legs crossed meticulously. He recognized the sign. "Yes. I know you are, Yuki," she said too precisely. "I wonder from what."

He sank lower in the plush chair, closed his eyes, rubbed little circles in the nape of his neck and let out a soft groan.

"I asked you a question, Yuki."

He stopped rubbing his neck but his eyes remained closed. "Oh, I didn't know it was a question. Would you care to repeat it?" He sounded like he was falling asleep.

"Stop playing games. I want to know what you're tired from . . . or of."

He sighed, eyes still closed. "Oh, maybe my job . . . maybe from living in this modern museum, in this dull suburb." He would string it out as long as he could.

"Maybe you're tired of living with me." Her voice was cool. "Open your eyes and look at me."

He opened his eyes. "It's not you, Harriet." His voice was gentle. "You should know that."

"I thought I did. I don't anymore."

He sat upright. "What's going on in that little head?"

"Do you really want to know?"

"Tell me."

She looked at him, compressing her bright red lips. "All right . . . I know what you're tired from . . . I know what you've been doing . . . and I think it's appalling. I thought you'd be the last person . . ." Her voice faded and she looked as though she would cry.

Oh, my god, she knows, he thought. What do I do now? I didn't want to involve her in this thing until I had to, until I could tell her the whole story. "How did you find out?" He tried to withhold his emotion.

"How did I find out?" Now that she had his admission she was irate. *"How did I find out?* You must think I'm stupid. . . . She called you here and left her number. That wasn't very bright of her. And all those nights you came home so late . . . those Saturdays you were away working on a special project." Sarcasm turned her sweet face into a caricature of her mother. She shook her head. "How could you go to bed with that . . . that girl? Don't I mean anything to you anymore—"

"*Dana?*" he said, smiling stupidly, delighted. "To bed?" He laughed out loud, relieved. "Oh, that's funny. You don't know how funny that is."

She stared at him. "It won't work, Yuki. I have the facts." She tried sounding cold but couldn't quite make it. "I know that you and *Dana,*" she said the name contemptuously, "spent the night—or at least part of it—in a motel, the Circle Motor Court, on route 28, the night of February twenty-fifth. You registered as Yukio Hirohito. I knew it was you . . . you used the same gag on our honeymoon when we registered at a hotel. That really hurt." She looked away, clenching and unclenching her hands. "And undoubtedly there were other motels on other nights. I wasn't about to research it any further."

Yuki looked at his wife, a sweet-faced, wounded girl. God, he loved her. He saw the laughing eyes and the generous smile and remembered her bubbling chatter that touched something in him the evening they first met.

"You don't know enough, honey . . . and that's the trouble. Let me tell you—"

"I don't want to hear it." She turned her head away.

"The trouble is . . . I don't know how to tell you. You're wrong about Dana and me. If you'll just listen, I'll try to make it clear to you." He shifted in his chair, took a breath. "First of all, Dana is Kermit's girl. They've been very close for a long time and I'm sure they love each other. She and I have no personal interest in each other . . . we've never shared a bed or a motel room, and that's that." He was beginning to feel a little angry. "I did rent a room—a suite in fact—at the Circle Motor Court that night. It was for a meeting on a very confidential project connected with my work—the same as all those other evenings and Saturdays I've been away. You've known that all along. If you had bothered to check with the clerk at the motel you would also have found out that there were two other people, both men, in the room with us. No, for god's sake, it wasn't an orgy. It was a long, serious *meeting.* I can't tell you who the others were and unfortunately I can't tell you much more about the project. All I can say is it's very important to our country and I've got to keep my mouth shut about it. You have to understand that and believe me. I'll be able to tell you the whole story next week." He got up from

116

his chair and sat down beside her on the sofa and touched her hand. "Okay?"

She pulled her hand away and turned suddenly to him. Her face was strained. "Tell me the truth, Yuki, are you involved in something . . . well, illegal . . . against the government? . . ."

An alarm went off in his head—she must be guessing. "Where did you get that? I told you it was a project important to the country. That's all I can tell you now."

"That's not enough. I want to believe you, but I can't." She looked frightened and close to tears.

He had to tell her something. "Harriet, listen to me. You know how I've felt for a long time about the problems of protecting satellite data transmission, and how hard I've worked on my own time to develop a series of defenses against satellite invasion, right? You also know those idiots wouldn't buy it. I just couldn't stand by and do nothing. Well I've found a way to do something about it. There are a few of us working together on this and we're all sworn to secrecy until we're ready to make it public. It's absolutely necessary, please take my word for it. I shouldn't even have told you this much but I had to make you understand. . . ." He looked at her neat, dark profile silhouetted against the champagne-colored drapery with the fading afternoon light filtering through. He put his arm around her and kissed her. "I love you, honey. You know that."

She began to cry, then stopped abruptly. Her eyes were staring into the deep pile of the rug. "I did something terrible." She seemed too stricken to go on. "I told my father two weeks ago that I thought you were seeing another woman. He became incensed—you know how he is —and he said, 'Don't you worry, sweetie, I'll take care of it.' I found out later he'd bugged our phones and there was a tape of a phone call you made to Dana where you said something about screwing up a data bank. He decided that you were involved in some sort of act against the government. You know, he wanted to believe it—all those night meetings, the weekends, the motel. He figured you had done me wrong and since most of your clients are government agencies, the data bank you mentioned had to be a government one. This made you a subversive as well as a cheating husband. . . . You know how he feels about his little girl." She looked up guiltily. "And he was not letting you get away with it. He told me last night . . . that he was going to report this to the FBI. I begged him not to, but he's so pigheaded. I don't know, he may have done it already. You remember how he acted the first time I brought you home. Oh god, I'm so sorry, Yuki, what are we going to do? . . ."

Yuki felt stunned. And yet he had to try to sort out the ruins. There was that one time he had spoken to Dana from the house . . . a pay phone was too far away and Harriet had been out. He saw Kermit just *looking* at him, and Dana and Duane staring accusingly. . . .

"Go over to your father's house right now and stop him from doing it. He may not have contacted them yet." His voice was deathly calm.

She got up, blank-faced, moved to the central hall closet, took her purse and walked out the door without turning her head. He yelled after her through the closed door. "Stop him, goddamn it."

He heard the quick roar of a car engine and the skid of the wheels as her car spun too quickly out of the wet driveway. As an afterthought, he walked over to a white telephone on a corner table, unscrewed the base, pulled out the small listening device, threw it on the floor and crushed it with his heel into the deep pile. That Purple Heart at Guadalcanal. . . . Her old man still hated the Japs.

A half hour later Harriet phoned from her father's house. It was hard to understand her at first. Through her sobs she managed to put together a complete sentence: "It's too late . . . he's told them already." Yuki hung up without a word, put on his raincoat, got into his car and drove off. He stopped at the first gas station he found that had a public telephone booth. He phoned Kermit at his apartment, gave him the number and waited for his return call. He told Kermit exactly what had happened and when he began apologizing for the inexcusable foul-up, Kermit silenced him. "Don't sweat it, it's not that bad. They couldn't possibly make anything out of that one phrase. And they have no reason to suspect you. It will all be over before they know anything."

But Kermit hadn't convinced himself. He called Duane, hoping to be reassured in turn. Duane listened, asked a few questions, then told Kermit that the FBI probably would refer the matter to their Boston field office for a routine investigation, but since no date was mentioned and the information was so vague, they would not be aware of any urgency and not likely to pick up Yuki for questioning until it was too late. And if they checked beforehand, his superiors at Parkinson Institute would give him a clean bill of health.

The weak link might be Harriet. She knew that Dana and Kermit were in some way involved in the project. Would she talk? Had she told her

118

father that much? They would have to assume, to be on the safe side, that Yuki might already be under surveillance. In any event, they both agreed, the project could not be stopped and would go off on schedule. They would have to wait and see if Yuki was picked up and play the timing of the press conference by ear, holding it as soon afterward as possible. But getting the media to attend without alerting the FBI would now be a very tricky maneuver indeed. Duane told Kermit to leave that up to him; he would figure out something.

As soon as he finished with Duane, Kermit phoned information for the telephone number of Yuki's next-door neighbor, whose name he remembered from their mailbox on the road. Mrs. Mueller answered the phone, and he carefully explained that he was unable to reach Mr. Ishizaka because his phone was out of order. Would she please go next door and give him a message because it was important he speak to him right away? She hesitated a moment and then agreed. He asked her to tell Mr. Ishizaka that Mr. Azimuth would like him to call him back immediately and he gave her the number of the public phone he was calling from.

When no callback came after ten minutes, he decided with a sick feeling that his ploy hadn't worked. Perhaps Mrs. Mueller hadn't bothered to deliver the message, or maybe the FBI was there already. Suddenly the phone rang.

Kermit briefed Yuki on his conversation with Duane, giving him their appraisal of the situation but trying to avoid any hint of the alarm he now felt. Yuki said Harriet would stand by him and not tell the little she knew. Only Dana's first name was on the taped conversation so if Harriet was questioned, she would simply say that she believed her husband had been seeing another woman, that she had no idea who she was and that what was on the tape may have been shoptalk and her father had probably gone off half cocked. No, she had told her father nothing else so there were no links to the other two.

That's the best news yet, Kermit thought. He told Yuki they'd consider him off limits until the press conference and he would let him know the date. If Yuki was still free, they could decide then whether it was safe for him to participate. Meanwhile, if Kermit had to contact him, he would ring once and hang up and then ring once more and hang up again. Yuki would then go to a public phone and call Kermit back at this same number, making sure he was not being followed. Yuki was not to call any of them unless it was an emergency.

Yuki apologized again for endangering the operation. Kermit reassured him that it would go off as planned even if they had to wing it a little. "In a few days, kid, we'll have made history."

As he hung up the phone and walked slowly to his car, he thought, I wonder what kind.

Chapter Fifteen

It was the weekend of the countdown: thirty-six hours until Saturday, March 15, the Ides of March, 10 A.M.

The Senate subcommittee hearings on S. 17, Morstan's bill, were rolling along, witness after witness savoring their hour or two before the TV cameras, biased for and against the bill, and being pecked at or stroked in turn by one or another of the cast of characters sitting augustly on the dais behind the microphoned, arc-shaped battlement. It was largely a replay, with names and faces changed, of the testimony of the first three days. A shifting tug of war and the name of the game was Who Is the Real Patriot?

As Dana and Kermit sat together in front of the television set, watching the taped subcommittee proceedings, they realized that none of this would have any bearing on the outcome of the subcommittee's vote. It was all preengineered in backroom caucuses. But the televised hearings would undoubtedly have an influence on public opinion. The question was, which way, ultimately?

Kermit and Dana noted that since the bill was first introduced almost two months ago and after a full week of nationwide exposure of the hearings, the public debate was still limited to the official statements of the usual organizations on both sides and to those of a handful of senators, congressmen and two liberal governors. Even the President was silent. It was an election year and no one was certain of where the people stood on this issue; except for a hardy few, the politicians were reluctant to commit themselves until they knew.

And in this climate of public apathy and political timidity, would the shock therapy the conspirators had designed have any effect? Would the patient even notice?

On Saturday morning Dana shook Kermit into consciousness. "Wake up darling, it's March fifteenth."

"Oh," he said, bolting upright, eyes half-lidded, "what time is it?"

"It's ten o'clock, give or take a minute. Happy Azimuth!"

"How did it get so late? . . . I wonder if it really went off. We won't know for sure until Wednesday at the earliest. If those hits are processed today, those millions of pieces of mail won't go out from the various regional offices till Monday and most of them won't arrive until Wednesday. I wonder how long it will take for the reaction. The first indication, I would think, will come from the press on the list of federal VIPs who are tax deadbeats. . . . I can't wait to see those headlines! *If* . . . things went off, that is."

It was a long, long weekend. They spent the next two days bike riding under warming skies, taking long walks through nearby wooded areas, cooking and savoring gourmet dishes they both prepared, going to the movies—and making love. And all the while, they wondered whether they would make it to the news conference. If the FBI got to them first, then their whole project would go down the drain and they would follow. Without that public forum to present their story, and their proposals, they would be branded subversives or worse in the press and certainly in the public mind, and it would be almost impossible to reverse the image later.

All day Saturday, they literally yearned to call Yuki. They wanted to hear him tell them that he was sure everything had gone off on schedule, that the deed was done and that at this very moment computers in IRS's ten Service Centers across the country were spinning out their hopes for an end to computer cannibalism. As far as they knew, Yuki had not yet been taken into custody for questioning by the FBI. The civil rights lawyer, Adam Greenfield, had agreed to represent Yuki when and if that happened, and he would have let Duane know. But Yuki might well be under surveillance, so they couldn't risk calling him. Instead they phoned Duane, and in a ten minute conversation, each standing in a public telephone booth in a different city, they tried to reassure one other.

On Monday morning, March 17, Hugh Gossage, the lean, forty-seven-year-old chief of *Newswatch*'s Washington Bureau, who looked more like a secretary of state than the incumbent, was handed six letters that were all addressed News Desk, Newswatch, Washington, D.C. They were dated March 14. The envelopes indicated they came from Internal Revenue Service offices in different parts of the country. He read them several times in disbelief. They all started out the same way: "The following is a list of individuals in the employ of the federal government who have delinquent tax accounts with the Internal Revenue Service in the sums and for the years indicated." And then each listed a number of names from their own part of the country—fifty-three names altogether—most of whom Gossage immediately recognized. There were senators, congressmen, commissioners of federal executive and regulatory agencies, federal district judges, two Cabinet officers and several he didn't recognize. They listed the amounts each owed and the years when the sums were due. This had to be some kind of put-on. It was illegal to make such information public this way. Someone must have gotten hold of letterheads and envelopes and pulled a gigantic hoax.

Gossage phoned the AP office. Yes, they had gotten the same letters and didn't know what to make of them either. The AP editor had also checked around and apparently other news media had gotten the same thing. It could have been some kook who stole IRS stationery or once worked there, or, the two men agreed, it might well be a political dirty trick to embarrass these high officials, especially if the information was true. But these individuals were members of both major parties. If this was a political trick, who could benefit? If it wasn't that, what was it?

Gossage phoned the chief Public Information officer at IRS's national headquarters building on Constitution Avenue. The P.I. chief admitted that he was at a loss. It was impossible for anyone on the outside to have access to that information and even on the inside it was virtually impossible. But he was looking into it. He suggested that Gossage call back in an hour. An hour later, he said the IRS would have no comment to make at this point but they were investigating the matter and would let the news media know when there was something to report.

Gossage called in one of his staff reporters and told him to get his ass

123

over to IRS headquarters. Duane was just arriving when the reporter rushed out the door. He grabbed him by the arm. "Where's the fire, Murray?" When he heard what the assignment was, he couldn't resist joining him.

A secretary met them outside the Public Information office. There was a temporary news blackout. No, they couldn't see anyone. Their office would be called as soon as there was any news.

Terrific, Duane said to himself. He got to a public phone and called Kermit's office. Kermit was conducting a class, April told him. He left word for Kermit to return his call at 12:15, and gave her the number of a downtown bar. He was feeling high. He was also feeling strangely horny. Maybe he'd see his girl friend tonight.

Duane was having his second drink when the call came. Kermit was, of course, ecstatic. But they both were mystified by the March 14 date on the letters. Everything had been set up for March 15. Yuki had been very specific about that. So they had lost the semantic drama of the Ides of March date. But they had their triumph. If Caesar had been assassinated one day earlier, he would have been just as dead.

Everything for the news conference was set on his end, Duane assured Kermit—the press kits containing the announcement statement, the comprehensive White Paper and thumbnail bios of each of them. The media invitation list was to be phoned at almost the last minute. Now the question was when to hold the conference. They had to wait until the event had made sufficient impact, but the longer they waited, the greater the risk of their arrest. All they could do was watch the situation closely and stretch it out as long as they dared.

An hour later, on the way to a routine interview he was assigned to with a congressman, Duane picked up a copy of the Washington *Star.* It carried a three-column headline on the right-hand side of page one: CONGRESS MEMBERS, FEDERAL OFFICIALS LISTED AS MAJOR TAX DELINQUENTS. The lead paragraph read:

Washington, D.C., March 17—In unprecedented letters received today by the Star and other news media, apparently sent out by several regional offices of the Internal Revenue Service, fifty-three high federal officials, including twenty-two members of the Senate and the House of Representatives as well as two Cabinet officers, were identified as having been delinquent in their payment of taxes from two to eight years for sums ranging from $3,400 to $297,000. IRS headquarters officials stated that the release of the list was unauthorized and that they had no knowledge of how it had occurred. However, they would not deny the accuracy of the information. An investigation of the embarrassing revelation is under way.

The next day, under pressure from the news media, IRS headquarters released a brief statement that the issuance of those letters was a procedural error which they regretted and was under investigation. A number of the senators and congressmen whose names appeared on the lists denied that they were delinquent or insisted that they were contesting the taxes claimed by the IRS. Some of them charged Lloyd Danziger, commissioner of the IRS, with conducting a vendetta against them and proposed that the IRS itself be investigated.

Every few hours there were reports of other irregularities. Other senators and congressmen not on the lists were said to have received simultaneous audit notices, and word leaked out from some of their staff people that they were incensed at what they considered to be unwarranted fishing expeditions into their financial affairs. A few heads of national unions were said to have complained bitterly to the Secretary of Labor that their audit notices were an attempt at antilabor intimidation by the Administration.

By Wednesday, the switchboards of IRS's regional, district and Service Center offices in every part of the country were swamped with telephone calls from individual taxpayers who had received copies of their IRS dossiers and were variously shocked, angered or petrified by the contents. Regional telephone companies around the country reported that their facilities were being seriously overloaded.

The FBI made the first move. Within hours after the news media had broadcast the sensational first development, FBI field offices around the country raided the homes of several hundred leaders of dissident political organizations and held them for questioning on the assumption that the illegal distribution of the list was an act of political sabotage. Although in most cases those arrested were released in a few hours, several civil rights organizations reacted quickly with denunciations of the rights violations of the individuals involved.

The following day several different groups staged separate protest rallies in Washington, marching around the perimeter of the White

125

House grounds and in front of the two-block-long IRS headquarters building on Constitution Avenue. Some opposed the violations of the rights of the political dissenters rounded up by the FBI and others were middle-of-the-road citizens who were angry because of the special privilege obviously accorded high-level tax cheats by the IRS.

Over the next few days, as the impact of Azimuth's revelations took hold, news reports from dozens of cities indicated that local citizen groups of wholly divergent political backgrounds were picketing the homes and offices of many of the senators, congressmen and other federal officials whose names were on the list of tax evaders, demanding their resignation or impeachment. Every night TV screens across the nation showed demonstrators from Seattle, Washington, to Tupelo, Mississippi, and Wilmington, North Carolina, shouting slogans and waving signs reading variously: IRS PROTECTS FEDERAL TAX CHEATS . . . PRIVACY YES, DOSSIERS NO, DANZIGER HAS GOT TO GO! . . . and CLOSE THE LOOPHOLES, TAX REFORM NOW. Viewers saw a two-minute film clip of a group of middle-American types in Saginaw, Michigan, burning a grotesque effigy of Lloyd Danziger in a public park. They were a community group who sought tax reform to end the legal tax breaks available to upper-bracket Americans. A sign on the chest of the straw figure curling in the flame read MR. TAX DODGE.

Each day produced new headlines reporting rumors from unnamed sources in the Justice Department and the White House identifying FALN, the Puerto Rican independence terrorists; the Weathermen; a cadre of electronic experts from a revived Symbionese Liberation Army, and even Cuban agents as being responsible for what was now recognized as sabotage.

On Wednesday at noon, the nation was treated to the spectacle, via live TV news coverage, of several hundred students from Boston University, Harvard and Emerson College, augmented by a few thousand applauding and participating local people, throwing stacks of IRS tax forms into Boston harbor from the end of a commercial pier. They had scooped up cartons full of the forms from banks and post offices and marched through the streets chanting, "Taxation without privacy is an abomination." Forty police officers assigned to break up the demonstration stood around, smiling. One discovered a carton of undumped tax forms and carried it to the end of the pier.

Pressure on IRS's national headquarters was coming from every possible quarter and the agency was in turmoil. The attacks on Commissioner Danziger from federal officials and from civic organizations were increasing. The American Civil Liberties Union called the revelations of the personal dossiers "another example of government tactics which violate the basis of individual rights guaranteed in the Constitution and threaten the process of democracy itself." The Union suggested that it would lead to the biggest class-action suit in the nation's history.

Chapter Sixteen

When Lloyd Danziger received a phone call from the President's secretary summoning him to the White House on March 19, two days after the news broke, he was afraid he would be asked for his resignation. When he was ushered into the French-windowed Oval Office, he was sure of it: it looked like a court-martial. Four solemn men sat around the room facing the President behind his large, elaborately carved oak desk. Only one rose to greet him. It was Paul Ives, the affable but tough-minded White House chief of staff. He placed one arm behind Danziger's back and propelled him with a gracious smile to the side of the room where the others were seated. The President shook his hand over his desk, smiling formally without rising.

Danziger knew them all, of course, but didn't have a particularly close relationship with any of them. They were Stuart Senseny, the boyish but abrasive Attorney General; Mitchell Storey, who resembled a successful sales manager more than an FBI director, and Percy Vandiman, the CIA director, who looked like the well-worn career diplomat he had been.

The President's full face was in soft, natural light, the low western sun through the three long windows behind his desk silhouetting the square of his shoulders. Danziger could see the long green lawns framed by those windows and, off to the left, a portion of the Rose Garden through the French doors opening out to the colonnade.

The President got right to it. "Tell me, Lloyd, what the hell is going on there at IRS?"

Danziger looked him in the eye. "Mr. President, I wish I knew. All we know for sure right now is that certain damaging instructions came through to our regional Service Center computers last Friday morning and entered our telecommunications network the way they normally do. But there is no record of their having come through our central system in Martinsburg, which is the command center where our master computer system is located." He held the President's eye, knowing that forthrightness was all he had to bargain with. "All programs and instructions to our Service Centers around the country originate in Martinsburg. They can't get there any other way. We haven't been able to find out yet how they went through Martinsburg to those Centers without being authorized and without leaving a record—a trace of any sort. We've been investigating since Monday and—"

"How is it that these unauthorized activities weren't detected last Friday when they started?"

"Our processing is almost fully automated and computer-controlled and the instructions came through the regular channel—the only channel we have, actually—and the work was processed automatically. The Service Centers had no reason to question the validity of the instructions. At headquarters, we had no way of knowing anything about it until we began receiving complaints on Monday. Then, of course, we moved on it at once."

The President slumped back in his seat, his arms folded across his chest, surveying Danziger. His voice was cold. "How *exactly* are you proceeding with your investigation, Lloyd?"

"We're exploring every possible avenue, overturning every rock, Mr. President, and we're doing it around the clock. I've put our best people on it from our National Office of Computer Facilities here in Washington —the people who create the programs and design the software. I've also ordered a top-notch consulting firm, Cybernet Associates, to work with our people. And IBM and Honeywell are combing through the various systems too. The investigation is covering Martinsburg and every one of our Service Centers and regional offices around the country."

"Have they found anything so far?"

"Only that the computer logs from our central system do not correspond with the logs in the Service Centers. The central system shows no record of sending out the instructions which activated these results. But the computer logs where these commands were received recorded them as coming from the central system. That's the mystery."

The President studied him for a moment. "I've been catching a lot of flak from all sorts of people in the last two days and I don't much care for it, I can tell you." He shook his balding head impatiently. "So let's get down to what this is all about, gentlemen. What would be the motive in making public the names of members of Congress, federal judges, commissioners and so forth who were delinquent in their taxes? Embarrassment to the Administration obviously, and to these individuals. But who would gain politically from this? These people represent both major parties and all shades of liberalism and conservatism so it doesn't make sense. They've made the whole of Congress hopping mad by ordering a mass audit. Maybe the whole thing is to embarrass this office."

The President suddenly leaned forward, his arms on the desk. "What I want to know, Lloyd, is what the hell is IRS doing with those computerized dossiers on half the country? They're loaded with all kinds of irrelevant junk that doesn't belong there. I thought that had stopped five years ago under one of my predecessors. I'm talking about that mess in South Florida . . . Operation Leprechaun, if I remember correctly. A cute name for a crummy operation. What have you done with it, Lloyd . . . revived it and spread it around the country? They'll cut us up on that one, on invasion of privacy and constitutional grounds. And they'll be absolutely right. Can't we run the government without these abominations? All our agencies are supposed to keep their houses clean, and I mean *all.*" His eyes roved the group.

Danziger was shaken. "Mr. President, I'm not sure how to answer that. The fact is that I inherited the program, I didn't start it. Project Pygmalion monitors various activities, some of them nonfinancial, of taxpayers above a certain income level and particularly in certain fields, and while many of the entries are technically irrelevant, I can tell you that it has proved extremely valuable in tax collections and an asset in other areas of government as well. Since its inception there has been a significant percentage increase in tax revenues from these sources. As I said, this has been an ongoing program and I assumed you knew about it—"

"You assumed wrong." The President glared silently for an endless

130

minute. "I'm going to ask you this question only once, Lloyd. From what you've said, I gather that it would be difficult for someone to activate your systems from the outside. Is it possible, then, that one of your own people could be behind this whole thing?

Danziger thought for a moment and made a decision. He got up slowly from his chair, his lean face drained white. "You can have my resignation now, Mr. President." His voice was low and precise.

"Damn you, Lloyd, sit down. When I want your resignation, I'll ask for it." Danziger sat down, feeling numb and humiliated. "If I thought you were involved, I wouldn't wait for your resignation—I'd fire you outright. Now will you please answer my question?"

That was as close to an apology as he could expect. "All right, I will." He took a short breath. "Yes, it's possible that one or more IRS employees somewhere in the computer network may have engineered this. I don't have anything to go on other than that such a person would be closer to the technology. I would like to think that our security is so good that this isn't possible. But no computer system is ever completely invulnerable. I hope to god it wasn't any of our people, but I must admit that we are looking into that angle too."

"Mr. President, if I may . . ."

"Go ahead, Stu." The President nodded at the Attorney General seated across from Danziger.

"I would like to pursue a different tack," Senseny began. "I would respectfully like to disagree with you both. I think we are asking too much to expect results from IRS's investigation in less than two days. And I think Lloyd is wrong in praying that it's not an inside job. I hope it is. That would surely be preferable to what I fear is the case. Let's analyze the little we know. If this was the work of some underground militant group seeking to damage, or at minimum to disrupt, the economy of the United States, how better could they do it than by stopping revenues from coming in to the government at this particular time. Obviously the motive was to cripple the inflow of tax-filing revenue when it would hurt the most. Otherwise why would they strike exactly a month before the annual tax-filing deadline?"

"You mean that people will stop sending in their tax returns because of this?" the President asked.

"Absolutely," the Attorney General responded with his usual certitude.

"What do you think, Lloyd?" The President turned to Danziger, hoping for a better answer.

"I think it's a real possibility."

"Therefore," Senseny said, resuming his summation, "we must assume that the people responsible for this ingenious strategy are either homegrown subversives or foreign agents, and in either case their motives are to damage our economy. So I think we can forget about a king-size dirty trick by the opposition or even by dissidents inside the IRS. I believe what we're dealing with, Mr. President, is far more serious."

Paul Ives, the White House chief of staff, leaned forward in his chair. "I'd tend to agree with that analysis. In fact, I'd go a step further. I'd say that this may be only a test of our vulnerability and how far these people can go. Since they were able to pull this off successfully, all our vital computer systems could be targets . . . the Pentagon, Treasury, Commerce . . . even the CIA. Maybe especially the CIA, if we're talking about foreign agents."

The President turned to Percy Vandiman. "What do you think, Perce?"

The CIA director's gray eyes were thoughtful. "If you were to accept these assumptions, I'd have to say that CIA would be a logical target, yes. But this is all sheer speculation. I don't think it forms the basis for any conclusions." One patrician eyebrow arched slightly. "In any event, the CIA operates on the assumption that hostile agents are always trying to infiltrate or penetrate us and our security apparatus takes this into account. I, for one, don't intend to panic, Mr. President."

"Famous last words," Ives mumbled to himself. He regarded Vandiman as a fatuous peacock.

"That's fine, Perce," the President said blandly, then took over. "Gentlemen, here's what we're going to do. I want the FBI and the CIA"— he turned his head successively to each of the directors—"to simultaneously investigate this sabotage at once . . . and I mean as soon as you leave this room. I want you to use any and all means at your disposal to find those responsible for this act and to determine how it was done. Use any methods of detection and surveillance that's necessary. The Attorney General will sign whatever authorization is needed. I want these people, whoever they are, located quickly. Clear?" He peered sharply at each, receiving their confirming nods, then he lowered the

132

register of his voice. "This Administration is being severely criticized for what has happened, not only by our opponents but by members of our own party and the public. And it's going to get a lot worse. Imagine having someone invade your money machine! We're being laughed at around the world. This Administration won't tolerate it and this country can't afford it. That's why we must have quick action on this. Any questions?"

"Yes," Mitchell Storey boomed. "I think this is strictly an FBI matter, Mr. President. My boys are in there already, as you know. Besides, Mr. Vandiman himself discounted foreign agents as the probable perpetrators. If both agencies were to investigate, we'd be falling all over each other's feet."

"Coordinate, gentlemen, coordinate." The President's tone was almost sardonic. "I want results . . . and fast." He got up. "I want to thank you all for coming—Stu, Mitch and Perce," he said coming around the desk and extending his hand. "Lloyd, I'd appreciate your standing by for another minute." He walked the other three to the door, smiling cordially. "No press comments or releases unless they're cleared with this office," was his final word.

The President turned to Danziger. "Sit down, Lloyd," he said pleasantly, leading him to the opposite end of the long room where a Greek revival fireplace was centered in the curved wall with gray upholstered sofas facing each other on either side and a round mahogany coffee table between them. They sat on opposite sofas while Paul Ives remained on the other side of the room pretending to read some documents.

The President smiled disarmingly. "I wanted to talk to you privately, Lloyd. I know I came down on you a little hard before. I'm really sorry about that, but I had a reason. We had company, remember, and I wanted to leave a certain impression. I don't entirely trust them. The fact is that I *am* aware of Project Pygmalion. I guess you can say I inherited it too. It was already in place when I arrived behind that desk . . . but I didn't know it had become so . . . so damned pervasive. These things have a way of proliferating and once they're rooted, they're hard to kill. That's the nature of bureaucracy, which I keep lecturing you people about. But I remember being assured, when I first found out about it, that it was not only contained but also secure, and that it was genuinely useful to the FBI, Justice and the Treasury, not to mention your outfit, and there was absolutely no chance it would ever surface to needlessly

133

embarrass us. Well, Lloyd, it has and now we have a serious problem—both of us. It's already started. You wouldn't believe the heat I'm getting, especially from our own party. Wait till the media jump into this, they've hardly started—they'll show no mercy, and a lot of folks around the country will be filling our mailroom and it won't be with votes of confidence. This is an election year. I may have to shift some of the heat over to you, Lloyd, and I'm going to count on your loyalty. We'll probably have to scuttle Pygmalion altogether at some point, at least downgrade it, but let's not worry about that. Keep in close touch with Paul and clear any press statements with him." He got up from the sofa and walked around the coffee table where Danziger was now standing and grabbed his arm and hand squeezing both with warmth. He walked the commissioner toward the door. "Don't worry, Lloyd," he said, smiling confidentially, "we've been through worse before."

After the door closed, the President walked over to the tall French doors lining one wall of the room and looked out beyond the Rose Garden. The sun was very low now, and the bare magnolia trees veined the pale rays. He stood there, his back to the room and let out his breath slowly. "You know, Paul, as of now we have no defense. Either we're guilty of flagrant mismanagement in allowing this to happen or we're inept at not finding the culprits and how it was done." He paused. "Do you realize, Paul, how incredibly clever these people must be? On the one hand, they make us look like we were carrying out some kind of vendetta in exposing and auditing these legislators and officials, and on the other they expose Pygmalion and make us look like damned peeping Toms to the people. Either way, they have us." He sighed. "I'd give a lot to know who the bastards are behind this thing. I'd cut their balls off. Personally."

134

Chapter Seventeen

Dana heard it first, on the radio at noon. The FBI announced on Thursday, March 20, that it was holding for questioning Dr. Yukio Ishizaka, director of systems security of the Parkinson Institute in Boston, in connection with the sabotage of the Internal Revenue Service's computer network. . . . Yuki had been arrested the previous night at his home. She and Kermit could be next.

Kermit had completed his classes for the day when Dana reached him with the news; she had invented a fever and left the Computer Center in the early afternoon. They drove to a gas station phone booth off the campus and phoned Duane at his office, where he wasn't, and then at his home, where he was. Five minutes later he returned the call from a public telephone. He had been trying to reach them for the previous hour.

"Well, it's happened," Duane told Kermit. "They got Yuki."

"I know . . . is Adam Greenfield representing him? I mean, is he getting him released?"

"I'm seeing Greenfield in an hour."

"I hate to think of Yuki being questioned by the FBI—"

"We may all soon be in that spot. They might get Harriet to identify you and Dana. She knows who you are, after all."

"I don't think Harriet would do that."

"Well, even if she doesn't we still could be picked up at any time. You and Dana especially. We don't know what else they've turned up."

"What do you suggest?"

"We'll have to hold the press conference tomorrow."

"Tomorrow? But that's only five days since the story broke. We were planning—"

"I know," Duane broke in, "we wanted to do more damage. But we've done pretty well so far. We'll just have to settle for that. Besides, a lot more trouble could come in the next twenty-four hours. We've *got* to go public tomorrow."

". . . I agree, we can't risk being picked up."

"Okay. You and Dana fly here tomorrow morning. Use that charter service you have in town. I'll meet you. Be here at nine-thirty sharp."

After phoning the charter service and arranging for a flight the next morning, Dana and Kermit lunched in her apartment, talking nervously about the next day. What should they wear? Should they pack extra clothes for a period of detainment after they were arrested? They even did a dry run of Kermit's news conference statement with Dana critiquing his delivery. Dana felt she should have some lines to read rather than just a walk-on part, and Kermit promised to let her field some questions from the press.

At dinner the radio news reported that the Senate Subcommittee on Government Operations had approved Bill S. 17 by a vote of twelve to five, empowering the federal government to unify and take control of the nation's computer systems, public and private, to improve government planning and operational efficiency and to strengthen the nation's security and ability to fight crime. The standing Senate Committee on Government Operations and the corresponding House committee were expected to likewise vote out the bill within the week.

Dana and Kermit looked at each other. It seemed like a ploy to forestall their next day's news conference. As though the enemy they were trying to stop was stalking them.

"Now *that's* what I call timing," Dana said with a bitter smile.

Chapter Eighteen

It was ten after seven when Kermit backed the low-slung car out of the driveway to pick up Dana. Now, finally, was the showdown. It was March 21, the first day of spring and it looked like it. The morning was cool and clear but was warming up under the early sun. It would be a perfect day for what they had to do. He hoped that the small plane he'd chartered for takeoff at eight o'clock would be ready on time.

As he approached the block where Dana's apartment house was set back on the landscaped lawn, something didn't look right. It was too early for two cars to be parked out front, one facing the wrong direction with a few men standing, feet planted, looking at the entrance door. As he came within one block, he saw that the one pointed the wrong way was a police car and he suspected the unmarked car belonged to the FBI. They were picking Dana up! He made a right turn the corner before, circled the block slowly, trying to decide what to do. He had to be sure. Maybe someone's apartment had been burglarized and a police car and detectives were sent to investigate. As he entered the street again, two blocks from the house now, he saw some movement on the walk outside the entrance, several figures huddled together. He tried to time it so he would pass in front to see what was happening without calling attention to himself. Half a block away he recognized Dana's figure in a yellow pants suit partly blocked by two men. He increased his speed somewhat and she caught his eye without giving a sign just before an arm thrust her into the unmarked car. In a moment he had cruised by, turned left on the next corner to get out of view and sped off for the highway.

He was feeling real panic now. This would be the end of the line. He had to get to Washington and tell his story to the world before they caught him too and official lies became gospel. He tried not to think about Dana. If he did he wouldn't be able to function at all.

Ten minutes later he jammed on his brakes in front of the hangar of the private air service with its three-plane fleet of Cessnas. He jumped out and ran into the tiny office. He was twenty-five minutes early, they told him, but the plane was warming up on the runway and they'd be ready to take off as soon as the pilot, co-owner of the service, finished his coffee. They poured a paper cup full for Kermit which he gulped down, looking out of the window for pursuers. A nervous ten minutes later they were airborne. He had dramatic visions of a jet fighter, manned by FBI men in blue serge suits, shooting them down in flames.

A nerve-racking hour later they landed in the private plane sector of the Washington National Airport in Alexandria, Virginia. It was 9:20. He feared that the FBI would be waiting for him there. He was grateful when he found Duane waiting for him instead. Driving into Washington, Kermit told him that Dana had been arrested by the FBI and how he'd barely missed being picked up himself. "I almost spent the night with Dana. . . ."

"Bad news about Dana . . . well, you've got to stay cool, and the first thing we've got to do is stash you away for a few hours. Until the press conference at twelve-thirty." He looked at his watch. "We'll be there by ten. I'm dropping you off at a friend's apartment in town. She's a PR gal and she'll be in her office. Here's what I've got worked out . . . actually it's a con game and the FBI is the mark. First, I'm calling a list of thirty news people I know well on all the major media. I'm getting on the phone as soon as I drop you. I'm going to tell each of them to meet me at the National Press Club bar at exactly twelve-thirty and not to ask me any questions. I'll guarantee it will be worth their while. I have enough credibility for them to believe me. I'm telling them that they must be there no later than twelve-thirty sharp or they'll be too late. Then, I grab them downstairs in the Press Club lobby as they arrive and hustle them into a bus parked around the corner. I don't want them to get together in the Press Club, where they'll attract attention. Oh, yes . . . I chartered a city bus for this.

138

All the while he'd been listening Kermit had also been fighting to keep his thoughts off Dana. . . . "Where are you taking them?"

"For a ride through the District. It'll be a news conference on wheels. Rigged up with a PA system like a sightseeing bus and the mike will be in your hand. You like it so far?"

"I don't know yet, do you think it'll work?

"That's just the beginning. I've rented a suite at the Sheraton-Park way uptown from the National Press Club, and we're scheduling a news conference there for three o'clock."

"I don't understand. I thought—"

"Wait a minute. This is just a decoy to draw attention—and I hope the FBI—away from the real news conference, which I figure should be over by one-thirty at the latest. That should give us enough time to turn ourselves in at our leisure."

"That sounds okay to me."

"Better than okay. I'm paying a PR woman . . . Marcia . . . the same one whose apartment we're going to . . . to phone a list of secondary media people—correspondents for regional news services, a few monthly magazine staffers, some reporters for a clutch of small dailies and a handful of independent radio and TV stations—and she'll tell them that a news conference is taking place at the Sheraton-Park at three o'clock to report a new development in the IRS computer investigation. She won't identify herself and she'll hang up. These people undoubtedly will check with IRS to find out what it's all about. IRS won't know a damned thing and they'll have to alert the FBI. But"—he held his hand up as Kermit started to interrupt—"she won't start making those calls until one-thirty and we'll be in the clear by then." He paused, turning off the parkway to the Fourteenth Street Bridge crossing the Potomac to downtown Washington.

"Won't it occur to them that it might be a phony?" Kermit asked.

"Probably, but they won't be sure. And when they find out that a suite is actually reserved for a news conference—I used a pseudonym—they'll have to show up just in case."

"But what about the girl . . . Marcia. Can you trust her?"

"She doesn't know a thing. She's not in PR that long and she still thinks a reporter is some kind of god. I told her a member of the Administration was leaking some information on this to the press and he didn't want his name used and I was doing him a favor, all very

139

confidential, and I needed someone to share the calls. She thinks I'm big stuff and she bought it. Besides, I'm paying her so it becomes a commercial assignment and she'll be in the clear. I gave her a personal check for fifty bucks and there'll be a record of that in case it comes up."

Duane pulled over to the curb in front of a four-story brownstone on East Capitol Street near Lincoln Park. It was ten minutes to ten. He gave Kermit the key to the second floor apartment and told him to make himself comfortable there and not answer the phone or a doorbell ring no matter what. He would phone him at the apartment at about twelve-thirty, ring twice and hang up. Kermit was to wait five minutes, then look out the front window until he saw a bus parked in front and come down immediately.

"One o'clock will be the deadline. If you don't hear from me by then, something's gone wrong. Take this number," Duane said, handing him a folded file card from his wallet. "It's the private number of Stan Michaelson. Stan's a good friend of mine. Tell him I asked you to call him on a high priority news item. He'll see you immediately. Just show him your statement and the White Paper and I'm sure he'll interview you live on his five o'clock news show on WTOP-TV. The rest of the CBS network is sure to pick it up. I've already primed him for a possible call. He doesn't know from whom or on what, but he knows it's important." He was talking fast, looking at his watch nervously. "It's not the same as a full-dress press conference, but at least you'll beat the clock. I've got to get the hell out of here. See you later."

Kermit slammed the car door, went up the flight of stone stairs feeling as though a bright target was on his back and a dozen guns were pointed at it.

In a pressure-cooked hour and a half in his own apartment, hunched over a disheveled desktop, Duane worked his way through thirty-three production-line phone calls, got through to twenty-four media people on his list and seventeen promised to meet him at the Press Club bar. A dozen accepted readily but he had to press for the other five he particularly wanted to be there. His cryptically urgent invitation piqued their interest. But it had taken longer than he'd expected and he felt under the gun. It was 11:40, he still had things to do and he wanted to be standing in the downstairs lobby of the National Press Club building by 12:15 at latest to make sure no early bird got away. He phoned the bus company to confirm that the bus would be in place as scheduled, then called Marcia to make sure she was all set. At five to twelve, he picked up a small suitcase filled with copies of the White Paper and Kermit's statement, which he would hand out to the reporters at some point during the bus ride. He hailed a taxi and ten minutes later was in front of the National Press Club building on Fourteenth Street near F Street, just a short walk from the White House.

He felt himself sweating with the pressure as he walked quickly around the corner where the bus was to be parked. It wasn't there. He looked at his watch. Ten after twelve. It was supposed to be there at twelve sharp. He didn't know whether he should wait there for it or rush back to the building lobby to corral his guests. Both ends were critical and he wished he had Marcia to split it with him and to shepherd the newspeople into the bus as they arrived. He was furious with himself for not thinking of it earlier.

He put down the suitcase, and told himself to calm down. An interminable three minutes later, as he picked up the suitcase to rush to the lobby, he saw the bus coming around the corner with a sign over the windshield reading TOUR CHARTER. The driver explained that he had to circle the block because there was no place to park. He parked it now in an alley between buildings on F Street. Duane put the heavy suitcase in back of the bus and hurried around the block to the building entrance.

Twelve-seventeen. Duane was stationed just inside the entrance doors, his eyes searching every face that hustled by. The lunch hour rush made it nerve-racking as faces were momentarily blocked: he could see only profiles or the receding backs of heads. He moved about trying to get a look at an occasional face he thought he might know. Suddenly he spotted Steve Hanna of AP coming through the swinging door. The largest national news service, a good start.

"I thought you'd be at the bar upstairs. What's up, Duane?" Hanna said.

"Hi, Steve, thanks for coming." Duane grasped his hand in genuine relief. "Please bear with me and don't ask any questions, okay? I promise you a hell of a payoff. Just hang around for a few minutes. I'm expecting some other people, and then we're taking a ride into the country."

Hanna looked at him closely trying to decide if this was a put-on. "Are you sure you haven't had one too many? April first is still a week away."

"Trust me."

"You give me no choice, old buddy."

Duane darted forward, grabbing the arm of Paul Englander, the ABC-TV newscaster, as he came through the door. Englander looked elegantly skeptical when Duane gave him a similar greeting. He looked to Hanna for confirmation and the AP man responded with a casual shrug, saying, "I'm going along with it."

And then they came through one or another of the glass doors in twos and threes: The representatives of NBC-TV News, United Press International, the *New York Times*, the Washington *Post*, the Newhouse News Bureau, NBC Radio, Group W Radio, the Knight newspapers, Hearst, CBS-TV News, the Los Angeles *Times*, Reuters and *U.S. News and World Report*.

Two of the seventeen hadn't yet arrived, but it was 12:35 and Duane decided not to wait any longer. He had to signal Kermit with a phone call, but he couldn't risk leaving the group. He turned to his friend Fred Baumritter of the Washington *Post* and in a whisper asked him if he would phone the number he handed him, hang up after exactly two rings, and then meet them around the corner on F Street in the parked bus marked TOUR CHARTER. Baumritter was nonplused, but shrugged, said, "Sure," and went off toward the public phones in the lobby.

Duane raised his voice. "May I have your attention? *Please* . . . may I have your attention? I appreciate your patience. I want to ask just one more favor. There is a chartered bus waiting outside that will take us to the source of a major news break. I'm sorry to be so mysterious but in a few minutes you'll all have your story. You all know me and I hope that will be good enough. If you'll please follow me, the bus is just around the corner and we'll board immediately. I'll be able to brief you then."

The group followed him out of the building, exchanging glances, a few of them hesitating and annoyed, others joking and intrigued. They filed onto the bus, querulous and good-humored in turn; Duane counted thirteen. Fred Baumritter made fourteen; one must have decided not to go along. As Duane gave the bus driver instructions for stopping in front of Marcia's apartment, Fred came running up and told Duane all the phones were in use and asked if he should keep trying. Duane looked at his watch—12:40. They were ten minutes behind schedule and with a busload of impatient, virtually hijacked passengers, he was feeling the pressure. "Let's go," he told the bus driver.

As the bus pulled into traffic heading east, Duane took the microphone from behind the driver's seat and, standing with his free hand grasping a support, began to speak. "Ladies and gentlemen . . . friends, I hope. . . . I've gotten you here today for a good reason—an extremely important news story. This bus will be the site of a rolling news conference in about ten minutes, as soon as we pick up the person who will make an important announcement and answer your questions. I apologize for this unorthodox, irritating procedure, but I think you'll soon realize why this was necessary. All I can tell you is that it would never have taken place if it was not done in secret." Questions were starting to arise from the middle of the bus, but Duane ignored them and leaned over to speak to the driver. In a few minutes, the bus was double-parked in front of the brownstone house a half mile east of the Capitol. Duane told the driver to keep sounding his horn as he bolted up the stairs to the second floor. He rang the bell, then pounded on the door when it wasn't answered promptly. Finally the door swung open and Kermit stood there, looking considerably more composed than he felt. Duane yanked him by the arm. "Let's go!"

The bus started off as soon as they entered. They stood together in front holding on to grab bars as Duane, using the mike, introduced Kermit, briefly giving his credentials. There was no sign of recognition from the media people and the only sound in the bus, as Kermit took the mike, was the low growl of the vehicle's rear engine and the noises of traffic.

Kermit looked around for a moment at the somber faces focused on him. It looked like a hanging jury. He cleared his throat, smiled self-consciously when the sound was magnified by the PA system. "Ladies and gentlemen, I'm very grateful to you for coming along on this rather unusual news conference and I want to apologize for the way you were, well, lured here. Circumstances gave us no choice." Their faces were immobile and their eyes stony. They wanted blood, he could feel it, for being manipulated.

He began to read from the typewritten sheets: "On Friday, March fourteenth, my associates and I invaded the national computer system of the Internal Revenue Service. In the process we also penetrated a COMSAT communication satellite." The faces remained immobile. "We did this to demonstrate the tremendous threat to our society of the misuse of computers and data banks. The decision to invade a government facility was a painful and reluctant one. We

143

made it because various efforts over the years, and in particular the efforts of an associate and myself over the past two years, failed to alert Congress or the media to those threats. As new developments escalate the threats, we're convinced that time is running out for viable democratic government in the United States. We hope that what we've done will stop the clock long enough to allow people to take a hard look at what is happening in this country and to decide if that is what they want for themselves and their children and, if not, to get angry enough to do something constructive about it—"

"Tell us how you did it," a loud voice interrupted from the rear of the bus. "You're giving us a lot of talk. How about some facts?" shouted another. "What group do you represent?" came at him before he could react.

Kermit held up his hand. "Please—hold your questions. Let me finish my statement first. I think it will answer most of your questions."

A groan filled the bus, subsiding to muttering.

"Before I go on, I want to identify the other people who took part in this project. Yukio Ishizaka holds a doctoral degree in computer science from the Massachusetts Institute of Technology. Dr. Ishizaka is the author of several theses and articles on computer protection and is manager of systems security at the Parkinson Institute in Boston. The other is Dana Haverhill, my colleague at South Hanover Institute of Technology. She has a master's degree in computer science from Stanford University, worked as a research assistant at Stanford Research Institute and is director of our Computer Center. I want to make it clear that we acted entirely on our own and that the institutions we work for were in no way involved."

"Excuse me, Kermit." Duane jumped up from his front seat and grabbed the microphone, his face flushing. "I'd like to add something to the record—something that Dr. Nordstrom generously left out. I too was, or rather am, a participant in this act. I'm the fourth member of the group and I was involved in the planning of the project and I fully support its purposes and methods. I did what I did without the knowledge of my employers at *Newswatch.*" He paused, he saw questions forming on the faces of some of his colleagues. "Well, now that you know who we are, I'm sure you can understand our need for holding this in secret. Dr. Ishizaka and Ms. Haverhill are already in the hands of the FBI. Kermit and I expect to be picked up at any moment." Surprised

144

buzzing darted around the bus. "So I ask you all to bear with us until this news conference is over, and not to leave the bus until then. This is our only chance to get the full story to you and to the public before the gendarmes close in. I'll distribute copies of the statement and also a White Paper, so there's no need to take notes. And please hold your questions until the statement is finished."

It was one o'clock, ten minutes since the bus had pulled away with Kermit aboard, and in the heavy lunchtime traffic they'd gone perhaps less than a mile. Cars pulled alongside or past them but no one paid attention to the chartered bus.

Kermit reclaimed the mike and resumed reading from the typescript. "None of us is a revolutionary or a subversive. All of us work within the establishment, but *we are* frightened to death by what's happening to our country in this Computer Age. This is a new decade and we've reached the point where we feel we must change course quickly or find our society changed beyond recognition. . . ." Impatiently he riffled through the next few pages and then looked up. "I'm going to skip a lot of this stuff—it's important but you can read it later from your own copies—I'll just hit the highlights, if that's all right with you." There were emphatic nods of approval. "We used a remote terminal to access the IRS computer network, and that involved the use of a COMSAT satellite. It was a complex operation and we don't intend to publicize the techniques we used. However, you should know that there are hundreds, possibly thousands, of computer experts capable of similar invasions. Our motives were to sound an alarm against runaway computerism and to prove how vulnerable data banks and communication satellites are. The motives of some others could be less benign.

"Okay," he said, settling on a page. "Here are the four areas we're especially concerned about: One is the invasion of privacy by computers on every level of government and in the private sector. None of this is new to you. There are a hundred thousand computer systems in the U.S. and tens of thousands are dedicated to compiling all kinds of personal, intimate information about every phase of our lives—what we do, what we think, whom we know, our political inclinations, organizations we join, how we pay our bills, where we travel, even with whom, and how, we have sex—I should be kidding but I'm not. Much of this information about us, in more data banks than we know, is irrelevant, inaccurate and illegally there. And even what is legal is frequently used for illegal

145

purposes. We spend our lives in dossier dungeons, subject to rape at the pleasure of bureaucrats both governmental and corporate.

"Let's get to number two—data surveillance. We've known since the early nineteen-seventies of illegal surveillance of law-abiding, nonviolent organizations and individuals by government agencies using illegally obtained data stored in data banks for unconstitutional uses. Okay, points one and two are certainly not hot news to you—although I must say that the media in general hasn't taken them very seriously except when a reporter's sources are involved."

Kermit's juices were beginning to flow, and he no longer felt so intimidated by his audience.

"Now for point three, which I doubt you're so familiar with. It is a fact that the government itself can be subverted, the economy wrecked and operations brought to a halt by electronic blackmail. It can be done by sophisticated computer-wise terrorists or by foreign agents using remote terminals. Perhaps a more likely danger is a coup d'etat from within the highest levels of the government itself—a sort of pushbutton palace revolution." Kermit saw a flicker of interest but no real concern. "Government computer systems *are* vulnerable—they *can* be penetrated. That's one of the things we set out to prove. And we proved it by successfully invading IRS's national network on our first try. If that doesn't convince the public, what will?"

"Don't you think your showing the way to terrorists is a disservice to the country?" a woman's voice accused.

"I'll answer that, but please let me finish first. . . . Which brings me to the fourth crisis area. Computer crime is rising at an alarming rate —another area that gets little exposure. A computer terminal in an expert's attic is more potent than a machine gun under a bandit's arm. It's easier to steal five million dollars with a terminal than fifty thousand with a gun, if you know how—and there's far less chance of getting caught. The threat grows as we train more bright computer people each year . . . this type of crime is very tempting . . . and now the crime syndicates are getting into it."

The fourteen faces in the bus were gradually changing from resentment and cynicism to open curiosity.

He flipped over a few pages and selected a spot for reference. "You're aware of the clandestine activities of the FBI, CIA, the National Security Administration, Army Intelligence and, yes, the IRS, using dossiers and

146

data surveillance techniques to spy, to harass, to intimidate and even blackmail those whose views or activities have been at odds with certain administration policies. But here are a few we came on that aren't known yet." He sensed a flurry and saw a few bring out pencil and paper. "It's all here," he said, holding his statement aloft, "so I don't think you have to bother with notes. . . . In IRS's central data bank in Martinsburg, West Virginia, we came across a program with the code name Project Pygmalion. This is a program which, as far as we can tell, compiles and stores irrelevant information on the personal activities, lifestyles, associations and X-rated data of the most intimate, scurrilous sort on certain categories of taxpayers. This program contains dossiers on possibly as many as five million citizens. Motive? To pressure . . . to put it politely . . . taxpayers."

Kermit looked down on the sheet again and then looked up. "When we invaded IRS's central computer system we discovered that we weren't the only invaders. We had some prestigious company. There was the—"

Suddenly the *wha wha wha* of a siren coming up fast behind them pierced their consciousness and every head swiveled. Especially Kermit's and Duane's. The story wasn't yet told. Two police cars came up on either side of the bus, which had slowed down to stop. Kermit felt a rasp drawn through his gut, and Duane jumped up, saying, "Of all the lousy luck. . . ." But the police cars kept going, speeding in and out of traffic until they disappeared. Nervous laughter broke out.

Dave Nielsen of NBC spoke up from an aisle seat. "For a minute we thought we were going to lose you. How about passing out those press kits now, Duane, just in case?"

"Okay, as long as you hold them 'til later," and he went back to the suitcase in the back seat of the bus and began handing out blue folders containing the news material.

Kermit reclaimed the microphone quickly. He was itching to hit them with the startling revelation. "Meanwhile, back in Martinsburg, as I started to say, we had some unexpected company. We ran into taps which we believe originated from the White House. Also NSA and Treasury, which could mean the Secret Service. At various times during the period our computer was secretly monitoring via a satellite the data traffic between IRS's central and regional Service Center computers, we picked up coded communications which were of a different pattern, and when we broke them down we found that computers, *apparently* from the White House and those other agencies, were talking at odd intervals to the IRS computers. Of course that direct access is illegal, which presumably is one of the reasons it's been kept secret." Judging by facial expressions and snatches of conversation, Kermit could see that these disclosures were making an impact.

Duane popped up from his front seat. "Excuse me, Kermit." He turned to the passengers. "I just want to say that everything Kermit is saying is being taped on a cassette recorder behind the driver's seat. It's a legal record for our own purpose, but I can arrange for copies to be run off for anyone who wants them." Duane turned and leaned over the driver's shoulder, directing him on a circuitous course of left and right turns every few blocks.

Kermit resumed. "We're not just trying to dramatize a national problem, we'd like to try to help solve it. The four of us have developed a set of proposals designed to control the cybernetic monster and make him work *for* the people. These are covered extensively in the White Paper so I'll just touch on them quickly now. First, we propose a full-scale investigation by a blue-ribbon committee of leading figures outside the government into the practices of all public and private computer operations.

"Second, we propose that legislation be developed to insure that certain types of information aren't computerized and that tight restrictions to insure privacy are enforced at all data banks, with serious penalties for violations. We urge that data banks be cleansed of existing data which is illegal or does not conform to upgraded standards. The legislation needs to prevent illegal access to data banks of government agencies and private systems under new and tough criteria.

"Our third proposal is to mandate the use of advanced protective techniques presently available in systems design, hardware, software and operating practices. There are a lot of soft spots in our current systems and we have a list of recommendations for tightening security on computer systems, land-based and in the sky—communication satellites. As an essential part of this we urge that the government fund a major research and development program by industry and the academic community to create new protective systems and techniques to prevent abuses and invasions.

"We also recommend setting up a separate regulatory agency—call it

148

the Computer Control Commission—to act as a permanent watchdog agency to monitor the operations of government computer systems, making them accountable to the public on an open, reporting basis. We believe this agency should also license and regulate every private computer system in the country that handles—"

Someone shouted from the middle of the bus. "That blue sedan . . . it's an FBI car . . . I recognize it." It was Max Garvey of UPI pointing at a car that had entered from an intersection and was now a block back in traffic.

Kermit dropped the mike to his side. He looked at Duane, standing next to him. "What do we do now?"

Duane yelled to the driver to keep going. He spoke to Kermit in a low voice. "I think we've run out our string. They'll have to get the rest from the press kit." Kermit nodded, Duane grabbed the mike. "It looks like the jig's up, friends. At least you'll be able to witness our arrest. I want to thank you all for—"

"Why don't we try to shake them?" Nina Paulsen of the Los Angeles *Times* interrupted from her third row seat. "I'd like to hear the rest."

"I've got a few questions that need answering and I suspect the others do too," Dale Warnecke of *The New York Times* added.

"I was hoping to do a videotaped interview when we got back," Mark Dunleavy of CBS-TV News said unhappily.

The FBI sedan was now just eight or nine cars back in the congested traffic. Duane looked at Kermit, who nodded in return. Forgetting the microphone, Duane shouted, "It's up to you people. Do we try to lose them and continue the news conference? We're willing to try it but it could get hairy. . . ."

"Lose them, lose them. . . ." The shouts began before he had finished.

Duane called out to the young driver for everyone to hear. "Carl, lose that car that's following. There's twenty bucks in it for you."

"Are you kidding? I know it's the FBI . . . make it fifty."

"You got it."

Suddenly the big vehicle shot out of its left lane and crossed over the double line, where there was a hole in opposing traffic, reached the corner and turned left as cut-off motorists blared their horns. It was a daring, neatly executed maneuver. The chase was on, and they all were involved . . . no more cool-eyed observers in the press box. They sped down a near-empty sidestreet, turned right in time to see the blue sedan turn swiftly into the block. It was obvious that they could not outrace the faster car; in a few seconds the chase would end. Abruptly, in midblock, the bus swerved at full speed onto the sidewalk and up the ramp of an old parking garage. None of the passengers who had been torqued over on their side during the sudden turn realized that the dark cavern they entered from the sunshine was a garage. They were momentarily shocked into silence as the driver swung open the door and got out to speak to the garage attendant. In a minute he was back. "I told him I thought my tire was flat." He sat down and turned the crank over his head which rolled the destination panel. "I changed it to read UNION STATION. That just might throw them off." Carl grinned, pleased with himself, backed the bus around and poked its nose flush with the doorway. Nothing in sight. He looked at Duane. "Let's *go,*" Duane said. The bus roared out and turned left, the opposite direction from where it had entered the two-way street, went two blocks, turned left again crossing the main thoroughfare from which they had turned off and then continued on that course at right angles to the original point of detection. Duane felt like he was riding shotgun, turning his head around to check out the rapidly moving streetscape, leaning over Carl's shoulder and issuing instructions. This was a good street to stay on for a while . . . traffic was light and they could use the distance.

Finally the sense of emergency of the last five minutes subsided some and Kermit, sensing the shift, took back the microphone. "I'll try to make this as fast as I can. They may have alerted other units. . . . There are just a couple of more things I want to say. We've not yet learned how to control the computer, and it's almost too late. Just consider the Morstan bill if you still have any doubts. This bill embodies all the violations of the privacy of individuals and the dangers to basic democracy we're warning about. It would actually legitimatize all the Watergate-type horrors by legalizing them, thereby turning them into a mandate for bureaucratic dictatorship. The raping of data banks, surveillance and intimidation of law-abiding citizens, control of data communication channels—all this would become *standard government functions* if that bill ever became law. And all in the name of national security, public safety. Whose security? Whose safety? I can't think of anything that proves our point better than this bill.

"The computer has turned our private lives public, and the political, legal, social and psychological effects on each one of us is just not understood, even though for the past fifteen years congressional committees have been *investigating* . . . and all that's come out of it is patty-cake legislation like the Privacy Act of 1974. Which, of course, is why the four of us felt we had to take this drastic route."

Kermit took a quick look at his wrist—1:33. It was quiet in the bus and they were moving along steadily in the moderate traffic. The faces were still focused on him and he felt their acceptance. He turned to Duane. "Just one more minute."

Duane nodded.

"In spite of all the alarms we've sounded, we want to make it clear that we're still convinced computers and data banks and computer communications in all their forms are essential to the proper functioning of our complex government and industrial structure. We're *not* against computers and computer technology, just the abuse of power that the corrupt use of computers represents. We're against the proliferation of computer crime for profit by individuals and by computer-based crime syndicates. We're against subversion of our government and society by computer . . . from the right, left, middle or from foreign enemies. We are *for* a better, saner American society. End of editorial. I'm damned grateful to all of you."

For a brief moment the only sound was the sullen growl of the engine in the rear. Then someone applauded lightly and it spread.

Duane, delighted, got up, said something to the driver, then turned around and announced, "We're heading back to the Press Club. When we get there Kermit and I are going to turn ourselves in to the FBI. I know you have a lot of questions. We'll answer as many as we can."

Mark Dunleavy of CBS-TV was the first. "This bus is equipped with a two-way radio," Dunleavy said. I'd like to call in to my office and have them get a camera crew in front of the Press Club waiting for us. I assume the other broadcast people want to do the same." They did and he took their news desk phone numbers and went up front and stood with the driver until the arrangements were made on the two-way radio. Meanwhile the question-and-answer period was under way as the bus got enmeshed in downtown traffic.

Steve Hanna of Associated Press: "It seems to me," he began, "that what you and your associates did, Dr. Nordstrom, was . . . well, unique. I noticed, though, you never called it sabotage. Regardless of your motives, isn't that really what it was—sabotage?"

151

"No, it wasn't. We didn't damage or destroy anything, except possibly the myth of invulnerability. We committed illegal entry and we created unauthorized programs, which undoubtedly upset a lot of people. But we also revealed some shockingly illegal practices. And our action should bring the government substantial tax revenues and, we hope, other long-range benefits."

Barbara Zimmer of Group W Radio had a question. "As I asked you before, Dr. Nordstrom, don't you think your showing terrorist groups that an important government computer system can be breached is a serious disservice to the country?"

"I don't think so. If someone broke into Fort Knox to demonstrate that the lock on the vault was inadequate and to get them to install a stronger lock, would you say that was a disservice to the country? Remember, we've been talking about this for a long time, but no one was paying much attention—including most of the media."

Dale Warnecke, *The New York Times:* "Dr. Nordstrom, do you anticipate that your act of . . . 'illegal entry' . . . will have any effect on the outcome of the Morstan bill?"

"We sure *hope* so . . . we hope that what we did and what we've exposed will shock the country into realizing the dangers while there's still time. We hope it will make them see the Morstan bill for the nightmare threat to democracy that it is."

Charlene Turner of the Newhouse papers: "Don't you think that national security should have a higher priority than individual rights, even privacy, when the two come in conflict?"

"I don't think we should have to make such a choice. When you start abridging rights like privacy, freedom of speech, press, assembly and so forth in the name of national security, well, you've lost your democracy anyway."

"It's ten to two," Duane pointed out. "In this traffic, it'll take us about fifteen minutes to get back to the Press Club. And then Kermit and I have a date with the FBI while you people go on to lunch."

"Since you've chosen to make yourself a martyr," Dave Nielsen of NBC spoke up, "I'd like to ask *you* a question. This is off the record as far as I'm concerned. Do you think it's proper for a newsman, an investigative reporter like yourself, to become an activist rather than carry out his function to uncover corruption and to report it?"

Duane thought for a moment. "I'll tell you, Dave, I made a choice

152

good or bad, you decide. Dr. Nordstrom gives the speeches, I'm lousy at them. But he speaks for me . . . every word. And you can put that *on* the record, if you want."

"I'd like to ask a question," Fred Baumritter, Washington *Post,* said. "What do you and your associates expect will happen to you now, Dr. Nordstrom, and what do you think it will do to your careers?"

"I'm not sure. I assume the government will charge us with a crime and we will do our best to defend ourselves. We don't know what will happen to our careers. But actually, we feel our day in court is today, now, this news conference. We're more interested in the court of public opinion. That's what this is all about."

Guy Ludlum, the *U.S. News* reporter who had sat rather subdued in the rear, spoke up in a low voice. "Have you ever thought of getting into politics?"

"No, I haven't, but I appreciate the thought."

Duane called Fred Baumritter over to him and gave him his Sony cassette recorder. He asked him to have twenty copies of the tape made up that afternoon and see that everyone in the bus who wanted one got one, and then to deliver the original and the remaining copies to Adam Greenfield, their attorney. Fred was a good friend and he felt he could trust him to do this.

"By the way," Fred said in the same confidential tone Duane had been using, "you should have seen Pierre Beauchamps' face when he saw us get into the bus. I guess he didn't like the idea."

"The Reuters man? . . . Oh, then he was the one who was missing. Yeah, he's going to be one sorry reporter when the story breaks on the other wires and Reuters doesn't have it."

From somewhere in the small circle around Kermit someone shouted, "Here we go again. It's the same blue sedan." They all looked to where he was pointing. It was the second car waiting on a red light at an intersection they'd just passed. So be it, Duane thought. We've done what we wanted. It was exactly two. The room would soon be filling up with newspeople at the Sheraton-Park for the news conference that wasn't there. He allowed himself a smile.

"What do you say we lose him again," Mark Dunleavy shouted from the back. "We've the camera crews standing by at the Press Club. We only need five minutes."

Duane turned to the others. "It's up to the rest of you—what do you say?"

"Lose him! . . . Lose him!" was the instant consensus.

Duane touched Carl on the shoulder. "You heard them, there's an extra ten in it for you."

The bus lurched forward, weaving in and out of the moderate post-lunch hour traffic as they headed for the National Press Club only about six blocks away. Carl made a careening left turn at the first corner where the sign read NO LEFT TURN, and veered around slow-moving cars. Just before they turned right two blocks later they heard a siren wailing, but it wasn't that close. And then they heard what sounded like a helicopter cutting through the sky. A few heads went through open windows, craning upward. "It's a chopper, flying low, about three hundred feet," someone said. "It could be tracking us." Duane looked out the window. It was a police helicopter and it was low, perhaps a thousand feet behind them and on the same path. The sound of the siren was getting closer but they couldn't yet see the car. Four blocks and three more turns to make it to the front of the Press Club building.

Kermit joined Duane in the front of the bus, crouching and looking out the window as Duane huddled with Carl on the strategy of slipping in and out of traffic moving in both directions.

The chopper was now circling back for another low-level pass, making a great racket. Coming right at them from that height, it looked like a huge weapon that might actually open fire. Then they saw the blue sedan wailing away two blocks back, getting its directions from the chopper overhead.

The streets were unexpectedly clear of other vehicles. Carl sent the bus around a corner and speeding down the block, the blue sedan one block behind. At the next intersection, another unmarked car, its siren blaring, joined the chase.

Carl was maneuvering like a stock car racer, taking advantage of every opening. One more turn and both FBI cars were tagged up behind, their sirens shattering the air. They were speeding down E Street, just one block from their target. Carl ran the red light as he swung the vehicle around the final corner onto Fourteenth Street, with one FBI car alongside and the other hugging the rear. The one alongside cut in front fifty feet ahead as Carl brought the bus to a halt almost exactly in front of the National Press Club building.

154

Four men in dark suits came running up with drawn guns before Carl could get the door open. They made everyone file out, ignoring the protests of the media people that they were members of the press, as well as Kermit's and Duane's attempts to identify themselves. The chopper was hovering overhead, another FBI car and two police cars came on the scene moments later. Two television cameramen were in front of the building and walked their hand-held cameras as close as possible to begin filming.

The FBI men began to search everyone until they recognized Dave Nielsen and a couple of the other newsmen, who explained that all these people being manhandled were press and broadcast representatives who had just attended a news conference. Duane and Kermit moved forward and said they wanted to turn themselves over to the FBI for invading the IRS computers. The FBI men recognized Kermit by name and description and immediately handcuffed him, his arms behind his back, but they told Duane they had no warrant for his arrest. "Look, I was a party to this," he told them. "Here's a press kit, you'll find my name in it as one of the . . . uh . . . perpetrators."

One of the older FBI men nodded to another, who swiftly handcuffed Duane as the first one took the press kit. Kermit and Duane were then led toward one of the FBI cars, with crowds watching from both sides of the broad thoroughfare.

As they neared the curb, Duane spotted a familiar face in one of the FBI cars. Pierre Beauchamps. As they ducked into the car ahead, Duane said, "I wondered how they spotted us so early. Good old lucky Pierre, he fingered us."

Chapter Nineteen

Within minutes after Kermit's and Duane's arrest just three blocks from the White House, the mild first day of spring was abruptly interrupted by radio and television stations breaking into their regular programming to broadcast a special news bulletin, announcing that four people had confessed to a conspiracy to sabotage the national computer network of the Internal Revenue Service. One of the group had been arrested yesterday in Boston. The bulletin identified the four and stated that they were all under arrest by the Federal Bureau of Investigation. It contained no information from Kermit's news statement. . . .

Kermit and Duane were driven to the FBI's field office in the century-old Old Post Office Building, a gray-block fortress at the corner of Twelfth Street and Pennsylvania Avenue.

"Do you know what's directly behind this?" Duane said as they were shoved up the stone steps. "IRS headquarters."

"Well," Kermit said, "the circles intersect—Azimuth."

They were led at once into a small workroom where they were photographed, fingerprinted and made to sign a form listing their rights. They were then allowed to phone their attorney, Adam Greenfield, who advised them not to answer any questions or make any statements. He would meet them later at the arraignment.

They were taken into a pale green, sparsely furnished interview room, where two men began questioning them. Duane and Kermit said they were exercising their right to remain silent. They were then hustled out of the building and driven a short distance to the U.S. District Court, a modern structure on Constitution Avenue and John Marshall Place, where they were turned over to a U.S. marshal—a tall, heavyset middle-aged black man with a fixed smile. Their personal belongings were removed and they were taken downstairs to a basement cellblock where they were placed in a large, steel-barred cell that served as a temporary holding tank. There were half a dozen other men in the cell waiting to be called before the magistrate upstairs for arraignment. . . .

An hour later daily newspapers coast to coast rushed out special editions with banner headlines across page one. Their stories carried detailed accounts of the arrests, the bizarre circumstances of the news conference, some background on the four conspirators and brief excerpts from the news statement about their motives. The evening TV news showed film of the arrest by FBI agents in front of the National Press Club building, with the helicopter hovering overhead, dramatizing the chase. Doug Hightower of NBC-TV News and Mark Dunleavy of CBS-TV News both gave balanced reports on the 6 and 11 P.M. network news, and this was the first indication for those who hadn't read the afternoon papers that the four were anything but militant subversives trying to wreck the government and harass law-abiding taxpayers. . . .

As they awaited their turn to be called, Kermit and Duane wondered where Dana was. Had she been taken to the nearest FBI field office, probably in Albany, or had she been flown directly to Washington? They assumed that Yuki was in Washington by now but they had no idea where.

Their questions were answered an hour later when they arrived upstairs in the Magistrate's Court. There was Dana in her lemon yellow pantsuit, dazzling the dull gray and brownness of the courtroom, sitting on a front row bench along with Adam Greenfield. A couple of minutes later Yuki appeared, led by a uniformed officer of the court. It was the first time the three of them had seen him in over three weeks. He seemed to be bearing up well enough, and his eyes showed his pleasure at seeing them. They had time just to say hello to Greenfield and to whisper a few words to each other.

Greenfield's appearance was a surprise to Kermit. He knew of him by reputation and expected to see a bigger and more impressive-looking

157

man. He was about five feet seven, at least a half a head shorter than Kermit and an inch shorter than Duane. He was slim, well-built, with finely cut features and a cleft chin, and quick, sensitive eyes. He looked more like an instructor in English literature than a high-powered civil liberties attorney.

When the four suspects were called before the bench, the magistrate asked the tall, youthful Assistant U.S. Attorney, a Mr. Wallendorf, for the charge against them.

He replied in a monotone: "The charges are sedition, conspiracy and destruction of government property under Title 18 of the U.S. Code, Section 2381 of the Federal Law. We believe that these four individuals conspired together to commit, and allegedly did commit, an act of sabotage on facilities of the United States Government, specifically involving the national computer system of the Internal Revenue Service." He stated in the same flat tone that two of them had been apprehended in the District of Columbia by the FBI after a chase, and that one, Miss Haverhill, had been arrested at her home in South Hanover, New York, and the fourth had been taken into custody one day earlier at his home outside of Boston. "I request that the four defendants be held without bail because of the serious and destructive nature of the crime against the government of the United States and the possibility that they might leave the country."

Greenfield began to speak, but the magistrate held up a delaying hand, looking at the Assistant U.S. Attorney. "What's the basis for your assumption that they might leave the country, Mr. Wallendorf?"

"The seditious nature of the crime and the conspiratorial aspects of it lead the government to suspect that the defendants might be affiliated with a foreign group or government unfriendly to the United States for the purpose of subversion, in which case we must assume that they would receive help to escape to another country to avoid trial."

"You're describing treason under federal law, as I understand it, Mr. Wallendorf. Do you want to change the charge?"

"No, your honor."

The magistrate eyed him. "Is that all you have to go on, then?"

The government attorney looked slightly uncomfortable. "We believe those are sufficient grounds, your honor."

The magistrate tightened his thin lips. "In that case, then, we'll set bail. What did you have in mind?"

"The government asks that a bail of one million dollars be set for each of the defendants."

The magistrate smiled slightly and turned to Adam Greenfield. "How do you feel about that, Mr. Greenfield?"

"I think it's amazing, your honor. I can't believe that Mr. Wallendorf is entirely serious. In my opinion no bail is necessary. The defendants are individuals of exemplary character, as I would be glad to establish, and it is ridiculous to even hint they would not be available for trial. The fact is, they welcome a trial."

The magistrate looked at the defendants. "In view of the seriousness of the charges, I'm setting bail at two hundred and fifty thousand dollars for each defendant."

Greenfield started to protest, but the magistrate stopped him with, "No use, counselor."

After conferring privately with Greenfield on how the bail could be raised, the four were led away by two deputy U.S. marshals. A few minutes later, at 4:30, they were placed aboard a small white bus marked U.S. MARSHAL, and driven to the District of Columbia jail, a dark red-block, T-shaped Victorian building on Independence Avenue. They would have to stay there in small cells until their bail was paid. It would be the second time around for Yuki.

Dana expected her parents to put up the money for all of them. After all, her father was chairman of the family-founded bank in Winston-Salem and had substantial real estate holdings. It should be no problem for him. Kermit had no one to turn to for bail; his widowed mother lived in modest circumstances in a Chicago apartment. Yuki would never accept help from the affluent father-in-law who had blown the whistle to the FBI in the first place, nor would it likely be offered. Duane was hoping he could persuade his publisher into coming through for him.

Dana's father had heard the radio report in the morning and had flown at once to Washington. Shortly after Greenfield left the U.S. District Court following the bail-setting, he arranged for Samuel Haverhill to visit his daughter in jail.

When she saw him entering the small interview room, she said, "Hi, Sam," hugging him tightly. "Hi, Irish." He kissed her forehead. It was her growing-up nickname, which he had given her when she was about six years old and her long, silky russet hair reminded him of their Irish setter.

159

A distinguished-looking man with lively blue eyes and thatched gray hair, he listened intently, trying to understand what she had gotten herself into. She gave him the story swiftly in great bursts, which he knew was her way, and he swallowed it stoically although it went down hard. At first he was outraged by her request that he put up the bail for Kermit and Yuki and Duane too if necessary, but he was finally persuaded—if he didn't bail out the others she would refuse to leave jail until the trial.

Duane's publisher and the editor of *Newswatch* came to see him later that afternoon. They weren't happy with his involvement and were astonished that one of their most reliable investigative reporters was a confessed conspirator in such a hairy enterprise, although they understood and to an extent sympathized with his motives. But they were relieved that he had made it clear that the magazine knew nothing about it. They offered to put up the bail money without his asking, and although he was on suspension he would continue to receive his salary until the case was resolved.

The President went on network television and radio at seven o'clock that evening and in a ten-minute statement condemned the confessed "saboteurs" for their criminal act against a vital government facility, praising the FBI for its swift and effective action in apprehending them. He ignored the professional stature of the four, their professed motives and their proposals. He said he would appoint a panel of computer systems experts to determine how the penetration was possible and to recommend corrective measures. He also announced that he had instructed Lloyd Danziger, Commissioner of the IRS, to cancel all unauthorized audits of individuals criminally ordered by the saboteurs and said that he would look into the alleged Project Pygmalion, which he had neither heard of nor authorized, and would take whatever action was required. His national broadcast on such short notice, itself unusual, gave the impression that a national emergency had been averted through decisivive action by the Administration.

Duane was free on bail by nightfall. His three friends had to remain in the old Victorian jail until eleven the next morning when Mr. Haverhill was able to collect enough collateral to cover their bail bond. They were then bused back to the U.S. District Court, where they retrieved their personal effects and were released.

160

That morning *The New York Times* and the Washington *Post,* and a few other major dailies, printed the full 17,000-word text of Kermit's statement and White Paper along with stories developing the details of the event.

At noon that day, Saturday, March 22, a large group of reporters were waiting when the three walked out of the courthouse building and were joined by Duane waiting for them in the lobby. Duane waved them smilingly away, saying to the dozen newsmen still following them, "We'll have something to say a little later, I promise you," and steered the three around clumps of gaping passersby to a waiting taxi. "There's going to be a lot more of that," he said as he directed the driver to a small quiet restaurant on Pennsylvania Avenue near Eighteenth Street, a couple of blocks the other side of the White House and a short distance from their attorney's office, where they had a two o'clock appointment.

As soon as they sat down in the small dining room, Yuki, looking unaccustomedly correct in a striped tie, white shirt and blue denim suit, said, self-consciously, "Isn't anyone going to ask me how come the Ides of March occurred on March fourteenth this year?"

"Okay, how come?" Dana said.

"Well, it seems I'm not such a whiz after all. I was so locked into higher mathematics I didn't bother to consult the calendar. I wrote the program the last week of February and I just counted the number of days from when I inserted the active command in the real-time clock in the satellite's computer to the number of days to March fifteenth . . . *but* I forgot that this was Leap Year and there was an extra day tagged onto February. So I was one day short and March fifteenth arrived one day early. I should have realized it on February twenty-ninth, but my head was somewhere else. Fortunately, it didn't matter—we were just in business one day early."

"It's the kind of mistake only a mad genius would make," Dana assured him.

When the drinks arrived a few minutes later, Kermit made a toast, waving his glass toward his former protégé. "Here's to Yuki, who made it all possible."

Yuki smiled, but seemed remote. Finally he said, "I wish Harriet were here. I haven't even spoken to her yet. I'm afraid her father has her intimidated. He always did. . . ."

After lunch, they walked to Greenfield's office on K Street at Twentieth, four blocks away. Duane thought he saw a young man following them, but he wasn't sure, and said nothing.

The building was a modern precast concrete and aluminum-strip structure. The marble and chromium lobby with its double bank of elevators was almost empty. They got off on the fourteenth floor and marched through the huge rosewood entrance door of the law offices of Leland, Hammerswak, Kaplowitz and Greenfield. The reception room was large with indirect lighting around the perimeter of the room softly illuminating the off-white stucco-stippled walls. There were two large abstract paintings and several pieces of modern sculpture in lucite, steel and wood on ebony pedestals.

There was no receptionist behind the long walnut table with the white telephone call director, but a secretary had her door open and was expecting them.

Adam Greenfield, jacketless and wearing a sleeveless pullover, came around his desk to greet them, then motioned them to the other side of the room, where they could sit around the coffee table.

"I just want to say you are the most respectable looking group of dissidents I've ever seen. You might even give the business a good name. I'm only half kidding about that—it could be a plus for our side. By the way, my name is Adam, not Mr. Greenfield, and I hope you'll extend me the same privilege. There are several things we've got to get done this afternoon. We've got to get to know each other. I need to know what makes you people tick." His eyes flicked around the semicircle. "I want you to get your view of what you did, why you picked IRS and what your motivations were—individually, not collectively. I want to know what you expect to accomplish through your trial and I'll probably louse up some illusions for you. I'm also going to set a few ground rules. The first one is plain talk. I'm going to be candid with you because I want you to go into this thing with your eyes wide open. It's not going to be any picnic, I assure you, and your idealism and purity of heart are *not* going to protect you from some rough times. I know you asked me to represent you because I specialize in civil rights cases and I've a pretty good track record. But my opinion of what you did won't help you in the slightest. You will be charged by the government with a long list of crimes and your civil liberties rationale—whatever it is—may have little bearing. One more thing, I don't mind questions. I want to make certain you have everything clear in your heads. But what I won't tolerate is not knowing

162

everything. I don't want to be kept in the dark about *anything*—I don't like surprises. Now, I want each of you to give me a biography of yourself from the day you were born . . . your parents, what they do or did, your education, your professional record, any honors, books or papers, special achievements, what organizations—political, social, whatever—you ever belonged to, your arrest record, if any . . . even a speeding ticket . . . any military service, your medical and psychiatric history, people you know or are related to in government, in any kind of public life, anyone who might be questionable or unusual. And *anything* else you think I should know. If you're not sure, tell me anyway. We're going to know each other a lot better before we're through."

For the next hour Dana, Yuki, Kermit and Duane—in the clockwise order they were seated—gave the details of their personal backgrounds, Greenfield repeatedly interrupting with probing questions, including many which challenged the sincerity of their political and social views. He sounded like a cross-examining attorney, and Kermit said he assumed Adam was testing their ability to stand up to such questioning. The attorney smiled. "This is just child's play."

Greenfield was particularly interested in Dana's family background, although he didn't say why. He also seemed fascinated by Yuki's ancestry and the fact that his grandfather had participated in the attack on Pearl Harbor. When the attorney heard Kermit say that he had once been a member of Students for a Democratic Society briefly back in the late sixties when he was a sophomore at Northwestern University, he questioned him closely about why he had joined SDS, how long he had belonged, why he quit.

"It's very important that I know all these things. You four, by your criminal act as a political protest, have, so the government will claim, set yourselves up as some sort of holier-than-thous. Which means you've got to be purer than the driven snow. You've admitted what you did . . . all we have to go on—at this point at least—is the justification for what you did. So you'd better be four little virgins four."

He then conducted another round robin asking each one what he expected to accomplish at the trial, and they each said pretty much the same thing: to make the public realize through the media the deep trouble the country was in from the long misuse of computer systems by government and industry and the imminent dangers of computer control if the Morstan bill should become law.

"Okay, let's talk about that," Greenfield said. "It's going to be very tough to get the judge to allow you to say why you did what you did. The prosecutor is going to keep objecting on the grounds that alleged government illegal behavior is irrelevant, and chances are the judge will agree with him. It will really depend on the judge we draw. And even with proof of computer illegalities by the government, he can still rule it irrelevant. And if he does, your whole rationale goes down the tube and all we're left with is how to keep you from wasting your lives in federal jails."

Kermit looked sour. "Damn it, Adam, you make it sound like it's over before it's started. We never expected a picnic, but there's got to be a way to—"

"I didn't say there isn't. I just want you all to know that it will be very tough, a real long shot, and I want you to be prepared for the worst. And speaking of the worst, I think you should know what the prosecution will probably try to do to you. Remember, they'll be under tremendous pressure from the Administration, from Congress, from the whole federal hierarchy to give you a good long ride. You made a lot of powerful enemies and most of your sympathizers are unorganized or have little leverage. So the government prosecutor is on the spot to produce, and besides this case will be a great showcase for him. He'll undoubtedly charge you with a whole laundry list of crimes beginning with seditious conspiracy, which carries a maximum of twenty years, and go on from there. A trial like this will cost the government several millions and you can bet that the prosecutor won't want losing it on his record. The whole world will be watching this one."

"That sounds pretty discouraging," Yuki said.

"It's supposed to. What do you expect? Your ass is up for grabs. You broke the law—a whole series of laws. And you picked the government of the United States—one of its most vital agencies—as your victim. You're a bunch of subversives, maybe revolutionaries, in the eyes of the government, and I would suspect in the eyes of most of the rest of the country too. This is an election year and you guys aren't exactly a popular issue. You and what you did may be the one thing the candidates can agree on."

"Okay, that's the good news," Duane said wryly. "What's the bad news?"

Adam didn't smile. "This is going to be a rough ordeal, and there's

164

no assurance of winning. I want to make sure that you're all tough enough to handle it. If not, let me know now. There's no shame or embarrassment at issue here. I just want to make sure that no one bails out later. If any of you want to discuss this with me privately, just give me a ring. I've got to know whether you'll stand together on this right through to the end." They all confirmed that they would.

"All right, now for the good news. From here on out, I'm the boss. I mean that literally. You can give me your opinions and you can curse me out if you disagree, but I call all the shots. That's the way it's got to be. Anyone who can't accept that, bail out now and get yourself another attorney. I'm very serious about this."

He got up from his chair, walked around in back of it and leaned over, resting his hands on its sides and looking at them thoughtfully for a moment. "Now that I've given you all those caveats and ultimatums, I'd also like you to know that I don't intend to lose this case. . . ."

It was nearly five o'clock when Adam finally walked the four of them down the wide corridor of the now totally empty offices. When they got to the reception room, Duane excused himself and said he was going to the john down the hall. Adam said, "I'll join you."

As they stood in adjacent urinals, Adam said, "I wanted to talk to you. I think Yuki is the weak link. That was one of the things I was probing for. With his personal problems with his wife and father-in-law, I wonder if he can stick it out. I suggest you and Kermit stay with him. Keep his back stiff."

Chapter Twenty

Newspaper headlines across the country: PRESIDENT DENOUNCES IRS SABOTAGE . . . CORPORATE LEADERS BRAND SABOTEURS REVOLUTION-ARIES . . . FEDERAL OFFICIALS DEMAND SWIFT JUSTICE . . . Some dubbed the conspirators the "Martinsburg Four."

Public reaction was a mixture of condemnation of the perpetrators and revulsion against the government for the Project Pygmalion dossiers, along with a strong undercurrent of vicarious pleasure from the embarrassment to high government figures, industry fat cats, the Mafia and union officials who were exposed as tax deadbeats. Some approved the rationale for the act but had reservations about the act itself. Most people, regardless of political stripe, were secretly amused or laughing outright at the fact that it was IRS, the taxpayer's hated nemesis, that was the subject of the attack. And there were rumblings that many would protest by not filing their tax returns.

In a Monday morning news conference Senator Morstan denounced the act as "treasonable" and the saboteurs as "academic revolutionaries of the type corrupting our American campuses." He went further a few days later on the floor of the Senate when he accused them of being radical militants out to subvert the whole government. He urged they be brought to quick justice and maximum penalties be imposed as an example to others. He cited the act as clear proof of the need to secure the nation's computer systems through the prompt passage of his bill.

Many members of Congress who had been targets of the penetration, either as now exposed tax delinquents or subjects of audits, were so relieved that it wasn't the Administration or the IRS out to get them that they felt free to jump on the bandwagon of condemnation. Only a handful of congressmen and federal officials stood up and disagreed with their colleagues.

The overseas press was, of course, vastly amused by the whole episode. "Uncle Sam's cash register is made to play a bogus tune by campus computerniks," one London daily put it. A Paris newspaper's headline read: "L'Affaire les Martinsburg Quatre Est une Tempête dans un Terminal."

The media in general was fascinated by the imagination and boldness of the Martinsburg Four, who represented a new type of American hero or villain, depending on your viewpoint. They were all highly respected professionals working within the system—attractive young people with impressive credentials. What, then, made them go off the deep end suddenly and become electronic guerrillas in one breathtaking act which shocked, intrigued and nearly polarized the nation? There was much probing into the backgrounds and personalities of the four. Before the week following the arrests was out, feature stories and separate photographs of the four hit the newsstands. Most found Dana and Yuki particularly interesting, for obvious reasons—she was beautiful, accomplished, intelligent, from a wealthy old-American family; he was oriental, a young genius, married to a Jewish girl whose own father had informed on them to the FBI!

On Monday, March 31, both *Time* and *Newswatch* came out with cover stories dramatically detailing the series of events beginning with the penetration on that fateful Friday when IRS's computers started spinning out their bogus commands. *Time*'s cover showed four rogues' gallery type photographs in rococo frames with large, bold type across the top reading THE IRS INVADERS. The *Newswatch* cover read THE GREAT COMPUTER RIP-OFF, with a line drawing of computer discs in the background.

Several psychiatrists always available for prime-time expertising gave their solemn opinions on what kind of people the conspirators were to commit this sort of crime. Fairly typical was the pronouncement from Dr. Simeon Golding, author of *Communicating with Your Subconscious* and analyst to the stars: "These individuals are undoubtedly victims of

167

a Robin Hood syndrome. They see themselves as a band of crusaders attacking what they think to be evil and then announcing their own purity of purpose to the world. This is not an uncommon form of group reinforcement where each one compounds an initial sense of outrage and raises it to the power of overt antisocial behavior. . . ."

At Duane's invitation, Kermit immediately moved into his friend's post–World War I, Federal-style apartment house on Wyoming Avenue off Connecticut in the old northwest section near the border of the District. They decided it would look best if Kermit and Dana lived separately at this point, so Dana rented and moved into a furnished sublet apartment in the Berkshire, a high-rise building on Massachusetts Avenue, a prestige area just north of Embassy Row. Yuki took a room at the Ramada Inn on Thomas Circle downtown, hoping that Harriet would join him.

And Harriet did come, a couple of days later. At first she was concerned only about Yuki. She kissed him lightly on the lips as she sat down next to him on the sofa. "Was it awful? Getting arrested and spending two nights in jail, I mean."

"It wasn't bad." He looked around the room. "This isn't the fanciest place in Washington. I hope you don't mind staying here."

"It's fine for now. We can make better arrangements later. Everything is so indefinite. We don't know what's going to happen to you. I feel at such loose ends. I hate that feeling."

Yuki tried to put his arms around her but she wasn't ready to be consoled. "Yuki, I'm not sure of anything anymore."

"Nothing has happened between us, we still love each other."

"Love isn't enough for a marriage. There has to be trust and sharing—"

"So?"

"You didn't trust me, didn't share this thing with me. You just froze me out."

"Are we back to that? I told you why I had to keep you out."

"I know what you told me. But I'm your wife. I'm not a child, not your girl friend. When you decided to get into this thing and put yourself on the line—your career, everything—you put *me* there too. You jeopardized our marriage. All you really thought about was your precious social convictions . . . your private world of protecting satellites . . . well, I have some social convictions too. I'm not just your, ha ha, JAP . . .

168

I might have gone along . . . but you never gave me the chance—"

"Harriet, please, you don't understand, I didn't want to *involve* you in a criminal conspiracy. I tried to protect you, so kill me . . ."

"That's not protection, Dana. That's treating me like an idiot child. I've been treated that way all my life. From my father to you. I want to be treated like an adult, for Christ's sake, an adult able to make my own choices—and mistakes—if necessary."

"But a criminal offense . . . you could have been called an accessory to the crime. I love you too much to let that happen—"

"You mean you couldn't trust me with something so earthshaking as a threat to our American democracy, a threat according to you and your buddies, that is. And you don't seem to realize that they *used* you—made you the triggerman. Without you, they couldn't have done it. And now Kermit gets all the credit—"

"You don't know what you're talking about, no one used me. I couldn't have done it alone. Kermit's the one who's taking all the heat. Anyhow, the fact is that you're not a party to it, and that's the important thing."

She looked at him. "Did it ever occur to you that you might be wrong about that? My father spoke to Max Ludwig, the criminal lawyer, and he said I could still be involved. He said that since I knew you were using your computer terminal in the house, and since I share the house with you, I could still be called in by the Justice Department as an accessory."

"But you knew nothing about what I was doing."

"That's right, but as your wife, and because the house is in my name, they would assume that I should know about it. And they're right, I should."

Yuki shook his head. "I think Ludwig is wrong, but I'll check it out with Adam Greenfield. . . ."

He pulled her close again. "Now, please, let me show you how glad I am that you're here." He put his hand on her breast. She didn't want to resist, and finally she didn't. . . .

Their closeness didn't last. After four days of phone calls from her father, and of reporters waiting for her whenever she went out, Harriet decided to go home. She hated the pressure and felt uncomfortable with nothing to do. Yuki was either working on his technical book or meeting with the others on legal matters. She decided it would be best if she stayed at home and visited him whenever she could.

As soon as she left, a despondent Yuki accepted the invitation to move into Duane's apartment with Kermit, and Duane moved into Marcia Milliken's apartment to make room for Yuki. That was his excuse, and he welcomed it.

Requests for interviews had begun immediately, and Duane tried to select the largest and most influential newspaper and broadcast media. Dana and Kermit kept their statements keyed to the issues of civil rights violations, to subversion potential against the government and computer-based crime. Their strongest fire was directed at the Morstan bill. Mindful of Greenfield's warning, they avoided any discussion of the charges against them or what they had uncovered during their IRS penetration.

The Assistant U.S. Attorney assigned to the case became alarmed at the defendants' media thrust and petitioned the U.S. District Court judge for a gag order to stop them from further pretrial publicity on the grounds that it was influencing public opinion and the subsequent jury. Greenfield argued that they had the constitutional right to present their views publicly under the freedom of speech provision of the First Amendment and hadn't said anything prejudicial to the case. The judge denied the prosecution's motion.

On another front there were more ominous noises. A nationwide advertising campaign, consisting of a series of full-page ads in several hundred daily newspapers with circulations of 100,000 and over, broke throughout the country the first week of April in support of Bill S. 17. Boldface headlines streamed across the page:

YOU CAN VOTE FOR A STRONGER AMERICA
Support the Morstan-Windmiller Bill
And Solidify the Nation

The subheads which separated blocks of copy read: PROTECTS THE NATION'S COMPUTERS; CONTROLS CRIME; STRENGTHENS NATIONAL SECURITY; AIDS PLANNING FOR A SOUNDER ECONOMY. Across the bottom of the advertisement signed by the "Committee to Strengthen America" were three coupon-size ballots which readers were urged to sign and send in to their two senators and their representative in Congress, demanding that they vote for the Morstan-Windmiller bill.

Meanwhile, Morstan was addressing large political groups as well as prestigious business and civic organizations in key areas of the country

170

at the rate of one a day. The news media were giving his speeches and his press conferences in each city heavier coverage than usual because of his vitriolic attacks on the Martinsburg Four.

On April 8, three weeks after the news of the satellite-launched raid against the IRS and two weeks after the culprits were apprehended, the first indication arrived of what the country thought about their act. The results of a Harris Poll revealed that 29 percent of the people considered it a criminal act as part of a national conspiracy against the government; 34 percent said it was a criminal act against the government but not part of a national conspiracy; 23 percent called it an act of protest with which they agreed; and 8 percent regarded it as an act of protest with which they did not agree; 6 percent had no opinion. But by adding up those who were opposed to the action, whether as a criminal act or as a protest, it was clear that the large majority of the country, 71 percent, was against the position of the Martinsburg Four.

Dana and Yuki were surprised and disappointed by the survey results, but Kermit and Duane felt that it was encouraging to know that nearly a quarter of the American public was on their side at this early stage and that 31 percent recognized what they had done as a political protest rather than as a criminal act. Greenfield said the only poll that mattered was the one the foreman of the jury would take after the judge charged the jury.

Chapter Twenty-One

Kermit was excited and a bit apprehensive as the taxi taking them to WTOP-TV, CBS's network affiliate in northwest Washington, hurried through the light after-hours traffic. He was to be interviewed on "National Newsmakers," one of the top three prime-time network interview shows in the country and certainly the most prestigious he had been on. Thirty million Americans would be watching.

Duane and Dana were with him this time. Duane had wangled Kermit's appearance on this program, which normally featured prominent public figures in the news, and now came along to thank the executive producer. Dana decided to go too and watch from the studio.

Kermit knew that what he said during the interview would be headlined. It was a marvelous forum and a challenging test. He had to handle it just right. When the three of them entered the modern office building at Fortieth and Brandywine streets, the lobby was bustling with people. They walked into the elevator with a half-dozen others. As it stopped at a lower floor, Kermit felt a sharp sting in his left forearm like a prick of a needle. People on either side of him marched out and the door slid closed. He abstractly touched his arm and felt nothing. The slight, momentary pain was gone. Dana looked at him inquiringly, but he dismissed it with a smile. Must have been a stray pin stuck to someone's clothing. . . . The elevator stopped at their floor and Kermit walked to a long white formica desk in a large reception area while Dana and Duane went to the studio lounge to watch the program.

Minutes later, as makeup was being applied to him in an adjacent room, Kermit felt himself becoming feverish. The strain of his upcoming performance was undoubtedly beginning to show. With all the exposure he already had on TV, this was the program that meant the most to him. He had to make sure he didn't come across like a radical college professor, which he wasn't and which was what too many people apparently suspected.

It was 8:56 P.M. when he was ushered into the large, brilliantly illuminated studio and introduced to Roger Morrisey, a barrel-chested man with the face of an urbane Saint Bernard. The noted television interviewer and news commentator greeted him warmly and reassuringly, joking about an upcoming sanitary napkin commercial. Kermit managed a brief smile.

The set was elegantly simple. Two honey-colored leather club chairs, separated by a low round lucite pedestal table, faced each other against a sharply defined photomural of downtown Washington showing both the White House and the Capitol Building on either end of Pennsylvania Avenue. A technician attached a tiny microphone to Kermit's tie. The two men, seated, faced three television cameras set at different angles and distances, and the long horizontal window of the control room in the background with a clutch of heads peering out. A casually authoritative voice cut through the fragmented sounds of cameramen adjusting their equipment and making small talk.

"Thirty seconds."

The room fell silent, action froze. The countdown, digiting in his head, seemed interminable to Kermit. His head was throbbing but his mind seemed clear.

"Ten seconds."

Roger Morrisey cleared his throat and looked up with his familiar tight-lipped smile. A red light lit up on the farthest camera focused on him and the photomural behind him.

"Good evening. This is 'National Newsmakers' and I'm Roger Morrisey. Our guest tonight is Dr. Kermit Nordstrom. As everyone is doubtlessly aware, Dr. Nordstrom is one of four individuals who invaded the computer network of the Internal Revenue Service—a system so sophisticated and safeguarded it was considered to be virtually impenetrable. And yet Dr. Nordstrom and his associates did in fact accomplish this remarkable feat. Whether it was an act of criminal sabotage or of social protest, as Dr. Nordstrom and his associates claim, is for the courts to decide."

Morrisey turned and faced Nordstrom. The red light went on in the closeup center camera.

"Dr. Nordstrom, you are a man of considerable academic and professional credentials. What you and your associates did was an unprecedented, an extreme act. I will not, of course, comment on its legality. But was there not some other . . . less extreme . . . way of registering your protest?"

"We needed a dramatic event to focus attention on this problem . . . a crisis, really, a crisis which we feel threatens the civil liberties of all of us. We tried conventional methods—meeting with congressional committees, speaking before civic groups, talking to the media. It didn't work. No one seemed to care enough." Kermit wrinkled his forehead and compressed his lips. "We felt that the country was running out of time and the best way was to, admittedly, shock the public into looking at what was really happening to them. Seeing how their privacy is being secretly taken away from them and how the democratic process itself is in real danger."

"But weren't you really committing a criminal act to protest one?"

Kermit was feeling feverish again. "In a sense, yes. But ours was a single demonstration of . . . whatever you want to call it . . . in the hope of reversing the loss of privacy and other constitutional liberties for over two hundred million Americans. We wanted to expose a lot of other computer-based evils by the government, by industry and by computer-wise criminals and terrorists. . . . It's a whole chamber of horrors . . . and all of us are the victims. . . ."

Morrisey's lips were moving and Kermit heard his voice but they seemed unsynchronized, as in a poorly dubbed foreign film. God, he was feeling strange. He squinted his eyes, trying to refocus.

"I'm sorry, Mr. Morrisey. Would you mind repeating the question."

Morrisey wasn't sure what to make of it. "Certainly. Many management people in and out of government feel strongly that an interlocking network of computer systems, both public and private, is essential to sound economic planning and growth. Why do you oppose that view?"

174

Kermit felt his head spiraling upward, upward through the violet reaches of space. It was a new and serene reality and he wanted to stay there. But he knew he couldn't. He clamped the lid back on hard.

"There is nothing wrong with the view per se," he heard himself say in a calm and reasoned voice, "but such a system without broad legal limits and an effective enforcement mechanism would accelerate the invasions of our privacy which already exist and make it far simpler for overzealous bureaucrats to compromise further our civil rights and for totalitarian politicians to . . ." He paused and took a deep breath. ". . . to seize control of the government," he blurted out quickly. He wanted to spell out the details of this rationale so they would be clear to everyone. It was a key question. But he knew he couldn't handle it. He felt himself slipping away again.

"I see." The creases around Morrisey's mouth deepened as he contemplated his next question. "That brings us to the next point. There's been a lot of speculation around Washington that your . . . *act* vis-à-vis the IRS was actually aimed against the Morstan-Windmiller Bill. That your real purpose was to build a case—and presumably to marshal public opinion—against its passage. Is there any truth to that?"

Kermit rubbed his forehead. He had to get through this somehow. "The fact is, Mr. Morrisey, that I've been crusading against the dangers of uncontrolled computerism for over two years—long before Senator—" Suddenly the studio became microscopic and he was looking down on the toys in the box. The next instant the scene exploded. The bank of overhead lights was crashing down on him. The room was expanding and contracting like a giant, overworked lung. His own chest was heaving with the deepness of his breathing and he felt tremendous strength vibrating in his limbs. He half rose from his seat and then flopped back heavily, grinning broadly.

Morrisey's face struggled between surprise and anger.

"Well, I'll tell you, Roger"—Kermit's voice was insinuatingly intimate—"that wouldn't be such a bad idea, now would it?" He waved a loose finger in Morrisey's shocked face. His eyes rolled around the room as though studying a hostile place, then fixed on Morrisey. "Morstan's bill is an abortion. It's shit. That's what S. 17 means . . . shit seventeen times over. . . ." His upper body was weaving from side to side.

Morrisey seemed immobilized.

". . . Who are those guys out there pushing those things around?"

175

Kermit was gesturing at the studio floor men. He turned back to his stunned interviewer. "The trouble with you people is you think you own the truth . . . well, that's shit and we've got to . . ."

Morrisey's face was a mask of disbelief. "I regret, ladies and gentlemen . . ." But the red light on the equipment was already shut off.

In the control room the director was screaming into the open mike. "Get Nordstrom out of there! *Geezus* . . . get the bum out!"

Kermit was standing now, wagging his head passionately, his eyes wide and glazed. Morrisey had retreated against the backdrop, eyeing him warily.

A cameraman and a powerfully built audio technician rushed forward and grabbed Kermit by the arms. He looked indignant and hurt. He shook one arm free and swung his fist catching one of the men flush on the ear. The fellow went down hard and stayed there. Kermit's other arm was twisted upward like a lever behind his back. He swung his free arm backward and caught the audio man behind the neck, then suddenly bent all the way forward catapulting his adversary over his head where he landed on his back with his legs raised against a TV camera.

For a moment the scene was a farcical tableau of disarray—a frozen frame in a silent film. No one moved in the studio or control room. The only thing playing was a visual on the TV monitor: DUE TO TECHNICAL DIFFICULTIES, THERE WILL BE A BRIEF DELAY. PLEASE STAY TUNED.

Kermit, looking and feeling paranoid, walked out of the studio and into the arms of two muscular security guards charging toward him.

Duane and Dana couldn't believe what they were seeing on the screen.

"Something's happened to him!" Dana called out.

Duane was on his feet. "It certainly has. He's coming apart. We better get him."

"It looks like a nervous breakdown," a calm voice across the room suggested. The man had been sitting there watching the program, but they hadn't really noticed him.

They didn't bother to answer, but ran down the hall in the direction of the studios. Before they could find the right one, two uniformed guards rushed past them and turned left out of sight. They followed, running, and in a moment they saw Kermit standing motionless and disheveled as the guards grabbed him, whipping his arms behind him and leading him away.

176

Duane touched one of them on the shoulder and said, "Wait a minute. He's not well. We'll take him to a doctor." The guards kept pushing Kermit ahead of them without saying a word.

Dana got in front of them, walking backward to keep ahead as she looked into Kermit's face. "What's happened?" she begged. He looked at her vacantly, eyes glazed. Her eyes filled with tears as she and Duane followed the unresponsive guards down two long corridors to the security office.

Two station executives and the chief of security were there waiting. The guards sat Kermit down roughly on a wooden chair and stood over him.

Duane recognized one of the executives, the station manager. "You know who I am, Mr. Tucker. This is Miss Haverhill. We'll take care of Dr. Nordstrom. He needs medical attention. We'll see that he gets it."

The security chief spoke up. "We can't release this man. This is a police matter. He assaulted two of our technicians. I've got to find out whether they want to press charges."

Tucker nodded. "You heard what the man said. It's his responsibility. Your friend here played hell with our programming, aside from the job he did on our personnel. We're getting calls from all over the country complaining about his obscenities. The network stations are furious." He turned to the security chief. "McVey, call the police."

"That's ridiculous!" Dana snapped. "Can't you see he's ill? He needs medical attention."

"The young lady is right," said a voice behind her. The man had just entered the room. It was the same man who had been sitting in the lounge with them. "I'm Dr. Corliss." He handed a card to the security chief. "I was in the reception room waiting for a friend to get off the air, and I saw what happened. This man is experiencing a major nervous breakdown. If he doesn't get medical attention quickly, the consequences could be serious. A go-round with the police is the last thing he needs. I practice at Washington General Hospital. I'll be glad to get him over there."

McVey nodded. "That's all right with me if it is with Mr. Tucker. We can see about those charges later."

"Oh, no you don't!" Dana said, walking over to where Kermit was sitting blankly, his cheek twitching. "I'm his fiancée and he's coming

177

with us. We'll take him to our own doctor." She put her arm around Kermit's shoulder.

"This man needs to be in a hospital and immediately," Corliss insisted. "Otherwise he could get violent again. That's the pattern in these cases. I'll have an ambulance here in two minutes." He started toward the telephone.

"Look, Tucker, I'm taking Nordstrom with us," Duane said. "We'll get him to our own hospital and you know where you can find us if there are any charges. I want you to release him to me *now*. Otherwise, call your boss Ellsworth Tully on the phone and tell him I want to speak to him. Shall I give you his home number?"

Tucker eyed him briefly. "All right, Crozier. He's *your* responsibility. Just get him the hell out of here."

The guards released their hold on Kermit. Duane and Dana helped him to his feet, put one of his arms over the shoulder of each of them and walked him out of the office, to the elevator and out into the street. Dana leaned Kermit against the building while Duane got a cab.

As they pulled away from the curb, they saw Dr. Corliss emerge from the building and stand there looking at them. On the way to a private hospital, Dana kept repeating, "This is no nervous breakdown, they did something to him . . . this is no nervous breakdown. . . ."

Chapter Twenty-Two

Come in, senator, delighted to see you." Mitchell Storey's deep voice resounded in the spacious seventh floor office of the J. Edgar Hoover building as he extended a strong hand to his visitor and led him to a brown leather drum chair. The square-rigged FBI director then circled his huge desk, settled into his high-backed swivel chair, and touched a button on his intercom. "I'm not in for any calls . . . and that includes the Oval Office." He was sure that would impress the senator. He hunched his shoulders and leaned forward, his hands on his thighs. "Well, Gunther, what do you think?"

Morstan got up and leaned over the desk, thrusting out his hand and shaking Storey's vigorously while clasping it with his other hand. "I congratulate you, Mitch. It was a masterful job. I don't know what you did or how you did it . . . I still can't believe it." He sat down, his lean, tan face radiating the pleasure and admiration he felt.

Storey smiled. "This isn't the Senate, you know. We're short on bullshit and long on action. You should know that. Especially on a high priority item like this one. I think S. 17 should sail right through now. Seeing that it does is *your* baby."

"You certainly turned him inside out—and before the whole damn country. Did you see what the papers are saying? Nordstrom's been discredited overnight. No one will touch him now. I couldn't believe the way he came apart on the tube. It was better than anything we could have dreamed up for him—"

"Except it was *exactly* what we dreamed up for him. You wanted him stopped and so did we. We need S. 17. We've got to be able to monitor every city and state police computer system in the country. Once we do that, then I'll show you what effective law enforcement is all about."

"I'm with you on that, Mitch. But I'm curious as hell how you got Nordstrom to go to pieces on that program."

"You sure you want to know? You might be better off not knowing."

"Trust me."

"Oh, I trust you." He was thinking of the things he had filed away on Morstan. He pressed a button on his intercom. "Roy, come into my office."

The senator raised a hand. "I'd rather not have anyone else in on this, Mitch."

"You don't have a thing to worry about. This was strictly a defensive operation for the Bureau as far as Roy is concerned."

He was lighting a discolored meerschaum as Roy Ebersole entered the office. "You know Roy, senator," he muttered through his pipestem.

Morstan nodded at Storey's deputy assistant, a bony, ascetic-looking man who had been with the FBI for twenty years. Storey had promoted him over the heads of several others three years earlier when he took over as director.

Roy, seated, looked attentively at his boss, waiting for him to speak. Storey took a few unhurried puffs, removed the pipe from his mouth.

"Roy, I want you to tell Senator Morstan how we helped put the college professor . . . in perspective."

Ebersole hesitated.

"It's all right, Roy. The senator is a friend."

Ebersole leaned forward and spoke in a slightly slurred Louisianian accent. "Last week—Thursday, to be exact—Mr. Storey instructed me to devise a plan to discredit Dr. Nordstrom in such a way that the propaganda he was spreading through the media would be aborted." He was beginning to enjoy his role, and it showed in his voice. "Mr. Storey and I decided that the best way would be to wait until he was on a live network TV broadcast—fortunately 'National Newsmakers' was coming up—and then make sure that he behaved in an irrational way that would shock the audience. Aberrant behavior, I believe the psychologists call it. I brought in a man from our forensic lab—he's an expert on chemicals and drugs. Well sir, he came up with a drug called Serpentyl. It's a compound made of the venom of the king cobra, which in itself is an extremely deadly substance but it's cut by another substance so that it's a slow-acting hallucinogen of short duration. It takes about twenty minutes before it really hits. In fact, I'm told they use it for therapy in some mental hospitals for serious psychotic disorders. All that made Serpentyl ideal for our purpose. If it was ever detected in Nordstrom, that would brand him a psycho. Or if he was using it on himself for a trip, that would make him look just as bad. But I understand the stuff breaks down in the bloodstream in about two hours and can't be detected. Of course, we had no intention of letting anyone test his blood during that time. The problem was to inject the drug into him without his knowing it, and at precisely the right time. That was tricky because we had only a thirty minute timespan on the show. We had three agents . . . two of them women . . . working together. Each one of them was equipped to do it. A quick jab in the arm and that was it. They could have given it to him as he got out of the taxi, in the elevator, the upstairs corridor or in the makeup room. It was a matter of timing and opportunity. It was a little tricky because two of his people unexpectedly showed up at the studio with him. But the real problem was to make sure he didn't come apart too soon or they'd keep him off the air—or too late when the show was over. It worked out just about right. And the nice thing is there's no way of tracing this back to the Bureau. I'd say we're home free."

"You did a fine job, Roy. I want to shake your hand." Morstan was on his feet and leaning over a pleasantly startled Roy before he could get out of his chair. "You did a fine job for the country, which is my only interest. *Our* only interest." It was obvious that he meant it.

"Thank you, sir."

"All good, Roy," Storey said, dismissing him. "I'll be talking to you later."

As Ebersole closed the heavy paneled door behind him, Storey said, "He's a great guy. Sometimes he scares me. Lives and breathes his job. No wife or girl friend. He isn't even interested in sports. Just watches TV and goes to prosties when there's a full moon. I tell him what I want and he's off and running. A jewel, that boy."

Morstan nodded solemnly. "We need people like that. Dedicated. People who do what they're told without question. These young smart-asses today think they have a right to know everything before they'll do it. They just don't give a tinker's damn for authority, or the country either." He shook his head. "But let's get back to Nordstrom. . . . I think we've got him stopped dead. The media won't come near him and the public has him pegged as a nut or an acid head. Still, I'd feel better if I could be positive that there was no way anyone could suspect his blowup of being caused by an outside source."

"You can forget about that, Gunther. There's not a damn thing that can be traced to this department or to anyone else for that matter. We had one of our people waiting to take Nordstrom to a hospital where a lab technician was primed to delay the blood and urine tests until the drug broke down. That bitch and Crozier hustled their pal away, but it doesn't matter. As Roy said, Serpentyl is used by psychiatrists for certain mental patients. He could have gotten it that way or taken a trip on his own. Either way, it makes him out a kook. His little performance on national TV is going to haunt him right through the courtroom and into the pen—along with his two pals and that piece of ass he's screwing. No jury will believe him now . . . no, my friend, that boy is *gone*. I guarantee it."

Morstan was pleased. "That's good enough for me, Mitch. I want you to know that once S. 17 gets through both houses—and I believe that the President has got to sign it—I'll see that your end gets hooked up fast. I intend to be behind the Oval Office desk next January and I'll be calling the shots. I won't forget what I owe you, what the *country* owes you. . . ."

"Don't give it another thought, Gunther. . . . I'll see that you don't."

Chapter Twenty-Three

The staff conference room of Valley Park Medical Center in Silver Springs was jammed with forty reporters seated on folding chairs and a dozen more standing in the rear and around the sides. Duane sat in the center of a long table facing the news people, with Kermit on his right and Dana and Yuki to his left.

Duane looked at his watch. It was 10:15. He stood up, looking very serious in a business suit with a tie and his thick hair neatly combed. "We invited you here today to present you with the *facts* of what happened last Thursday night, April tenth, on the 'National Newsmakers' show. There have been many statements by public officials and others concerning Dr. Kermit Nordstrom's behavior on that program. Most of these allegations are wild and slanderous and they are based on nothing more than surmises and in some cases, I suspect, on some wishful thinking. We're here this morning to give you all the available facts about what actually happened four days ago.

"We have three highly reputable medical doctors"—he nodded in their direction—"who will report their findings. I'll first introduce Dr. Donald Hollander, who is chief of staff of this hospital." Duane took his seat as Dr. Hollander stood up. He was a pleasant-looking man in his mid-forties.

"My associates and I take no position in this matter other than as medical doctors who participated in Dr. Nordstrom's treatment at this hospital. Dr. Nordstrom was brought here last Thursday evening in a catatonic state. Dr. Fingerhut, the head of our psychiatric wing, and I examined him and determined that it was not a nervous disorder. We had a blood chemistry workup and a urine analysis done in our laboratory and we found traces of a rare drug we believe is Serpentyl. We can't be positive because this drug quickly breaks down in the bloodstream, and in its broken-down state resembles one or two other exotic drugs, which are likewise hallucinogens."

Low conversation spread around the room. "Yes, Serpentyl is a powerful hallucinogen and that jibed with our further examination of the patient. He was tractable when he was first brought in and sometime later he had another hallucinogenic episode in which he was feverish, disoriented and rather abusive. These symptoms disappeared completely within twelve hours, which is characteristic of this particular drug, and Dr. Nordstrom has been entirely normal ever since. We have copies of the lab report and of our findings. I'm now going to ask Dr. Fingerhut to report his findings concerning this patient."

The older, dignified man to his right got up as Hollander resumed his seat. He put on a pair of metal-rimmed eyeglasses he'd been polishing and cleared his throat. "As Dr. Hollander has told you, we both examined this man when he arrived. I observed him closely those first twelve hours and, once the symptoms disappeared, I conducted a comprehensive psychiatric examination over the next three days—until yesterday afternoon, to be exact. My conclusion is that Dr. Nordstrom is in an excellent state of mental health and his abnormal behavior on that television show—I studied a videotape of it—and the episode which occurred afterward were the result of the foreign substance we found in his blood chemistry. I called in a consulting psychiatrist, Dr. Maxwell Ames, for a second opinion. He examined Dr. Nordstrom and confirmed my findings that the patient's brief hallucinogenic experiences were the result of the drug found in the lab tests. He also concurred as to the general state of his health. Dr. Ames is here on my right."

Duane was quickly on his feet. "I'm sure you have a lot of questions."

Several hands shot up and Duane pointed to one.

"I'd like to ask all three of the doctors whether they were paid to present these findings to us?"

Hollander got up. "Certainly we're being paid for our professional services. Your question seems odd."

"I don't mean for treatment and consultation," the reporter persisted. "I mean for standing here and giving us your opinions."

"Yes, we plan to bill the patient for the time we spend presenting our findings."

"At your regular rates or—"

"Frankly, I don't like your implication."

The reporter was not about to be denied. "I think the press has a right to know whether you're being given a financial incentive to give these opinions."

"You're asking whether we've been bribed to give false information, and you should be ashamed to suggest it." He sat down.

Duane stepped in. "I think the question is improper but in view of the serious issue it raises"—he turned to Dr. Hollander—"I hope you will be willing to answer it."

Hollander rose, red faced. "The answer is that we would never accept a financial incentive to report our professional findings, nor was one offered." He sat down quickly.

"Thank you, Dr. Hollander. Next question, please."

"What is Serpentyl used for and what symptoms does it produce?"

"I'll answer that," Dr. Fingerhut said, remaining seated. "It has been used experimentally in chemotherapy on psychotic patients, but the results are not conclusive. It produces hallucinosis and aberrant behavior of short duration depending on the dosage."

"I'd like to ask a follow-up question of Dr. Fingerhut," another voice said. "What about the one or two other drugs which Serpentyl resembles, since you're not sure which one it was?"

"They're of the same spectrum and act in a similar fashion."

"How was the drug administered to Dr. Nordstrom and couldn't he have given it to himself?" was the next question.

"Apparently through his arm," Dr. Fingerhut replied. "Dr. Nordstrom indicated that he felt a pinprick in his left arm while riding in a crowded elevator on his way up to the television studio." A murmur swept around the room. "We found a tiny puncture and discoloration on the fleshy part of his upper left arm. I suppose he could have injected it himself, but I don't know any way he could have obtained the drug. It's strictly controlled and we would have trouble getting it ourselves. And I don't know why anyone would want to do it to himself—it's an extremely unpleasant experience."

"Couldn't the drug have been LSD or mescaline or speed or some other available hallucinogen?" a woman reporter asked.

"No, the symptoms are very different. Besides, as we said, our pharmacology department established that it was one of the three controlled drugs mentioned."

"Dr. Ames, you're an eminent psychiatrist and I believe past president of the American Psychiatric Association. Since you were called in as a consultant on this case, do you have any opinions that vary from those of Dr. Hollander and Dr. Fingerhut?" The questioner was Max Garvey of UPI.

Dr. Ames stood up, a surprisingly large man with luxurious white hair. "Thank you for the plug," he said. "I do indeed confirm what my colleagues have said about Dr. Nordstrom's symptoms, their cause and the present state of his mental health." He sat down.

"If there are no more medical questions," Duane said, anxious to move on to the next phase, "we won't take up any more of your time, doctors. Thank you for your help." The three men left. "Kermit Nordstrom will now make a statement," Duane announced, "and then he'll answer your questions."

Dana looked anxiously at Kermit as he stood up. He still looked a little peaked and his eyes were bluer than usual, she thought. He stood with his weight on one foot, and a hand in his pants pocket. He let his eyes wander around the room before he spoke. He could feel the silent disbelief mixed with curiosity; he was some kind of a freak now.

"I don't really have a statement. I have a story to tell you. Last Thursday night when I was in the elevator on my way up to the TV studio, I felt what seemed like a pinprick on my arm." He placed his hand on the spot. "The car was crowded and I thought I had bumped into a pin sticking out of someone's clothing. I thought nothing more of it but I gradually became feverish and things started going out of focus, really out by the time I was into my interview with Roger Morrisey. You know the rest. When I saw the videotape, I couldn't believe it was me.

"Obviously, I was drugged—you heard the doctors' reports—and I wish I knew by whom. The question is, who would have a motive for drugging me and why? The only thing I can think of is that those who want to stop me and my colleagues from speaking out against the Morstan-Windmiller bill and against the abuses of computers and data banks would have good enough reason to discredit me. But that covers a lot

186

of people, as you know. So as of this moment all we have is circumstantial evidence—the proof that I was drugged—and some suspicions."

Duane felt that Kermit's sincerity was coming through, but he had no idea whether anyone out there was buying it.

"Thanks to the doctors' reports," Kermit went on, "I think it should be clear that I'm not a kook, not an acidhead and not mentally unbalanced. I have no medical or other history that would indicate anything like that. I'd like to remind you that such information is computerized and is available, unfortunately, to anyone who knows how to pry. You can investigate that if you like. I'll be glad to cooperate. I'd also like to point out that secret druggings aren't unknown within the intelligence branches of various government agencies. I make no charges because I have no proof. But I think most of us are aware that the CIA and the FBI, to name two, have used drugs—some of them quite exotic, some of which they developed in their own laboratories. I'm not telling you anything you don't know. All I know is it happened to me. You'll have to draw your own conclusions." He took a breath. "I'll answer any questions now."

"Dr. Nordstrom, what individuals or agencies do you *suspect* may have drugged you?"

"I'll tell you which ones had a motive, that's all I can do. Senator Morstan . . . Representative Windmiller . . . the FBI . . . the CIA . . . army counterintelligence . . . IRS . . . Office of Budget and Management . . . Committee for a Stronger America . . . you can take it from there."

"Aren't you being paranoid in suggesting that any one of those individuals and agencies would go in for anything as extreme as having you drugged? And wasn't your behavior on 'National Newsmakers' another example of *your* paranoia?"

"Let's start with the fact that I *was* drugged on national television. Wouldn't it be logical to suspect those who had a motive? In my place, wouldn't *you?* As for my actions on the show being paranoid, the doctors have already said what it was. So I ask *you*—who is paranoid? . . . the *victim* of a drugging, or those who would carry out such an act?"

Another voice: "You say this was done to discredit you. There's another side to the coin. Isn't it possible that you drugged yourself just so you could make this charge?"

This was one Kermit hadn't anticipated. It made him boil inside but

187

he had to control himself. "Hardly. I don't know how much credibility I've built up by presenting the facts. Unquestionably, I've lost a lot by what happened on that show."

"If what you say is true," began a reporter Kermit recognized from that bus ride, "your opposition is dangerous. Aren't you afraid it will . . . well, strike again?"

Kermit didn't smile. "It's occurred to the four of us. I don't know if there's much we can do about it. But I feel that a second attempt would be too obvious, though that may be wishful thinking."

"Do you think the Harris Poll may have been a factor in someone deciding to do you in? Just two days before this happened, it showed that almost a third of the country felt that what you did to the IRS was an act of protest rather than a criminal act."

Ah, a friendly question at last, Kermit thought. "That's an interesting idea. I really don't know. I wonder what such a poll would show now."

A ripple of brittle laughter died as soon as it started.

"Since you're convinced someone drugged you to discredit you or to stop you from speaking out, do you plan to investigate further to find out the guilty party?"

"Well, it was obviously a very professional operation. Whoever was responsible will be hard to track. We intend to try, though."

"Do you have any clues?" the same voice asked.

"I'm going to let Duane Crozier answer that." He sat down, relieved that his ordeal was over.

"You anticipated me," Duane said. "I have a statement to make which will answer that question and I think a lot more. Miss Haverhill and I were in the viewing room at WTOP-TV last Thursday night watching the broadcast. When the guards hauled Dr. Nordstrom off to the security office, a man showed up and identified himself as 'Dr. Corliss' and tried to talk the station executives and the security chief into releasing Dr. Nordstrom into his custody so he could take him to Washington General Hospital for treatment. He said Dr. Nordstrom was having a nervous breakdown. He was very insistent and said that it was urgent that Dr. Nordstrom be hospitalized immediately and he'd get an ambulance there in two minutes. Miss Haverhill and I didn't know anything about this man and we wanted to have Kermit taken care of ourselves. I knew Dr. Hollander and that Valley Park had an excellent psychiatric section, so we persuaded, fortunately, Mr. Tucker, the station manager, to release

Dr. Nordstrom to us. Afterward, I checked with Washington General and they said they had no doctor by that name practicing there nor did they know of him. Then I contacted the local chapter of the A.M.A. and they had no record of a Dr. Corliss anywhere in this area. The telephone directory turned up nothing either. This man had been in the viewing room with us watching the broadcast. He said he was waiting for a friend. That turned out to be false too. Obviously the man was a plant who was conveniently there to take Dr. Nordstrom away to prevent the blood tests from taking place before the drug broke down . . . in two hours it wouldn't have been detectable. As it turned out, it still barely was . . . I don't expect you to take my word for this so I asked Harry Tucker, WTOP-TV's station manager, to be here. He was in the security office and witnessed the whole thing."

Tucker had come into the room ten minutes earlier and had taken one of the empty seats at the table.

Before he could get up, half a dozen voices shouted, "Is that true?"

"Yes, that's just about what happened. He just walked in and claimed to be a doctor. I asked Mr. McVey, our security chief, for the doctor's card afterward, but he couldn't find it. He said he recalled the first name was James and the address was somewhere in the District. We investigated but no one on staff or any of the talent knew a Dr. Corliss. I checked the Washington General Hospital myself and it's true they didn't know him. Thinking back, he seemed pretty anxious to take Dr. Nordstrom to a hospital and I didn't know who he was, so I wasn't about to hand Nordstrom over. I felt it would be safer for us to release him to Mr. Crozier and Miss Haverhill."

"Any more questions?" Duane said over the din of excited conversation.

"Yes," a voice shouted from the rear of the room. "If this phony doctor was planted there to take Dr. Nordstrom away, as you say, and this was a professional operation as you and Dr. Nordstrom seem to believe, do you think they'd be clumsy enough to plant an agent there who would just let you walk out with their target and get his blood tested?"

"Even the pros make mistakes, get overconfident. They must have assumed that Dr. Nordstrom would be alone, the way he was on all his other radio and TV interviews. It was a coincidence that Miss Haverhill and I were there. Even the FBI and the CIA can foul up. Remember the assassination attempts against Castro and others that misfired? I have a feeling that Dr. Corliss, whoever he is, is catching hell right now."

The news conference broke up with small knots of reporters arguing, shaking heads and trying to digest the bombshell they had heard. Fred Baumritter came up to Duane and Kermit—who were talking animatedly with Dana and Yuki—and shook their hands. "I'm buying," he said. "But I don't know about the others." . . .

Within minutes after the news conference ended radio and television programs were interrupted with special news bulletins reporting on the charges by Kermit and his associates that he had been drugged on the network TV show and that they suspected, among others, Senator Gunther Morstan and a bunch of federal agencies. The statements by the two doctors, corroborated by the noted psychiatrist Dr. Maxwell Ames, carried a great deal of weight. But the eye-opener was the revelation that an unknown person posing as a doctor had attempted to take custody of Dr. Nordstrom. It made the charge that someone was trying to stop Dr. Nordstrom from speaking out more believable.

Over the next few days, news commentators and newspaper editorials seemed to indicate that while much of the credibility of the Martinsburg Four had been restored, many people still remained uncertain. A number of prominent people in and out of government, including Senator Morstan, suggested that the phony doctor might have been planted there by the "saboteurs" themselves to substantiate their version of the drugging. "Why would it be surprising that confessed conspirators would conspire again to hide their criminal designs?" Morstan asked. The question apparently made sense to those who still preferred to continue believing that the four were subversives. . . .

The word among the members of the Washington press corps was that tax filings were running about 30 percent below the previous year at this date and that an estimated fifty billion dollars in taxes was being withheld —a sum so staggering that editors agreed not to print or broadcast it because of the panic it might cause in financial circles. The rumor was silently substantiated when, on April 15, the President issued a statement through his press secretary that the deadline for tax filing this year would be extended to May 15 "because the temporary disruption in the Internal Revenue Service's computer operations has delayed the processing of tax returns." The statement also indicated that triple penalties would be

190

invoked for late payment, by executive order, for those who didn't have a valid reason. The end result could not be predicted. . . .

Almost unnoticed was the fact that the full Senate Committee on Government Affairs had approved S. 17 with insignificant modifications from the subcommittee version. Windmiller's House subcommittee had earlier marked up and put through their identical version of the jointly sponsored Morstan-Windmiller bill, and the full House Committee on Government Operations had likewise approved it, after some bitter infighting, under bill number H.R. 191.

Yuki shook off his wet trenchcoat and handed it to Dana. "April showers, ugh!" he said, wrinkling his nose. "Well, it's good for the cherry blossoms, I suppose."

The others were already seated about Dana's large, modern living room talking. "Hi, Yuki, grab a chair," Kermit said. "Duane was just saying that he's been sampling media reaction around the country and he's convinced that we've come back in fairly good shape. He thinks I should start speaking out again."

"What do you think?" Yuki said.

"I'm not sure. That's one of the reasons for this meeting. I think maybe I've said enough. I don't know what else can be accomplished between now and when the bill comes up in the next few weeks."

"I'm worried about Kermit exposing himself so much," Dana said. "We've seen how desperate they are. We don't know what they might try next. I'm damn scared."

Yuki nodded to Kermit. "I think she's right. You've done everything you can—"

"Not everything," Duane said. "I still say you can use the media to gain some crucial mileage in the next couple of weeks. But I agree that there's a risk involved. . . ."

"*His* risk, not yours," Dana said, obviously annoyed. "I say it's too damn dangerous."

"I think what we need to do," said Yuki, stepping in quickly, "is to find out who drugged Kermit. If we can do that, it would be the best protection of all and maybe it would give us the ammunition to stop S. 17."

No one spoke for a long moment, then Kermit said, "I doubt that we'll ever find out. You know who we're up against."

191

"Don't be so sure," Duane said. "As I pointed out at the news conference, pros make mistakes too. They've made one already. I think Yuki's right. We should hire a top private investigator right away and let him start digging. It's a longshot, I realize, but it's certainly worth a try. Maybe he can give us a little protection, too, at the same time."

Dana, relieved that it wasn't all on Kermit's shoulders, said, "All right, let's do it, and don't worry about the money."

"Do you know anyone you can trust?" Kermit asked.

"Let me think about it," Duane said.

"It's got to be someone you *know* you can trust," Dana emphasized. "And then we can decide better whether any more press interviews would be safe."

The following day the four defendants were surrendered by their attorney to appear before the grand jury, where they were promptly indicted. The formal charges under Title 18 of the Federal Code included Seditious Conspiracy; Conspiracy to Commit Offense Against the United States; Embezzlement and Theft of Public Records; and Concealment, Removal and Mutilation of Public Records and Reports. The maximum penalty on the first charge alone was twenty years in jail and a $20,000 fine.

Chapter Twenty-Four

Dana and Kermit were startled when they got their first look at Cynthia Kellogg. Duane had told them that the private investigator he hired, subject to their approval, was an attractive, thirty-one-year-old woman. That was surprise enough, but they weren't prepared for what they saw. She was a tall, dark-haired beauty with dark, intelligent eyes and a shapely athletic figure.

Duane had been specific about her background and qualifications. He had met her in Madison, Wisconsin, two years before when he was investigating a corrupt congressman from that area. She had been a much-decorated police officer but had since become a free-lance private investigator. Nobody had anything bad to say about her, although admittedly Duane wasn't looking for such information. He had been impressed with her skill in helping him dig up some critical, hard-to-come-by facts about the congressman, and they spent more than one friendly long weekend together. He said he believed that her experience as both a police officer and an investigator, and the fact that she wasn't known in Washington, made her a very good candidate for the job. She could also provide protection if necessary.

Now, as the five of them sat around Dana's living room, Cynthia Kellogg was the center of attention. The men were intrigued with her sexiness, but Dana viewed her with objectivity.

"We're all impressed with your qualifications, Miss Kellogg," Kermit began, "but—"

"Cynthia," she corrected.

Kermit smiled. "What I started to say, Cynthia, was that I'm curious about why you'd come east to take on an assignment like this."

"Several reasons. One is that it seems to be much more interesting than the cases I've been handling in Wisconsin. You know—infidelity . . . industrial theft . . . missing persons. The second is that I've never worked the Washington area before and it will be a change of pace for me. I guess the third reason is that it pays well. And I suppose I should say"—she looked at Duane—"because my friend here asked me to."

"It could be dangerous. I guess Duane told you I was drugged last week. The people who are trying to stop us are pretty powerful."

"Yes, Duane gave me the highlights. I'm a professional, I can handle it. As Duane knows, I'm a very good investigator, but I've got to know a lot more about the whole deal here before I know where to begin. Why don't I just go to the powder room while you people decide whether I'm what you want." She got up and walked out of the room.

"She's right to the point, I must say that," Dana began.

"She's bright and seems to have a lot of guts," Yuki said.

"And aside from her qualifications," Duane said, "she's unknown in these parts. She can be your secretary, Kermit, go with you whenever you go out, and it's a good cover for her. It should take whoever's trying to stop you a while to catch on, and by then, if we're lucky, she might come up with something. The fact she's a good-looking woman makes it easier for her to operate, I've seen her in action. . . ."

"But can you completely trust her? I mean, we have a pretty good idea who's after us and there's no telling what they'll pull."

"What can I tell you, Kermit? I can't guarantee anyone. I've never really checked her out over a period of time, but it hardly seemed indicated. I think what we get is what we see. Those I've talked to say she's a hell of an operator. Also, remember, I contacted *her* on this. So far as I know she has no connection with anyone in this town, but the decision is yours."

"Why don't we have Greenfield's investigator check her out?" Dana suggested. "He's working on our case anyhow."

Kermit nodded. "Good idea. Let's tell her she's hired, it would be bad to put her off. But we won't go into any details with her until we get word from Greenfield's office. I'll see if they can do it overnight." . . .

The next morning Cynthia Kellogg was back in Dana's apartment for a thorough briefing. Greenfield's investigator had made a telephone call to another private investigator in Madison and was told that, as far as he could reasonably determine, she was known to be reliable and competent.

Now Kermit, Dana and Duane gave her the whole story, including their suspicions that someone representing Senator Morstan, possibly the FBI, the CIA or the Pentagon, might be involved.

"You can back out now if you like," Kermit told her. "You didn't know before who you'd be up against."

"No thanks. It's more than I bargained for, true, but all *I'll* be doing is investigating. I don't think anyone will try to blow me away for that. Besides, I doubt they're any tougher than the Mafia."

Dana eyed her curiously. "We'd like you to live here with us—use this apartment as a base. You'll be Kermit's secretary. You can use the extra bedroom."

Cynthia nodded. "That's fine. I'll use the name Karen Cooper."

Ménage à trois, Dana thought, and then, Oh well, I guess there's no way around it. Still, I'll have to keep my eye on this one. . . .

Lyle Gabriel had to bend his bony frame in half as he folded himself into the new dark green Jaguar parked in the L'Enfant Plaza in the southwest section of the District. He had just had lunch in the Loew's L'Enfant Hotel. The sports car was his birthday present to his wife Marilyn, and he had promised to take it back to the dealer to have a faulty windshield defroster adjusted.

As he pulled out, he saw Morstan get out of a taxi in front of the hotel and walk over to a car parked at the curb. He didn't understand it. An hour ago in the senator's office Morstan had told him he had a three o'clock appointment with a group of influential fundraisers from his home state in their suite at the Sheraton-Carlton. That was on the other side of town on K Street. Lyle looked at his watch; it was five after three. Why would Morstan lie about a routine appointment to his own speechwriter?

The car, a silver Mercedes, pulled away and Lyle couldn't get a look at the driver. Curious, Lyle decided to see if the car was headed uptown toward K Street. Within two blocks it headed in the opposite direction toward the Fourteenth Street Bridge. He decided to follow at a safe distance, knowing that Morstan had not seen his new Jag.

Once across the Potomac, the Mercedes headed west in the direction of Dulles airport. As the traffic thinned, Lyle kept a couple of blocks back, then dropped back further as they entered Route 7 and the road opened up. Ten minutes later, when Lyle was convinced that his boss was headed for Dulles, the silver car abruptly pulled off the road and stopped in front of a boarded-up gas station. It was obvious from the broken pavement with weeds growing through it that the place had been abandoned for some time. A tall erect man got out of the car with Morstan and they entered the small building through a side door.

Lyle continued on, fascinated by this mysterious meeting in an out-of-the-way spot in Tyson's Corner. He certainly wouldn't be able to approach the car now to get the license plate number. He was glad he had had the good sense to memorize it when the Mercedes pulled out of L'Enfant Plaza.

"I found out something today that may be important," Duane said as he entered Dana's apartment. "Are the others here?"

"Here," Dana said breezily. "All these meetings are draining my liquor supply. This better be important."

He followed her into the living room where Kermit and Yuki were sitting, Kermit puffing an after-dinner pipe. Cynthia Kellogg was standing in a corner next to a tall Dieffenbachia plant, holding a glass of sherry.

Duane flopped wearily into a deep chair and stretched his legs. "I found out today that Morstan is meeting secretly with a Colonel Neil Quaritius. Anyone here ever hear of him?" Negative head shakes all around. "Me neither. Well, a couple of days ago the two of them took the trouble to meet in a very unlikely place, an abandoned gas station about twenty miles out of Washington, a town in Maryland called Tyson's Corner. That doesn't sound very exciting, but Colonel Quaritius turns out to be a retired spook for the Counterintelligence Analysis Division of the Pentagon. I checked around and I understand that the man lives in high luxury—far more than a twenty-year pension would provide. The word is that he occasionally takes on special assignments for his old service and for others who can afford him."

"CIAD," Kermit said. "That's the outfit that surveilled and computerized dossiers on everyone who sneezed during the Vietnam War. They had tens of thousands of names in their data bank in Fort Holabird. It was later ordered destroyed."

"Right," Duane said, "and our colonel had a secret copy made of it and squirreled away somewhere in the Pentagon."

"So Morstan meets secretly with a free-lance spook," Dana said. "What's the connection?"

"I don't know, but when a man like Morstan who's trying to foist his god-awful bill on the country and at the same time bulldoze his way to the Presidency takes such pains to keep a hush-hush meeting in an abandoned shack with an undercover operator like Quaritius. . . . I'd say it's got to be something pretty important."

Cynthia put down her wine glass and sat on the arm of an empty club chair. "I agree. You said that Morstan was your number one suspect in Kermit's drugging, right? It could be that Quaritius handled the operation or is working on something else for the senator. By the way, how did you get this lead?"

"I've got sources, it's one of the advantages of being a reporter. I can't tell you who it was. Besides, some of it I dug up myself. Once I learned about the meeting and knew Quaritius's name, I ran around to get a line on his background. I have some friends at the Pentagon who know Quaritius and aren't particularly fond of him. They considered him too gung ho, even for the CIAD. One of my contacts there seems to know something about the kind of free-lance work he's doing and intimated it wasn't too pretty. I'm going to see if I can get some specifics from him —like what kind of assignment he's taken on for Morstan."

"What about the CIA or FBI angle?" Yuki asked. "That still seems the best bet to me, but they wouldn't have done it on their own. Someone with enough clout must have gotten them to do it. Couldn't that have been Morstan?"

"I think it *had* to be Morstan," Kermit said, "but how do you prove it?"

"Well," Dana said, "we can start with the fact that Morstan and Mitchell Storey are close friends, Morstan helped push through Storey's confirmation in the Senate—"

"And Morstan's bill would give the FBI control over all police agencies in the country, which Storey would give both arms for," Dana added.

"Which means Storey *owed* him, and he didn't need any coaxing," Duane said.

Yuki looked worried. "But how can you ever prove that?"

"It's tough, but it may not be impossible. There had to be at least half a dozen people involved in the drugging operation and maybe a few more who knew about it. This is top secret stuff, of course, but somewhere there may be a loose link. You know the FBI isn't the monolith it used to be under Hoover. There's been a lot of upset in the Bureau since the old man died. I've got to find some well-placed malcontent who just might be able to turn up something for us, and I do have a couple of sources in the Bureau. Or I did. . . . I hope you don't think I'm crowding you, Cynthia—"

"No sweat, I've got my own leads to keep me warm. It doesn't matter which one of us nails Morstan, although I'm betting I get there first." She smiled. "I've even made a little progress on the drugging business in the last couple of days, found an employee of WTOP-TV who saw a private ambulance parked around the corner from the TV station during the 'National Newsmakers' broadcast and he remembered the name. I checked with the company, Medicorps Ambulette Service, and they denied any such call. They wouldn't let me see their records, said they were confidential, but I hung around a bar near their office and found one of their drivers who knew another driver who was on duty then. Being a shameless type, I used my natural assets to get him to tell me that he was assigned to have his ambulance in that spot at nine o'clock sharp to pick up a patient. At 9:25 a man came over and told him the ambulance wasn't needed and to get out of there fast. He didn't know who the man was but from his description it could have been your Dr. Corliss."

"Did he know where he was supposed to take the patient?" Kermit asked her.

"No. He said someone was to come along and direct him. Naturally they wouldn't let him know in advance. My guess is that they were going to take him to a safe house—the FBI's or the CIAD's, whoever was running the show—and hold him for two hours until the drug disintegrated."

"And then take him to a hospital," Yuki added.

"Probably."

"How would they cover up the two-hour time lag before getting me to a hospital?" Kermit asked.

"When I find *that* out I'll have the whole story. But another possibility is that they would have taken you directly to a hospital and arranged to delay the blood tests on that end. Believe me, it's not difficult."

"Oh, by the way, here's another incidental bit from my same source," Duane suddenly remembered. "Morstan has had a mistress for some time—it's been one of those rumors that insiders don't talk about. Her name is Jacqueline Lardner. She's a former airline stewardess and occasional actress. Well, it seems that Jackie is disenchanted with her lover because he's been spending too much time away from her, allegedly because of his campaign commitments. She mentioned this to a man she spent the night with, an economist for the Brookings Institution who happens to be a friend of my source. He passed it along only because he hates Morstan's guts and he's strongly opposed to his bill. I don't know how sore she really is, or whether you can make anything of it, Cynthia. . . ."

"It's interesting, but her kind of lady often has more mouth than guts. If it comes to a showdown, I suspect she'd hang in there with him. Right now I've got some more urgent business—"

"What do you plan to do?" Kermit asked.

"I've made some progress on the drugging. Now I'm going to find out who Dr. Corliss *really* works for. I've got a couple of things going that just might pay off. . . . After all, I can't let Duane make me look bad."

Dana turned away, not appreciating her style. "And if *that* doesn't work," Cynthia said more sarcastically than she wanted, "there's got to be a dossier of some sort on Morstan at the FBI or maybe the General Accounting Office. He's not exactly Mr. Clean. If necessary, we can run a computer probe with a terminal and maybe turn up something interesting. . . ." She was less hopeful than she sounded.

The taxi stopped under a street light near the corner of Thirtieth and Olive Streets in Georgetown. A man in a tan twill topcoat got out and stood there until the cab disappeared from view. He looked down the dark row of neat early nineteenth-century attached structures, then turned right onto Olive Street and walked quickly to the middle of the block. He paused in front of a narrow, three-story, white-brick town house with the shades drawn, looked about once more, then walked to the heavy oak-paneled door and rang the bell.

The door opened instantly. The visitor looked into the face of a tall figure standing inside the dimly lit doorway. "You didn't give me much time, colonel. This better be important."

"Give me your coat, senator. We'll talk inside." He hung the coat in a hall closet beneath an ornately balustrated ascending staircase and led his guest into a high-ceilinged sitting room furnished with fine eighteenth-century English furniture.

Quaritius motioned Morstan to a Queen Anne sofa and dropped into a damask-covered wing chair.

Morstan looked impatiently at Quaritius. "What the hell is this all about? Calling me on such short notice and getting me to come all the way across town at this time of night."

"Are you certain you weren't followed?" The voice was all business.

"Of course I'm certain . . . I took all the precautions." He glared at the handsome, assured man sitting across from him. "I don't like being rousted like this."

"Something has come up that we have to talk about and this is the safest place to do it. This house belongs to a businessman who's in Europe with his family. So we can relax and talk." He paused. "Would you like a drink?"

"No, let's get on with it."

Quaritius unhurriedly reached into his jacket pocket and brought out a gold cigarette case, took out a cigarette and lit it. As he expelled the smoke, he looked directly at Morstan. "Senator . . . we have a problem. Earlier this evening I audited some tape from the wall bug we maintain at that Berkshires apartment. It seems that our *friends* are sharper than we thought. They apparently know a few things they ought not to know."

Morstan's eyes were stony. "Such as?"

"Such as that you and I met in that abandoned gas station in Tyson's Corner."

"How would they know that?"

"It seems that Crozier has some contacts in the right places. Could there be a leak in your office?"

"No one else knew about it," the senator shot back resentfully. "Besides, what could they make of it? Do they know any more than that?"

"Well, the fact is that Crozier has dug into my background and he knows the kind of work I do. They've made some very accurate surmises about what we've been cooking, but at this point they have no actual evidence—"

"What do you mean 'at this point'? Is there any danger of their finding out at some *other* point?"

"I doubt it, but it's a danger signal. What I'm more concerned about is that they seem to know about you and Mitchell Storey. They've figured out that you and Storey are responsible for drugging Nordstrom on that network TV program. Crozier seems to have contacts in the Bureau too, and while Storey is a thorough guy, somewhere down the line there could be a loose tongue. He doesn't run nearly as tight a ship as J. Edgar did. There was one foul-up on this already—that agent who was supposed to get Nordstrom into a hospital and let him get away."

"I see." Morstan looked serious.

"No, you don't, there's more. They hired a private investigator, a former cop—a woman named Cynthia Kellogg. She's out there digging too. She's already made contact with the ambulance driver who was supposed to pick Nordstrom up at the TV station and take him to the hospital. I've checked on her, she's a smart, tough pro. This whole thing could break apart. I don't like it at all."

"Even if they found out the Bureau was responsible, they couldn't tie me to it. No way at all."

"Maybe, maybe not. But we don't want the Bureau embarrassed either, do we? Storey wouldn't like it."

"Neither would I. If the media got hold of it, it would hurt S. 17's chances. We can't let that happen."

"I'm glad you agree, senator. There's a lot at stake here." His tone was didactic.

"Obviously." Morstan didn't like being preached to by a hired hand. "I'm sure you have something in mind."

"I do. We've got to cut down the tree."

Morstan was stopped by the expression, then . . . "You mean stop them forcefully?"

"I mean stop them permanently."

Morstan suddenly realized what he was dealing with. He didn't conceal his feelings. "I won't have that, there's got to be another way—"

"What would *you* suggest, senator?"

"You've been in the intelligence business long enough to know what should be done. Intimidation, blackmail, bribery . . . my god, there's got to be another way . . . why don't you just buy off their private investigator. She's a woman, you should know how to handle her."

Quaritius smiled. "A good thought, senator, but I'm afraid it's gone beyond that. Those four just know too much, and remember that Crozier is a very competent investigative reporter. If we bought off the girl, they'd find out and then go hell bent for leather. That's the problem in dealing with dedicated amateurs, especially capable ones like these. They don't know when to stop."

Morstan's face was tight with anger and frustration. "I don't give a damn. I won't be involved in . . . violence. I've been in tight corners before and I always managed to turn things around. Ten years ago there was this hotshot young assistant attorney general from my home state who thought he had me—never mind for what. He *could* have ruined me. Well, I turned that around in short order and had the guy make a public apology." He smiled at the memory. "And then about four years ago, I think it was, I'm sure you remember when Senator Whiting tried to unseat me from my chairmanship of the Armed Services Committee and—"

"Fish and fowl, senator. Not the same animal at all. We're not talking about political gamesmanship. We're talking about the future of America."

"Don't you lecture me about America, colonel." Morstan was on his feet. "I helped write the book." He glared down at the lanky figure in the chair. "Your assignment was and is to discredit those four saboteurs so that they cannot interfere with my legislation or with my campaign for the Presidency. That's *all* you need concern yourself with."

Quaritius rose languidly to his feet. "That's exactly what I am concerned with. And the only way I can guarantee that those four won't interfere with your bill—which I happen to believe in—or ruin your try for the White House is to stop them, once and for all. Otherwise this whole thing may blow up in our faces. It's either them or us. Take my word for it."

Morstan was shaken. He walked away a few feet and stared into the empty fireplace. "Let's for the moment assume you're right. I still won't be a party to what amounts to murder. I'm a U.S. senator, not some Mafia don, and I won't authorize a contract for murder." He turned to Quaritius. "You'll have to find another way, and that's final."

The colonel measured him. "Let me ask you a question, senator. Is it possible that there's a damaging dossier on you in some government data bank? Because if there is, there's an outside chance those crazy computerniks will figure out a way to dredge it up. They've already said as much. Would you care to hear the tape?"

Morstan turned back to the fireplace, looked at the fake flames licking up from no visible source of fuel, and wondered . . . *Could there be such a dossier, I think he's trying to stampede me, but what if—*

"It doesn't really matter," Quaritius continued. "The decision has already been made. Someone else has taken the responsibility. It's a pragmatic decision based on a realistic assessment of the risks." His rich voice suddenly became soothing, all sympathy and understanding. "You needn't concern yourself with it. You are not involved in any way, I personally assure you of that. Just forget about it. But you had to be told."

Morstan's erect posture failed him and his face was dead weary. "You know my position. I don't want to hear any more about it." He turned and quickly walked to the entrance hall.

As he helped Morstan with his topcoat, Quaritius said with a straight face, "This meeting never happened, Mr. President."

Wearing a smart pantsuit and high black boots, Cynthia looked like a thousand other D.C. secretaries as she moved into the lobby of the old but still decorous Mayflower Hotel in the downtown shopping district. She was barely through the door when the bell captain, a corpulent fatherly type, came up to her.

"Karen Cooper?" he inquired solicitously.

She nodded, surprised.

"Go right up . . . suite eight-seven-two. You're expected."

"I was supposed to meet someone here in the lobby."

"Yes, I know. You're to go right up. I was asked to tell you that."

She looked at him closely. "By whom?"

His fleshy face creased into a reassuring smile. "Oh, it's perfectly all right, miss. I know the man. There's nothing to worry about."

She pursed her lips. "Eight-seven-two?"

As she walked into the empty elevator and pressed the button, she wondered who or what she would find at the other end. She didn't like walking into a blind situation. If she were still back on the Madison police force, her reflex would have been to call for backup. But a private investigator had to take chances a police officer wouldn't. Her informant had given her a number to call for information on Dr. Corliss. A well-spoken man on the other end of the line said he had the information she wanted, suggested that they meet in the Mayflower lobby. No, he couldn't give his name on the phone for reasons he would explain later.

The door to 872 was already open and a tall, distinguished, athletically built man in a well-cut suit was poised in the doorway.

"Miss Cooper . . . please come in." His voice was resonant and warm.

She smelled the aroma of an excellent eau de cologne as she walked by him into a large, elegantly furnished sitting room with a distinct oriental decor.

He took in her figure as she moved into the room. At the same time he reached into his jacket and his hand came out holding a dull-black automatic. He pointed it at her back.

She caught the action instinctively out of the corner of her eye, pretended not to notice. As he drew close she wheeled swiftly and moved her flattened hand in a chop across his wrist. The weapon rumbled to the floor. In a continuous motion she grabbed his lowered wrist with one hand and his upper arm with the other and, using his arm as a lever, yanked him forward, arching his body in a circle. He landed on his back in the middle of the room, his head just missing the corner of the coffee table. He lay there a moment, stunned and surprised, looking into the barrel of a snub-nosed .32 caliber revolver she had taken from her boot.

Suddenly, he broke out with laughter. A silver-brown forelock hovered over one eye and the laugh lines creased his tan cheeks. "You're very good, *Cynthia,*" he said. "I had to see for myself."

She allowed him to get up, holding the gun on him. "Who are you?"

"Can I fix you a drink?"

Bullshit. "Who are you?"

"Mind if I have one?"

"Stay where you are. Why did you call me 'Cynthia'? My name is Karen Cooper."

"I thought Cynthia Kellogg would be too formal. I know you quite well." His deep-set brown eyes were no longer amused. "Shall we sit down and talk?"

She paused, nodded. As he sat down on the sofa, crossing his legs and winging his arms on the side cushions, she bent down and picked up his gun.

"It isn't loaded."

She pulled out the clip, and it was empty. She flipped the weapon sharply at him, and it bounced off his thigh.

She was seated now in a club chair facing him. "So you know who I am. Now I'd like to know what this is all about." She held the gun on her lap still pointed at him.

"Okay. I owe you an explanation. I'm Colonel Neil Quaritius, retired U.S. Army intelligence. We've had you under twenty-four hour surveillance since you went to work for Nordstrom and his people. We know every move they make too." His lips tightened momentarily and his thickly lashed eyes regarded her steadily. "We've got a line on you from the moment of your birth . . . February 19, 1953, at 6:09 A.M. . . . to the moment you walked into this room. Your parents, Thomas and Marie . . . your two younger brothers, Gary and Evan . . . the schools you attended . . . when and where you lost your virginity. Say, you were precocious." He didn't smile. "You went to Westlake Junior College, dropped out after one year. The report was that you assaulted the wife of your psychology instructor when she accused you of body contact sports with her husband. You were also an excellent athlete in other sports—wrestling, track—the 440 was your specialty . . . junior swimming championship in high school, rifle marksmanship, black belt karate a bit later on. You weren't a bad student either, but too much of a renegade to stay with it."

The gun rested limply in her hand as she stared at him.

"After Westlake you joined an acting group in Eau Claire, then you did some summer stock—painting sets mostly. You got in some trouble there when the gay producer wouldn't give you a featured role. You worked him over. You're a tough lady, Cynthia, when you think someone's done you in. You're also an expert at survival, at recognizing the main chance and taking hold of it." He paused for a reaction but she just sat there, returning his gaze. "After that you headed for the West Coast and became a stunt driver in a couple of made-for-TV movies. Finally you drifted back to Wisconsin and got on the Madison police force. I understand you were a superb police officer, got more citations in three years than any other officer, male or female, on the force. Then suddenly you quit. Or I should say the department asked you to resign. It seems you did a little free-lancing on the side that they didn't approve of, made a couple of hits for the rivals of a loan-sharking syndicate. The department found out but they couldn't get anyone to testify, so to save themselves the embarrassment of charging you with two murders they couldn't prove, they let you walk out and kept their mouths shut. Then you went into the old private-eye business, and after a boring couple of years you hit what seemed the jackpot. You got the job of protecting and helping the most dangerous subversives in this country: Nordstrom and his computerniks." He smiled a Q.E.D. smile, letting it sink in.

Cynthia hung tough. "So you've looked me up. Is that supposed to impress me?"

"No, it's supposed to persuade you."

"What are you selling?"

"Don't be stupid, Cynthia. Once you drifted into this Nordstrom business, you became fresh meat for us. We can *persuade* you to do whatever we want you to do."

"Really? . . . okay, persuade me. And by the way, who or what is 'we'? I thought you were retired from army intelligence. I thought I'd covered my tracks pretty well . . . you sound like you've got the whole CIA and FBI going for you. Who *do* you work for now?"

"*We* . . . is a private coalition of highly placed individuals in and out of government who are dedicated to keeping this country strong and free. Sounds corny but we mean it. We believe that the first priority for America right now is to make it impossible for computer terrorists like Nordstrom and his bunch to invade our vital government agencies, breach our national security and finally take over the government itself. There is only one thing that can prevent that from happening—the Morstan-Windmiller bill. S. 17. It's obvious that whoever controls the nation's computer networks can control America. This bill will guarantee that control where it belongs . . . don't you agree?" He watched her closely.

"Kermit Nordstrom and the others had it the other way around. It made sense the way they explained it." She too was testing.

"They distorted the facts, Cynthia." A note of irritation, impatience, edged his voice. "They're trying to fool the country. You're too intelligent for them. I mean it. You're a former law-enforcement officer—and a damn good one. You know how critical it is for us to have every possible tool in fighting crime and subversives. And how tough the courts make it to put away those people. Let me ask you a question. As a police officer in a patrol car or on the beat, where would you have been without the FBI's computerized National Crime Information Center to give you a rundown on the suspect you were tracking? S. 17 will add muscle to every local police precinct and law enforcement agency in the country. It will tie all police computer systems together so that the FBI can help eliminate the vermin. If you believe in the law and its enforcement, as I think you do, you *have* to join with us, not just because of what I know about you but because of what you are, what you believe."

"Of course I believe in law and enforcement. But what I came here for was to find out about Dr. Corliss. You said you had the information I wanted."

Quaritius looked annoyed. "And you told *me* you were a secretary named Karen Cooper. Never mind that. I do have the information you want and a good deal more. All right, you already know that Dr. Corliss was a phony. He's an agent who messed up his assignment. He's been transferred to Siberia, also known as Utah. Which is why I'm running the show now."

"You work for the FBI, CIA? I thought—"

"No, I don't work for them. I work for that group of important, dedicated individuals who want to see S. 17 passed for the good of this country. But some other powerful organizations are cooperating with us."

Cynthia was thoroughly puzzled. "I don't understand. You know who I work for and what I came here to find out. Aren't you taking a chance in telling me as much as you have?"

"No. Because I know everything you know and everything your ex-employers know."

"*Ex*-employers?"

"I say 'ex' because as of now you don't work for them anymore." This time his smile was unpleasant. "I know you found out about my meeting with Senator Morstan and that you're familiar with my background. I also know that you have an eyewitness who spotted that ambulance and that you managed to get the driver to talk." His eyes fondled her full breasts and long legs. "I'm aware of your talents—and I have a feeling that given time, you'd find a way of getting the rest of the story. That's one of the reasons you are here . . . oh, don't bother about the gun." He had seen her hand tighten on the weapon resting on her lap. "You won't want to use it when you hear what else I have to say. We know that Nordstrom lied to you about the National Personnel Advisory Council and made you think it was a clandestine operation to blackmail good people rather than a defense against subversives infiltrating the government. And we also know that he's been meeting in the apartment with bleeding-heart senators like Hugo Kammerer and those other so-called civil rights mouthpieces. When I took over I had acoustical wall spikes installed through the adjacent apartment, and they've given us the whole litany. Also, the new doorman at the Berkshires works for us."

"Why shouldn't I kill you now and go back and tell Nordstrom what I found out?"

"The bell captain saw you come up here, and he knows who you are. Anyway, I think you're finally beginning to believe me." His deep-set eyes held hers.

"What are you getting at?" She was still guarded.

"We want you to help us stop Nordstrom and his people."

" 'Stop' them?"

"Cynthia, we want you to kill them."

She suddenly *felt* the power, and threat, of this man, but also realized she was not repelled by it. "I won't do it."

"I think you will. Remember that we know about your killing the two people who finked on your clients . . . and that the Madison police department couldn't get anyone to testify against you." He paused. "Well, Cynthia, we have someone who *will* testify. Do you remember Manny Oldrich? He's in Lewiston Penitentiary now, for extortion. We arranged a deal for him . . . he'll testify. His lawyer is waiting for our call."

"He's a convicted felon. His testimony would be worthless."

"Not quite. Didn't he give you the gun for the job, a .38, so you wouldn't have to use your service revolver, which could be traced to you?"

She didn't answer.

"He promised to dispose of it afterward, correct?" He was enjoying her predicament. "Well, he didn't. It still has your prints on it and we know where it is."

"I don't believe you." It was a reflex without conviction.

"Of course you do. This isn't Wisconsin, Cynthia. It's called the big

208

leagues. You'd better believe me, for your own sake." He paused, giving her a last chance to make up her mind.

She sat there silently, weighing the odds, looking abstractly at the painting of a delicate Japanese landscape reflected in the ornate, gilt-framed mirror.

"You know, Cynthia, you're a beautiful woman and a very capable one too. I think you believe in what we're doing for our country, and you could be a tremendous asset to us. I shouldn't have to blackmail you into doing something you really believe in. I certainly have no desire to hang you for murder. But believe me, I will if I have to."

She didn't have to look at him to know that he would, and could. She'd been foolish to have returned the borrowed .38 to Oldrich; she should have disposed of it herself. She hated being vulnerable. "Isn't there some other way? Nordstrom and Crozier are really very nice guys."

"Delightful guys, I'm sure. But the country can't afford them. When they hired you and started getting close to who was responsible for the drugging and then discovered the senator's connection with me—well, they pretty much asked for it. And that notion of searching for an incriminating dossier on the senator—obviously we can't allow that to happen."

"Then it doesn't have anything to do with that bill."

"It does and it doesn't. We had Nordstrom completely discredited on that TV show. If he hadn't gone to all that trouble to clear himself, S. 17 would have been a sure thing and the four of them would have been put away until they collected Social Security. Now it's gone beyond that. That subversive SOB can ruin the career of one of the great men of this country. A man we all badly need in the White House to turn this country around."

She sat there, eyes examining her boots, feeling peculiarly defenseless. He got up and walked over to her chair. She was conscious of him but did not look up. He put his hand on her shoulder, then leaned over and took the gun lying on her lap.

"You won't need that."

She looked up. "I guess I'll take that drink now."

She admired the square of his broad shoulders and his long, straight back as he walked to a small ebony bar on the other end of the room where two bottles and two glasses stood next to a silver ice bucket.

"Canadian Club on the rocks okay?" His back was still turned.

"Fine."

He returned with a glass in either hand and gave her one. He raised his and looked down at her. "Here's to S. 17." He took a long swallow.

Cynthia raised hers silently, looked at him over the rim of the glass.

He put his glass on the low walnut coffee table and took a long white envelope from his breast pocket. "This is for you."

She looked at it in surprise.

"It's ten thousand dollars," he said. "There will be forty thousand more later—a bonus for a job well done."

Cynthia got up quickly. "I'm not doing it for the money. . . ."

"Of course not. We're all in this for the best of reasons. And by the way"—he raised one hand for emphasis—"you will not be using a gun. Too crude. This will look like an accident because it will *be* an accident. There must be no possible suspicion of foul play. None whatsoever. We know they'll be taking a car trip for the weekend, right? They will die in a car crash, and there must be no witnesses. That shouldn't be too much of a problem for an experienced stunt driver like you." He took her drink from her hand, put it on the coffee table next to his. "We can discuss the plan later." He went to her, slowly unbuttoned her jacket and unsnapped her bra, all the while looking at her dark, wide-open eyes. His hand took hold of one full breast, and as his other arm pulled her hips against him, he said, "All right, killer. Unzip my fly."

Chapter Twenty-Five

A steady rain was peppering the long, narrow, neatly curtained dinette window in Marcia's apartment in the four-story brownstone where Duane Crozier was rereading yesterday's Washington *Post.* It sounded like the scurrying of mice on a wooden floor, but it was nonetheless a comforting background as Duane sat in his pajamas drinking his second cup of coffee an hour after Marcia had left for work and keeping posted on the personal and political notes titillating the nation's capital. It was one of the few days lately when there wasn't some news or feature story concerning the Martinsburg Four or of some vaguely related development.

Suddenly it came together. Why not? Turnabout is fair play. He remembered what Lyle had told him the other day about Morstan gradually drawing away from his mistress and her resentment of it. Then he thought about the new information on the secret meetings with Colonel Quaritius. He had this wild idea that might just possibly work. If he got nowhere, what was there to lose? If he hit pay dirt—yes, "dirt"—it might turn up something which could help them discredit Morstan. He'd give it a try. . . .

In the taxi ride across town, he planned how he would handle it, even his opening remarks. It was making him edgy and he gave it up. He would play it by ear.

It was 11:15 when the cab pulled up to a two-story garden apartment complex on North Queen Street, in suburban Rosslyn, Virginia, about half a mile west of the Potomac. It had stopped raining. Duane found the right entrance, looked at the mail boxes, noted the apartment number and walked in. It was on the second floor. He smoothed back his thick, rumpled hair, cleared his throat and rang the bell. There was no answer, and he hesitated to ring again. In another moment he heard footsteps on a hard floor. A light voice through the peephole said, "Who is it?" "Duane Crozier," he answered. "Who?" the voice seemed higher. Before he could respond, he heard a click and the wood-grained metal door swung open. A slender, very pretty young woman of medium height stood there in a bright green street dress. The light through a mesh-curtained double window some thirty feet behind her silhouetted her trim figure. Her features were small and even and her eyes were widely set and remarkably green. Her light brunette hair was medium length. It was easy to see the airline stewardess she had been and the part-time actress he had heard she was.

"Miss Lardner?" he asked diffidently.

"Yes, I'm Jacqueline Lardner. What do you want?" Her voice was bright but her manner was crisp, almost brusque. It was obvious she didn't much welcome the intrusion.

"I'm Duane Crozier, and I would very much like to talk to you for a few minutes."

She stood there, her hand still on the knob of the half-opened door, looking at him carefully. "About what?"

He had a feeling that this was as far as he would get. He smiled and angled his head self-consciously. "It will take more than a minute to tell you. I'd appreciate it if I could come in and talk to you. I'm the reporter from *Newswatch* who . . ."

"I *know* who you are, I read the papers, but I have nothing to tell you. So, if you'll excuse me—"

He saw that her hand on the knob was starting to move inward. "I have something to tell you, something I think is important . . . to both of us."

Those intelligent green eyes stayed on him for a long moment and then the door swung wider and she said in a low voice, "Come in."

She led him into the living room and sat down primly on the light blue velvet sofa, sleek legs crossed and pulled in at the ankles, arms folded across her bosom. Duane took a matching club chair across the room from her.

"This is very difficult for me and I hope you'll bear with me." He decided on the sincere-young-man-in-pain approach. Besides it was true. He felt pretty rotten about what he was trying to do. He looked down at the blue and yellow and gray Chinese rug between them and sighed. "I have something to tell you and it isn't very pleasant, but after you hear it, I think . . . I hope . . . you'll understand why I had to tell you." He looked up at her. Her face was expressionless, but he sensed that her curiosity was piqued.

"As you know, Miss Lardner, I'm an investigative reporter and I naturally have a number of dependable sources which often provide me with confidential information. What I'm about to say is very embarrassing but there is no way around it." He cleared his throat. "Your relationship with Senator Morstan has been rumored in certain Washington quarters for some time, but the word now is that the senator is leaving you for another woman, and I thought—"

"If you're trying to trap me into admitting a relationship with the senator you're wasting your time. What right do you have to barge in here anyway and tell me this garbage?"

"I'm not asking you to admit anything. I'm telling you what I learned, and what I think you already know, because I thought we might be able to help each other."

She looked at him closely, trying to appraise his sincerity. "My friendship with the senator is none of anyone's damn business. But I can't believe you'd have the gall to come here and tell me all this . . . gossip, which happens not to be true. The senator and I are still good friends. You must have a motive for doing this. Exactly *why* did you come here?"

Well, she's curious at least, Duane thought. "I thought that if the senator had walked out on you, he might have hurt you badly enough for you to be willing to help us. You probably know better than anyone else what kind of a man he is. Senator Morstan will stop at nothing to hurt us—he's already proven that. We're certain he was responsible for the drugging of Kermit Nordstrom. I thought you might know something that we could use to defend ourselves when our trial comes up in a few weeks—"

"Why would I want to do that?"

"Because you may want to pay him back. Or because it's in a pretty good cause. I don't want to bring politics into it, but the fact is that the four of us are just what we said we are, social protesters, not subversives. We hope to prove that."

Jacqueline Lardner smiled. "You thought I might just have a taped conversation lying around of the senator confessing that he drugged your friend?"

"No, but I was hoping that you might remember something that could help us . . . names of people he may have mentioned, for example." A sudden thought occurred to him. "Incidentally, Miss Lardner, if it turns out I'm right and the senator does walk out on you, I think you have a story quite a few people would like to read. It would be highly salable as a magazine series or a book, or both. I have contacts in publishing and I suspect I could help you make a substantial deal."

"That sounds like a bribe."

"I'd call it a quid pro quo. You help us, I help you."

"Look, you don't know the sort of person I am and yet you barge in here without even a phone call and ask me, just like that," she snapped her fingers in the air, "to do something underhanded. I'm more than insulted, I'm shocked. You must think I'm some sort of . . . what's that girl's name who ratted on Congressman Wayne Hays? . . . oh, it doesn't matter. The point is, I'm not!" She looked genuinely upset. "I'm really amazed that a man like you would suggest such things."

Duane rose from his chair with melancholy dignity. "You're right . . . I shouldn't have come here . . . I *am* ashamed, but this man is so dangerous and I'm looking for a way to prove it."

She was standing now too, her hands clasped primly at her waist. "Don't you really mean dangerous to you and your friends and your case?"

"That too," he conceded.

She took a step forward. "You've said enough. I suggest you go—*now.*" She led the way to the door, opened it wide. The slamming sound behind him punctuated the gamble he had lost. He wondered how much more it might cost.

Chapter Twenty-Six

The trees on Massachusetts Avenue and on the Berkshire's landscaped hillside were in full chroma, the early morning beads of dew still clinging to the leaves and grass. The only missing ingredient for a lovely April day was some sunshine to dapple through the leafy canopy. It looked as though it might burn through the lavender-gray sky later on and make the day humid.

It was 8:20. Upstairs in Dana's spacious apartment, Cynthia answered the phone. It was the doorman reporting that the car rented for the trip had just been delivered and was waiting out front. They had insisted that Yuki come along. He needed a respite from the book he was working on, and it would be nice for them all to spend a long weekend together now that there were no more interviews to be given and the trial was just a few weeks away. At Dana's suggestion, Yuki had asked Harriet to come along too, but she didn't feel comfortable about spending a weekend with the group. Cynthia would, of course, be with them to provide security since it would be a four-day period of exposure.

The five of them had already breakfasted. They were anxious to get off to an early start on their long drive to Blowing Rock, North Carolina, some 375 miles to the southwest. It was to be a long-planned weekend of relaxation at Dana's parents' country retreat—a hiatus between the pressures which had built up and the greater ones to follow.

A few minutes later, the five got out of the elevator, each carrying a small case. The muscular young doorman helped them load the luggage into the trunk of the red Oldsmobile sedan parked at the front entrance. They drove down the winding driveway, with Kermit behind the wheel and Cynthia next to him; Dana, Yuki and Duane shared the back seat. As they entered Massachusetts Avenue and the stream of southbound traffic the doorman looked about carefully, then held a small black plastic box to his mouth and spoke briefly into it.

The traffic became heavier as they passed the scores of impressive foreign embassies and elegant old mansions and skirted the edge of Georgetown heading for the Roosevelt Bridge. Once across the fog-laced Potomac, they picked up Route 50 at the north end of Arlington National Cemetery and sped through the suburban Virginia communities where much of the District of Columbia lived. Most of the traffic was headed the other way as the workday was beginning in the nation's overcast capital. Ten minutes later they turned into U.S. highway 211 at Fairfax, heading due west toward Skyline Drive and the thickly forested mountain roads of the Shenandoahs some eighty miles away.

The sky was dramatic with dark amoebic shapes skimming across the horizon followed by unexpected kites of bright jagged light jigsawing the landscape into huge swatches of abstract greenish shadows and highlighted hilltops.

Kermit, behind the wheel, settled down for the long, interesting trek ahead despite the unsettled weather. He was peering intently at the road, but his eyes were preoccupied. "I can't help thinking about that damn bill." He shook his head. "I sometimes wonder if we—"

"That's a no-no," Dana interjected sharply. "We agreed not to talk shop for the whole weekend. This is a holiday and we want to get our heads clear of all that and have some fun. Next one who slips has to walk the rest of the way."

"I'm for that," Duane agreed.

"That and tennis . . . on your father's court," Yuki added. "It used to be my specialty."

They chatted animatedly about tennis, what Dana's family's country place was like, what Blowing Rock had to offer and what they would do on Saturday night. After a while the conversation played itself out as the changing landscapes and miles sped by.

It was now 10:15. They had been driving an hour and three quarters, done about seventy-five miles. They had just passed the town of Amissville. Ben Venue was coming up next. In the distance they could see thunderheads boiling up.

Fifteen minutes later they came abreast of Sperryville, the last town before they entered the Shenandoah National Park seven miles away. The clouds were now so low they seemed to be sitting like giant cushions on the shoulders of the mountain.

"Okay, Kermit," Cynthia said suddenly as the road to the park entrance started to rise. "Pull over. It's two hours. My turn to drive."

"I don't mind driving. I'm not tired."

"We made an agreement. We change every two hours. It's my turn. Shove over."

He parked at the side of the road and walked around to the other side of the car. She eased herself over the console between the bucket seats and took the wheel. He stretched his legs as far as he could on the upslanting floorboard and brought his arms back, flexing his shoulders until his bones cracked.

"I guess maybe a change of horses is a good idea," he conceded.

She put the car in gear and they took off in a cloud of road dust.

A few minutes later they were ascending the mountains, past Panorama and finally into Skyline Drive. Driving with obvious finesse and great concentration on the twisting forested single lane road, Cynthia was noticeably silent, and laconic when he tried to lead her into conversation. The others in the back seat were too involved in their own conversation to pay attention.

Kermit decided to try once more. "Tell me, Cynthia, what's it like to be a private eye?" He smiled a little.

She was focused on the serpentine road and for a few seconds it seemed as though she wouldn't answer. Finally she replied. "Sometimes interesting, sometimes dull. Depends."

He wouldn't accept her nonanswer and tried again. "It must be very different from being a cop where you're visible in the community and carry a lot of authority."

She exhaled a deep breath. "That's right."

Kermit gave up. She was tense about something. She had clammed up as soon as they entered Skyline Drive. It was as though the dark canopy of trees had dropped a curtain inside her. Perhaps it was just her concern for their safety as she concentrated on this difficult mountain road. Meanwhile, the three in the back seat were chatting away. Suddenly, they stopped talking and Dana said, "How about turning on the radio, Kermit." He dialed some country music.

The clouds opened and sheets of water whipped through the heavy branches overhanging massive rock outcroppings on both sides of the road. Cynthia slowed to 35 miles an hour and turned the windshield wiper to the fast position. Visibility was still difficult although the wiper was clicking away like a hopped-up metronome. She cut her speed further as she eased through a succession of sharp turns.

This doesn't make things any easier, Cynthia thought. I've got to be able to see the markers on the side of the road. Finally, through the momentary clearing of the wiper blade swipe, she spotted one. STONY MAN—4,010 FEET ELEVATION, it read. My god, she said to herself, we've come further than I realized. I must have missed at least one marker. Only seven miles to Hawksbill, then. Her eyes were fixed grimly on the undulations of the rainswept road.

She was sweating now in the humid cubicle. She turned on the defogger and it quickly cleared up the smoky windshield, but her scalp was prickly with sweat. She rolled down her window a bit but water splashed in, so she closed it and turned on the air-conditioner. That felt better. And the rain was slowing.

"It's my turn to drive next," Duane said. "This is a rugged road in this kind of weather. When you get tired, let me know and I'll take over, Cynthia."

She didn't reply. The only sound was that of a country music group thwacking away on guitars overlaying the roiling hiss of tires squeegeeing water. She was measuring the miles with her eyes, searching the surrounding hills, sudden ravines, rock formations and dark thickets as they flashed by, her hands gripping the wheel tightly. Then she saw it ahead: an eight-foot pole planted on the right edge of the road with a soggy red flag flapping limply. Her eyes widened.

Kermit saw it too. "Looks like the surveyors were at work," he observed casually.

She didn't hear him. A thousand feet more. There would be a sheer drop down the mountainside. Right after the next marker. She pressed down on the accelerator—up to fifty now rocketing through a long curve.

"What are you doing? Slow down!" Kermit commanded.

"Are you crazy? Slow down!" It was Dana.

She paid no attention. There it was . . . the sign coming up on the right: HAWKSBILL—4,049 FEET ELEVATION. She could see the hairpin turn ahead swinging sharply to the right, and beyond that open space where the edge of the road fell off to an unseen bottom. She leaned lightly on the door latch and felt it give without opening the door. The car's velocity would keep it closed until she was ready.

Suddenly, a set of headlights appeared drilling through the mist. Crazy coincidence but it didn't matter. She was into the sharp turn and would be at the cliff dropoff on the right in a matter of seconds. A rocky wall of outcropping rimmed the left side of the road. Then a second set of headlights was there. They were side by side on both sides of the road bearing down swiftly on them, forcing them toward the cliff.

Quaritius's words flashed in Cynthia's head. *There must be no witnesses.* Both sets of headlights were 500 feet away and closing fast. She could make the cliff but with no room to jump. They would run her down.

Kermit suddenly understood too. *"Turn left, turn left!"* He thrust his arm to turn the wheel but she had already jerked it sharply to the left as she jammed her foot to the floorboard. The red car leaped across the path of the oncoming headlights just feet away and skidded obliquely off the road, across a grassy shoulder. A dark monolith of upthrust rock rose before them. The crash of metal and glass exploded in Kermit's brain. He heard a scream, and then everything stopped.

He didn't know how long he had lain there. The pelting rain on his face seemed to revive him. He tried to remember where he was, what had happened. Lying on his back he saw a mottled gray sky filtered through a linear network of what he gradually recognized as tree branches. He felt water soaking his back and he slowly became conscious that the wail he heard in the background somewhere was a horn continuously blowing, sounding its alarm through the fastness of the mountain.

He raised his head and felt a terrible pain through his shoulder and chest. Then he saw the crushed red vehicle. Dana . . . and the others . . . they were in it, he had to get to them . . . he raised himself painfully onto his elbows, took a deep breath, forced himself to a sitting position. One upturned car wheel was at a crazy angle, and he could see the undercarriage dripping liquid. The acrid smell of hot chemicals and oil was in his nostrils. He couldn't see into the car from this position.

Slowly, he crawled forward on the mossy forest floor and pulled himself up on the slanting wheel. He stood erect for a moment, accustoming himself to the shooting pain in his upper chest. Then he looked into the twisted open door on his side from which he had apparently been projected by the force of the impact on the driver's side. Yuki was trying to get Duane and Dana out the open door. The other side was crushed. He heard them moaning. Yuki turned to him. "Are you all right?"

Kermit nodded. "How are they?"

"They're badly hurt. Give me a hand."

Yuki eased Duane out of the back and up the incline of the side-angled car. Kermit helped walk him to a tree, where they sat him down. Duane's forehead was cut and blood was pouring from his nose, but he was smiling weakly. They pulled Dana, unconscious and bloody around the head, out of the back seat and carried her to a spot where they propped her against a large rock. Kermit's heart sank when he saw her face, and he forgot his own pain.

"What about Cynthia?" Kermit asked.

Yuki shook his head. "Bad."

"Stay with them," Kermit said, and lurched his way back to the wrecked car. Cynthia was draped over the steering wheel, which was crushed into her chest, her head hung sideways against the smashed window. He couldn't see her face. The lurid sound of the horn was piercing his brain. He maneuvered his body into the bucket seat torn from its moorings and took her limp elbow off the horn. The awful sound stopped. Instead he heard the radio. It sounded like an old Elvis Presley record.

He couldn't tell if she was alive. Leaning over her, he saw blood covering her turned-away face, matting her long dark hair and staining her yellow blouse a rust color. He gently, tentatively, touched her shoulder, but she did not respond. He tried to get his hand to her chest to feel for a heartbeat, but the steering wheel was too tight against her. When he took his hand away it was sticky with blood. He thought he would throw up.

Then he heard her moan softly. At least she was alive, he'd have to get help. . . . "Cynthia . . . can you hear me?" She moaned again, and he thought he heard something mumbled. Her face was turned away, her words unintelligible. "Don't try to talk, I'm going for help."

Before he could extricate himself from the crushed area he saw the back of her head move slightly. A whisper came from her. "Tried to . . . kill me too . . . double cross . . ."

Kermit waited a moment. "Who, Cynthia? *Who?*" He heard a mumble and it stopped. He stumbled out of the sprung door and fell to the soggy ground. The pain filling his whole upper body was unbearable. He passed out.

As Adam Greenfield walked into the neat Colonial building past the sign reading, PAGE COUNTY MEMORIAL HOSPITAL, Luray, Virginia, he remembered visiting the Luray Caverns in this small agricultural town ninety miles west of Washington when he was a teen-ager.

"Hi, you two," he said, entering the hospital room Kermit and Duane shared. "How do you feel?"

Kermit nodded from his pillow and grinned self-consciously, raising his lower right arm, which was in a cast. A canvas sling, stretched tightly across his right shoulder and chest, was visible under his loose white hospital gown.

"Like I had an accident," Duane answered, lying half upright in the adjacent bed. "I hurt all over." His nose was swathed in bandages and adhesive tape crisscrossed his face like a goaltender's mask.

"You both got away lucky," Adam said. "How's Dana doing?"

"She got the worst of it," Kermit said. "Three broken ribs, a dislocated shoulder and some lacerations of the scalp. The doctors thought at first she might have a skull fracture but it turned out to be a bad concussion. Yuki is visiting her now. He's the luckiest. Just some bruises on his right side."

"I see you've got a broken nose, Duane. Is it painful?"

"They reset it and taped it up, but it hurts like hell. And I've got a nonstop headache from a brain concussion. But I guess I shouldn't complain. Kermit broke his collarbone and his arm."

Kermit pointed to a chair with his cast. "Sit down, Adam. Let's talk. But if I fade away, it's because of the Demerol they're feeding me."

Adam pulled the chair near Kermit's bed. "The first time I saw the four of you in my office, I said you were the most respectable-looking

221

dissidents—or was it subversives?—I had ever met. You look more in character now. Like the gendarmes did a number on you."

"Somebody did," Kermit said. "It was no accident. They tried to kill us."

"What are you talking about? The news reports said it was an accident, that the car skidded off the mountain road in a blinding rainstorm. They said you would have dropped down a sheer cliff if the car had skidded to the right instead of the left. They said also . . . I guess you know this by now . . . that Cynthia Kellogg was identified as a private investigator and she was killed when the car impacted with a boulder on her side and crushed her against the steering wheel."

"I probably would have been killed too," Kermit said, "if the door on my side hadn't sprung open and tossed me out. Dana was on the left side and she got the impact. The park rangers said we all would have been killed if the undercarriage hadn't hit some rocks and slowed us down."

"I landed on Dana and Yuki landed on me," Duane put in. "She cushioned the impact. Then the Shenandoah Park Service called the hospital, and the Luray Volunteer Rescue Squad picked us up in two ambulances. I was riding with Cynthia. . . ."

Adam looked mystified. "I don't understand, you had an accident. How could it be anything else?"

Kermit told how Cynthia had become strangely silent once they entered the mountain road, how she seemed to be searching for something and how the two cars had suddenly appeared and headed toward them on both sides of the one-lane road, forcing them toward the cliff. "If Cynthia wasn't such a skillful driver, she wouldn't have been able to turn off the way she did. It saved our lives. It also cost her hers . . . no, it was no accident. Two cars coming straight at us to send us off the cliff . . . *she* knew it was no accident . . . just before she died I heard her say, *'tried to kill me too, double cross.'* "

"That sounds like she was involved. Who do you think she meant?"

"I wish I knew. After all, she was working for us and doing a good job—"

"Whoever had Kermit drugged was behind this," Duane said. "No question."

Adam looked skeptical. "Morstan? Somehow I doubt he would dare go that far. He wouldn't take the chance a second time. Besides, we don't know for sure that Morstan was connected with the drugging—"

222

"You don't know the man—he's kind of crazy," and Duane heard Lyle's voice echo in his ears. "It's not only that bill of his anymore. It's beyond that . . . it's his ambition for the Presidency—that's worth daring to take the chance to stop us—or anybody else—a second time, or as many as it takes."

"I can't buy that," Adam said. "I don't see the necessary connection—"

"Don't you *see* . . . he had all of us in the car at the same time," Duane said. "He wanted us *all* dead—not just Kermit. That means he thought we were all a threat to him and—"

"He must have figured we knew something that could expose him," Kermit interrupted. "If one of us found it out, we all must know it. . . ."

"The drugging? . . . the Quaritius connection?" Duane said. "Cynthia and I were working on both angles. Maybe he found out we were making progress. We were moving around, asking questions. He must have gotten on to it."

"It's beginning to fit," Kermit said, propping up his pillow and easing his body higher. "This is the first chance we've had to talk about it since the crash. Quaritius may have had something to do with it. We know that he was meeting with Morstan. And if they thought that Cynthia had found out something, they'd want to kill her too. Jesus. . . ."

Adam shifted in his chair. "From what you tell me, Kermit, Cynthia seemed to know who *they* were . . . you said that she said 'double cross.' That must mean she was in on it too. . . ."

Duane shook his head emphatically. "I don't buy that. I knew her pretty well. . . ."

"Not well enough, apparently." Kermit looked at his friend. "What other conclusion could you come to?"

"We'll never really know, will we? I prefer to leave it that way. What's to be gained now that she's dead?"

Adam and Kermit exchanged glances, thinking the same thing.

"Well, since the news media have reported it as an accident," Adam said, "I suggest that for now we let it go at that. We can't prove otherwise and going to the media accusing a senator of murder with only suspicions could be dangerous stuff. No one will believe you. In fact, it might raise doubts about the credibility of your drugging story and about your motives generally. Let it go as an accident unless we can come up with some proof. And I think it would be dangerous even to try to look for it. You've been lucky twice now. . . ."

Kermit massaged his almost two-day stubble. "The question is, how do we protect ourselves from here on?"

"We could ask for police protection, but I'm not sure we'd get it, since we can't say this wasn't an accident. Or you could hire a private security service and hope they can't be reached or infiltrated."

"I guess the best protection would be to avoid exposing ourselves together at any one time," Kermit said. "If they can't get us together, they're not likely to try separately. Do me a favor, you two. Play this down with Dana and Yuki—they're shook up enough already."

Adam nodded. "Do you think you'll be well enough for the trial? The preliminary proceedings begin in about two and a half weeks."

"I think so," Kermit said. "Dana's the only question mark. We can check that out with her doctor. By the way, her father and mother were here this morning. They're very nice people. They want to move her to a hospital in Winston-Salem, where they live. Dana would have none of it."

Adam slapped his thighs decisively and rose to his feet. "Well, I've spent enough time jawing with you two bums. Besides, I think you're really goldbricking. I'm going to drop in on Dana now and see how she's getting by."

Chapter Twenty-Seven

In the beginning of May a one-week radio and television blitz of one minute commercials in support of the Morstan-Windmiller bill was launched by Americans United. It saturated the airwaves for a concentrated period just in advance of the bill's coming up for debate in the Congress.

Kermit, Dana and Duane, lying in their hospital beds, heard the commercials and kept turning them off. Yuki had already returned to Duane's apartment, and Harriet had joined him there.

On Thursday, May 8, S. 17 was brought up for debate in the Senate. Because of the highly controversial nature of the bill, the Senate Policy Committee and the House Rules Committee each allowed three full days for their consideration. Predictably, the debate aroused violent passions and opposing speakers hurled at each other charges of "un-American," "unpatriotic," "left-winger," and countercharges of "totalitarianism," "police state" and "computerized McCarthyism."

By noon on a rainy Saturday, the third day of the virulent confrontation, the Senate was anxious to bring the controversial measure to a vote. There was no way to tell from the polemics which way the battle was going, and the leadership of both sides remained closed-mouthed about anticipated support. The only thing apparent was that senatorial reactions to the bill crisscrossed party lines, so that liberal Democrats and many conservative Republicans were surprised to find themselves on the same side opposed to the bill while many conservative Democrats and moderate Republicans teamed up arguing for it.

When the vote was finally taken and announced in the Senate chamber there was a moment of shocked silence, then pandemonium broke loose. The vote was fifty-five to forty-three in favor, an unexpectedly large margin.

Kermit, Dana, Yuki and Duane were shocked by the news, which they did not hear together. Kermit was getting around in a motorized wheelchair he manipulated with his left arm and spending several hours a day with Dana, who was still in pain but mending well. Duane had left the hospital after five days and gone to Marcia Milliken's apartment and her ministrations; both his eyes remained blackened from the nose fracture. Yuki and Harriet were still together and getting along reasonably well, but below the surface Harriet was apprehensive about their relationship.

Duane phoned the hospital that Saturday night and the three talked for a long time, Dana and Kermit taking turns on the phone. They wondered whether a similar result might be lurking in the House wing of the Capitol, which would send the bill to the President for signing, and make everything they had done seem for nothing. They would just have to wait and pray. Their upcoming trial seemed an almost distant fantasy. . . .

The day after the car crash Duane had told the others about his contretemps with Jacqueline Lardner. No one was in a mood to fault him for what he'd done, but he hadn't been ready to discuss it with Adam Greenfield when the attorney had visited them that first day. But soon after he returned to Washington Duane did report the episode to Greenfield, who said it was interesting and important he know about it. Having said that calmly, he then criticized Duane sharply for meddling in a situation that could affect the outcome of the case, warning that if he couldn't be a client rather than an investigative reporter, the four of them would have to get another attorney to defend them. He pointed out that, given certain circumstances, Duane might have turned the senator's mistress into a very effective witness for the prosecution. Duane got the message, although he resented the tongue-lashing. He had also made no progress with his Pentagon and FBI contacts in trying to get something definitive on Quaritius's connection with Morstan, or on the drugging episode. He was beginning to feel very much like a bungler (he didn't even want to think about the fact that it had been he who'd introduced them to Cynthia, though she *might* have been innocent . . .).

Chapter Twenty-Eight

On May 15—two days after Kermit and Dana returned from the hospital—the month's extended deadline for filing of tax returns expired. The government made no announcement about the result, but newsmen who covered IRS learned off the record that close to the normal number of returns belatedly came in. The fifty-billion-dollar emergency seemed over. The tax strike had lost its steam, but the widespread protest gesture *had* made its point. . . .

That morning Charles Windmiller, acting as floor manager for the bill here labeled H.R. 191, introduced it on the floor of the House. The debate was as bitter as in the Senate a few days earlier, but this time those opposing seemed better organized. An unprecedented number of the 435 House members were on hand. The head of steam generated the first day exploded by midmorning of the second. Amendments to modify the bill in opposing directions were proposed and struck down. Several congressional leaders representing the Administration tried to work out a compromise acceptable to both sides through an amendment which would give a joint congressional committee an oversight role in the event private computer systems were taken over by the federal government in a declared national security emergency. But Representative Windmiller, after conferring with Senator Waggoner, his opposite number in the upper chamber, would have none of it.

By early afternoon on Thursday, the second day of the debate, the

228

House was ready to vote. The representatives rose in ragged clusters and assembled around the forty-eight electronic voting stations throughout the chamber on the aisles. One by one they inserted their computer-coded plastic I.D. cards into the slot and pressed either the "yea" or "nay" button. Behind the Speaker the electronic board lit up the names of the representative in green or red in rapid succession in the yea or nay column. On the walls to the right and left of the Speaker, on the level of the overhead galleries, electronic scoreboards flashed the changing totals in amber as the voting proceeded. The vote had to be completed within the allotted fifteen minutes and the clock was counting down to zero. With four minutes to spare, the total vote was frozen in amber on both sides of the chamber. The gaunt, dignified Speaker of the House gave it voice in a broad western accent.

"The final vote on H.R. 191 is 213 for"—he paused to clear his throat uncomfortably—"and 213 against." A loud buzz darted about the huge chamber and he gaveled it down. "Is there anyone who has not as yet voted? Very well, in view of the tie vote, I elect to exercise my option so that a clear-cut decision will be rendered on this important legislation by both houses of Congress." The detritus of random sounds was suddenly gone. He spoke clearly and slowly into the microphone before him, his hairless, parchment-like pate shining with sweat. "On H.R. 191, the Speaker votes . . . 'yes.' "

Duane got the word within minutes from *Newswatch*'s man on the Hill. He immediately dialed Dana's apartment, where she and Kermit were waiting for the call and told her the news.

"It couldn't have happened," she said distractedly as she hung up the phone, but the disaster was in her eyes.

Kermit read them. "My *god,* it passed. . . ."

Dana picked up a Lenox china vase and flung it crashing against the opposite wall. "No, no, no, it couldn't have happened. Don't they *know* what they've done? Didn't we accomplish *anything?* We almost got ourselves killed and those dumb bastards sit on their iron asses and vote democracy into the ashcan. Fuck them, fuck them one and all—"

She burst out sobbing and Kermit took her in his arms. His own anger and misery was smothered in her. She'd said it all. Now the only thing that could prevent the final debacle was a Presidential veto, which wasn't worth thinking about. The Administration's attempt to secure passage through a compromise amendment was confirmation of that. The only thing left was the trial, to try to show the country there that the defendants should really be the plaintiffs, suing over the dangers they'd tried to expose, and that the government should be the defendant for having created those dangers. That was one hell of an assignment.

That evening after dinner Duane met with Kermit and Dana in her apartment. Yuki, deeply upset by the news, had gone home to Chelsea with Harriet for the weekend.

Dana's ribs still pained her and the healing wounds in her scalp were itchy. The cast had been removed from Kermit's arm, but he wore a sling to keep it immobile and his collarbone was still strapped. Duane's black eyes were now a pale purple and a small white triangular patch covered his nose; with his full lips and unruly hair he had the look of a tribal medicine man.

But there was nothing therapeutic in the atmosphere. They still felt in danger of their lives. And they were now convinced that their chances of coming out on top in the trial were not good. Even if they won the case and convinced the country of the need for sweeping reforms in computer control and management, the new Federal Computer Management Law, as it was now being called, would make such legislation impossible. And with Morstan riding high on the passage of his bill and the momentum it added to his candidacy, there was a better than good possibility that the resident of 1600 Pennsylvania Avenue come next January would be President Gunther Morstan. Which was the most chilling prospect of all.

The jury selection was scheduled to begin on Monday, May 19. The last weekend was an almost metaphysical experience for Kermit and Dana. They spoke very little and yet somehow communicated at a deeper level. He felt her fluttering apprehension and fear, so strange to this independent, freewheeling woman. For the first time in her life she was in a situation that threatened her because she couldn't outwit it, outfight it, laugh at it or, face it, let daddy buy it off. She was too gutsy and proud to voice her feelings except to say, "I love you, Kermit," many times, in many places, but her wide-set gray-green eyes said it all.

Chapter Twenty-Nine

It wasn't the bright sunshine through the bedroom window that awakened Dana and Kermit earlier than usual on Monday, May 19. It was the alarm clock on the night table. They were to meet Adam Greenfield in the courthouse at nine o'clock. They had slept peacefully, despite the portents of the next day, after a single, tender act of lovemaking—a sensuous amulet to ward off, as it were, impending evil? Afterward they'd held each other tight until sleep overtook them.

Now they dressed and breakfasted quickly, emerging downstairs in front of the Berkshire. They found a cab on Massachusetts Avenue and drove downtown to Duane's apartment, where they picked up Yuki, dressed in a dark blue lightweight suit, white shirt and a conservative tie, looking like he was going either to a bar mitzvah or a wake. Nobody mentioned the latter.

They continued on to the U.S. Court House occupying the entire block on Constitution Avenue between John Marshall Place and Third Street. As they started across the long walkway to the main entrance of the modern, squarish, six-story building, they sensed that once through those portals they would never be again as they were at this moment.

Dana took hold of Yuki's and Kermit's hands and the three marched toward the entrance, Kermit's arm still in a sling. They took an elevator to the second floor and went to the Attorneys' Lounge where they met Adam Greenfield. It was ten after nine, and Duane was already there talking with Greenfield and Andrew Bonaventura, who had done much of the legal research and would assist in the trial. Bonaventura was a dark, slender man of medium height with a round pleasant face and small dark eyes. His thin-rimmed glasses and slightly cherubic lips gave him a bemused, scholarly appearance. Greenfield introduced his young associate and told them that while Kermit was the only one of the four he planned to put on the stand, he might decide to call any one of them as the trial developed.

Promptly at nine-thirty, he led them down the long, spacious corridor to courtroom number three. A large group of people, held in check by two policemen, were lined up to one side of the entrance. To the right of the large double doors, a framed panel listed the plaintiff and defendants in the trial. It looked very official and ominous as it caught the eye of the four.

The courtroom was sizable and functionally modern but not as large and impressive as Kermit expected. He knew they would be living here for a good part of the month and he found himself oddly interested in the details of the scene, as though he wanted to file it for future reference. The room was brightly lit with recessed lighting in the slightly vaulted three-story-high ceiling, and the windowless walls were surfaced with light walnut panels. As they walked by them Kermit took in the ten rows of heavy, clean-lined walnut benches on both sides of the rear portion of the room. In the open middle area were two long conference-type matching walnut tables, each with six dark-red vinyl-covered chairs. The table to the left had a small printed sign reading PLAINTIFF, while the one to the right read DEFENDANTS. The judge's bench in front of the room was a bow-shaped wooden affair raised a couple of feet above the broad, curved enclosure of the court clerk's and stenographer's desk. A lectern stand in front of the clerk's enclosure held a microphone sticking out like a short mast. The jury box against the left wall held two rows of eight chairs each, the rear row on a higher level. A narrow desklike table stood to the right of the defendants' table. Centered on the front wall directly behind the judge's bench was a huge embossed-gold Seal of the United States set in a wide, floor-to-ceiling dark-green marble slab. The only people in the courtroom were two policemen standing just inside the entrance door, a court clerk wandering around checking on things, and a fortyish woman sitting sedately in the court stenographer's box.

Greenfield assigned seats around their table, putting Andy Bonaventura to his right, Kermit next and the other three on the opposite side of the table. A few minutes later, the U.S. Attorney, Eric Hinckley, entered briskly with two assistant U.S. attorneys carrying two attaché cases each which they slapped down on their table. Hinckley was a compact, middle-size man in his late forties with a Vermont churchgoer's flat-cheeked face capable of wrathful scowls and quick charming smiles. His faded brown hair was stranded with gray and his blond eyebrows were invisible. Deep creases parenthesized his thin mouth. The opposing attorneys obviously knew each other, shaking hands, joking about missing Judge Sirica's old Watergate courtroom number by one. It was the fraternal joviality of professionals displaying their coolness before the shoot-out.

At 9:45, a woman in her mid-thirties arrived with a stocky man a few years older and they conferred with Greenfield and Bonaventura briefly out of earshot of the four, then took seats behind the small table off to the right. Bonaventura moved over to sit between them for the jury selection process. Greenfield explained to his four clients that the woman was a professor of psychology at the University of Maryland and the man a sociologist with the research firm which had done the Community Profile study he had ordered for the case. They would help eliminate prospective jurors most likely to be hostile to the defendants. He invited the four to feel free to comment on the prospective jurors or "PJs," as he called them.

Almost precisely at ten o'clock, Federal Judge Frederick Huddleston entered, heavy-set and dignified in his black robe, and sat behind his broad elevated bench. His deep-set eyes hid under prominent brows which curled upward at the ends, and his protruding jaw jowled into his neck. After ascertaining that the prosecuting and defense attorneys were ready, Judge Huddleston ordered fifty prospective jurors led into the courtroom and seated in one of the two sections of spectator seats. He looked directly at them. "I want to thank all of you for giving us your time today. Before we begin the jury selection process, I would like to ask if any of you feel you should be excused or disqualified from serving on this jury for any reason. If so, please raise your hand and state the reason."

Seven hands went up and one by one the judge let them speak. He denied three as being invalid reasons, but did let four leave because of personal hardship or obvious bias. The judge then turned to the clerk seated below him. "Draw the names," he directed. The clerk spun the small drum on his desk, withdrew the names and read them aloud, requesting those called to occupy the jury box.

When the jury box was filled, the judge explained the *voir dire* procedure of questioning and qualifying jurors. Then he asked each one in the box a series of questions which were basically the same but varied somewhat in the follow-up questioning depending upon their initial answers: "Do you know anyone connected in any way with this case, either Mr. Hinckley or a member of his staff, or Mr. Greenfield or a member of his firm or any of the four defendants or any of the witnesses? . . . Are you related to anyone who is employed by the Internal Revenue Service? . . . Have you read press accounts or heard broadcast reports concerning this case or charges against the defendants? . . . As a result of what you heard or read, have you formed any opinions? . . . Despite any opinions you now have, can you hear the evidence that will be presented and without fear or favor make an impartial decision?"

After dismissing several of the candidates on the basis of their responses, Judge Huddleston asked each of the survivors a variety of questions about their backgrounds, vocations and affiliations. Then, with inevitable repetition which sometimes was amusing, Judge Huddleston queried each of the remaining individuals: "Do you think breaking the law is ever justified? . . . Do you think the government is always right? . . . Do you feel that citizens have a right to protest against government policies or practices? . . . Do you think the government has the right to violate individual privacy for the benefit of the country? . . . Do you believe that individual rights are more important than the national security? . . . Are you familiar with the Bill of Rights? . . . Do you disagree with any of its provisions? . . . Do you think that college instructors have the right to express their political views to their students? . . . Do you think that many college instructors are too liberal for the good of their students? . . . Do you have any strong objections to the policies or practices of the Internal Revenue Service?" Those who showed a pattern of consistent bias were dismissed and replaced by others.

The slow process ground on during the day, interrupted quite often by requests by one of the assistant U.S. attorneys or Andy Bonaventura for further questions to a particular individual. Both sides were making notes, listing those they wanted as jurors and those they would challenge.

Bonaventura conferred in low tones with the psychologist and sociologist sitting on either side of him. Greenfield was keeping his own score on a yellow legal pad, and occasionally one or another of the defendants would express an opinion.

Periodically the court clerk approached Hinckley and Greenfield to receive their peremptory challenges. After he conferred with Judge Huddleston, people would be thanked and dismissed, new names would be drawn and called from those remaining in the spectators' section and they would fill the empty seats in the jury box and the process would repeat itself. By four-thirty, only six of the required fourteen, including two alternates, had been agreed upon and chosen and only three of the original pool of fifty remained uncalled. The judge, weary, announced that the Court would adjourn until nine the next morning.

After the four defendants left the courthouse and broke through the cordon of reporters, they made a point of going their separate ways for security reasons: Kermit and Dana took a taxi together and Duane and Yuki went to their separate apartments. They still had that overriding fear to contend with.

When court resumed the next morning a fresh batch of prospective jurors was shepherded into the spectator section; this time there were seventy-five. Judge Huddleston called Hinckley and Greenfield to the bench.

"Gentlemen," he said in a low voice, "we can speed up the *voir dire* without diminishing your clients' interests if you will cooperate. You've both used up most of your peremptory challenges and I will permit very few challenges for cause unless they have substantial merit. You both did too much nitpicking yesterday. I have no intention of wasting the Court's time and the government's money on trivial objections. Understood?"

The admonition worked. After using up their remaining peremptory challenges, the prosecution and the defense attorneys challenged more selectively, citing their reasons. Face followed face—a young housewife, a nervous middle-aged government statistician, a thirtyish stockbroker, an auto mechanic, a pharmacist, a rather effete government clerk, a self-assured industrial salesman, a smiling practical nurse, a taxi driver, a vice-president of a nonprofit foundation . . . a succession of sweet-faced and complacent, prim and diffident, urbane and talkative women and men, black and white, of various ages, most of whom worked for the government. Their faces tumbled past like the names in the spinning

235

drum from which they were drawn. This was a random selection of citizens from the District of Columbia where America's black minority was the majority, though they were clearly less than a majority in this courtroom.

The procession of faces and voices and mannerisms, the droning questions from Huddleston, the dismissal of people for cause, the spinning of the little wooden drum, the new cards of candidates replacing the old in the portable panel board, Bonaventura's steady conferring with the psychologist and sociologist, the low-voiced, bench-side discussions among the judge and Hinckley and Greenfield continued during the long morning and resumed after the lunch recess. By four o'clock, eleven jurors were selected and were seated in the box.

Anxious to wind up the tedious process, Huddleston, his face strained and his voice acquiring a rough edge, decided to press on a bit longer. By 5:15, the twelfth juror, a shoe store proprietor, was selected along with two alternatives. The judge adjourned court until ten the next morning, rose and disappeared through the left side door to the robing room. Hinckley and Greenfield shook hands cordially, each feeling that he had come away with an advantage in the completed jury as the result of astute maneuvering.

Chapter Thirty

The next morning running the gauntlet of the crowds gathered on the broad walkway leading to the entrance of the U.S. Court House, was a unique and frightening experience for the four. It was such a contrast in volume from the previous two days, as though the street throng separated the preliminaries from the main event and now sensed blood. The four of them couldn't help wondering whether those pressing in on them didn't include a potential assassin. And the feeling persisted when they emerged from the elevator on the second floor; several hundred noisy people were queued up and kept in double rows by policemen outside the courtroom doors.

The plaintiff and defendant tables were occupied by the opposing attorneys with their papers neatly stacked. The court stenographer and clerk were in place behind their long, curving enclosure in front of the judge's bench. Several attendants and policemen were moving about. At 9:45 the doors were opened and the policemen at the entrance fed in a stream of people with passes in their hands. The news media people filled most of the two-hundred-seat capacity of the two sections of ten rows of benches, leaving only a few dozen reserved for interested parties and selected members of congressional staffs and government agencies. The door from the front left opened and the court clerk intoned, "All rise, the Honorable Frederick Huddleston, Federal Judge of the U.S. Court,

District of Columbia." The gray-haired, severe-looking jurist entered and took his place.

Yuki was startled when he caught a glimpse of Harriet in the second row. He wondered how she had arranged to get a ticket. He had left her in Chelsea the previous week and she had said nothing about coming to the trial. He was glad she wanted to be here with them.

The austere, official singsong voice of the court clerk rang out again: "The United States against Kermit Nordstrom, Duane Crozier, Dana Haverhill and Yukio Ishizaka." It sounded like the damn voice of doom. Judge Huddleston looked around the crowded courtroom, raised his head and said in a deep, measured voice, "I realize that there is special interest in this trial and there are controversial questions that will be decided here. The facilities of this courtroom are being severely taxed, and I must insist that the rules of the court be strictly obeyed. There will be no talking, no outbursts, no interruptions from any of the participants, members of the news media or other spectators while this court is in session. I will not have this court turned into a circus. I hope I have made myself clear."

Adam Greenfield looked at Andy Bonaventura. The old boy was starting out in character.

Huddleston looked at the chief prosecutor. "Mr. Hinckley, will you proceed with your opening statement."

Eric Hinckley rose with conscious solemnity, walked toward the lectern, then turned and faced the jury box with his feet planted slightly apart and his hands clasped below the waist. "May it please the Court, ladies and gentlemen of the jury. The government will prove beyond a reasonable doubt that the defendants, Kermit Nordstrom, Duane Crozier, Dana Haverhill and Yukio Ishizaka, are guilty of the charges of Seditious Conspiracy; Conspiracy to Commit Offense against the United States; Concealment, Removal or Mutilation of Public Records and Reports; and Embezzlement and Theft of Public Records. The government will prove that these four defendants did conspire together with malice aforethought for the purpose of damaging a vital agency of the government, namely the Internal Revenue Service, and in fact did carry out a destructive act of sabotage to impede that agency in carrying out its legal functions as the collector of taxes. We will prove that their intent was to weaken the economy of the United States to make it vulnerable to subversion by those, like themselves, who wish to change

238

our form of government by stealth from the democracy it is to something alien to our Constitution and to all loyal Americans."

Kermit listened intently to the compact figure with the clipped New England speech as, step by step, Hinckley made the formidable list of serious charges sound plausible and the proof of their guilt inevitable. Kermit noticed that during the damning statement, a number of jurors looked at the defendants as though trying to equate those young, intelligent faces with the heinous crimes. He himself was impressed with the force and seeming credibility of Hinckley's ten minute presentation. It made him shiver inside.

Greenfield was on his feet the moment Hinckley started back to his seat, even before the judge nodded for him to open. He faced the judge and then turned to the jury, his hands at his sides. His voice was calm but emphatic. "Your Honor, ladies and gentlemen of the jury. The statement you have just heard from the U.S. Attorney was eloquent and interesting. It contained all the assumptions and suppositions about this case the government would like you to believe. I am certain that Mr. Hinckley believes all these statements and charges himself. I have always known him to be as sincere as he is persuasive. But I am forced to say that these charges are the biggest collection of fantasies I have ever encountered in a courtroom. As the facts emerge from the evidence you will have the opportunity of determining for yourselves that what these four young people did could not have been an attempt to overthrow the government of the United States—and that is what Seditious Conspiracy is. Nor did they conspire to commit an offense against the United States, but rather they acted to *protect* the United States from the offenses of others. Nor did they conceal, remove or mutilate public records and reports—because the records and reports of the Internal Revenue Service are intact and operating, as those of you who have filed your returns and paid your taxes know. As for the fourth charge, the government will be unable to prove that any public records were embezzled by the defendants because such an act did not take place."

Greenfield paused and scanned the faces of the jurors, then put his hands in his jacket pockets, relaxing his stance. "The defense will readily admit that the four people you see before you did indeed cause the computers of the Internal Revenue Service to perform certain unauthorized tasks, but none of these tasks in any way damaged the facilities of that agency or weakened the economy of the country, nor was it their

239

intention to do so. On the contrary, the defense will show beyond the possibility of reasonable doubt that the only intent of these four people was to *preserve* our democracy by demonstrating two things to the American public—one, that very serious and continuing violations of the privacy and of other civil rights of each one of us is being committed every day by the federal government—the same government that accuses them—through illegal use of computer systems and data banks. And, two, that the government itself is *vulnerable* to access by computer and must be protected from potential enemies in the interests of our nation's security. What these four dedicated people have done is the highest form of citizenship—to alert the country to these dangers they put their professional careers and futures in jeopardy. Once you have heard the evidence, I am sure you will have no trouble in deciding that my clients are *not guilty* of *any* of the charges and indeed that they are guilty only of being dedicated to their country and to constitutional democracy."

He walked back to the counsel table and the voice from the elevated bench reached out through the silence. "The government may call its first witness."

A stocky man in his late thirties with thinning dark hair and a squarish, pleasant face came forward with the bouncy gait of an athlete and sat in the witness chair. He was duly sworn in by the clerk.

Hinckley approached him. "What is your name and occupation, sir?" His voice was dry but friendly.

"Gilbert Eisenstadt. I'm systems director of the National Office of Computer Facilities of the Internal Revenue Service in Washington."

"How long have you been in that position, Mr. Eisenstadt?"

"Four years. I was assistant systems director for three years before that."

Hinckley extracted the highlights of the witness's impressive professional background, including his doctoral degree in computer science from Carnegie Institute of Technology, his positions as a systems analyst and designer at IBM, and his work as a systems consultant at Rand Corporation before joining IRS. Hinckley immediately began referring to him as Dr. Eisenstadt.

"What are your responsibilities now as systems director?"

"Well, the function of our division is to design the systems and create the programs for our computer network and to select and test the equipment and systems purchased from various manufacturers before they're

240

installed in our computer network. My job is to supervise this function."

"That sounds like a key position requiring broad expertise. Would you say that you have thorough knowledge of the systems which operate your agency's nationwide computer network?"

"I would say I do."

"Would you describe for the court the Internal Revenue Service's computer network in nontechnical language and give us an overview of how it operates?"

Eisenstadt raised his eyebrows in thought for a moment. "There are ten computer centers throughout the country. We call them Service Centers. To put it simply, these Service Centers do all the actual computations on the quarterly and annual tax forms which come in, and they send the verified accounts to the National Computer Center in Martinsburg, West Virginia. That's the heart of the network where the master data bank is located. Martinsburg has the programs which process the incoming accounts and makes the decisions on each one and issues them in the form of instructions to the originating Service Center. There the various notices—for hearings, audits, bills, refunds, whatever—are processed and sent out. That's about it."

"So we have ten Service Centers around the country and we have the Central System in Martinsburg. How do they send this data and instructions back and forth to each other?"

"The computers talk to each other, in digital code, over telephone company wires. In most cases distances are involved so the messages are bounced off a communications satellite at great speed."

Hinckley folded his arms over his chest. "In your expert opinion, is it possible for anyone outside of IRS to gain access to your computer operations through a remote terminal or in any other way?"

"It's always theoretically possible. There's no foolproof system. Any computer system, regardless of safeguards, theoretically can be accessed by someone with sufficient expertise and intimate knowledge of the system. But where the systems architecture and the procedures down the line have the built-in safeguards that we have, that every important federal agency has, the possibility of unauthorized access is so remote as to be virtually nonexistent."

"Well, sir," Hinckley said with anticipation, "how do you account for the fact that IRS's entire computer network was successfully invaded

241

and sabotaged by these four defendants, none of whom are in any way connected with the Internal Revenue Service?"

Greenfield was on his feet. "Objection! The prosecution has offered no evidence tying my clients to any acts of sabotage. It is the defense's contention that the defendants committed no acts of sabotage and unless and until the prosecution can prove otherwise, I must insist that Mr. Hinckley refrain from making that statement or any such implication."

Huddleston nodded. "Sustained. Counsel will withdraw or rephrase the question."

Hinckley really didn't expect to get away with it, but he'd gotten it out, the jurors heard it. "Dr. Eisenstadt, since you say that the possibility of unauthorized access to your computer network is virtually nonexistent, although theoretically possible, then what kind of person or persons do you think would be able to pull off such a job? What qualifications would they need?"

"Objection," Greenfield said routinely without rising. "It calls for a speculative answer."

"Mr. Hinckley?" the judge said.

"We've already established the witness's authority in this area. We're asking for his professional judgment, not speculation."

Greenfield suddenly thought he saw a hole in the U.S. Attorney's question; he'd let him fall into it and use it in his cross-exam. "I withdraw the objection," he said casually.

Hinckley looked at Greenfield curiously and then turned to the witness. "Do you want me to repeat the question?"

The IRS man smiled. "No, I remember it." He paused, then spoke slowly and deliberately. "I'd say that an individual capable of accessing our network and making our computers behave the way they did would have to be an extraordinary person in many ways. He would have to be a brilliant systems specialist with exceptional knowledge of the most advanced technology in hardware, including built-in and procedural safeguards, as well as in software. As I said before, he would also have to have intimate working knowledge of our entire system and tremendous motivation. It's a monumentally difficult thing to do."

"Would you say that the person or persons who illegally accessed IRS's sophisticated computer network and wrought such havoc on its operations would have to have had a special entree to the system—some privileged opportunity of penetration other than a remote terminal?"

242

"Definitely."

"You stated before that your agency's Service Centers and Central System in Martinsburg communicated with each other's computers through a communications satellite. Is that correct?"

"Yes it is."

"Would you say that someone who worked with the computers of the Communications Satellite Corporation, commonly known as COMSAT, and had authorized access to those computers would be in a unique position to figure out a way to penetrate your network through a satellite?"

"I'd say he'd have the best chance."

"Do you know of another way?"

"None that I think would work."

Yuki shifted in his seat and looked uncomfortably at Greenfield across the table. The attorney leaned over and whispered assurances, but he knew that Hinckley was leading up to the testimony of his next witness to nail Yuki as the triggerman.

Hinckley then questioned the witness about the abnormal performance of IRS's computer network on March 14 and he produced several documents—described as Prosecution Exhibit A—which Eisenstadt identified as printouts of the five sets of unauthorized instructions, and which were allegedly activated by the defendants. Hinckley did not ask the witness to describe the contents of the printouts, but asked why the unauthorized instructions couldn't be detected and what were the findings of IRS's own investigation.

Eisenstadt replied: "We came to the conclusion that since the Central System had no record of the false instructions being issued from there to the Service Centers, even though the messages carried the proper identification code from Martinsburg, the Central System had been bypassed and the messages originated from another source. The only possible source was through a communications satellite computer."

Hinckley had skillfully steered his witness to pointing for the second time to someone privy to COMSAT computers. "Your witness," he said to the courtroom in general, pleased with the testimony he'd gotten.

Huddleston had other ideas. "It's too late in the morning to begin cross-examination. This court is adjourned until one P.M. Jurors are cautioned not to discuss this case among yourselves or with the press or with anyone else. I hope that's understood." He rose and hurried to the door leading to his chambers, his flowing robe transforming him to a huge black bird in passage.

As the attorneys pushed their chairs back from the table, Andy Bonaventura said, "He sure seemed in a hurry to get out of here."

Adam Greenfield smiled. "It's his famous weak bladder."

The defense entourage of two attorneys and the four accused were mobbed before they got out of the courtroom, pressed by reporters bombarding them with questions. When they got to waiting taxis to take them to nearby restaurants, Yuki wasn't with them. Duane spotted him running for a taxi around the corner on Connecticut Avenue with Harriet on his arm and two photographers in pursuit. . . .

Court resumed at one o'clock. Gilbert Eisenstadt took his seat in the witness box and was reminded that his oath was still in force. On signal from Judge Huddleston, Adam Greenfield approached and addressed the witness. His tone was conversational.

"Dr. Eisenstadt, your testimony this morning was expert and useful. But you used a few terms which are not familiar to most laymen. I think it would be helpful to the jury and to the rest of us if you would clarify them. Would you please define the terms "hardware" and "software," which you used in referring to knowledge of advanced technology."

"Certainly. Hardware means computer equipment of any kind, and software refers primarily to programs which operate computers."

"Thank you." The request was simply to put the witness at ease for the cross-exam and possibly earn a few credits with the jury. "You testified this morning, Dr. Eisenstadt, that anyone capable of accessing IRS's complex computer network would have to have exceptional knowledge of the most advanced technology, an intimate working knowledge of your entire system and tremendous motivation. I think those were your exact words. Is that correct?"

"Yes."

"All right. In your expert opinion wouldn't it be possible for someone with those qualifications to be an employee or an ex-employee of your agency's computer network in Martinsburg or in some other strategic IRS post? . . . and in that way to have an intimate working knowledge of your entire system?"

Eisenstadt sat there studying the loophole and deciding how to handle it. He became cautious. "I would say that is extremely unlikely because the system is so complex that no one person among our computer personnel knows everything he would have to know to access the system in the way this was done."

"Even you?"

"Even me."

Greenfield hid his disappointment. "I know that IRS has a computer research division and I believe that one of their chief functions is to develop more efficient procedures and better safeguards for your data processing operations. Is that correct?"

"Substantially."

"Please answer yes or no."

"Yes."

"As systems director of IRS's National Office of Computer Facilities, you testified that your division's function was to design the systems and programs used in your network. Am I correct in that?" Greenfield was taking no chances, leading him in small steps.

"Yes." Eisenstadt's complacency was starting to slip. He didn't know what the defense attorney was leading up to.

"In designing systems and programs, aren't you and certain individuals in your division involved in the security of your network and in your intercity data communications?"

"I can't answer that with a flat yes or no."

"Okay, answer it your way."

"The fact is that my work is primarily administrative. There are several people in my division who are concerned with systems security as one of the considerations in systems design and operations."

"I assume that you are similarly knowledgeable about network security, despite your administrative duties, or you wouldn't have been involved as an expert in your agency's investigation. Isn't that correct?"

Hinckley was on his feet. "Objection! This man is not on trial, Your Honor. Dr. Eisenstadt is a prosecution witness and defense counsel is exceeding his mandate under cross-examination, as he's well aware."

"I have no intention of impugning this witness's motives or his actions in any way. I am simply leading up to a point relevant to his earlier testimony, which is basic to the defense's case."

Huddleston puffed out his lips. "You may proceed subject to connection."

"Would you like me to repeat the question?" Greenfield said, turning to the witness.

245

"That won't be necessary," Eisenstadt replied coldly. "Yes, I do have an overall knowledge of our security technology but it is not one of my responsibilities."

"How about outside organizations which make some input to your systems, such as manufacturers of equipment used in your network—IBM, Honeywell, Control Data Corporation—or outside consulting firms such as Cybernet Associates which, I understand, has a consulting contract with IRS. Some of their top systems experts served on the investigating committee appointed by the President to find out where and how your security was penetrated. It's pretty obvious that all these experts are knowledgeable in your security technology and procedures. Wouldn't you agree to that?"

Eisenstadt sat there, his arms now crossed at his waist. "Not entirely. I doubt that any one of them knows it all. Each one is familiar with his own area."

Greenfield felt he was on the edge of something. He turned away from the witness and spoke with deliberation, facing the jury. "Dr. Eisenstadt, if several systems experts got together, and each one knew a portion of IRS's computer system security, isn't it possible that they could gain access to your network if they had some reason for doing so?"

Hinckley didn't even bother to get up. "Objection," he announced in a bored voice. "The question is sheer conjecture. Any answer would be the same. The defense is fishing in an empty lake."

"The last comment was gratuitous," Huddleston growled. "The U.S. Attorney knows better. Objection sustained."

Greenfield was somewhat relieved when Huddleston ruled against him. He felt that his question left a logical, positive implication. A negative reply would have washed it away. . . . "In view of your testimony that several people in your division are involved with IRS's computer network security, and systems experts from manufacturers whose equipment is used in Martinsburg and in your Service Centers around the country are also knowledgeable in portions of your security technology, and at least one consulting firm has people who are similarly knowledgeable, then it would seem an inescapable conclusion that there are quite a few people around the country who have an overall or partial knowledge of your protective technology. There also—"

"Objection!" Hinckley said from his seat. "Defense counsel isn't asking a question, he's editorializing."

"It's the basis of the question I'm about to ask."

"Then ask it," Huddleston told him impatiently.

"In addition to former employees of your division and also ex-employees of the other organizations mentioned who were privy to this same information, how many people would you estimate would have this knowledge of IRS's security?"

Eisenstadt shrugged. "A dozen . . . ?"

"Objection!" It was a shout.

"Sustained."

Greenfield decided not to contest it. He was sure the jury got the point. He returned to the witness. "Dr. Eisenstadt, the prosecutor showed you Government Exhibit A, which you identified as five sets of printouts of unauthorized instructions which allegedly caused IRS's Service Centers to perform certain functions." He took the sheets from the clerk and handed them to the witness. "Would you examine and summarize the contents of these printouts."

"Objection," Hinckley said. "The witness is not prepared to interpret processed data he's not familiar with."

"I can't believe I heard the prosecutor correctly," Greenfield said, turning to Hinckley. "A few minutes ago he asked this man, his own witness, to identify the prosecution's exhibit and now he doesn't want its contents described. Is he embarrassed to have this data revealed in open court?"

Hinckley was angry. "I object to the inflammatory nature of the defense counsel's remarks and I must insist—"

Greenfield was facing the bench. "Your Honor, whatever was admissible as evidence during the direct can be brought up during the cross. . . ."

Huddleston glared at both men. "Counselors," he said, "your display does you no credit. As for you, Mr. Greenfield, I don't need a lesson in the rules of evidence." He paused and lowered his head. "The witness will answer the question."

Eisenstadt summarized the five sets of instructions in a flat monotone and twice Greenfield told him to speak louder. When he finished describing the instructions which activated the Service Center computers to send to the news media the list of high federal officials who were long-time tax delinquents, the spectators' section broke out with laughter and Huddleston warned them against another outburst. Eisenstadt then described the instructions to mail the secret dossiers containing intimate data and other personal irrelevancies to the several million individuals so filed in the Project Pygmalion data bank.

As soon as Greenfield excused the subdued witness, Hinckley was on his feet. "Re-direct," he announced. Huddleston nodded wearily. It was getting on in the afternoon.

"Just one question, Dr. Eisenstadt. Mr. Greenfield led you into a blind alley when he asked you what individuals were knowledgeable in your agency's security technology. What he failed to ask you—and for obvious reasons—was whether a systems security expert with authorized access to COMSAT's satellite computers wasn't the most qualified of all to penetrate IRS's network. I ask you that now."

"Objection," Greenfield said routinely. "The prosecution asked that question in direct examination and received an answer. It's on the record."

"I'm asking the question now in the context of the inadequate testimony on this point elicited by the defense counsel, so the jury will not be confused."

"You're reflecting on the intelligence of the jury," Greenfield slipped in, "but go ahead—"

"*Mister* Greenfield," Huddleston said, "the court can manage without your side remarks." He cleared his throat. "The witness may answer the question."

"The answer is *yes.*"

Hinckley smiled. "No more questions. Re-cross, counselor?"

"No thanks, we're fine," Greenfield said.

Huddleston consulted his watch and then asked both attorneys to approach the bench. After a three-way discussion on the probable length of testimony of the next prosecution witness, the judge decided that there wouldn't be enough time and he announced that court would adjourn until ten the next morning.

Greenfield was noncommittal, but privately he thought at best it had been a draw.

Chapter Thirty-One

The bell rang as Kermit and Dana were getting ready to dress for dinner. Dana was in the shower. Kermit went to the door in his trousers and undershirt, his arm still in the sling. It was Nelson Gerard, Senator Kammerer's administrative assistant. Kermit was mystified. He had last seen Gerard over a year ago when they had lunched in the Senate cafeteria, following a meeting with Kammerer. They had remained friendly, but Kermit wasn't prepared to see him at this moment and certainly not in these circumstances.

"Hi, Kermit," Gerard said, smiling uneasily in the doorway. I'm afraid I'm barging in, I can see I came at a bad time . . . but it's rather important. Can you spare me a few minutes?"

"Oh, sure . . . come on in. I was just dressing for dinner."

They sat on facing chairs in the living room and Kermit eyed him curiously, wondering why he had come to the apartment without phoning. "This is a surprise. What's up, Nel?"

"I'll come right to the point. I know you're tied up now"—he made a small grimace—"this is going to sound sort of dramatic. I'm here on a confidential mission for the White House. Paul Ives, the President's chief of staff, asked me as a special favor because he figured I had some, you know, rapport with you. So what I'm about to tell you is as an emissary—it doesn't reflect my own feelings. Let's be straight on that."

"I understand," Kermit said, puzzled and intrigued.

"The White House wants you to turn over the magnetic tape and transcript showing the accessing of IRS's computer network by the White House, NSA and Treasury. They don't want it made public in your trial or anywhere else. It would, frankly, be a political disaster for the President and the party if it were—especially with the national elections coming up. In return, the U.S. Attorney will drop the two conspiracy charges and ask for a light sentence on the other two indictments. They feel they're sticking their necks out going that far, but they must have that tape and the printout." He rushed out the last words as though to disgorge the distasteful thought from his system. He paused, drew a small breath. "I want to make it clear that I'm just a messenger, and I can tell you I'm not one bit happy about it."

"Did your boss ask you to do this?" Kermit was curious because Kammerer was one of his staunchest supporters in the Senate.

"He left it up to me. I couldn't turn Ives down. He said it was an important service to the White House and he thought it would be to you and your friends too. I thought he might be right."

Kermit thought for a moment. "Is the President going to sign the Morstan-Windmiller bill? It's been on his desk for at least three days now."

"I don't think there's much doubt about it, Kermit. Ives didn't say so directly, but that's the impression I got. I feel the same about it as you do and, of course, you know where Kammerer stands."

Kermit liked Nelson, trusted him. "Tell you what, Nel. You go back and tell Ives that I'll be delighted personally to deliver the stuff to him as soon as the President vetoes that monstrosity. I mean it—you tell him that."

"Oh come on, Kermit. You can't seriously expect the President to make a deal like that. You just don't say, Look, Mr. President, if you veto a bill which Congress debated and passed and you were about to sign—then I'll give you what you want. I can't go back and tell Ives that."

"You said you were just a messenger boy. Well, that's my message. Give it to him."

Gerard sighed, smiled, shook his head. "You're really serious. All right, I'll deliver the message. But I wouldn't hold my breath if I were you." He suddenly looked concerned as though recalling a bad scene. "Oh, I think you should know how serious they are. The FBI has been monitoring your conversations here through an acoustic device attached to the wall of the apartment next door. The White House knew nothing of what the FBI was doing until Storey told the President what they had uncovered. The bugging's been going on since you first moved in. That's how they know about your plans for using that tape and transcript as evidence in court. You must have discussed it recently. They may still be listening even though they've been told not to—I don't give a damn. But I would be very careful if I were you," he said, and got up.

"Yes, thanks," Kermit said abstractedly, reeling the sound track backward to things said there in recent weeks. Suddenly the sky opened up. . . . That's why someone tried to murder us . . . they knew that we'd found out about Morstan's and Quaritius's secret meetings and seemed about to find out the rest . . . they knew we were getting closer on the source of the drugging, that Duane would use his contacts in the FBI to try to connect Morstan with Storey in the plot . . . they knew about Dana's proposal to hunt out a dossier on Morstan . . . and even that we'd discovered that Morstan's affair with his mistress was going on the rocks. We'd been tracked all along! . . . The threats of exposure must have been too much for Morstan—he'd have been afraid it would ruin his chances for the White House. . . . We weren't only expendable, we *had* to be gotten rid of. . . .

"Are you all right, Kermit. You look a bit wobbly. I know you've had a bad time, the accident and all. . . ."

"No, I'm okay. I was just thinking. How did you find out about that bug in the wall?"

"I just found out today. Ives leveled with me when I asked him how he knew you had the tapes and were planning to use them. I repeat, it was strictly an FBI operation."

Dana marched in wearing a white terry cloth robe, her hair in damp disarray and her face glowing. "Oh, I thought I heard someone talking."

Kermit smiled at Gerard's discomfort. "Dana, this is Nelson Gerard. You've heard me speak of him."

"Hi, there . . . don't rush off. I have to dress anyway." She turned to go.

He nodded. "I've got to go too. Good luck to you both." He took Kermit's left hand and shook it. At the door, he turned and paused,

"Yes, one more thing—this conversation never happened. If it's ever made public, I'll have to deny it."

Maurice Stendahl, a fiftyish bullfrog of a man, sat uncomfortably on the witness stand, his palm raised woodenly during the court clerk's rapid-fire swearing-in litany. He had a broad face with puffy cheeks, swollen neck and wide-set eyes magnified under thick-lensed glasses.

Hinckley, fresh-eyed, moved briskly from the prosecution table and faced the witness with a cordial smile. In a series of pro forma questions put forth with conspicuous courtesy, the U.S. Attorney quickly established Stendahl's credentials as a former professor of electrical engineering at M.I.T. in charge of Project MAC, a former computer research specialist with the National Science Foundation, the author of several books and numerous papers on esoteric aspects of computer technology, chairman of prestigious professional seminars and, for the past nine years, executive vice-president of Parkinson Institute responsible for research and consulting services.

Bit by bit Hinckley drew out the dry, thin-voiced professorial witness on his relationship with Yukio Ishizaka, how long the young man had worked for Parkinson, the exact nature and scope of his responsibilities, which clients he serviced, what security clearance he had on sensitive government accounts and what resources and confidential data files and systems he had access to. Stendahl's terse, objective testimony clarified the fact that Ishizaka had top security clearance from the government and, as manager of systems security for Parkinson clients including the Department of Commerce, Health, Education and Welfare, the Export-Import Bank and the Communications Satellite Corporation, as well as industrial corporations, it was Ishizaka's job to test the vulnerability of client computer systems and to develop solutions for plugging up the actual or potential leaks.

"In other words," Hinckley summarized, "Mr. Ishizaka knew the weaknesses in your clients' computer systems and how they could be penetrated. Is that correct?"

"Yes. Certain clients hired our organization to protect them from unauthorized penetration, data theft and various forms of tampering. That was Mr. Ishizaka's function."

"Dr. Stendahl, would you describe for the court Mr. Ishizaka's work on the COMSAT account?"

252

"Yes, well, he was on the COMSAT account for about two years. For most of that time he worked with the systems people at COMSAT Laboratories on the security factors in their design of a highly advanced computer system for communications satellites. Subsequently he discovered a potential flaw—after the new computer system was operational. As a result, he developed and proposed a corrective solution to the problem."

Hinckley took a few steps away looking at the jury. He walked back and faced the witness, hands on his hips. "I see. And was this corrective solution incorporated in the new system?"

"No, it wasn't. The client felt that the flaw was so minuscule that it wasn't worth the time and expense of modifying some of the hardware."

"Tell me, Dr. Stendahl, could this same, uncorrected flaw have provided access to IRS's computer network?"

"It could provide potential access to all integrated computer networks which use the satellites for data communications," was the unhesitating response.

Hinckley had his arms folded in front of him. "If I understand you correctly, then, IRS could be penetrated from the outside by a person who had full knowledge of this flaw and full access to COMSAT's computer systems?"

"Yes, that is correct."

Hinckley turned to the jury and, scanning the faces in the box, repeated what he wanted to drill into them. *"Yes, that is correct."* He said it like a pronouncement, wagging his small, neat head affirmatively. He faced the witness. "Dr. Stendahl, do you know *anyone* who would have the special knowledge of communications satellite security, and as ideal an opportunity as Mr. Ishizaka, to penetrate the IRS network?"

"Objection." Greenfield was on his feet. "The prosecutor is asking for conjecture."

Hinckley turned quickly to the bench. "Your Honor, I'm asking this witness, out of his professional knowledge and experience, to give the court his opinion on a point vital to the government's case."

"Still an opinion," Huddleston said. "That doesn't serve a useful purpose at this point. Objection sustained."

Hinckley persisted. "An *expert* opinion, Your Honor, and one which—"

"Sustained, Mr. Hinckley."

"Very well . . . would you say it was possible for Mr. Ishizaka, using Parkinson's computer facilities and confidential data files, to penetrate IRS's computer network?"

"Unfortunately, yes."

Jackpot. Hinckley's smile gave the jury the benefit of it.

The U.S. Attorney advanced on the uncomfortable figure in the box, radiating certitude. "You stated that Mr. Ishizaka had at his disposal all of your company's security facilities, code-breaking programs and confidential data bank files, and he knew your clients' security secrets because that was his responsibility. You also testified that he discovered the flaw in COMSAT's new computers and he knew exactly how it could be penetrated. Was anyone else in your organization as well equipped as Mr. Ishizaka"—he swiveled about and pointed his extended arm accusingly at Yuki seated at the defendants' table—"to use this weakness he discovered in COMSAT's satellite to penetrate IRS's computer network?"

Stendahl paused and then his monosyllable dropped like a stone into a deep lake. "No."

"Your witness, counselor."

Greenfield approached the witness. "Dr. Stendahl, doesn't Yukio Ishizaka have a doctoral degree in computer science from M.I.T., one of the nation's leading universities, and wouldn't that entitle him to the courtesy of being referred to as *Dr.* Ishizaka by Mr. Hinckley?" Hinckley started to rise from his seat, then changed his mind.

"He does and it would."

"How did you happen to hire a man as young and inexperienced as Dr. Ishizaka was three years ago?"

"We had read his doctoral thesis, *Computer Penetration Technology and Protective Counter Mechanisms,* and my associates and I thought we should see him. It was one of the most brilliant dissertations on the subject of computer system security that I had ever read. We felt that he had an enormous potential in this area and we had a need for such a person. So we interviewed him and hired him."

"Before you hired him for such a sensitive and responsible position involving the security of the computer systems of government agencies and other clients, did you investigate his background to determine his loyalty and trustworthiness?"

254

"Certainly. He was checked for government security clearance by the FBI and we ran our own check."

"Did he ever do anything during his employ with your organization, up to the time of his arrest, which was suspicious or which caused you to distrust him?"

"No."

"Do you recall that approximately a year ago Dr. Ishizaka informed you of the vulnerability, the flaw, he found in testing COMSAT's new computer system?"

"Yes I do."

"And isn't it a fact that a short time later he drew up a comprehensive proposal for eliminating that security flaw, and he submitted it to you and your associates?"

"Yes."

"Isn't it also a fact that as one of the nation's leading computer scientists, you approved his proposal and submitted it to the management of your client, the Communications Satellite Corporation in this city?"

"Yes, I did."

"What was their response?"

"They turned it down. They felt it was too costly and not necessary."

"What was Dr. Ishizaka's reaction to that?"

"I recall that he was very disappointed. He—"

Hinckley was up. "I object to this line of questioning. It is immaterial and irrelevant."

"Overruled," Huddleston noted methodically. "The witness will continue."

"He felt they were wrong and that the security risk was unacceptable."

"Did you agree with him?"

"Not entirely. But it was the client's decision. We're hired to consult and advise."

"Did Dr. Ishizaka ever discuss this matter further with you?"

"Yes, several times."

"Would you describe those discussions to the court?"

"He was very persistent and felt that the client should be urged to consider the proposal further."

"To eliminate the security flaw in their new system?"

"Yes."

255

"Did you or your associates do so?"

"No. We felt we had done everything we should to apprise them of the situation."

"Did Dr. Ishizaka ever bring this up again?"

"Yes, at a meeting with the president of our organization and myself. He made a strong appeal, but we felt that our client's decision was final."

"Dr. Stendahl, would you say that Dr. Ishizaka's behavior in this entire matter—his working out the solution to correct the weakness in COMSAT's security, his conviction that the problem was a vital one and his frequent urgings that something be done about it to make COMSAT's global communications secure—would you say that this was the behavior of an extremely conscientious man more concerned with his security responsibilities, and with the integrity of computer communications, than he was with irritating his employers?"

"Yes, I would."

"Would you mind repeating that?" He held his hand to his ear. He wanted to make certain it registered on the jury.

"I said, yes I would."

"Thank you. In that event, do you believe that a man who would go to such lengths to protect the security of a vital communications system would then use that system to sabotage or damage the computer system of another agency?"

"Objection! Defense counsel is asking the witness to—"

"Sustained. You know better than that, Mr. Greenfield." Huddleston shook his head.

Greenfield looked philosophical. He hadn't thought he could get away with it, but it didn't hurt. The jurors had heard the question. He resumed his questioning.

"Did you fire Dr. Ishizaka because you felt he had been disloyal to your company or that he had committed an illegal act against the government?"

"No, we just knew that he had been arrested and charged with a crime."

"But you had no reason to believe he was guilty of the charges?"

"We didn't know what to believe."

"Then why did you fire him? Why didn't you just suspend him until the issue was resolved in court?"

"Because the reputation of Parkinson Institute was at stake. We have

256

a great deal of privileged information concerning our clients so that when our credibility was brought into question, we felt we owed it to our clients, as well as to ourselves, to end all doubts."

"Then your firing of Dr. Ishizaka did not in any way indicate that you knew or felt that he had done anything wrong?"

"That is right."

"No further questions."

"Re-direct, Your Honor." Hinckley was already standing. He walked over to the witness box. "Dr. Stendahl, you testified before that Dr. Ishizaka was very disappointed when his proposal for improving security on COMSAT computers was rejected. You also stated that he was very persistent in trying to persuade you to get COMSAT to change their minds. And that he was rejected by you as well. Knowing him well as you obviously do, wouldn't you say that it was logical that this brilliant young man who was so compulsive in this matter might seek revenge for the rejection of his ideas by using the flaw he had discovered to damage the heart of the establishment—a vital government agency?"

"Objection! The question calls for a psychiatric judgment for which the witness is not qualified."

"Overruled."

Greenfield was surprised, got up slowly. "On what grounds, Your Honor?"

Huddleston *never* liked to have his rulings questioned. He peered at Greenfield. "Mr. Greenfield, the witness is qualified to give his layman's opinion on the temperament of an employee he was familiar with. It could shed some light on his motives."

Greenfield couldn't believe it. This was the first bad ruling the old man had made. "Exception," he requested.

"Exception noted," Huddleston said dryly. "The witness will answer the question."

Hinckley was eager. "Shall I repeat the question?"

"No, I couldn't forget a question like that." His thoughtful eyes were huge under the thick lenses. "I don't really know whether he was disturbed enough to do something like that. I certainly didn't think so at the time."

"But you wouldn't rule it out?"

"No, I couldn't do that either."

"Re-cross?" Hinckley offered, satisfied.

Greenfield shook his head.

As Huddleston started to announce the adjournment until the afternoon, a rush began for the double doors. The reporters were in a hurry to get to telephones or back to their typewriters. The judge's gavel and the two policemen stationed inside the doors couldn't hold them back.

Court reconvened at one o'clock but a few minutes later the jammed courtroom still resounded with people settling into seats, shuffling papers and chatting across the benches. The gavel came down hard twice. Judge Huddleston continued to glare until all noise stopped and then devoted the next five minutes to lecturing the news media people on their lack of respect for the dignity of the court by bolting out of the courtroom prematurely. He seemed to benefit from this verbal catharsis, and he actually smiled as he invited the prosecution counsel to call the next witness.

When Gideon Chappell took the stand, his large, pink face, cerulean eyes and silver-black hair gave him the look of an aging, handsome choirboy. His eye involuntarily caught Kermit's and went glassy. Kermit wondered what he could say that would be damaging enough to justify the prosecution calling him as a witness. How he loathed that damned shining face.

With an obvious display of courtesy designed to underscore the prestige of the witness, Hinckley drew forth Dr. Chappell's credentials: Dartmouth, Harvard for his advanced degrees, the university president's scholarly accomplishments and honors, his leadership in national associations of higher learning, his progress from a professorship to administration at Hamilton College before being appointed president of the South Hanover Institute of Technology almost five years before, an institution which, Hinckley pointed out, had flourished under the witness's administration. The prosecutor methodically questioned Chappell about his relationship with Dr. Nordstrom, the latter's work at South Hanover, and then about Dana Haverhill's position at the university. Chappell's answers were open and seemingly innocuous. Then Hinckley launched into questions about Kermit's lobbying in Washington.

"Did you ever object to his lobbying activities concerning computer legislation?"

"No, I did not. I strongly believe in freedom of speech and in full academic freedom for members of the faculty, including the right to

258

engage in political activities as long, of course, as they are not inimical to our national security."

Kermit leaned over and whispered to Greenfield. "That's a lie, *of course.*" Greenfield nodded without taking his eyes off the witness.

"Aside from his lobbying in Washington, did Dr. Nordstrom engage in politicizing on campus which you considered to be a threat to our national security?"

"Yes, I'm afraid he did."

"That's a damn lie," Kermit whispered urgently.

"Relax," Greenfield said, "it's going to get worse."

"Dr. Chappell, would you tell the court from your personal knowledge the exact nature of those activities?"

"He was advocating the overthrow of the system as a means of serving the people's interests."

Greenfield got up. "Objection!"

Huddleston gaveled the courtroom into silence and Hinckley quickly said, "Your Honor, I'll validate that testimony with my next question, or I'll agree to have it stricken."

"Very well, ask your next question."

"Did you personally hear him make such a statement?"

"I did."

Kermit said, "My god!" The other three shook their heads in dismay.

"Would you describe the circumstances under which you heard him make such a statement?"

"I called Dr. Nordstrom in for a meeting in my office—I believe it was in January of this year." Chappell's voice sounded rich and well groomed in the hushed courtroom. "I told him I wanted to talk to him because I had heard numerous reports that he was proselytizing students in his various classes on his radical political views. Some of the faculty had mentioned—"

"Objection!" Greenfield was advancing toward the bench. "Your Honor, this is hearsay. I must insist—"

Huddleston held up his hand. "I agree with you, Mr. Greenfield." He turned to the witness. "Dr. Chappell, can you tell this court what statement Dr. Nordstrom made to you personally without referring to other sources?"

"I was about to. I was just describing the circumstances of our meeting so that it will be clear how he happened to make that statement to me."

"Proceed."

"I told Dr. Nordstrom that I had heard reports from students and faculty that he had been advocating that the system be overthrown as the only means to effect social change. I asked him if this was true. He didn't deny making those statements and he claimed his right of academic freedom. When I challenged him on the propriety of a faculty member advocating views on campus which were seditious and a threat to our form of government, he laughed and said it wasn't sedition, he was simply proposing that our so-called military-industrial dictatorship be eliminated in favor of a people's democracy. He said it couldn't be done in the voting machine anymore—it would have to be done by computer terminals. He said that didn't constitute the violent overthrow of the government—it was just a nonviolent way of giving the government back to the people."

An undercurrent rolled through the courtroom, and Huddleston halted it with his gavel and formidable glare.

"You are certain of what he said?" Hinckley was nailing down his trophy.

"Absolutely. It's a close paraphrase of his exact words."

"I see. And how did that interview end?"

"I told him I couldn't tolerate his preaching subversive doctrines on campus. I told him it was dangerous, and I urged that he reconsider his position and stop airing those views or it would be necessary for me to terminate his services in fairness to the students, their parents—"

"And did he stop?"

"Yes. Instead he went underground to practice what he preached."

Kermit's groan was buried by Greenfield's demanding voice. "Your Honor, the witness's statement is incompetent, inflammatory and prejudicial. I must insist that it be stricken from the record."

Huddleston nodded. "The stenographer will strike the witness's last statement from the record and the jury is instructed to ignore it." Hinckley could not care less. He had himself a great witness. "What was the professional relationship between Dr. Nordstrom and Miss Haverhill?"

"Their work brought them into close contact."

"Isn't it a fact that they lived together as well?"

"Objection!" Greenfield was genuinely angry. "The question is irrelevant, immaterial and malicious, and the defense resents its implication."

"Sustained. I'm surprised at the U.S. Attorney. The question is improper."

"I apologize to the court," Hinckley said with a pious face before the judge could censure him further. But he knew he had succeeded in calling attention to what must have been on the minds of some of the jurors. "Your witness."

Greenfield approached the witness in an easy but businesslike manner. "Dr. Chappell, I'm aware of the reputation of the South Hanover Institute of Technology . . . even if it doesn't have a law school." He smiled. "It is one of the best universities in the East and you certainly are to be congratulated."

Chappell wondered what was behind the flattery.

"Isn't it a fact that like most colleges and universities, you operate with a board of trustees, which appointed you as president and has the authority to approve of your policies?"

"That's correct." Chappell looked wary.

"Do you meet regularly with the board of trustees?"

"Several times a year and there may be special meetings from time to time."

"I assume you are in contact with the chairman of the board more often?"

"Objection," Hinckley said, "this line of questioning is immaterial and irrelevant."

"Your Honor, I am laying the foundation for something which will quickly become evident."

"Overruled."

Greenfield turned to the witness. "My question was whether you are in contact with the board chairman more frequently than just at regular meetings."

"Somewhat more, yes."

"Isn't the chairman of your board of trustees a Mr. Vance Lockwood who is also the largest private donor to South Hanover?"

"Yes, I believe Mr. Lockwood may be our largest donor."

"Dr. Chappell, isn't it a fact that Mr. Lockwood is also president of Commonwealth Electronics, a defense contractor for the Pentagon, and it was he who persuaded you to try to stop Dr. Nordstrom's political activities?"

261

Hinckley stood up decisively. "Objection. Counsel is making an unfounded accusation. Nothing has been established to show—"

"Yes," Huddleston agreed coldly. "Sustained."

"Isn't it a fact that the political activities you wanted Dr. Nordstrom to stop were not on campus at all, but were rather his lobbying activities in Washington to promote legislation to control the abuses of computer operations and civil rights violations by the government and by industry?"

"No, it is not." His eyes had become hostile, and Greenfield knew he would have to keep boring in.

"Isn't it a fact that Dr. Nordstrom never advocated the overthrow of the system or the government and that there were no such reports on campus and you never heard him make such statements?"

"That's not true." His mouth was tense.

"Before we go any further, I want to remind you that you are under oath and if you perjure yourself in this testimony you will be subject to criminal penalties." He paused, monitoring Chappell's eyes, and then continued. "Isn't it a fact that when Dr. Nordstrom met with you at your request in your office on January fourteenth of this year at three P.M., you told him that if he discontinued his lobbying in Washington for corrective legislation against computer abuses, you would name him for a full professorship and also recommend him for a major grant to conduct an important computer study for an unnamed government agency?"

"No, that's not a fact!"

Greenfield shook his head in dismay for the benefit of the jury. "Isn't it a fact that you did *not* discuss his advocacy to students of anything political, subversive or otherwise, because there was no basis for such a discussion?"

"That's not true."

"And that the only reason you met with him was to induce him with offers of that professorship and that handsome grant to drop his perfectly legal lobbying activities in Washington?"

"That's a lie!" All the pinkness drained out of his face.

Hinckley was on his feet and motioning decisively. "Your Honor, defense counsel is badgering the witness. He seems to have forgotten that he is cross-examining and that the witness is not on trial."

262

"Your Honor, this witness has made a serious charge against one of the defendants. It gives me the right to ask questions which go to the credibility of the witness."

"Overruled."

"Dr. Chappell, are you a friend of Senator Gunther Morstan?"

A murmur of surprise went through the courtroom, followed by an expectant silence.

"I know him slightly. I wouldn't call him a friend."

"What would you call him?"

"Someone I've met once or twice."

"On what occasions?"

"I don't recall exactly."

"Try."

Chappell stared at him. "I may have met him through a mutual friend and again when he addressed a gathering I attended."

"Those were the only times?"

"Yes."

"I believe you graduated from Dartmouth University in 1952, is that correct?"

"Yes, that's right."

"Did you know that Senator Morstan was a member of the Dartmouth class of 1951?"

The witness frowned. "I don't recall that."

"That's odd. You both were members of the same fraternity at the same time—Sigma Alpha Epsilon. Do you recall that?"

"Objection."

"Overruled."

"Come now, Dr. Chappell, would you forget a fraternity brother who became a prominent United States senator and is now aspiring to the highest office in the land?"

The pressure was stiffening the university president's face into a mask. "I didn't know him that well."

"Since he was your fraternity brother, how is it that you didn't recall his being a fellow alumnus at Dartmouth?"

"I had forgotten. . . ."

"Did you also forget that you attended several fraternity reunions together, the last one two years ago in Hot Springs where you spent a weekend together along with your wives?"

Chappell sat there looking at the rear wall.

"I asked you a question."

"No, I didn't forget. I didn't think it was important." He looked at Greenfield with defiance.

"You admit now that, despite your previous testimony, you in fact knew him as a fraternity brother and spent periods of time with him on a number of occasions?"

He was looking at his feet. "Yes, but we never became friends."

The beginnings of laughter died quickly under Huddleston's gavel.

"You stated before that you may have met Senator Morstan through a mutual friend. However, you actually knew Gunther Morstan as a fellow undergraduate and as a fraternity brother. Isn't it a fact that the mutual friend was Vance Lockwood, the chairman of your board of trustees?"

"No!"

"And it was *you* who actually introduced Lockwood to Senator Morstan because the senator was chairman of the Senate Armed Services Committee?"

"No, it wasn't."

"And since then, Lockwood's company, Commonwealth Electronics, has received multimillion-dollar contracts from the Pentagon through the Department of Defense?"

"I know nothing about that."

"Objection! Defense counsel is—"

"Both counsels will approach the bench." Huddleston's face was lined with concern. At the sidebar, he leaned forward and spoke in serious, confidential tones. "Mr. Greenfield, you've entered a new and highly sensitive area of inquiry which is unacceptable. Moreover, you've involved the name of a U.S. senator, who is also a potential candidate for the Presidency, in a most pejorative way. Exactly what do you have in mind?"

Greenfield kept his voice low. "Your Honor, I have good reason to believe that this witness has perjured himself many times and that his motive is to protect others who conspired with him to make these false charges against my client. I must be allowed the opportunity to pursue it."

264

"Mr. Hinckley?"

"It's ridiculous to think that Senator Morstan would be involved in anything as shabby as Mr. Greenfield implies. And it's unconscionable to bring the name of a respected U.S. senator into this on the defense counsel's assumption. Unless Mr. Greenfield can produce some hard evidence, I think we can assume he's just throwing up a smoke screen."

Greenfield focused right into those deep-set eyes. "Your Honor, I realize the seriousness of the course I'm pursuing. Believe me, I do. I have no hard evidence but I believe I can get at the truth through this witness. I am well aware of the political overtones of this trial. It's unfortunate if the mighty get some mud on them, but my responsibility is to get justice for my clients and I can't do that if my hands are tied."

Huddleston compressed his lips, and his eyes reflected on a distant place. Finally he said, "I'll go along with you for a while Mr. Greenfield, but remember you're on dangerous ground."

"Thank you, your Honor." He turned back to the witness. "Dr. Chappell," he began, consulting a small sheet of notepaper in his hand, "I have information showing that Vance Lockwood contributed $200,000 to the South Hanover Institute of Technology in 1981, $250,000 in 1982 and $350,000 last year. Is that correct?"

"I believe so."

"Was this the result of your personal fund-raising activities?"

"Yes. Mr. Lockwood is a very public-service-minded man."

Greenfield walked over to Bonaventura, who handed him some papers. "I have here a U.S. Government record showing Department of Defense contracts for the past ten years. I offer this as Defense Exhibit A to be marked and entered." The court clerk took it from him, returned with it to his desk and then handed it back quickly. Greenfield looked down at the finely printed sheets. "These documents show that Commonwealth Electronics received Department of Defense prime contracts in excess of seventy-eight million dollars in the past four years and none in the years prior to that. Would you like to verify these facts for yourself, Dr. Chappell?"

Chappell shook his head. Greenfield motioned with the documents in his hand. He spoke slowly. "You have been president of South Hanover Institute for five years. Mr. Lockwood's company has been receiving large defense contracts for four years. He became chairman of your board of trustees three years ago and he has been contributing large sums

265

to the university for the past three years. This is a rather tight pattern of relationships. Would you have the court believe that it is all coincidental?"

"I draw no conclusions from it."

"I didn't think you would. Tell me, Dr. Chappell, what conclusion would you draw from the fact that the hotel register shows that Vance Lockwood was at the Hot Springs Inn the same weekend, two years ago, that you and Senator Morstan were there together at your fraternity reunion, and that both your bills were paid for by Commonwealth Electronics? Do you deny that?"

Chappell looked startled. "I don't recall who paid my bill."

"There are many things you don't recall. I can refresh your memory by subpoenaing the hotel records and calling you back to resume this cross-examination."

"That won't be necessary. . . . I believe that Mr. Lockwood did pick up the tab for both of us."

"Isn't the reason for Mr. Lockwood's company's generosity the fact that it received those profitable military contracts *after* you introduced Mr. Lockwood to the senator, and isn't that the same reason Mr. Lockwood has been so generous to the university?"

"No, there is no connection in any of this."

"Did you know that Vance Lockwood is a founding member of the Committee to Strengthen America, which ran full-page ads and radio and television commercials in support of Senator Morstan's legislation, which was passed by a single vote in Congress last week?"

"Yes, I did."

"Isn't that why he pressured you, in behalf of Senator Morstan, into getting Dr. Nordstrom to stop the lobbying which opposed his bill?"

Chappell's gaze fractured, scattered. He looked empty and ill. "No. . . ."

"And isn't that the reason you lied to this court about Dr. Nordstrom advocating the overthrow of the government and why you branded him a subversive . . . because Vance Lockwood asked you—perhaps forced you—to do this for your mutual friend, Senator Gunther Morstan? Before you answer that question, I want you to consider what compounding perjured testimony can mean. You would risk being indicted on a criminal offense." He paused and momentarily studied the now rigid figure before him. "Now, will you please answer the question?"

266

Chappell sat erect, eyes glazed and mouth twitching slightly at the corners. He made no sound, as though he hadn't heard.

Huddleston leaned sideways toward the witness box. "The witness will answer the question."

Chappell sat there, apparently shattered, and unresponsive.

"Are you ill?" Huddleston asked with concern. "If you are, you may come back tomorrow and answer the question."

Chappell's eyes blinked, he seemed to be recovering. He shook his head slowly. "No," he said almost inaudibly.

"Then you will answer the question."

"No," he repeated, "no. . . ."

Huddleston leaned back in his black leather high-back swivel chair. He pulled on his long earlobe and studied the mannequinlike figure in the witness box. Several alternatives went through his mind. He leaned forward and spoke to the witness.

"Dr. Chappell, if you refuse to answer this question, you will leave me little choice. I will have to hold you in contempt of court and the testimony you have given will be stricken from the record."

Excited chatter boiled up in the crowded press section. Huddleston gaveled it down. He instructed the police guards not to permit anyone to leave the courtroom until adjournment was announced. Then he turned to Chappell. "I will give you until tomorrow morning at ten o'clock to reconsider. If you still refuse to answer the question at that time, my decision to hold you in contempt and to void your testimony will be in effect."

Court was adjourned, and Hinckley, his face tight with anger and frustration, followed the judge's black flowing robe to his chambers.

Dinner that evening in Dana's apartment was noisy. Harriet was there with Yuki. It was the first time Harriet had met the other three although she had seen them in the courtroom. They made her feel welcome and their high praise of her husband brought out her quick, vivacious smile. She watched the way Dana looked at Kermit and realized how foolish she had been to suspect Yuki of infidelity.

They all felt freer now. Yuki had carefully checked out the apartment next door under the guise of being interested in renting it, but there were no bugs anywhere. He had found two small spots the size of quarters in the common living room wall which looked as though they had been freshly patched and neatly blended with paint. Obviously, the FBI had been careful to make the small holes virtually invisible. With the FBI's audio surveillance ended, they felt they were probably in less danger now and could speak freely.

Kermit had an elaborate Chinese dinner delivered from a Szechuan restaurant in the neighborhood, and they complemented it with a California chablis. They talked spiritedly about the details of Dr. Stendahl's and Dr. Chappell's testimony, particularly the latter's cross-examination and how Greenfield had punctured his credibility.

Kermit had invited Adam and Andy Bonaventura to stop by for a drink after dinner, and when they arrived a little after nine, Dana greeted each with an enthusiastic hug and kiss at the door.

"I'm afraid I can't accept that in lieu of fee," Adam said with a straight face, "my stuffy partners wouldn't go for it."

Dana raised her glass toward Adam and Andy, and said, "To Batman and Robin—for beating the bad guys at their own game."

They all laughed. But when they sat down, the talk turned serious.

Kermit started it off. "I was amazed at all the things you were able to throw at Chappell—the fact that he and Morstan were fraternity buddies, the weekend the three of them spent together, with Lockwood that is, and his company's fat contracts with the Pentagon and so forth and so forth. I had no idea you had all that."

"That's what we pay a private investigator a hundred and fifty dollars a day for, plus expenses. Andy worked closely with him, fed him leads, made him shake his tail."

Andy concurred. "He's really one of the best in the business. He used to be with the Philadelphia police department. He quit about ten years ago when they told him to cut his hair. His name is Gaetano Lasagna."

"Lasagna?" Harriet laughed. "Gaetano, I would believe."

"Now that you've established that Chappell was lying, how do you see the effect on the case?" Duane asked.

"Well, we haven't proved that he was lying but we made it pretty obvious. We undid the damage he did—and it *was* damaging—in his direct testimony, but, more important, we also discredited the prosecution some in the eyes of the jury. That's something they'll have to contend with as long as they go along."

"What about the next two witnesses—my hostile colleague from the

Light Engineering department and my favorite ex-student pain-in-the-ass? They certainly will try to bury me," Kermit said.

"Sure they will. They'll probably testify along the same lines as Chappell—unless he gives them a new set of answers by then. We don't have anything on them to pin them to the mat. The only prosecution witness I can't figure out is the one Hinckley's bringing over from the General Services Administration. GSA has statutory power over interagency pools of data processing systems, but I don't know what the devil Hinckley plans to have him say that can do us in. Anyway, this trial has been loaded with Ph.D.'s. It will be nice to be able to call a witness 'Mister' for a change."

"GSA is the key authorizing agency on the huge multi-access, time-sharing systems used by the major government agencies," Kermit pointed out. "One of their concerns is the security of those systems. Maybe this guy, whatever his name, will come to tell the court how serious and damaging what we did to IRS can be to the government's total operations."

"That's an angle," Andy said. "I'll look into it."

"I'd like to ask you a question, Adam," Yuki said self-consciously. "Do you think that Chappell will answer that question tomorrow rather than be charged with contempt of court? And if he does answer it . . . I mean if he lies about it . . . what effect will it have?"

"I don't think he will answer the question tomorrow. In fact I think that Hinckley might even tell him to get sick so he won't show. But if he shows up and takes the witness stand tomorrow morning, and lies his way through it, it's pretty late. The jury saw and heard."

"I was really shocked to see a man in his position fall apart that way," Harriet said.

Adam nodded. "The way he was stonewalling it through the first half, I frankly didn't think it would happen. But once I caught him in a few lesser lies about how well he knew Morstan and began building on them, he sure came unstrung. He thought I had more than I did and that I'd keep throwing new stuff at him. The fact is, I was fresh out. And then he got caught between the threat of criminal perjury from me and contempt of court from the judge. I guess it was too much. Guys like that are often tough to a point, then suddenly collapse. They just have no flexibility. . . ."

At the other end of the large living room Dana turned on the color

TV console facing diagonally into the room. "It's five after ten. Let's see what we can get."

Webb Vanderzee, NBC's noted Washington newscaster, was just finishing a report on the trial. ". . . to obtain large military contracts for Commonwealth Electronics. The entry of Senator Morstan's name in this already sensational case adds a dimension of potential political scandal which will further rock the nation and could have a decided effect on the Presidential elections. On the legislative side, the President today vetoed a bill jointly sponsored by both houses to provide the elderly—"

Dana switched off the set. "So what else is new?" She walked over to an end table and picked up a cigarette.

"I hate to spoil this nice party," Adam said as a general announcement, stretching his legs with studied deliberation, "but I'm afraid there *is* something else that's new. I was stalling about telling you. . . . Our office safe was broken into last night. . . . I know, I know, shades of Watergate, but desperate people do desperate things. . . . The only things that were taken were the magnetic tape and printout you gave me which I planned to use as evidence of government penetration of the IRS. We discovered it this afternoon when—"

"Oh, my god!" Kermit slapped his hand over his face. "Gerard must have given my message to Ives immediately and they decided to go after the tapes themselves."

"You didn't expect they'd take no for an answer, did you?" Adam said. "Obviously he called Mitchell Storey and told him to go get it. The FBI must have guessed it was in my office safe."

Kermit looked disgusted. "That wall bug next door I told you about. We must have mentioned sometime where the tape was kept and those spooks picked it up. But why didn't they just steal it before, instead of the White House bothering to try to make a deal with me?"

"Maybe," Duane said, "they wanted to see how the trial was going before they made up their minds. Besides, they're not keen on break-ins if there's an easier way. You were the easier way—until you issued your ultimatum to the White House."

"Exactly." Adam nodded.

Kermit massaged his chin. "That means the President is definitely going to sign the bill." The grim import of that seemed to make everything else irrelevant.

270

"It also means we've lost a valuable piece of evidence," Adam said. "I was counting on it as the clincher to prove that the government was doing exactly what it was accusing us of doing . . . only on a larger scale and with less wholesome motives. Oh, well, there's not a damn thing we can do about it. It's a real loss, of course, but we'll have to manage without it. I reported it to the police just so the theft will be on record. But they realize it's an inside political job and almost certainly nothing will be done about it. Not for now, anyway."

He got up suddenly from the sofa, stretched, and buttoned his sport jacket. His eyes seemed strained. "Let's get out of here, Andy, we've got work to do tomorrow. And it's not going to get any easier."

After the door slammed, the trailing silence seemed ominous, Adam's news having chased whatever festive or even hopeful feelings the evening had started with.

They were the four conspirators again. And feeling overwhelmed by the lengths the country's most powerful forces seemed willing to go to.

Chapter Thirty-Two

The walnut-paneled courtroom was jammed on Friday morning.

Judge Huddleston settled into his high-backed swivel chair, looked up and said, "Mr. Hinckley, I don't see Dr. Chappell in the courtroom. Is he in the witness room?"

Hinckley stood up. "No, Your Honor. I received a telephone call this morning from Dr. Chappell. He was back at the university. He told me that he wouldn't answer the question and he didn't wish to appear in court. He was very definite in his statement. He asked me to convey the message to you and to apologize to the Court for any inconvenience this may cause."

"Does Dr. Chappell understand what the consequences of his refusal will be?"

"He does. I explained it to him very carefully."

Huddleston shrugged his shoulders, massive under his black robe, and shook his head. "Very well. The court stenographer will strike all of the testimony of Dr. Gideon Chappell from the record." He turned to the jury. "Members of the jury are hereby instructed to disregard all the testimony you heard from Dr. Chappell and the proceedings related to it. I hope each of you understands that." He faced the courtroom. "The court will hold in abeyance the contempt of court citation against Dr. Chappell until a later date. Mr. Hinckley, you may call your next witness."

Kermit and Dana were waiting with odd anticipation for Professor Eli Greenwalt of South Hanover's engineering department to occupy the witness box. Hinckley rose and faced the judge. "Your Honor, the government will call as the next witness a person who was not on the scheduled list of witnesses, and we are prepared to justify our action. The government calls Eloise Geist."

Greenfield turned quickly to Bonaventura, who shrugged. Then he turned to Kermit and the others. "Do any of you know who this is?" None did. He got up. "I object, Your Honor, to calling this witness at this time. This is a surprise witness, and we have no knowledge of who she is or the area of her testimony."

Huddleston looked at the prosecutor. "Mr. Hinckley, what is your justification?"

"Your Honor, our investigation in this case is open-ended and continuing, and it was only last night that we came into possession of important information directly relevant to the government's case. In the interests of avoiding a lengthier trial than necessary, we feel that this witness should be allowed to testify without delay."

"The court is inclined to agree, Mr. Greenfield."

Adam knew in advance that he couldn't stop it. "In that case, we request the right of adjournment to cross-examine the witness next Monday."

"That's agreeable. You may proceed, Mr. Hinckley."

The witness was a woman in her late thirties who looked like so many of the hopeful young women who came to Washington from small towns hunting for excitement and opportunity and ten years later were resigned to routine lives, still working for the government. Miss Geist's title was assistant director of the Retrieval Section of the National Personnel Advisory Council, McLean, Virginia. Under questioning Hinckley established that she was in charge of record retrieval for the agency, then walked back to the prosecution's table and took a single long sheet of paper from the outstretched hand of one of his trial assistants. He returned to the witness and handed her the paper.

"Miss Geist, would you identify this document?"

She glanced at it. "This is a printout of a computerized dossier from the data bank of the National Personnel Advisory Council."

"The government offers this as Prosecution Exhibit B."

Greenfield was up and walking forward in one motion, his arm outstretched. "May I see that?"

"Certainly." Hinckley handed it to him.

He read through it hurriedly, then looked up. "Your Honor, I object to the introduction of this *document*"—he flavored the word with sarcasm. "The U.S. Attorney is well aware that this dossier is not an exception to the hearsay rule and therefore cannot be used as evidence of *anything* except the overzealousness of our government's secret intelligence agencies."

"Mr. Hinckley, what's your position?"

"Your Honor, it is perfectly clear that this dossier is an official document of a government agency whose function is to investigate, collect and store data of this sort and it is part of their standard recordkeeping system. Therefore, it must be considered an exception under the hearsay rule of evidence and must be admitted."

Greenfield's voice grew sharp. "I suggest, Your Honor, that this *cannot* be considered an official government record by any reach of the imagination. It does not contain established facts. It is simply a report of presumed activities—raw information which has not been verified. Unless the prosecution can produce witnesses who will testify to their firsthand knowledge of the accuracy of this report, I object to its being placed in evidence."

"Let me see what we're talking about." Huddleston nodded to the court clerk, who took the long sheet and handed it to the judge. He held the paper a long distance away and read it carefully for a full two minutes. Finally he put down the paper and looked up. "There is a valid question of judgment here concerning the character of this document. Because seditious conspiracy is at issue here, I am inclined to admit this record as evidence under certain conditions. The government must show the chain of custody of this document to prove its legitimacy and also that the information it contains is part of the standard recordkeeping procedures of this particular agency. If the government can do that, I will let the evidence be introduced subject to a caveat I will issue to the jury concerning its interpretation."

"Despite these qualifications, I still note my exception," Greenfield said.

"Your exception is recorded. What is your answer, Mr. Hinckley?"

The prosecutor seemed relieved. "The government is prepared to show what the court requests. Miss Geist, in her capacity as assistant director of the Retrieval Section of the National Personnel Advisory Council, is the person most qualified to verify the legitimacy of the document and the procedures under which the information was obtained, recorded and retrieved. That is why she is here."

"Very well, proceed."

How the devil could Hinckley have come across that dossier last night and gotten the NPAC to make someone available to testify this morning? Greenfield wondered. But what mattered was that Huddleston had taken a flyer by allowing the dossier as evidence. He was convinced that it was inadmissible and that his client's rights were being violated. If things went really badly and the jury brought in a guilty verdict on the conspiracy charges, he at least had a basis for petitioning that the conviction be put aside. Small comfort. . . .

Hinckley routinely elicited from the witness, sitting hands folded primly, that she had retrieved the document from the NPAC's data bank at the request of the U.S. Attorney's office with the concurrence of her superior. In answer to further questions, she stated that one of the functions of the agency was to receive data from various intelligence agencies of the government, verify the accuracy of the input through their field investigators, and integrate the resultant information through their computer system and data banks. She said that the data she had retrieved would necessarily have gone through this process and it had been in the data bank in the DSM file which, she blandly explained, meant Dissidents, Subversives and Militants.

Adam quickly spoke up. "Your Honor, I would like to cross-examine the witness on the basis of the testimony she has just given, and reserve the right to cross-examine her again following the government's introduction of the evidence referred to as Exhibit B." He wanted to undercut, if he could, the validity of what he knew was coming before it made its impact on the jury.

"That's an unusual procedure, but I don't object if Mr. Hinckley doesn't."

The prosecutor waved his arm generously.

Greenfield approached the witness. "Miss Geist, how can you justify releasing an obviously classified printout from your data bank—containing confidential information collected by secret intelligence agencies of the government—to the U.S. Attorney's office?"

She seemed ready for the question. "This is covered by a standing written agreement between the National Personnel Advisory Council and the Department of Justice."

Greenfield hid his surprise. "All right then . . . isn't it a fact that much of the data in the DSM file is *raw* data from the FBI and other intelligence agencies, based on reports and other information never verified by firsthand competent witnesses?"

"That is not correct. Any raw data which comes in is field-checked and verified before it goes into the DSM files."

"Since your responsibilities are in the Retrieval Section, how would you know that for a fact?"

"I worked in the Investigative Section as a clerk and then as a supervisor for the first six years. I am familiar with the practices."

"But you weren't in a position to know whether those practices were always carried out, that all data was fully and properly verified in the field?"

"No, but I had no reason to think otherwise."

"Is there any record, coded or otherwise, on the dossiers in this file indicating which intelligence sources the data came from?"

"Not on the individual dossiers. That information is stored in another file and is classified. I don't have access to it."

Greenfield knew he would get nowhere with Eloise Geist. She was hard-core. But he decided on one more try. "Isn't it possible that someone who was intimately familiar with the working of your system—perhaps a current or ex-employee—could produce a counterfeit dossier and insert it in the system to look like any other?"

"That would be impossible, our security precludes that."

He was glad to release her.

Hinckley rose and walked briskly to the witness. He handed her the printout which the clerk had listed as Prosecution Exhibit B. "Miss Geist, is this the same document you identified before?"

"It is."

"Will you identify the subject of this dossier?"

"The subject is Kermit Nordstrom."

The gavel sounded as soon as an undercurrent from the spectators began.

"Would you read the relevant section of the printout?"

Eloise Geist looked down, then looked up. "After the usual biographi-

276

cal data, there is a list of affiliations and activities, as follows." She began reading from the long sheet in a clear, unemotional voice.

Member, Students for a Democratic Society, 1967–1969. Visited Cuba with SDS group in 1967, despite U.S. Government sanctions, as guest of Premier Fidel Castro. Member, Weathermen, 1969–1970. Participated in bombing of ROTC facilities on Berkeley campus, University of California, U.C.L.A., and at University of Minnesota. Member, Symbionese Liberation Army, 1972–1974. Held several clandestine meetings in 1973 and 1974 with Sergei Nicolai Kulchenko who held title of deputy economic counselor to the Soviet Embassy, Washington, D.C., but operated as KGB agent in the U.S. and returned to Soviet Union in 1976 at request of U.S. State Department.

Kermit's mouth was open in disbelief. He turned to Greenfield and Bonaventura. "They made it all up!" His voice was odd.

"We'll talk about it later," Andy said, touching his arm.

Dana, Yuki and Duane looked at Kermit. "It's Watergate and McCarthy time again," Duane whispered across the table.

The reporters, frustrated and irritated that they couldn't rush to phones, settled for cynical exchanges, the commotion shattering the austerity of the courtroom. Huddleston repeatedly rapped his gavel until it stopped, then severely warned against further outbreaks.

Hinckley was waiting for the judge's signal to resume, impatient to complete his coup de grâce. "Miss Geist . . . do you know the purpose of this file category maintained in NPAC's data bank and, if so, would you describe it?"

She nodded with a tight little smile. "That category, DSM, was set up as a separate data file following the riots in Watts in 1965 and various bombings and other acts of violence on college campuses and in center city areas around the country a short time later. Its purpose was and is to keep watch on those individuals and organizations who could be a threat to the internal security of this nation, or to any federal, state or city agency, or to the safety of the President or other government officials. This is a vital service to all the people."

Bullshit, Adam said to himself as Hinckley said, "Thank you, Miss Geist. No further questions. Your witness, Mr. Greenfield."

The defendants wondered whether Greenfield would cross-examine the witness now or postpone it till Monday as Huddleston had agreed. The spectators and the jury wondered the same thing. It was still Friday

277

morning and none of the defendants wanted to see the vicious, damaging lies in the counterfeit dossier survive over the weekend. They wanted Greenfield to demolish them now. He looked at his watch—it was 11:15 —and then leaned over and whispered to Bonaventura, who nodded.

Greenfield stood up. "Your Honor, I would like—"

"Just a moment, Mr. Greenfield. I want to make a statement to the jury first." Judge Huddleston swiveled around to face them, speaking slowly and deliberately. "Pay careful attention, please. I will now instruct you concerning the testimony you have just heard from the witness, Miss Geist. You must regard her testimony, particularly the reading of the material in the dossier concerning Kermit Nordstrom, as going to the weight of evidence rather than being admissible evidence by itself. That is a subtle but important point and I want to be absolutely certain that you understand it. What that means is that you can consider that as testimony only insofar as it adds weight to similar testimony, but if you hear no similar testimony then you must disregard it. Is that clear to all of you?"

Greenfield saw several uncertain faces among the jurors but none spoke up. It could raise hob in their eventual deliberations.

"Mr. Greenfield, do you wish to cross-examine the witness?"

"Not at this time, Your Honor. But I will use my option to do so on Monday morning when court reconvenes."

"Very well. The members of the jury are instructed not to discuss this case in any way among yourselves, with members of the news media or with anyone else. Is that understood? Good. This court is adjourned until Monday next at ten A.M."

The defendants and their attorneys waited until the courtroom cleared and then another few minutes. But it didn't help. Greenfield and Bonaventura, trying to run interference for the entourage, elbowed their way through the throng of reporters and photographers waiting in the corridor and downstairs. But everyone wanted Kermit, thrusting toward him, jostling him and throwing the same kind of question from every angle. "Are you still a Weatherman?" . . . "Were you involved in any other bombings?" . . . "What was the purpose of your meetings with the KGB man?" . . . "Are all four of you involved in any of these organizations?" It was a long, long way to the protection of taxis.

Greenfield had suggested that they all meet in his office at one o'clock for a quick caucus on the morning's damaging testimony and the options open to them. After a hasty and silent coffee shop lunch for which they had no stomach, the four trooped into the offices of Leland, Hammerswak, Kaplowitz and Greenfield. A secretary brought them down the long hall into Greenfield's large office.

He and Andy Bonaventura, both shirt-sleeved, had apparently been in deep discussion about it when they arrived. Motioning them to seats without getting up, Greenfield immediately summarized the situation for them. It was his opinion and Andy's that Huddleston had made a serious judicial error in allowing the contents of the dossier to be read, his caveat to the jury didn't diminish the damage. He said that the testimony would confuse the jury and provide the basis for a possible reversal of conviction on appeal. But *meanwhile* the defense had suffered a very serious blow. Which was of paramount importance now.

"Why do you suppose Huddleston made that decision? He must have known better," Dana said.

"I think he looked at the printout and believed it—he had no reason not to. He must have figured, My god, we've got a real live dangerous revolutionary sitting here in court. I suspect he was so impressed with the data that it got the best of his judgment and he rationalized a way to let it in. Judges have emotions and biases like the rest of us, and occasionally they make a mistake."

"Adam, why did you insist on postponing cross-examining that Geist woman till Monday?" Duane asked. "By then the media will have massaged the story to death and everyone in the country will have convicted and crucified us all, along with Kermit."

Greenfield pulled out a lower desk drawer and rested his legs on it, leaning back in his swivel chair. "I have absolutely nothing to counter this witness with. She's a low-level government functionary in a secret agency. I doubt that she would know that the dossier isn't authentic. If I cross-examined her today I would get nothing and it would look worse. I've got to have some ammunition." He picked up a pencil and began twirling it between his fingers. "I spoke to Hinckley on the phone a little while ago. I was curious how he learned about the dossier and why he didn't get hold of it until last night. He told me—and I believe him—that one of his investigators was tipped off only yesterday that there was such a dossier buried at NPAC. He wouldn't tell me where the tip came from, naturally, but I'll try to find out in court. I don't think I'll get anywhere, though."

"I can tell you where the tip came from," Kermit said. "Morstan had to have a hand in this."

"The question," Adam said, "is why would he be involved in a phony dossier? What would he gain? He's already gotten his bill passed."

"The same reason he tried to murder us. He's out to destroy me because he knows what we know about him through that wall bug the FBI was monitoring. We were getting close on the drugging and we knew of his connection with Quaritius and the kind of work Quaritius does. And he *does* know we're aware that the car crash was no accident and he may be worried that Cynthia told us something before she died that might incriminate him. I think he's afraid that we can ruin his chances for the Presidency, and that he can't and won't risk."

"The trial is the only opportunity he has to stop us," Dana added. "If he gets us convicted on conspiracy, we can't hurt him."

"Because our credibility would be zero and we have no hard evidence," Yuki finished.

"In other words," Adam said, "you know too much. Of course I could challenge the legality of making a classified dossier public in violation of my client's civil rights. But if I objected to its being made public, that would lend credence to the authenticity of the dossier, regardless of the grounds. Besides, it's been read in court already and nothing will take that back. Except proof it was phony." He shook his head. "They've got us mousetrapped—at least for now."

Dana grimaced. "So what do we do now?"

"We have two and a half days to dig up something or else we take on Hinckley Monday morning with an empty gun. Andy has already called in Gaetano Lasagna and we're expecting him any minute. We've got to find a way to *prove* that every charge on that phony printout is a lie."

"It's not *all* a lie," Kermit said. "I told you, Adam, I did join SDS in 1967 and I did go to Cuba with a group. I was a freshman then and I stayed in five months, just long enough to take that trip. It was a way of demonstrating for greater student representation and also protesting the war. But I didn't like the way the SDS leadership operated. It was completely undemocratic and besides they really had no program except to attack the system. It made no sense to me so I got out. But there's no truth to any of the rest. I never joined the Weathermen, never even

280

lit a firecracker. The part about the Russian spy is, of course, total bullshit."

"But since part of the thing is true, it's tougher to discredit the rest. Something like being only a little pregnant."

Kermit looked irritated. "What can we do about it?"

"Hope that Gaetano can find someone who was involved in phonying the dossier and scare him into testifying. Then we'll just deny the whole thing."

"What about the SDS part?"

"If we can prove that the dossier was counterfeit, then the logical assumption is that everything in it was."

"Do you think Gaetano can dig up what we need by Monday morning?" Kermit asked.

"It's not likely but we've got to try. If he comes up with something later in the trial we can still use it."

"And if he doesn't come up with anything?"

"It will be that much tougher to beat the conspiracy charges."

The phone on his desk rang. Adam picked it up quickly. "Gaetano is here," he said to Andy.

Andy quickly headed for the door. "I'll put him to work."

Samuel Haverhill was furious when he phoned his daughter that evening.

"You must have known that Nordstrom was a revolutionary. The man's a *bomber,* for god's sake, and very likely a traitor too—meeting with that Russian spy . . . how could you possibly—"

"*Wait* a second, daddy," Dana broke in, "you're wrong about that, Kermit isn't any of those things—"

"Don't tell *me* he's not. It's in all the papers, it's on radio and television round the clock. It comes from official government records. How can you—"

"That dossier is a *phony.* It was made up to smear us all so that we'd be convicted of conspiracy and those other charges. Not a word of it is true except that part about SDS. Kermit did belong for a few months but then he got out. A lot of students belonged then to protest the war."

"You know better than that. No one could falsify a dossier and get away with it. I read that woman's testimony very carefully. She described how those records are thoroughly checked out before they go into the data bank and—"

"Senator Morstan is the phony," Dana snapped. "He's the one who had that dossier made up and inserted. It's a counterfeit."

"What are you saying? A man like Senator Morstan would never stoop to what you're suggesting."

"He's screw his own mother if it would get him into the White House."

"What did you say?"

"Forget it, forget it . . . you know that car accident we had that nearly killed your precious daughter? Well, it was no accident. Morstan was behind that too. He tried to kill all of us because we know too much about him—"

"Dana, I don't believe a word of this. I think you're deluding yourself. Senator Morstan is from South Carolina. He's an outstanding senator and a fine American—"

"You go on believing that, daddy, if it makes you happy. The point is that Kermit is no more a revolutionary than I am."

"That's what I'm afraid of. You've gotten yourself mixed up with a bad crowd and I don't know what you're up to anymore."

"You mean you don't trust me?"

"You know I always have. I don't know what to think now. You've deceived me on this whole affair. You told me you did this thing with the IRS as a social protest to protect civil rights. I thought it was a terrible idea but I agreed to pay the legal costs for all of you to get you in the clear. Now I find that these people—at least Nordstrom—are subversives and *my* money is defending them. You know, Dana, our family helped settle this country almost three hundred years ago and we helped build it. You must know how much it hurts me to have you even indicated for sedition against the government, and now it turns out the man you're involved with is a revolutionary and maybe a traitor."

"You're wrong, but I don't know how to make you believe me."

There was a pause on the other end of the line. "There's a way. You can break with him and the others. You can tell the judge you didn't know about Nordstrom's background—he deceived you—and ask to be separated from the trial. I'll get you the best criminal lawyer available and he'll—"

"You'll do no such thing. I love Kermit. He happens to be the finest man I know. None of us is guilty of anything except what I told you. We're going through this trial together."

"If you persist, I won't pay your lawyers. All I've sent them is the retainer so far."

"You stop now, daddy, and you'll never see your daughter again. I mean that."

There was a long pause before he answered. "You play rough, Irish," he finally said, using her childhood nickname. "It's a lousy ultimatum." He paused again. "I guess I've got to go along."

"Thank you, Sam," she said with deep affection. "I know I'm being hard on you, but believe me we're really on the side of the good guys—you'll see. Your ancestors might even be proud. Just *try* to believe me. . . ."

"I'm trying to believe." She heard his voice break and he sounded suddenly old. "I think you should know I intend to vote for Senator Morstan for President."

"I love you anyway. And give my best to mother."

On Sunday night at ten o'clock Andy reported to Duane that Lasagna had still come up with nothing. NPAC was a top secret agency and it was impossible to penetrate its security shield. He had checked with Colonel Quaritius's past and present associates and friends and no one knew anything or would say anything that didn't make him out an all-American hero and a superb professional whose integrity was impeccable. Even two former girl friends had only good things to say about him. Lasagna had spoken to friends of his at the FBI, at CIA and at State Intelligence for a clue about how a dossier could be inserted into NPAC without going through official channels. He finally concluded that it must have been done *through* official channels and on a level so high that no one would know about it. If that was the case, it would be impossible to get at the truth unless someone confessed. And it was twelve hours to show-and-tell time.

Kermit and Dana disposed of Sunday by losing themselves in another dimension, where the stroking of flesh and the rapture of the senses was all the reality they needed. The third time she was on top on her knees and he was manipulating her soft, small breasts. When orgasm finally shattered their quiet and they lay against each other, he kissed her hair and said, "I love you, Dana. If something goes wrong, if we go to jail, how will we manage without each other?"

"Let's not think about it," she whispered. And moved herself even tighter to him, as though to make sure they were forever joined.

Chapter Thirty-Three

On Monday morning at 7:45 when the phone rang in his Georgetown home, Adam Greenfield had just finished shaving. He ran to the bedroom to answer.

"Yes, it is . . . no, you didn't wake me. Who is this? I see. Yes, I know who you are. You have *what?* Yes, I certainly would—it could be important. Exactly. I'm glad you feel that way." He looked at his watch. "Can you meet me in half an hour—all right, forty-five minutes, at my office. Got a pencil? It's 1980 K Street, near Twentieth Street, on the seventeenth floor. Eight-thirty sharp and bring it with you."

He stood there a full minute, hand resting on the phone, dressed only in undershorts, a quizzical expression on his smooth face. It was hard to believe. If only it contained what she said. . . .

At 8:25, he got off the elevator with two containers of coffee and two pieces of danish in a paper bag. He sat on the edge of the reception desk in the large, deserted room and began drinking his coffee. Five minutes later he heard the elevator close and a very pretty young woman in a clinging blue and white knit dress came through the heavy rosewood door.

"Miss Lardner?"

"Yes."

"I'm Adam Greenfield. Please come with me to my office." He picked

285

up his coffee and the paper bag. "Our breakfast," he smiled. "I'll take it with me."

He seated her at the end of the room and put the coffee and pastries on the low table between them. She refused any breakfast but as she accepted a cigarette, he noted the shapeliness of her legs and her strikingly wide-set green eyes.

"Did you bring it with you?" he said.

"Yes." She took a tape cassette from her white pocketbook and handed it to him with a nervous look.

Adam went to his desk, brought back a Sony cassette recorder and placed it on the coffee table. He opened the little clear hatch and snapped in the cassette.

"This is very difficult for me." Her voice was unsteady.

He tried to reassure her. "Yes, I know. Let's see what we have first, okay?" He depressed the playback key.

There was a dead-air sound of revolving blank tape for a few seconds followed by faint classical music overlaid with unidentifiable muffled sounds and then a woman's high conversational voice caught in midsentence. ". . . want to ask you. What would happen if those four on trial get off free? Would it hurt your campaign for the Presidency in any way?" Silence except for the music softly in the background. Muffled sounds, the woman's voice again, now recognizable as Jacqueline Lardner's. "Aren't you going to answer me, Gunther? You know how upset I get when you don't answer me." A man's low voice: "For god's sake, Jackie, this is a hell of a time to talk about such things. Come here, baby." Jacqueline's voice: "Not until you answer me. You always shut me up whenever I want to talk about anything but sex. You treat me like I don't have a brain in my head. I'm fed up with it"—her voice was high, petulant—"and maybe with you too." Morstan's voice: "Where's the bourbon?" Hers: "On the night table." Muffled sounds of movement over the music—of liquid poured, of an object against a hard surface, then no sound but music again, and then Morstan's gruff southern-accented voice: "All right, what's bothering you? Those three SOBs and their little piece? You don't really think I'd let them get away with it, do you? They won't, take my word for it. And now, may we resume? . . ." Rustling noise and what sounded like a barely audible weather report, then Jacqueline's voice, plaintive and frustrated: "That's all you ever want from me. You don't think of me as a person anymore, if you ever did."

286

His voice, very southern now: "Look honey, I'm sorry, but you've gotta understand something. I'm under tremendous pressure these days . . . not only in the Senate but from the national committee and my campaign for the Presidency. I've got enemies all over trying to stop me from getting the nomination. You know I never like to bother you with shoptalk, but I'm going through a very rough time. That's why I need you more than ever, sugar . . . you know how important you are to me. . . ." The sound of a deep breath, her voice: "Take your hand away. One more move like that and I'm getting out of bed." His voice, a little thick: "Okay, okay. You wanna talk, we'll talk. I'm listening." Jacqueline's voice: "You used to be *with* me. We'd have long talks and nice long romantic dinners. You'd tell me you loved me and I believed you. And then we'd make love. It was really nice. . . ." A pause. "Now all you want to do is grab, screw and run. Sometimes you make me feel like a call girl . . . well, I am *not*. I don't think you even like me anymore." The sound of soft weeping. His voice: "That's not true, sugar. Of course I like you, and much more than that. Now stop that sniffling." Her voice: "I told you not to touch me." His voice: "You're murdering me, sugar. I've got this here fine upstanding erection and no place to put it." Her voice: *"Good.* I hope you're suffering. Now you know how I feel when you treat me like a convenience. I will not make love with anyone who doesn't care for me." His voice, entreating: "That's not true, Jackie. I told you, I never stopped caring for you and now I need you more than ever." And in spite of himself, god help him, it was true. Her voice: "Like shit. If you even came close to caring you'd sit and *talk* to me . . . like a *person.* I'm interested in the things you're doing and I don't want to be shut out. I still love you, damn you, and I want to feel I'm part of your life. Gee, honey . . . I'm worried too that those four characters are going to get away with it, like all the others seem to. That Jew boy lawyer of theirs has done it before and now—" "Not *this* time!" Morstan's voice broke in. "Where have I heard that before?" Her voice seemed taunting. "There isn't a damn thing you or anybody else can do. Well, is there? . . ." His voice: "Something's being done—now forget it. I've already lost my erection . . . what are you doing? Oh, sugar . . . that feels marvelous. Now it's my turn to . . ." Her voice, teasing: "Uh, uh—not yet. I asked you a question." Morstan, groaning: "You're a bitch, do you know that? A beautiful one, but a bitch for sure. . . . You're driving me out of my mind. You want to know about those four little motherfuckers? . . . it's

287

all taken *care* of. I've got something that will hang that Nordstrom—along with his floozie, that reporter and the Jap. . . . Where's the damn bourbon?" The clatter of bottle and glass, a pause, then his voice again in a thick drawl: "I'm going to take a dossier out of a data bank and shove it right up Nordstrom's ass. Simple as that. . . ." His words became increasingly slurred. "That dossier is going to prove that he's a goddamn revolutionary instead of the boy scout he says he is. . . ." Laughter. "Hell, I should know, I wrote it myself, a lil ole made-to-order dossier tied up with a nice red ribbon . . . that's what I call poetic justice . . . right? He who lives by the sword shall die by the sword, and so forth. . . . Enough talk for you, sugar? Now c'mere, talking about swords, I've got something for you. . . ." Muffled sound with soft music, a click, dead air space.

Adam ejected the cassette and weighed it in his hand. "There's everything we need here." He looked at her. "You're an extraordinary woman. I know what this must be costing you."

She looked up gratefully, guiltily, then lowered her head as though she might cry. "I'm terribly embarrassed by this. Bringing this very personal and sordid conversation to a stranger. And I really didn't mean what I said when I called you a Jew lawyer. I was just baiting him to get him to say *something* . . . I was awful mad. . . ." She was blushing and her eyes were on the floor.

Greenfield nodded.

"I just couldn't let it happen this way. I know what kind of a man he is but I still didn't think he would do it. When Mr. Crozier came to see me some weeks ago and asked me to help him with information that would incriminate Senator Morstan in some way, I was furious. I thought he had a lot of nerve asking me to do a thing like that. But it gave me an idea. I at least realized that he was right about the senator getting ready to walk out on me." She smiled wanly. "I could see it coming but I guess I was trying to believe it wouldn't happen. So I decided that the best way to protect myself was to have something on tape that I could hold over his head just in case. I've been secretly taping for a few weeks, but most of it was meaningless. But this one time he said something I knew could hurt him if it was true. He's usually very closed mouth, as you heard, but this time I guess I pushed him pretty far." She blushed again. "It took me all weekend to make up my mind to give it to you. I still don't know if I did the right thing."

"It was a tough thing for you to do, we appreciate—"

"No, *please*—let me finish. I really did this for my own protection, not for any high-minded reason. I'm certainly no Snow White, but when I heard they were using that dossier he made up, I was horrified. I couldn't believe that anyone could be so . . . ruthless . . . I don't know if those four are guilty or innocent, but I believe everyone deserves a fair trial, and I guess that deep down . . . well, maybe I just don't think a man like that should be President. I can still remember Watergate, how naive I was then and how ugly it made everything seem . . . even the President. . . ."

Adam looked at her. "I admire you very much, Miss Lardner. It took guts to come to me with this. I mean it . . . oh, by the way, I may need you to appear in court to verify this tape as evidence. I hesitate to ask you but . . ."

She nodded. "I thought you might . . . but will I have some, you know, protection?"

"I'll see that you have as much protection as possible. But you also know the senator. No question he'll try to make life miserable for you. He's a vindictive man. I think it would be best if—"

"I know. I plan to go away very soon. Probably to Hawaii. I have friends there."

"A foreign country might be better—and as soon as possible."

"I'll think about it."

He walked her down the empty corridor to the reception room. As the elevator door opened, he took her hand quickly and pressed it. "Good luck. And, again, thank you."

It was nine o'clock, one hour until trial time. Adam phoned the U.S. District Attorney's office and spoke to Hinckley.

"Eric, I have bad news for you. I just listened to a tape of Senator Morstan admitting that he counterfeited and planted the dossier that your witness, Miss Geist, read in court last Friday."

There was a silent moment on the other end. "Would you repeat that, Adam?" He did. "Either you're crazy or you've been taken in. What would *Gunther Morstan* have to do with this? Whatever you have is a phony. I'm amazed at you."

"I can understand your reaction. It does sound wild. But I have the person who recorded the tape and she'll testify that it's Morstan's voice on it. I'd like you to meet me in Huddleston's chambers at nine-thirty. I'll play the tape for both of you."

"Who is your witness?"

"You'll get the whole story in half an hour."

"I don't know what you're up to, but—"

"Look Eric, the government's case is badly damaged, and this doesn't make your office look too good either. I'm going to see Huddleston in chambers and play this tape for him. I'm sure you'll want to be there."

When he hung up, he walked down the hall and took hold of Bonaventura by the arm. "Andy, I want you to make a copy of this tape immediately. It'll give you a chance to hear it. Jacqueline Lardner, Morstan's mistress, gave it to me a few minutes ago. It changes the ballgame. I'm meeting Huddleston and Hinckley in chambers at nine-thirty. Step on it!"

He dialed Huddleston's office in the U.S. Courthouse. It was ten after nine. When Huddleston picked up the phone he seemed reluctant to be disturbed before trial time. Adam quickly summarized the situation and the judge said okay, he would meet with both attorneys if it was that important.

Ten minutes later Andy came into the office. "Wow! Really hot stuff," he said, handing the copy and original to Adam. "This should turn it around. What are you going to ask for?"

"The moon." Adam grabbed both cassettes, snapped the original in his cassette machine, gave the copy back to Andy and called, "Put it in the bank vault, I'm taking no chances with this," as he ran for the elevator.

The second floor of the U.S. Courthouse was already half choked with press, police guards and various courthouse personnel. Adam snaked through and walked down a short corridor between two courtrooms to the judge's chambers. Winnie Conway, the judge's assistant, led him through the four-room suite to the long office.

Huddleston put down his newspaper, got up gingerly from his wing chair and greeted Adam. Without his imposing black robe and the judicial bearing which went with it, he came across as a genial, portly man with animated eyes—an aristocratic-looking grandfather. Hinckley hadn't arrived yet so Huddleston invited Adam to join him in a cup of coffee that a secretary brewed in an adjoining office.

While they were waiting Adam told Huddleston about Jacqueline Lardner's early morning phone call and visit to his office with the incriminating tape. He also mentioned that he had heard through an informed source that NPAC was not averse to cooperating with certain government intelligence agencies in hanky-panky involving the use of dosiers. Huddleston was stunned and then dubious when Adam told him what was on the tape. As Adam was finishing the summary, Hinckley walked in, looking perturbed and suspicious.

He shook hands with Huddleston, lowered himself into a chair. "What the devil is this all about, Adam?"

"I was just telling the judge how I came into possession of this cassette."

"Now tell me."

Adam did, and Hinckley's eyes hardened.

"I'll play it for you," Adam said, getting the black compact cassette recorder and playback and setting it on a low table in front of both men. He walked to the door, closed it and sat down and pressed the PLAY key. Huddleston's face went from a peculiar smile to a grave expression as he listened. The hostile expression that Hinckley started out with changed to disbelief to shock to anger. Adam turned off the cassette with a click that seemed to punctuate the finality of the episode.

"What proof do you have that this isn't counterfeit?" Hinckley snapped.

"I have Jacqueline Lardner. She'll testify. Good enough?"

"No, it's not. She could have set this whole thing up—had someone impersonate the senator's voice, an actor. She's an actress, you know, and obviously a woman scorned."

Huddleston's forehead was deeply furrowed. "This tape could have the most serious consequences. I'm sure we all realize that. As to its authenticity, that's easily settled. I'll call Senator Morstan and ask him to come right over. It would be best to confront him with this in private. Then we'll know very quickly if this is genuine and we can save him the humiliation of playing the tape before the jury and the press in open courtroom. I think we owe him that much in any case, and I insist upon handling it in this way. Meanwhile, I suggest we assume that the . . . shocking piece of dialogue we've just eavesdropped on is authentic because if it is, it would seriously alter the entire nature of the government's case."

Hinckley was far from ready to concede that. "Assuming this is genuine, all it would mean is that the prosecution's Exhibit B has been discredited, that we lost the evidence concerning the background of one of the defendants. But we have two other witnesses who have firsthand knowledge of Nordstrom's—"

"And will lie their heads off iike Chappell did," Adam put in.

"Are you accusing me of suborning the witnesses?" A vein stood out in his neck.

"Come on, Eric. We know each other better than that. You've just been unlucky. The suborning was done by Morstan and Lockwood for obvious reasons. But so much of your case depends on this fabricated testimony—Chappell's has been stricken and he may be cited for contempt, and now this. I frankly think you're over a barrel."

Huddleston nodded. "I have to agree. Your sedition and conspiracy case has been compromised. Even if your subsequent witnesses are reliable and they can produce testimony on the conspiracy charges, their credibility would be open to question because of your last two witnesses. I know that's not a legal consideration, but it is a practical one. If Adam were to ask me to dismiss the two conspiracy charges in view of what has happened or to declare a mistrial, I'd have to consider it seriously."

Hinckley was stunned. Before he could respond Huddleston continued. "Let's postpone this until we know exactly what we're talking about." He walked to the other side of the room and sat down at his desk, picked up the phone and asked his assistant to come in. A moment later when the woman appeared, he said sternly, "Winnie, I want you to find Senator Morstan wherever he is—try his office first. I must speak to him right away."

A few minutes later a buzzer sounded on Huddleston's desk. He picked up the phone. "Senator, this is Fred Huddleston. Yes, well we're all doing our best. Senator, I must ask you to do me a favor. Can you come right over to my chambers? I need you to help clear up an important matter. I'd be very grateful. Ten minutes will be fine." He pressed the intercom button to Winnie's desk. "Have the clerk announce that court will be convened at ten-thirty instead of ten o'clock. I'm expecting the senator in a few minutes. Send him right in."

They withheld further conversation pending Morstan's arrival. Hinckley thumbed impatiently through the pages of a law journal he picked up, and Adam busily reversed the tape on the cassette to its beginning. He felt like he was reloading a revolver.

Morstan came through the door, all grace and ease. A near-overpowering charisma radiated from him, and Adam suddenly felt that the room was too small for the coming explosion.

"Judge Huddleston, gentlemen." The well-tanned senator greeted them with a public smile. "I am delighted to see you. If I can help you in any way . . ."

"You can, senator, please sit down." Huddleston motioned him to a chair and took a deep breath. "Senator, I have just come into possession of a piece of evidence which concerns you, and frankly it disturbs me . . . disturbs all of us . . . very much. This is very awkward because it is of an intimate nature and yet it could have an important bearing on this trial. We are trying to determine—"

"For god's sake, Fred, stop palavering. You sound like a New England senator filibustering on a military appropriations bill." He smiled easily. "What's on your mind?"

Huddleston looked solemn. "We have a tape we'd like you to hear and then you'll understand." He nodded to Adam.

Adam leaned forward and pressed the key on the little black box.

As soon as Morstan heard Jacqueline Lardner's voice, he broke out with, "What the *hell* is this!" and half rose out of his chair.

"I think you better sit down and hear this out," Huddleston said quietly.

As the damning conversation emanated from the spinning tape, Adam couldn't help feeling sorry for the man.

Morstan got up, unsteadily. "If you think I'm going to sit here and be intimidated by this filthy garbage . . ."

"I advise that you do, senator." Huddleston's tone took on an edge.

Morstan sank slowly into the chair and his eyes turned inward as he heard his voice utter the fateful words. And then the tape went blank and Adam clicked it off. The room was like a mausoleum for a long moment until Huddleston broke the silence. "I'm deeply distressed that this was necessary, senator. You must understand our position. We do not want to play this in open court, and there is no need for this ever to be made public. You have my assurance on that. However, you must recognize that the fraudulent dossier made a great impact on this case and on the

293

rights of the defendants to a fair trial. The record must be corrected at once in the interest of basic justice. I cannot allow it to stand."

Morstan rose imperiously, seemingly in full command of himself once more. His face was a cold mask, his eyes deadly. "This tape was illegally made and obtained. How did you get it?"

"Miss Lardner brought it in of her own free will," Adam replied. "None of us had any knowledge of it before I received it."

He turned on Adam. "You paid her to do it!" Then back to Huddleston: "It was obtained by stealth in violation of my privacy and therefore is not admissible."

Huddleston eyed him sadly for a moment. "You know better than that, senator. Besides, as I said, I do not plan to admit it in evidence—unless I have to. I'm hoping we can save you the embarrassment of public exposure. I want you to take the witness stand and testify that you have direct, personal knowledge that the dossier is fraudulent."

The muscles in Morstan's cheeks tightened. "I have no intention of doing that. What you have on that tape is a clear case of entrapment by a vicious woman who was paid to do it. I was drinking, Fred . . . all right, I'm no angel and like most men can sometimes make a horse's ass of himself over a woman . . . the worst kind too . . . I just told her what she wanted to hear so I could get back to business with her . . . I would have said anything at that moment, for god's sake . . . you heard it yourself, if that's a crime, I'm guilty. It was just one of those stupid situations that any *one* of us can get into. . . ." He smiled confidentially. "Man to man, I'm sure each one of you understands. . . ."

The judge was unimpressed. "I'm sorry, senator, but this isn't a matter of a sex scandal. I'm not interested in your private life. On that tape you said very clearly that you were going to hang Nordstrom and the other three defendants with a dossier you had written yourself to show that he was a known revolutionary. And then a dossier to this effect is introduced as evidence in court. I can't believe in that much coincidence. If you persist in taking that position—and legally you have every right to —then I'll have to ask you to take the witness stand and defend it."

"You mean you'll play the tape in court?"

Huddleston nodded. "I would hope not to."

A shade descended over Morstan's eyelids and when it came up, the look in his eyes was savage. "You're railroading me, damn it . . . what I did was absolutely justified . . . the damn government's case was falling apart, all I did was try to save it . . . those four are as guilty as hell, and that's what's important—even Greenfield here admitted it in his opening statement. They should be tried for treason. If I didn't step in they'd have gotten clean away with it and you *know* it."

Huddleston shook his head and said nothing.

Morstan softened his expression. "Good lord, Fred, you don't want that much." He paused. "We can surely work something out . . . there are matters at stake that transcend—"

"I'm afraid there's no other way, senator. I'm sorry."

He switched to truculent. "All right, I'm going to tell you something, *judge*. I wouldn't expect anything else of Greenberg here, defending these radicals, these so-called *civil libertarians* . . . should be called civil libertines." His words were venom. "But you, Fred, and Eric—you're both officials of the government sworn to uphold the Constitution of the United States. . . ." (It occurred to Adam, watching him turn inside out, that the man was entirely, horribly sincere. . . .) "Are you going to let these people tear down everything we've built up these last two hundred years? Do you remember what happened when that *Ellsberg* got off with *stealing* and *publishing* the Pentagon Papers because a soft-headed judge let him off? Every government agency started leaking like a sieve and the CIA, army intelligence and FBI lost their balls . . . which is exactly why America is where she is now, shit on by every two-bit sheik and nigger honcho in the U.N. . . . We've been kicked out of Southeast Asia, our NATO defense has gone to hell, we've been outflanked and outgunned by the Russians . . . even our so-called friends are laughing at us. Why? . . . because we've lost our guts." He paused, and a more evangelical look took over. "Gentlemen . . . it can all stop *here* . . . in this very room. Don't you see that?" His eyes searched theirs. "We must reverse the process . . . stand by our government . . . stop these subversives in their tracks. This trial can be the turning point—make an example of them. My bill is about to become law . . . the President promised to sign it today . . . and then we'll put control of our national computers where it belongs —in the hands of those elected to run the country, those who love and respect it and would die for it . . . instead of those who would destroy it with their treachery and secret terminals in some dark cellar and all the rest. . . ."

Huddleston touched Morstan's arm lightly and spoke in a soothing though firm voice. "All right, Gunther, you've made your point. And now I want you to go home and simmer down, relax. We've all been upset by this and need a little time to adjust. I'm going to postpone court until two this afternoon. That's over three and a half hours. And then I want you to come back and take the witness stand and testify truthfully. If you refuse, I'll have no choice but to cite you for creating false evidence and obstruction of justice. Neither of us wants that, so you just be back here at two and we'll straighten out the record—"

Morstan pulled away with a look of betrayal. "Damn you . . . I don't need your favors or your sympathy, and *don't* call me Gunther—I'm Gunther to my *friends*. . . ." He examined Huddleston with a ferocious intensity, beyond reason. . . . "You're one of them now, aren't you? Standing up for that SOB Nordstrom, that Jap and that penny-ante muckraker . . . *and* the rich young cunt who pays off Mr. *Greenberg* here. . . . Oh, don't think I don't know, I've got you all pegged. . . ." He was hissing, like a drake at bay, his head moving from side to side. . . . Suddenly he squared his shoulders and looked from one to the other with high disdain. "America will survive *despite* its traitors!" Whereupon he turned for the door. Before he went through it, Huddleston called after him. "I'll see you here at two o'clock, senator. . . ."

The slamming of the door was a stagy punctuation to the awful, scary performance.

"I'm afraid the senator's come unstuck," Huddleston said sadly. "It's terrible to see a man of that stature come apart like that. I'm sorry I had to be a party to it—"

"He did it to himself," Adam said, still shaken by what he'd seen and heard. "Do you think he'll come back and take the stand?"

Huddleston sighed. "I think so, I hope so . . . he's already blown himself out, he's a practical man . . . he'll come to realize it's at least the lesser of two evils."

Adam looked skeptical. "Providing he's capable of that much rational thought. . . . In any case, . . . he's blown himself out of the Presidency. And for that we can all be grateful. . . ."

Huddleston looked sharply at him. "I'm not grateful where a man of the senator's stature is compromised—even if he does it to himself. He's been terribly wrong in his behavior, but he is as convinced of the right of his positions as you are of yours. Give him that. . . ."

Adam nodded. "I'll try, Your Honor, but it isn't easy. . . ." To which the others gave a silent amen.

Huddleston called in Winnie and told her he wanted her to announce that the opening of court would be postponed until two o'clock due to an unforeseen development. She was to instruct the jury to be back at 1:45 and to continue maintaining their silence about the case.

"I think you gentlemen better put your heads together and work something out," he said. "I'll be here if you need me."

"Well, what did you have in mind, Adam?" Hinckley's manner was more tractable now, though still cautious.

"Withdraw all charges."

"You can't be serious. Your clients invaded a vital government agency, played hell with its vital services and stirred up a hornet's nest in Congress where it hurts the most—in their personal tax records. Not to mention embarrassing the Administration—."

"All of which in our view is a public service. None of these things did the slightest damage. To the contrary . . . they exposed high government tax cheats and deadbeats who weren't being prosecuted, they exposed IRS's Pygmalion invasion of personal privacy—it was worth the effort for that alone—and they shook up the cheats and fat cats in Congress, in industry, the unions and the Mafia. They should have a special medal struck in their honor, not a criminal charge."

"Well . . . I'll drop the conspiracy charges, I think that's more than fair—"

"You're being very generous," Adam said sarcastically. Actually it galled him that he still didn't have what could be his biggest gun—the tape stolen from his safe by the FBI and no doubt in possession of the White House now. But he had no intention of letting that slow him down. "You may as well know what you're facing, Eric," he said quickly. "I have witnesses who worked in government agencies who will testify and produce documents on serious computer violations among various major agencies—some of it by secret agreement among themselves, others by illegal invasion. Now I would call *that* conspiracy by the government against the people, including some cases during the current administration. Add to that the government tax cheats and the Pygmalion invasion, and it would be obvious to the jury that the real conspirators were all government agencies, not my clients. In short, who's the plaintiff and who's the defendant? . . ."

"Is there any reason I should take your word for it? Besides, that doesn't lessen the culpability of your clients on the two other charges."

297

"After the jury hears the blockbuster illegal acts by *government* agencies, they'll consider my clients at worst rank amateurs. . . ." He decided on a pressure tactic. "Look, Eric, I don't want you to take my word for it. I wouldn't, of course, if I were in your shoes. I can have four of my witnesses in your office by this afternoon. You listen to them and *you* decide."

Hinckley looked sharply at Greenfield and made a decision. "If you say you have the evidence, I'll take your word for it"—he'd better trade here rather than in court, he decided. "I'll drop the third charge too—Theft of Public Records. I'll have to get the Attorney General's approval, of course—"

Adam wasn't through horsetrading. "Not good enough. I want *all* the charges dropped. Otherwise we'll continue the trial and use everything we've got. How will the White House take to that? I'm looking forward to my summation."

Hinckley studied him. "Look, Adam, let's be practical. Your clients committed an illegal act when they penetrated that satellite and pressed that button on IRS, *regardless* of their motives. They put it on the public record themselves when they held that press conference, and you did too in your opening statement. You can't expect the government or a court of law to ignore it. The whole world knows about it. It would set a precedent which is indefensible legally, morally and politically. Let's not beat a dead horse. I'll even agree to a light sentence on the Concealment and Removal of Records charge, if I can get Senseny to go along with it."

"How light?"

"Six months plus a two thousand dollar fine, for each."

"Six months, suspended sentence, and I'll go for the fine," Adam countered. "I'll have to speak to my clients, naturally."

Hinckley nodded. "A deal." It could have been worse. The destruction of his case by the flagrant perjury of a prosecution witness and his own unknowing introduction of vicious, false evidence were things he couldn't have contemplated. He wouldn't come out looking good, but at least his superiors would understand, and he was relieved to make a clean break.

Huddleston looked up. "I've been eavesdropping, counselors. I think you've both made a wise decision. I'll go along with it."

When Hinckley went into the next room to make a call in private to

Attorney General Stuart Senseny, Adam went to consult with his four mystified clients waiting impatiently in the empty courtroom.

"I have news for you," he announced.

They sat around the defense table in the empty, unnaturally quiet courtroom, and in ten minutes he compressed the incredible events of the morning, from Jacqueline Lardner's surprise phone call and the playing of the cassette, to Morstan's terrible outburst of a few minutes ago.

"What do you suppose made Jacqueline Lardner decide to do that?" Kermit asked.

"Duane must have done a better job than he realized," Dana said quickly.

"Is Morstan actually going to get up and admit he was behind the fake dossier?" Yuki asked.

"And how come Hinckley—" Duane began.

Adam waved his hand. "Later," he said. "How would you feel about pleading guilty to the charge of Concealment and Removal of Records? All the other charges will be dropped."

"That would be great," Duane said. "But what about the two years in prison?"

"How about six months, suspended sentence, and a two thousand dollar fine?"

"*Fabulous,*" Dana said, and hugged him. "You're not kidding us, are you?"

"I never kid a paying client," he said with a sly smile. "By the way, you should thank Duane for having the right hunch about the lady and the senator. . . . Well, I've got to finalize this with Hinckley and Huddleston. Wait for me here, I won't be long. I'm buying lunch. We don't have to be back until two."

Over an early lunch at the Sheraton Carlton, three blocks north of the White House, they toasted Yuki for his brilliance in developing the intricate electronic pattern for accessing the network, Kermit and Dana for originating the concept and motivating it, Duane for spotting Morstan's weak spot, and Adam for keeping them out of jail. "Here's to Andy," Dana said with her second whiskey sour held aloft, determined to leave no one out, "for seeing that Gaetano Lasagna was out there hustling his pasta."

Adam mentioned that Huddleston in chambers had helped him

persuade Hinckley to cooperate in withdrawing most of the charges.

"I can guess the reason," Andy said. "He was anxious to wipe out his decision to admit the phony dossier in evidence. It was a bad decision to begin with and it turned out to be a disaster. Withdrawing the charges cleared the record so we couldn't ask for a dismissal or a reversal on that basis."

Adam nodded, then turned to the others. "Well, now that the Martinsburg Four have saved the nation, where will you strike next?"

"If only that were true, Adam," Kermit answered with sudden melancholy. "I guess we've saved ourselves, but once that damn bill is signed, who'll care about or even notice such niceties as a phony dossier or invasion of privacy or even mass surveillance by computer? Not the bureaucrats with the Federal Computer Management Law in one hand and the other on a terminal. The Bill of Rights will become an artifact of the Bicentennial. . . . Sorry to throw cold water on the celebration, but I'm pessimistic as hell about the future. The only thing going for us is the new Senate Select Committee on Computer Operations headed by Senator Kammerer. He's a decent man and I know he'll conduct a thorough investigation, but it will be like a rape victim making a protest speech at a Rapists' Convention. Not a damn thing will come of it. Yuki and I have been invited to testify, and we'll go, of course. . . ." He shrugged.

Yuki nodded. "I'll finally, I hope, get my chance to sound off about the dangers of communications satellite penetration and what can be done about it."

"My proposals," Kermit said, reviving somewhat, "will cover the other side, the gamut of abuses in government and industrial computer operations. Lord knows, we have enough scandalous examples to trot out in front of the committee, including the new ones Yuki discovered . . . oh, hell, I doubt anything will come of all of this, but we just can't stand by and do nothing after what we've come through."

Adam nodded. "I think you've already accomplished a great deal. I wouldn't put that down. At least the country is now aware of the seriousness of the problem, even though they managed to jam that bill through Congress. If Kammerer's committee does the job, it's got to get to the Supreme Court on constitutional grounds. It's turned the First Amendment into a piece of Swiss cheese. . . . Well"—he looked at his watch—"it's about time. We better get going."

Chapter Thirty-Four

The mood of the courtroom at two P.M. on Monday, June 2, was electric. Over two hundred fidgeting bodies were squeezed together on the wooden benches, separated only by the middle aisle, and police guards were permitting a dozen more to stand near the double doors.

The two postponements in the convening of court—from ten to ten-thirty, and then until two—were more than enough tip-off that an important news break was in the making. The prevailing wisdom scuttlebutting around the National Press Club bar through lunchtime was that Greenfield's investigator had gotten onto something damaging involving Morstan and Lockwood's company.

Ten minutes later court was convened by the clerk's intonation and Judge Huddleston walked in, adjusting his robe as he sat down. He scanned the courtroom unhurriedly, then summoned the clerk. He leaned over and chatted with him at the side of the bench, keeping an eye on the door. Then he straightened up and sounded the gavel repeatedly until the hubbub subsided.

"Will counsels approach the bench?"

Both men arose simultaneously and went forward to the sidebar. "He hasn't arrived in the building yet," Huddleston said in a low voice. "Winnie checked with his home and office and they know nothing of his whereabouts. Do either of you have any suggestions?"

"He could be at his club, with a bottle of bourbon," Adam said matter of factly. "I think we can assume he's not coming."

Hinckley nodded. "I would have to agree."

Huddleston looked unhappy. "We certainly can't wait any longer. I'll decide later about asking you to consider charges against him, Mr. Hinckley. Meanwhile, we'll have to proceed as planned."

Both men returned to their tables but Hinckley remained standing, facing the bench.

Huddleston banged the gavel once to clear the background hum which had gathered. "You may proceed, Mr. Hinckley."

"Your Honor, new evidence has come to our attention which alters the government's position in this case. As the result of this evidence, which we became aware of for the first time this morning, the government has decided that justice would best be served and—"

Huddleston's gavel came down hard and his voice boomed out. "What is the disturbance in the rear of the courtroom? Bring that man to me!"

All heads swiveled to watch a slight, sandy-haired young man in a business suit being hustled up the aisle by a bulky, middle-aged police officer. The young man turned and looked anxiously at the prosecutor as he passed, then stood in front of the lectern.

"See what this is all about, Jim," Huddleston snapped irritably to the clerk seated in front of him.

The clerk came back a moment later with a note the young man handed him. As Huddleston read it, his jowels seemed to sag and his head remained lowered as though he was having trouble understanding it. Finally, he looked up. "Do you know this man, Mr. Hinckley?" His voice sounded distant.

"Donald Neff—a law clerk from my office," he responded, bewildered. "Anything wrong, Your Honor?" He took a few steps forward.

Huddleston looked abstractedly over the courtroom, then took a deep breath. He looked very tired.

"Ladies and gentlemen," he began solemnly, "I have just received shocking news. I have been informed by this report from the District of Columbia police department that Senator Gunther Morstan . . ."—his deep voice wavered momentarily—"shot and killed a young woman named Miss Jacqueline Lardner and then shot and killed himself. Apparently this happened within the last two hours. I have no information other than that." He paused to compose himself and his words took their

302

effect throughout the stunned assemblage. He continued, his voice low. "This court is deeply grieved by this tragic news. However, we will carry on the business of this court. I will expect everyone to cooperate. . . ."

A susurrating whisper swept around the room, but Huddleston didn't bother to silence it, and it dissolved when he resumed. "Before you proceed with your statement, Mr. Hinckley, I would like to describe for the record, and for those present in this courtroom, a meeting which took place this morning in my chambers . . . a meeting which, I am fearful, is directly related to this terrible event. It is important that it be understood. . . . This morning at nine-thirty a tape recording was played in my chambers in the presence of Mr. Hinckley and Mr. Greenfield. What the three of us heard was an admission by Senator Morstan, in his own voice, that the dossier on Dr. Nordstrom presented to this court was fraudulent in all respects, and indeed . . . it was he who authored it and contrived to have it inserted in the data bank files of the National Personnel Advisory Council. The tape made it clear that his purpose was to discredit Dr. Nordstrom and reinforce the conspiracy charges against him. I want it known that the U.S. Attorney and his office had no knowledge that the dossier presented in evidence was fraudulent and designed to obstruct justice." He paused and contemplated the courtroom with melancholy. "At ten A.M., I called Senator Morstan into my chambers and played the tape for him. Mr. Hinckley and Mr. Greenfield were likewise present. His response to us confirmed that the voice on the tape was his and that he had indeed made those statements and falsified the dossier. The tape was a recording of a conversation between himself and Miss Jacqueline Lardner, who recorded it without his knowledge. This is the chain of events that apparently prompted Senator Morstan to take Miss Lardner's life and his own. I had hoped that he would return to this court and set the record straight himself." He made no attempt to hide a deep sigh. "This court is deeply distressed that this distinguished senator, who has served the country and the state of South Carolina so well for *many* years, felt it necessary to end his life and his career and that of an innocent young woman. We extend our deepest sympathies to their families and many friends." He lifted his thick, upturned eyebrows in somber appraisal of the scene around him. "And now, Mr. Hinckley, will you please proceed?"

A dozen or more reporters slipped past the two police guards and out of the courtroom before they could be stopped.

The gavel came down repeatedly before Hinckley was able to speak. "I would like to say that the government deeply regrets the unfortunate events of this day and we are profoundly shocked by its tragic conclusion." He shifted his stance. "Your Honor, in view of the evidence that was brought to our attention this morning, which you've just described, the government will withdraw both Conspiracy charges and the Theft of Public Records charge against the four defendants. However, the Concealment and Removal of Public Records charge remains. It is my understanding that the defendants wish to plead guilty to that charge."

"Is that correct, Mr. Greenfield?" Huddleston asked, going through the prescribed motions.

Adam half rose in his chair. "That is correct, Your Honor."

"Very well." Huddleston turned his drained face to the jury. He looked at them thoughtfully before speaking, his vision still on that turbulent scene in his chambers this morning which had exploded into murder and suicide. "Ladies and gentlemen of the jury, you have participated in a trial of national and perhaps historic significance. However, the unfortunate circumstances which have led the government to drop the major charges against the defendants, and their plea of guilty on the remaining charge, means that this trial is terminated. The court wishes to thank you for your time and patience in willingly performing your civic duty. This jury is accordingly dismissed. If you wish to remain in your seats until court is adjourned shortly, you may do so."

The jurors glanced questioningly at each other but none of them moved. Having sat through the drama, they apparently wanted to stay for the final scene.

Huddleston shifted his spiritless gaze. "The defendants will approach the bench."

The four rose, stepped back from their chairs and then lined up in front of the lectern facing the judge. Adam stood on one end next to Dana.

"Are you all aware of the penalty for pleading guilty to the charge of Concealment and Removal of Public Records?"

They each acknowledged they were.

"How do you plead to the charge?"

They went down the line—Yuki, Duane, Kermit and Dana. "Guilty" ... "Guilty" ... "Guilty" ... "Guilty."

"All right, then. Normally, I would set a date for sentencing, but in view of today's events I prefer to dispose of it immediately."

The courtroom was hushed and waiting. "I hereby sentence each of you to a six months jail term, sentence to be suspended and . . ."

Pandemonium. Those in the front row may have heard the judge conclude ". . . and a fine of two thousand dollars each," but it hardly mattered.

Huddleston stood up in his black robe, tiredly surveying the chaotic scene, intoned, "This court stands adjourned," which almost nobody heard, and then turned and fled through the door to his chambers.

Kermit, Dana, Yuki and Duane were overwhelmed and somewhat disoriented by the demonstration around them. They were pleased, but in some way they felt there was a smear of blood left over to stain them. Duane felt it most directly. If it hadn't been for his rather farfetched notion and his visit to her apartment that rainy day earlier in the month, that remarkable green-eyed girl would be alive right now and so would the senator. None of them wanted him dead. And the vision of Cynthia's crushed body came back. All a high and unexpected price to pay for their act, however important. . . .

As if on signal, as soon as the judicial robes disappeared from the courtroom, the defense's table was surrounded by the mob of reporters pressing in, pushing against their chairs, shouting and obliterating one another's questions in tangled voices.

Adam and Andy led them into the refuge of the judge's chambers some thirty feet away. Duane, staying behind, managed to get over to the lectern where the P.A. system was still operating. Waving his arms above his head, he shouted hoarsely into the mike. "Hold it, hold it. I'm Duane Crozier. Quiet down for a minute—I have something to say." The noise subsided enough for him to be heard. "If you'll all calm down and take your seats, I'll see if I can arrange a press conference here, right now, so we can answer all your questions. Okay? It's either that or nothing. Look, I'm on your side, remember? All right, sit down and give me five minutes. I'll see if I can arrange it with the judge."

He made his way through and entered the judge's chambers. Dana was in the ladies' room, Yuki was in the men's room and Kermit was waiting his turn. What is there about crises, or the end of them, Duane thought, that calls to nature?

"Tell me something, Duane," Kermit said on seeing him, "your friends out there—what kind of people are they? How can they react this way after hearing that terrible news only a few minutes ago?"

Duane shook his head. "You've got it wrong . . . they were shocked by this too. But they're also excited by our . . . well, partial victory, I guess you could call it. Four dedicated nuts beat the odds and the system, at least for now . . . especially after losing that big one to Congress. There's a saying in our business—inside every cynical reporter is a sentimental optimist. Reporters want to believe in Tinkerbell too. What you heard out there was two hundred basically decent citizens blowing off.

Kermit smiled, understanding, and Duane grabbed his arm. "Oh, by the way, I promised them a press conference—right now—if Huddleston will let us use the hall. Why don't you take your leak and then get ready to answer some questions." He rushed down the corridor to find Adam and enlist his help.

A few minutes later, Duane emerged from Huddleston's office, gathered up Dana and Yuki and Kermit, who had freshened up, and were in the judge's reception room. "Come on, terrible four, the world's waiting to hear from us."

Dana took Kermit's hand. "I missed the bus the first time. I don't intend to miss this one."

As she walked at his side toward the courtroom door, Kermit thought of what the four of them had been through together—how it started that sleety day in January in Dana's bed and how it ended in a crowded federal courthouse in view of the world, with trauma and with very little victory. . . .

The courtroom was a surprise. Everyone was seated on the walnut benches they had occupied before, and except for a low, conversational hum, the room was quiet. The three network television cameras had appeared, were set up and ready. Duane turned the lectern with the live mike around so it faced the press. Yuki and Dana seated themselves behind the court stenographer's and clerk's long desk and Duane sat on a corner edge.

Kermit stepped behind the lectern. "I'll take the first question." He pointed to one of the waving hands.

A thin, serious-faced man got up. "Hank Kellerman, the St. Louis *Post-Dispatch*. Dr. Nordstrom, now that the President has vetoed the

Morstan-Windmiller bill and there's no possibility of an override, do you feel there's still a need for—"

"The President has vetoed the bill? . . ." Kermit stood there slack-jawed. ˢ ˢⁱⁿg like a schoolboy struggling for comprehension. "Are you serious?" His voice was unnaturally thin.

"His press secretary announced it half an hour ago—just before Court reconvened."

Kermit turned and looked at Dana, his face glazed with astonishment. The President vetoed the bill on the seventh day. It was some sort of miracle. What made him change his mind? Was it somehow the confirmation of evil in the shocking deaths of Morstan and his mistress? Had he finally seen the dangers of such a law? Was it that he had the tape incriminating the White House safely in his possession and was free to follow his conscience? Perhaps he'd been vacillating all along. He had taken seven days before he acted. But whatever, it *did* happen . . . that was the bottom line. Crazy, terrible, how things got done . . . on a breath, a whim, a sudden insight. . . . But now there was time, and maybe even hope—even if there still was no guarantee.

Dana was at his side, squeezing his hand; he squeezed back, hard. Yuki and Duane crowded close, arms circling waists, and the quick looks they traded were personal gifts, private and transcending the moment. Above their heads was the Great Seal of the United States.

Kermit turned facing the television cameras. "Mr. Kellerman, for once in his life, this professor is speechless. Thank you."

307